Amanda
Roberts

First published in Great Britain in 2023 by
Hickory Press, Oxfordshire, England

ISBN 978-1-915787-91-0

Typeset by Hickory Press
Produced in the UK by Biddles Books Ltd

A catalogue record for this book is available from the British Library.

Cover: Original artwork by William North, www.williamhnorth.co.uk
Design by Stuart Hubbard, Concept Creatives

www.amandarobertsauthor.co.uk

The Woman
in the Painting

AMANDA ROBERTS

Hickory Press
Oxfordshire, England

Also by Amanda Roberts

The Roots of the Tree

ONE

Hannah
2019

IT WAS ONE OF THOSE left fork/right fork moments. I'm sure you know what I mean. Turn left and you bump into the class geek who's morphed into a demi-god in the years since you left school. He asks you out. You accept. Two years later, you're walking down the aisle. Turn right and you arrive at the supermarket without incident, clueless about what you've just missed.

I'm talking about the day we dug the footings for my deck and boat mooring. When I say 'we dug' I don't mean I was actually doing the digging. That was in the hands of a builder - his name was Dave. I had cast myself in the role of director, but he was doing a good job of ignoring my instructions.

If I hadn't chosen that exact spot. If we'd dug a few inches to the left or the right. If I'd had my eyes closed, or been looking in a different direction at that split second when it became visible, before it was covered over again by dirt. In any of those scenarios I wouldn't have found it and my life would have gone spinning off in a different direction.

I wouldn't have met Matt.

It's funny as well, looking back, the pointless details that have stuck in my mind about that moment.

I remember it was a cool, dry day.

I remember getting my new flower-patterned wellington boots stuck in the boggy ground on the river's edge.

I remember fighting in the wind with the zip on my old fleece and breaking it.

So there we were, at the bottom of my garden in this most

perfect, idyllic spot. If I said that this was the reason I'd chosen this cottage, I wouldn't be exaggerating. I could have bought one of the modern, much larger houses elsewhere in the village for the same money - or less - but I wanted the river frontage. The cottage is charming - too small, but still charming. It was converted from some sort of outbuilding that would once have held stores for the nearby mill, or so the agent said. Not that the mill was working any more. It was just a house these days.

What makes this spot so special to me? The riverbank flattens out between two willows making a sort of beach area that's sheltered, secluded, and from where it's possible to launch a boat or a kayak. That's it, in a nutshell.

But since I moved in just after Christmas, the weather has been against me. Of course, the Cherwell floods and we had a particularly wet winter, which continued into early spring. I had to wait for the river to retreat to its well-defined channel, constrained by steep nettle-filled banks, lined by willows that tickle its surface with their elegant boughs. I also had to wait for the ground to dry out to Dave's satisfaction for the job to be attempted.

I thrust my hands deeper into my pockets and watched, excited, as he handled the digger with a great deal of skill, extracting earth and stone and depositing it in a pile to one side. The rhythm of his movements - scoop ... swing ... release, scoop ... swing ... release reminded me of learning to waltz at school. It was during one of the release movements that something caught my eye. A slither of something that didn't belong in the dirt and rubble.

I jumped between the machine and the pile of debris. 'Stop,' I yelled, hoping my voice would carry above the throaty noise of the digger's engine, and that he would break with tradition and do as I asked. 'Idiot,' I added under my breath. I turned my back on him, trusting that he would have the brains to see me and stop. I bent over the clumps of clay-like soil, rock and stone, brushed away the top surface and there it was. A tarnished metal chain. I pinched it between my thumb and forefinger and gave it a gentle tug, but it was stuck. Not wanting to break it, I rubbed at the dirt to work it free, which is when I realised it was attached to something that looked like a ring, but it had been buried for so long that the hole in the middle was full of hard, compacted soil. I picked it up and ... ouch ... dropped it. A shock, like a blend of static and an oven burn, raced along my fingers.

Dave climbed down from the cab of the digger.

'Look, love, if you don't mind I need to get on - I've only got this hired until midday and if I don't get it back on time there'll be a fine.'

I rubbed my hand and examined it, expecting to see blood, but there was nothing.

He was looking at me as if I were a few pixels short of a picture. 'Is there anything wrong?'

'I thought ... no, never mind, I'm fine.'

I reached back into the pile of debris and used a loose edge of my fleece to wrap around the ring and chain. I picked them up and slipped them into my pocket. My eye was caught by another object in the now disturbed earth. 'Just a minute. There's something else in here.'

Dave stepped towards me until he could peer over my shoulder. I brushed away some more dirt and picked out three roughly circular discs of metal in my uninjured hand. They were so dirty I couldn't make out what they were. I turned them over.

'They look like old coins to me,' Dave said. 'You find all sorts of stuff when you start digging with one of these,' he waved his hand towards the digger. 'Can I get on now?'

I nodded, wondering if I ought to hire a metal detector and see if there was anything else buried in my garden. I added the coins to my pocket with the ring and chain. 'Yes. I'll leave you to it. Give me a shout if you need anything.'

I kicked off my muddy wellington boots at the back door and slipped my feet into furry, lion's-head slippers. I ran some clean, warm water in the kitchen sink, immersed my hands in it and washed the dirt off my fingers and from beneath my nails. When I had finished, I turned my hands over and over to inspect them from every angle. There wasn't a mark on them, but then I hadn't imagined that sharp, burning sensation. I could still feel it now, although it had faded to a tingle. So what had caused it?

I spread some old newspaper across the kitchen table, turned the pocket of my fleece inside out and allowed its contents to slide onto the paper. Ignoring the ring, I decided to start with the coins, but I wasn't sure what to do. I thought I'd read somewhere that you're not supposed to use anything like soap and water on old coins. Under the sink I found a toothbrush that I used to clean the grout between the bathroom tiles and a rag torn from an old tea towel. I made some coffee and sat down. Picking up the toothbrush, and using gentle strokes, I brushed the dirt from each coin. Sipping my coffee, I examined them one-by-one. They were very tarnished, so it was difficult to make out any of the detail. I peered at them and thought I could identify a monarch's head on one side. Well done Sherlock! All coins have the monarch's head on them don't they? Not that what I could see looked very regal - it could just as easily have been Humpty Dumpty. On the other side was what could have been a shield. They were so worn that it was impossible to read the lettering around the edges.

I put the coins down and jabbed a finger at the ring. The stabbing pain I was rewarded with made me curse and snatch my finger back. I held my hand up in front of my face and examined it. Once again, there was not a mark to be seen.

I frowned. There's got to be a logical explanation for this. Perhaps I'm allergic to the metal. I chewed my now clean fingernails for a moment, thinking. Somewhere I had one of those special cloths you can get from a jeweller's for cleaning silver. I bounded up the stairs to my bedroom and rummaged in a drawer until I found it. In the bathroom I took a pair of disposable gloves from a basket beside the sink.

Back in the kitchen I put the gloves on, screwed up my eyes,

4

took a deep breath and reached out to pick up the chain and ring. Nothing. What a relief. I brushed the chain with the toothbrush to loosen the dirt that clung to its links and then rubbed it using the cloth until the layers of tarnish began to yield to the pressure. A delicate, pale silver emerged. It sparkled when I held it up to the light, like fairy dust sprinkling from the wand of a Disney princess.

I watched it for a moment, a smile spreading over my face, before lowering it back to the table so I could focus on the ring. Using the handle end of the toothbrush I pushed the compacted soil out from its shank, and then brushed the dirt from its surface. My breathing quickened as the metal shed its coat of grime to display its true colours. Gold. Not a brash, over-bright yellow gold, but a deep, luscious, golden gold.

I picked up the jeweller's cloth and polished it, allowing the ring to reveal more of its character. It was a signet ring, and a little out of shape. Its flat face had a curious engraving, and an oval of bright green glass was set into the left side. A curved line around the glass set with black beads gave it the look of a human eye fringed with lashes. To its right there were some small letters that I couldn't read. Between them was something that could have been a tree or a branch. I rubbed a bit harder and squinted at it, trying to work out what the picture was supposed to be. Puzzled, I put the ring down on the table next to the coins and stared at it, certain I'd seen something similar to this before, but I'd no idea where.

TWO

Catherine
Friday, April 18th, 1645

THE FINE, SILK-LIKE THREAD OF a cobweb clung to her hand as she traced the outline of the engraving on the smooth stone with her fingertips.

John Meakin
17th July 1643, Aged 25

She knew what it said, even though she struggled to read the words.

Kneeling by the side of the grave beneath a tall yew tree, the moisture from the damp grass seeped through Catherine's skirts. In one hand she held two posies of bluebells tied together with string. She had gathered them in the forest on the edge of the village. People said it was enchanted, but she had picked bluebells there since she was a young child and had not yet been taken by the fairies. She'd woven two into a bracelet that she wore on her wrist, concealed beneath the cuff of her gown. It was a small act of defiance, and one which gave her great pleasure. She leaned forwards and pressed her free hand into the grass in front of the stone, moulding a sort of cradle into which she placed one posy. Her fingers stroked the delicate flowers, their vibrancy already beginning to fade as their fragile life ebbed away. Her gaze lingered on the stone, the permanent reminder that her beloved John had once walked this earth, but now he existed only in her memory, alongside the ghost of their dreams for the future. That's all they would ever be, memories and dreams that became less vivid with every day that passed.

She stood up, and picking her way with care between the graves she meandered towards the stone wall that enclosed the graveyard. There, she stooped, placed the second posy down on the ground in front of her, and stepped back.

The inscription on this marker stone was also simple - the stonemason charged by the letter.

Catherine Bramble
19th July 1643, Aged 53

It still hurt to know that she would never see them again in this world. Two of the people she had loved the most, taken by the fever that had spread its poisonous vapour through the village, not caring which lives it destroyed and which it spared.

With one last glance at her mother's grave, Catherine turned away. She had to focus on the present. On the living.

Her eyes sought out the small figure perched further along the boundary wall, head turned towards the lane, long black hair hanging in a tangle down her back. It could have been her 20 years ago. How she loved her little girl. Sometimes the emotion was so strong that it was quite overpowering, and she had to steady herself with a few deep breaths. This was one of those moments.

Catherine waded through the longer grass that bordered the wall until she reached her daughter. She leaned with her back against the warm stone and lifted her face up to the sun. On this sort of pleasant spring day, she found it easy to forget the harshness of the recent winter, which had coated the village in a blanket of sparkling white, and frozen the water on the ford under the bridge so the children could skate across the river. She raised her arm and Matilda - Tilly - ducked under it, burying her face in her mother's neck.

'Why do people have to die, mama?'

'It's God's will my love.' She stroked her daughter's hair, fingers teasing at the knots, and Tilly relaxed into her side. Catherine knew

Tilly's memories of her father and grandmother were disintegrating as they aged, like the cloth of an old gown, and one day the gaps would be so large she would no longer be able to patch them.

'But why?'

Catherine didn't know how to answer. In public she wouldn't dare to question, but in private she had doubted the wisdom of a God who would take someone as kind and gentle as her mother, or as caring and loving as John, for himself. It seemed like a selfish act, to deprive this world of those who could do such a lot of good, yet leave others behind.

Others who were cruel and mean.

She must not think such wicked thoughts. Who was she to question these things, when for generations educated men who had travelled and studied accepted that the will of God was sacrosanct?

The church clock chimed. Catherine glanced up at the tower, shielding her eyes with her hand so she could see the face. It was half past three.

'Come. Let's go home. Grandpa will be back soon for his supper, and I haven't made the bread yet.' At the thought of her father the warmth of the sun on her skin seemed to fade. She glanced up, expecting to see a cloud hovering between them, but the sky was a perfect blue canvas. Catherine lifted Tilly down from the wall and took her hand, swinging it to lighten her mood as they crossed the graveyard.

Several Royalist soldiers were smoking under the elm tree on the other side of the gate. The Earl of Northampton's regiment had been quartered in Islip for some time, keeping the road and the bridge over the river Ray open whilst the King was in Oxford. On market days this area would be heaving with stalls, people and animals, but today it was peaceful. One of the soldiers winked at her beneath his plumed hat. There was a time when she would have laughed and winked back. She turned her head away and hurried past.

She reached the cobbled High Street and glanced to her right, wondering if her father would already be drinking in the King's

Head. To her left, across the road, a man dismounted and tethered his horse in front of The Prince's Arms. He had one hand on the door when he looked up and saw her, removed his hat and bowed. Catherine's cheeks glowed with heat that was nothing to do with the sun.

'Who's that?' Tilly asked.

'That's Thomas Marlow.'

'Why did he bow to you?' Tilly raised enquiring eyes to her mother.

Trying to sound casual, Catherine replied, 'He was just being polite. That's what gentlemen do.'

Tilly thought for a moment. 'So why doesn't Grandpa bow to people?'

For the second time in the space of a few minutes, Catherine found herself unable to think of a sensible answer that would satisfy her audacious daughter.

A carriage pulled by four horses rattled past. When the dust had cleared, Catherine could see that Thomas was striding across the road towards them. Her fingers worried at a loose thread on the cuff of her gown.

'Run on home Tilly my love. I'll be right behind you.' She flashed an encouraging smile at her daughter. Tilly dropped her hand and dashed across the road, jumping over the puddles that lingered in some of the deeper ruts. Catherine watched her go. From the corner of her eye she could see Thomas approaching, but she didn't turn towards him. She watched Tilly until the little girl reached the track that led to their house and vanished from sight.

'Mistress Meakin.' Thomas reached her side. A plague of insects fluttered inside her chest. The bluebell bracelet was just visible under her cuff. She focused on it, allowing her nerves to calm, and adjusted her cloak. It was an old one her aunt had given her and it was too big. Catherine almost disappeared within its folds, but she loved its colour - a shade of deep bronze that made her feel like a tree in autumn.

'I am so pleased that I've seen you. Let me escort you home.'

She raised her head. 'It's only across the road, sir. There's really no need.'

'I want to, and besides, I need to talk to you, away from the eyes of others.'

He nodded in the direction of the soldiers who did not appear to be paying them any attention. Catherine's gaze shifted from them to Thomas. He seemed ill at ease. His brows were knitted together obscuring his eyes, and his expression was sombre, or was that just the shadow cast under the brim of his hat, which he had returned to his head? The impression he gave was of a man with a weight pressing on his mind. What could he want to talk to her about with such urgency? And in secret too. Something must have happened since their paths had last crossed, but she could think of nothing. Her stomach clenched, as if it were being squeezed in the mangle she used for wringing laundry at the manor, but whether with fear or excitement she could not tell.

She puzzled over his choice of words as she walked, conscious of him by her side, a scent of leather and horses hovering in the air. If the soldiers were watching them, she could imagine what they would be thinking. The thought made her uneasy and she was reminded how fragile her good name was in this community. She folded her hands in front of her and her fingers connected with the petals of the bluebells. The feel of their cool flesh calmed her and she forced her chin up. She had done nothing to be ashamed of.

As soon as they had turned down the dirt track and were out of sight of anyone passing along the High Street, Thomas stopped. 'Wait, please,' he said, and reached out as if to touch her arm but dropped his hand before it made contact with the worn wool of her cloak.

Catherine could see her house, tucked into the middle of a ramshackle row of timber-framed farm workers' dwellings just a few yards away. It was a low building with two tiny windows hanging beneath a thatched roof, like glassy eyes under bushy eyebrows.

Tilly had left the front door ajar. She yearned for the security of its humble walls, within which she could cocoon herself and Tilly away from the world and its dangers. But she was also drawn to Thomas. There was a powerful intensity to him and his strange behaviour that both fascinated and excited her.

'There's something I want you to have.'

He held out a small velvet pouch. She backed away from him, her hands held in front of her as if to push him away if he came any closer, and shook her head. 'Sir, you must know, I cannot ...'

'You must take it ... please,' his voice had a supplicating quality that was quite at odds with his usual air of total confidence. 'It's difficult to explain, but I feel there is a darkness gathering around you. This is a talisman. Please, I want you to have it and keep it with you always.'

He pressed the pouch into her hand. The softness of the velvet caressed her palm like the fluffy, warm down of a young chicken. Catherine stared at it. He must know she couldn't accept a gift from him. What would people think, and say? She opened her mouth, closed it again, eyes fixed on the pouch, and her opportunity to speak was lost, swallowed by her hesitation. He turned and strode back to the road. She should follow him, insist that he take it back, but before she could move, she heard him greet another passer-by. She span around and hastened to her front door. On the threshold she hesitated, curiosity overcoming caution. After a quick glance over her shoulder to make sure she was still alone on the narrow track, she pushed her fingers into the neck of the pouch and opened it just far enough to peep inside. Disbelief dropped, as a veil, clouding her vision, and the mangle tightened its grip on her stomach. She jerked her head around again. She was still alone. Her fingers fumbled on the drawstring as she stepped into her house and closed the door behind her.

Catherine gulped in the welcoming aroma of fresh rosemary that lingered in the small room. With shaking hands she removed her cloak and looped it through the rungs of the short ladder that led up, under the thatch, to the platform that was just big enough for the straw mattress she shared with Tilly. The leather satchel that had belonged to her mother, and in which she kept her precious drawing materials, hung from a hook beside the ladder. She slipped the pouch into the satchel and turned, eyes searching for her daughter. The room was dim. Daylight tried to filter in through the small panes of glass in the windows above her head, but failed to penetrate the dense shadows that hung in the corners.

'Tilly,' she called, hoping her voice wasn't as shaky as her hands.

Her daughter's head appeared from the top of the ladder, hair streaming towards the floor. 'Here Mama,' Tilly giggled. For a moment, Catherine forgot the pouch, Thomas Marlow, and his darkness. Here, in this room, was all that mattered.

She took four brisk paces across the stone floor and opened the back door. Light flooded in, racing across the room, caressing the well-scrubbed surface of the table in its honeyed glow before spreading its fingers into every nook and cranny, chasing away the gloom. Tilly slid down the steps and scampered past her into the garden.

'What shall I pick?'

'Spinach, please, my love, and then you can play outside.'

Catherine paused in the doorway and allowed the soothing familiarity of the view to calm her nerves. Her eyes scanned the panorama, from the formal structure of the bridge that spanned the Ray with its neat stone arches, around to the untamed wetlands of Otmoor. It was a scene that shifted and changed with the seasons and the moods of the weather. Whatever face it presented, its wildness and untamed beauty never failed to please her.

She smiled as a loud honking noise rent through the still air and a skein of geese emerged, their shapes in flight forming fluid black letters against the pale blue sky. She shielded her eyes and watched until they were mere specks in the distance. It was very tempting to fetch her charcoal sticks and lose herself and her worries in a new sketch, but the church bells chiming the hour reminded her she had jobs to do. First, though, she must do something with the contents of that pouch.

With an effort she dragged her eyes away and turned back to her kitchen. The table filled much of the space, apart from which an oak chest and four hard-backed chairs comprised the only furniture. Along one wall, shelves attached to the building's timber frame from waist height to the ceiling held cooking utensils, earthenware bowls, mugs, platters and her meagre pantry. Bunches of herbs and wild flowers were strung along the solid beam that ran the length of the room. They danced in the breeze that drifted in from the open door.

She opened the small chest in which she stored her few household linens and her sewing materials. On the top was a metal box, inside which she kept the few items of jewellery her mother had possessed - a brooch, her wedding ring and a St Christopher on a long silver chain. Simple trinkets to many, but precious to Catherine. She unfastened the clasp on the chain and let the charm slide back into the box. She clicked the lid shut, closed the chest and retrieved the pouch that Thomas had given her from her satchel. Checking that Tilly was still occupied in the garden, she took the chain and the pouch to the table and shook the contents out.

In the few minutes that had elapsed since she'd peeped into the pouch, Catherine had been hoping that she'd imagined its contents. She hadn't. The ring landed on the table with a solid thump. She swallowed, hard, and stared, unwilling to believe her own eyes. Her overwhelming instinct was to put it back in the pouch and return it, somehow, to Thomas. But how could she do that? She couldn't turn up on his doorstep and ask to see him. Nor could she give it to one of his household staff and trust them to return it without questioning how it came to be in her possession, or mentioning it to someone else.

She had to do something to make it disappear. Her fingers reached across the table, and with a quick, furtive movement as if she were being watched, she picked it up. It was chunky and heavy. Catherine raised it to her eye level, and studied it. This was no cheap trinket. A large, oval-shaped green gemstone was set into the gold on its flat surface, partially ringed with smaller black stones, and it had a curious engraving of a human figure who appeared to be about to fall from the branches of a sapling, next to the letters 's l i p'. As she studied the design, puzzling over what it meant and twisting the ring between her fingers, the gemstone caught the shaft of sunlight penetrating the room from the open door and it seemed to pulse with life.

Catherine gasped. It was the most beautiful object she'd ever held. Seconds and minutes slipped by and still she stood, staring at the ring, unable to decide what to do. Tilly singing nearby spurred her to action. She threaded the ring onto the chain, fastened it around her neck and slipped it inside her gown where it seemed to burn into her skin.

Her head was buzzing now, remembering Thomas's words. She plucked some sprigs of thyme and added them with a venison bone to the stockpot. Whatever he had meant still eluded her. She poked at the fire in the hearth. It crackled and spat in protest. She fed it another log, hung the stockpot above and started work on the bread dough. What was the darkness he had referred to? She didn't understand, but if there was any chance that Tilly might be in danger, Catherine was in no doubt she would do anything in her power to protect her daughter. She was also certain that the ring was unique and valuable. No-one could see her with it, especially not her father. She shivered, although the room was not cold, wondering what state of inebriation he would be in when he came for his supper.

The spinach leaves that Tilly picked were thick with woody stalks. Catherine washed and trimmed them, chopping the stalks into fine slices and adding everything to the pot. As she worked, she listened for the stomping of her father's boots on the path outside. She lost count of how many times the church bell had marked the passing of the minutes and hours and there was still no sign of him. Tilly was hungry. Catherine spooned some broth into a bowl and tried to ignore her own rumbling stomach, knowing her father would expect them to sup together. She lit the candles, which cast grotesque shadows over the grey walls, sent Tilly to bed, and sat at the table with a pile of sewing by her side, straining her eyes to see in the dim light, and screwing her nose up as the acrid smell of tallow filled the room.

The needle slipped with ease through the delicate fabrics, guided by her nimble fingers, but her mind was elsewhere, thinking of the events of the last few weeks, and recalling the incident that had stirred her former zest for life. Zest that had gone stale since John had died. Shrivelled up like a strip of lemon peel.

She'd been walking down the High Street, battling against the strong wind that had been funnelling up the hill between the buildings towards her. As a man on horseback had trotted past, a vicious gust had swept his hat from his head and slammed it into her face. She'd had no time to think. Her arms had moved of their own accord, and she'd caught the hat. She had stood still, feeling foolish. The man and horse had swung around and trotted back towards her. As he'd drawn closer, she'd recognised him as Thomas Marlow. His father, Richard, was one of the wealthiest men in the village, as well as being her landlord and her father's employer. John, too, had worked on the Marlow estate as a gamekeeper before he died.

She'd held the hat out to Thomas, and he'd leaned over to take it, grazing her fingertips with his own. He'd paused, staring at her, his expression puzzled, as if he thought he knew her but couldn't quite remember who she was. Embarrassed, she'd dropped her hand and backed away. He'd replaced his hat and nodded to her with a smile that started with his eyes, before he'd turned and spurred his horse into a trot.

It had all been over in a matter of seconds, but she had wandered home in a daze, seeing that smile in front of her instead of the road.

Then, after church the following Sunday, she'd had the sensation that someone was watching her. She'd turned around and there he was, across the graveyard, standing between two giant yew trees in a group that included his father and Sir Henry Gilder, the most powerful man in Islip. Thomas's head had been angled towards Sir Henry, but his eyes were looking beyond the older man's shoulder in her direction. She'd turned, certain she would see someone approaching on the path behind her, but there was no-one. Feeling exposed under his scrutiny, Catherine had been grateful for Tilly pulling at her skirts, wanting to leave the churchyard.

Since then, it seemed that she had encountered him around the village almost daily; at the market, on the way to her aunt's house, or to the manor delivering or collecting sewing. She was beginning to suspect that those meetings were not by chance, but design. The thought both worried and excited her.

The candle flickered and her needle slipped, stabbing into the tender skin at the side of her fingernail. A droplet of blood glistened. She put her sewing down and sucked her finger. The church clock chimed, pulling her back to reality. This was her life. This small house in which she spent most of her non-working hours; cleaning, cooking, and waiting for her father to return so that she could serve him food.

There was still no sign of him. She clicked her tongue, trying not to give into the annoyance that was swelling within her. He was spending more and more time in one of Islip's many alehouses, but still he expected her to cook and wait on him, returning to her home in the evening rather than his own, kicking off his working boots, planting his feet under her table, as if they belonged there, and lingering in front of her fire.

She heard him before he pushed the door open, cursing as he stumbled in the lane outside. She poured warm water into a bowl and placed it on the table with a towel for him to wash.

'Where's Tilly?' he asked.

'In bed. It's late.' She kept her voice even, careful not to imply any criticism of him in her tone.

He stripped off his shirt and stood, stooping, in his breeches to scrub the day's grime from his hands and body. William Bramble's face was weathered, with heavy lines around the eyes, but he was lean and muscled, accustomed to hard physical labour. Catherine averted her eyes and focused on putting the food on the table. The broth was thick, swimming with spinach and turnips. The bread had cooled but was still fragrant. She poured a mug of ale for each of them from an earthenware jug.

He slurped his broth and tore off a large chunk of bread, pushing it into his mouth whole. Catherine tried to ignore the sound of him eating, and swallowed the sour taste that rose in her throat. She crumbled her bread between her fingers and lifted a smaller piece to her lips.

'Curse that Richard Marlow,' he spat out between mouthfuls. 'Thinks he's better 'n the rest of us. Just 'cos he was lucky to be born a landowner, don't make him a better man than the next one.'

Catherine gulped in air, and bread, and almost choked. Her father couldn't know of her encounters with Thomas Marlow, but his words were a brutal reminder of the difference in their positions in life. The faint tingle of the ring against her skin was reassuring, and she had to resist the impulse to feel for the chain around her neck, reaching instead for her ale and taking a sip, whilst she tried to recover her composure.

'Someone has to be in charge, Father,' she kept her voice light and studied him from behind her long, black lashes, hoping he would not notice the scrutiny, trying to judge his mood.

'I know girl, but it don't mean he shouldn't treat us with respect. They're all the same. We do a hard day's work for what? For a wage that would insult a rat, and then they demand half of that back. 'Got to do our bit for the King's men'.'

She put her spoon down and pushed her bowl away. His mocking tone and the pitch of his voice cautioned her that tonight's ale had put him on the brink of belligerence.

'He, and others like him, they don't understand the mood of the country. Of men like me that do all the work for the scraps they care to throw at us while they pocket the big profits. But still they want more from us. We have to pay for their war. It 'ain't right and happen we won't have to put up with it for much longer.'

He spoke with a sneer; a man with a secret that he can't wait to share.

'The mood of the country! What do you know about 'the mood of the country'?' She snatched her hand to her mouth and pressed it there, trying to force the words back in. Swallow them. She daren't blink. Her eyes did not leave his face, waiting for a change in his expression as her words sank in. Her other hand gripped the table.

'You mark my words girl.'

Catherine relaxed. She might not have spoken, for he was not listening. He dipped his bread in the broth and waved it in front of her, splattering droplets onto the table.

'Preacher man spoke to us in the lane. Says Parliament is building this new army that's going to defeat the King. That ambitious pup - Cromwell - is in charge.' There was intensity to his expression, as if he'd been given something to believe in and he was determined to defend it.

'While they're busy fighting each other, honest men in this country are going to start standing up for themselves and may the devil take the rest of them.'

He thumped the table with his fist, making her jump.

She concentrated on keeping her voice calm, all thoughts of Thomas Marlow banished from her mind. 'Father, you can't say that. The King is still the King, chosen by God. He'll come to terms with his Parliament.'

How often had she heard John say that Parliament couldn't keep denying the King's demands? But it was nearly two years since John had died and there was still no agreement between them, yet she had never thought to question his view. Even as she spoke John's words, her mind was busy with the meaning of her father's. Was he saying he was going to fight? Against the King's men or even the Parliamentarians with their weapons and horses. With what? With words?

He spat on the floor. She turned away. He was still her father and she did not want him to see the disgust written on her face. 'You mark my words girl. There's going to be change, and those who are lording it over the rest of us today might find they've got nothing tomorrow.'

'But how will that help?' Catherine's chair legs screeched across the stone as she pushed away from the table and leapt to her feet. She was struggling to follow his argument, which seemed idealistic and lacking in substance. She could feel her anger bubbling up within her like the broth in her stockpot. 'Who's going to pay you to work then?'

He leaned across the table, hands stretched out towards her. 'Do it for myself won't I. He's no better 'n I am.'

'But you need tools and seeds ... and ... and animals and land and people to sell to. How are you going to get all of those things and what are you going to live off before you've got anything to sell?'

'I don't expect you to understand, girl.'

His voice was full of a new self-importance that sickened her. 'I always told you I was going places, didn't I?'

He poured more ale into his mug, spilling it down the side so it slopped onto the table. He smeared it with the sleeve of his shirt.

Catherine had heard enough. She cleared the table, wiped out the bowls and put them away. He started filling his pipe with tobacco, staring into the glow of the fire.

She stood by the table, arms folded in front of her. 'Goodnight Father.' She didn't look at him, directing her eyes instead towards the door.

Slowly, he folded his tobacco pouch and put it in his pocket. His hands moved by habit, unguided by his eyes, which had lost their animation of a few minutes ago and now appeared cloudy and unfocused. 'You want me to leave?'

She nodded.

'Aye. I suppose it is late.'

He pulled his boots back on, lit his pipe and sucked on it for a few moments, taking his time.

Catherine waited in silence, sensing that to say anything more would not encourage him to hurry. 'Goodnight girl,' he said. He strode across the kitchen, and in seconds had let himself out of the house, allowing the door to swing closed behind him. Catherine listened to his footsteps receding as he plodded down the track to his own house at the end of the row.

The cool night air that had pushed its way into the room when her father opened the door blew away her anger. But the chill that crept from her feet to her shoulders was not due to the change in temperature. She recalled his words and his bravado. Fear nibbled at her stomach.

'Fool,' she muttered. 'No, dangerous fool.' If he got involved with some ill-advised scheme he could lose his job and his freedom, perhaps even more than that. His actions could cause trouble for her and Tilly as well. But what was he getting involved with?

She pondered that question whilst she slid the bolts into place to secure the door, scrubbed the table and banked the fire, but she was unable to find an answer.

It struck her as well that it was more than a little hypocritical of him to talk about people taking from others when he expected her to provide meals for him every day, but had not once offered her so much as a half penny towards the cost.

It was so typical of her father. Never a thought for anyone but himself.

She was assaulted by a sudden, unexpected memory of her mother. It was so powerful that when she closed her eyes she could see her mother with crystal clarity as if they were together, in the same room, except she was back in her parents' house and there was a vile smell that made her clamp her hand over her nose. Her mother lay on a straw pallet in the corner of the kitchen where her brother slept, arms wrapped around her stomach, a bucket by her side. Catherine could hear her moaning. And then, her father's voice. Angry. Shouting. There was no supper. The young Catherine had cowered on the top rung of the ladder, too scared to go to her mother's help until her father had stamped out of the house, slamming the door behind him. Then she'd crept down the ladder. Rushed to her mother's side. Thrown her arms around her. Wished she could take away the pain.

Catherine's eyes jerked open. The muscles in her legs twitched with tiredness. She should go to bed, but her mind was too busy to yield to sleep. Just beyond the circle of dim light cast by the candle, she could make out the outline of her satchel. She fetched it and pulled out a charcoal stick and a sheet of paper, frowning as she saw it was her last. She folded it in half, tore it carefully along the crease and returned one half to her satchel. The other she laid on the table and started to sketch, not thinking about what she was drawing, but allowing her thoughts to express themselves across the paper. When she was finished, she sat back and looked at her work. She had sketched three panels of her father. In the first he had two faces - one looking forwards and one backwards. In the second, he still had two faces and his feet were in the same position, but he was smaller, and his body was twisted to one side as if he was unable to move in either direction. In the third, only his two faces were visible, dissolving into a plume of grey dust rising from the hooves of the horses pulling Richard Marlow's carriage over Islip bridge on the road to the south, and London.

She stared at it for a few minutes, puzzling over what it meant. Was this how she saw her father, or was this how he saw himself? Was he disappearing because he was escaping what he saw as the unfairness of a world that was holding men like him back, or was the act of living itself destroying him and others like him? She could not say.

And then there was Thomas.

The ring. That changed everything. What did he mean by insisting she have it? She shouldn't have accepted it, but if she kept it close and was careful to ensure no-one saw it. What harm could it do? The ring could even be a symbol that her life might be about to change, as though she were waking from a long sleep. It may be that it was time to start living again.

How she had loved John, and always would, with his lazy smile that turned his mouth into a crescent moon and his eyes that sparkled like the frost in moonlight. But it wasn't his face she saw now when she closed her eyes, but Thomas Marlow's, and his confident smile that carried just a hint of arrogance in the curve of his lips.

Catherine's fingers fumbled for the chain around her neck. She twisted it, feeling the tingle of the ring against her skin where it nestled between her breasts. A frisson of excitement fizzed in her veins, and she allowed it to spread around her body and infuse her thoughts, welcoming its warmth and energy. It was time she moved on, but she was foolish to think of Thomas Marlow in that way. There could be no future for her in that direction. Or could there? She stroked the bluebell bracelet, now hanging limp and withering from her wrist and thought of her daughter, sleeping peacefully upstairs. This could be her chance to grasp a more secure future for Tilly and she wasn't going to let it pass her by.

THREE

Hannah

OXFORD CITY CENTRE. IT'S ONE of my favourite places. I think it's the way the old and new don't so much mingle as co-exist, meshed together by the colleges of Oxford University that straddle the two - with one foot in the modern world and the other in their historic past.

I was standing on the High Street. Cornmarket, with its smattering of historic buildings wedged between purpose-built, bland retail was behind me. The ancient spire of the University Church rose in front of me. I blinked, and it was as if a shutter fell and my imagination projected a vision of this scene but from centuries ago. The gentry stepping out of their carriages, the ladies stretching out their dainty ankles and holding up their skirts to avoid the steaming horse crap on the cobbles.

I stepped off the pavement to overtake a tour guide waving a yellow flag surrounded by his flock of tourists, and hopped straight back on to avoid the cyclists hurtling past, competing for space with an endless procession of buses, all heading towards Magdalen Bridge.

I turned left, following a chattering group of students laden down with books onto Turl Street and the transformation was as sudden and surprising as Alice's world on the other side of the Looking Glass. Here, the backdrop is the golden glow of the high stone walls of Oxford's Colleges - I'm never sure which. This is a world of narrow, medieval lanes or alleys populated by the tiniest pubs imaginable, restaurants that ramble over many levels separated by heavily-trodden stone steps, and dusty shops with doorways that even I have to duck to enter. They trade in high quality goods that lack the designer-label appeal of the retailers in the nearby Westgate Centre, or specialist antiquities, for which serious collectors would part with substantial sums of money.

Turl Street is stuffed with history and one-offs. I can happily lose myself here, idling away an afternoon, discovering the treasures that might be hidden in the cramped interiors that lurk behind the bright facades. Today, though, I had a purpose. I lingered in front of a shop front displaying worn, leather-bound books and the urge to push the door and enter was difficult to resist. 'Maybe later,' I told myself, the voice inside my head insistent. I didn't have time to browse.

Like Lewis Carroll's white rabbit, I was going to be late.

According to the lady I'd spoken to on the phone, I should find Denton's Collectables at 36A, accessed by a green front door between a leather goods shop and a jeweller, specialising in coins, maps and postcards - sales, valuations and sourcing. Sure enough, there it was. I rang the buzzer - viewings here were by appointment only - and gave my name. A click indicated the lock had been released and I pushed. The door swung open. I ducked and followed a narrow corridor that led in a straight line back from the street to another door that stood ajar, dispelling a shaft of light to show the way.

I pushed this door and stepped into the most peculiar room. It seemed to have modelled itself on Oxford's brand of old and new. It was very wide. One side was low and dark as if it were burrowing into the rear of the building. It was lined with thin wooden drawers from the floor to the ceiling. The other side was flooded with natural light from the double glass doors that opened onto a courtyard. The ceiling was much higher, as if a floor had been removed and it was occupying the space of two storeys. A grey metal desk was dominated by a massive computer screen, which dwarfed its keyboard. In front of it was one of those ergonomic swivel desk chairs that are supposed to mould themselves to your posture and cost a fortune. Along the far wall a table was covered with a black cloth above which adjustable spotlights were suspended on a sort of metal beam.

You might think it's strange that I would notice this level of detail in a room, but you see it's what I do. I'm a photographer and although I earn a living doing the usual - wedding photos, family portraits, dog shows and the occasional corporate deal - it's the contrasts that fascinate me and I long to capture in my images. Light and dark, new and old, mono and colour - I'm sure you get the idea. And this room was just packed with it. I could feel my fingers twitching and if I'd had my camera with me I'd have whipped it out and started snapping away. It was all I could do to stop myself reaching for my mobile and I probably would have done if the man leaning against the glass doors, fingers hooked in the pockets of black designer jeans, hadn't interrupted me.

'This bit's modern - built in the '60s I suspect. Don't know how they got away with it really. Bit of an eyesore when you look at it from outside.'

He must have noticed my expression, or perhaps he was used to this reaction from his customers. Don't think for one moment that because I haven't mentioned him already I hadn't noticed him. He was hard to miss. For one thing, he was tall. If he ever ventured into that burrow of drawers he would have to do it on all fours. For another, I couldn't help but notice that he was gorgeous - toe-tinglingly gorgeous. I had almost forgotten what that sensation felt like. He had long, wavy dark hair held back from his face by a blue bandanna and heavy, dark eyebrows beneath which his eyes were striking, light and grey with silver flecks. I felt sure he'd be more at home with a guitar in his hands than a load of dirty old coins.

'I'm Matthew - call me Matt.' He held out a hand and I shook it.

'Hannah,' I said.

'Have a seat.' He pulled out two chairs that had been tucked beneath the table. He took one himself, and stretched his long legs out until they must have been touching the back wall. I shrugged my jacket off and sat in the other.

'So, you've found some old coins?' From a box on a shelf by the table he withdrew a sheet of black felt and spread it out in front of us.

'Er, yes.' I reached into my bag for the jewellery pouch I'd put the coins into and handed it to him. He tipped them out, picked them up one-by-one and inspected them.

'I did my best to clean them up, but they're a bit battered.'

From his box of tricks on the shelf he plucked a cloth and a bottle of something. He waved them at me. 'May I?'

I nodded and watched him polish the coins, taking delicate strokes with long, slender fingers. Just as I was thinking it was almost too bad I was still off men, the door through which I had entered burst open and crashed against the wall. Startled, I looked up to see a young woman backing into the room. She was curvy, with blonde hair tied back in a pony tail that swished almost to her waist. Dangling from one hand was a paper bag and in the other she held a takeaway cardboard carry tray containing two cups of steaming hot coffee with *The Varsity Cafe* scrawled across the side in a script typeface. She dumped them on the shelf, reached into the bag and pulled out a muffin, which she bit into before leaning over Matt's shoulder.

'Lauren, please.' He raised his shoulder to shrug her away and continued his scrutiny of the coins, now peering at them through a magnifying glass - not the kind that I remember using as a kid to burn holes in paper - a proper, serious, grown-up kind of magnifying glass. She threw him a sulky glance, which he didn't appear to notice, took one of the coffees and moved to the other end of the table where she leaned against the wall.

'Civil War. Definitely.' He put the magnifying glass down on the table and pushed his chair back. 'The date is quite difficult to read, but I think it's 1644, and see this plume of feathers?' He flipped one of the coins over. 'It's from the badge of the Prince of Wales. Charles I included it on all the coins he had made in provincial mints to pay his soldiers. It distinguished his coins from those of his enemy.'

'You mean it was made here in Oxford?'

'Minted, yes,' he corrected me. Lauren smirked and I could have kicked myself for showing my ignorance. If my history teacher at school had looked like Matt Denton perhaps I would have paid more attention.

'War is an expensive business, and Charles had lost control of the mint in London to the Parliamentarians. He had to make more money. He had set up an alternative parliament here in Oxford and he had a mint here too. He also changed the inscription.'

He thrust the magnifying glass into my hand and pointed to a coin. 'It's only just legible, but see here - it says *Iustitia thronum firmat.*'

I was about to ask him what that meant, but he must have read my face. '*Justice strengthens the throne.* It was the King's way of saying that he was the rightful ruler. Where did you say you found them?'

So I told him the story.

'Don't get too excited about how much they're worth. Charles was minting coins faster than McDonalds turns out burgers, so although they're old, they're not particularly rare. I doubt any museums or private collectors will be very interested.'

I shook my head. 'No, I don't care what they're worth. I want to know about them because I found something else with them.' I pulled out the other jewellery pouch into which I'd placed the ring and chain. I tipped them onto the felt next to the coins. Lauren leaned forward, the flash of gold no doubt attracting her attention. Her eyes gleamed and her mouth formed a perfect but silent 'o'.

I ignored her and focused on Matt as he picked up the ring and unfolded a polishing cloth. He rubbed at it, applying pressure in firm, smooth strokes on its surface and inside the shank. There was no reaction from him, not a thing.

'Didn't you feel anything?'

He raised his head and looked at me. His eyes were questioning, silver flecks in a slab of granite. Great. The most attractive man I'd met in a long time and he already thinks I'm a loon.

'When I picked this up I got a massive shock from it - like an electric shock - and every time I've touched it since ... the same.'

Lauren smirked again. She'd only just met me, but she was

enjoying watching me make a fool of myself. I know that what I'd experienced when touching that ring was real - I could still feel it burning my skin - but to anyone else it must sound crazy.

'Maybe I'm allergic to the metal,' I mumbled. But even as I said it I knew how ridiculous a suggestion that was. Whoever heard of a metal allergy giving you an electric shock? A nasty rash maybe.

Lauren giggled, but Matt seemed to consider my words with more seriousness than they deserved. He adjusted the angle of his chair and leaned towards me.

'This is gold.' He looked at my hands and pointed at my gran's wedding band that I wear on my little finger. 'Does that bother you?'

'No.'

'Can I look at it?'

I slipped the slim band off and handed it to him. He turned his magnifying glass scrutiny to it.

'This is also gold, but not as pure. I don't think you're allergic.'

'It's a mystery then. Can you read the letters?'

'Yes.' He held the ring out, flat side turned towards me. It sparkled with the brightness of the Crown Jewels. Not that I'd ever seen the Crown Jewels. I peered at it. The engravings were now very clear, sharply defined, as if they had been done just yesterday. There was a stick figure man in a tree and some letters. 's l i p.' I read them aloud one-by-one.

He nodded. 'And this green stone on the other side is like the iris of an eye, with the black stones being the eyelashes, so I'd say that if you put the two together it says Islip.'

I couldn't drag my eyes away. It was like a picture, telling a story. But of what? I sensed Lauren staring too, as she sipped her coffee.

'So, this ring is somehow associated with the village? Which is where I found it? And where I live?'

Matt shrugged. 'I'm not a specialist in jewellery. I've no idea what it means.'

I felt as though I'd run slap bang into that well-worn cliché - the brick wall.

'Wait, you said green stone? That's a piece of glass surely.'

Matt shook his head. 'Like I said, I'm no jewellery expert, but I'd stake a lot of money that what is set into that ring is not glass.'

'Maybe I should take it to the jeweller next door.' I pondered.

Matt coughed. 'I wouldn't,' he said.

I looked at him in surprise.

'He has a bit of a reputation.'

What sort of reputation I wanted to ask, but Matt appeared preoccupied. He turned the ring over and ran his fingertips over its surface.

'I've got a friend who knows a lot about the English Civil War.' I tried to focus on what Matt was saying. 'Joel Fielding. He's based here at the university. Shall I call him and see if he might be able to help you?'

I nodded. 'Thank you, that's very kind.'

Matt moved to his desk and made the call while I waited. Lauren sat down in his chair, held her hands out and stretched her fingers, admiring her glossy fingernails. I wondered if she behaved like this with every client who visited or if she just didn't like me.

'He can see you tomorrow,' Matt said. 'Is 2pm good for you?'

'Great,' I nodded.

He hung up whilst I gathered the coins and replaced them in one of the pouches. 'Would you mind putting the ring back in here?' I passed the other pouch to Matt. Touching it and giving myself a shock that would make me yelp was not appealing, especially with an audience.

'Sure. Could I just take a photo of it first? I'll do some research, and I'll call you if I find anything interesting.'

I wrote my number on a post-it note he pushed towards me whilst he took a few snaps on his phone.

I left with both my jewellery pouches, the phone number and address of Professor Joel Fielding, and a sensation in the tips of my toes that I hadn't experienced for a very long time.

I walked straight past the bookshop, forgetting that I had promised myself some time between its cramped shelves and returned to where I'd parked my car on a meter.

Islip was busy as I drove back into the village. It was school pick-up time and mums lingered in small groups talking, or were being dragged by their kids to the play area next to the village shop. The car park was full and some people were fixing posters to gates and telegraph poles along the lane. More posters decorated trees and fences on Mill Street, and when I got to the entrance to the Confessor's Walk - named in honour of Edward the Confessor who was born here - a banner had been erected with various slogans: 'Islip says NO,' 'No new road here,' 'Ban the bridge'. The campaigners had my support. This was just a scheme by the landowner to cash in on the pressure to build houses in this part of Oxfordshire. The new bridge, at the point where the rivers Ray and Cherwell converge, would divert traffic away from the picturesque and narrow old stone bridge in the centre of the village, but it would also open up the fields bordering the proposed route for massive housing development in the middle of the green belt, turning this rural backwater into an urban landscape.

Less than a hundred metres further on, I pulled into my drive. I went straight through to the kitchen and opened the back door. The weather was warming up and the forecast was for an early mini heat wave to arrive in the next few days. I was eager to see what progress Dave had made on my deck whilst I'd been out. The scars that he and his digger had inflicted on my garden were still visible. I walked around the area that would be the deck. The footings had set, or gone off, or whatever concrete does when it's poured into a hole - and the legs for the platform were in place. I perched on one of them and watched the light changing as fluffy white clouds flirted with the sun, and shadows danced along the stone wall that was the border of my garden. It was as close to perfection as I could imagine. I fetched my camera, selected a lens, and captured it all in pixels. Red kites were hovering overhead, swooping and soaring. I lay down in the straggly grass that should be my lawn and took frame by frame of these beautiful birds. A family of deer ran across the field on the other side of the river, and I just managed to fire off a series of shots before they vaulted over a low hedge and disappeared into a wooded area.

The light was fading, and when I checked my watch I was surprised I'd been out here for over an hour. It's not unusual for me to lose all sense of time when I'm alone with my camera, but having realised it was getting late, cold and hunger soon followed. The shadows were deepening across my garden and I shivered, struck by the sudden sensation that I wasn't alone. I spun around but I was being foolish. There was no-one there. My thoughts returned to the ring and what this friend of Matt's would be able to tell me - if anything - as I replaced my camera in its case and returned indoors.

It was during my dinner-for-one - vegetarian chilli with nachos, eaten from a tray on my lap in front of the TV - that I remembered something. When I first moved to Islip I had bought a book on its history from the village shop. What did it say about the Civil War? I couldn't remember, but something was tugging in the far recesses of my memory, and if there was anything it was bound to be in that book. After I'd finished eating I scoured my bookshelves. It didn't take long to find it - wedged between my bible of photographic techniques and a walking guide to the Brecon Beacons. It was a small book - only 40-something pages. It fell open in the middle and I flicked backwards - and there it was - Islip in the Civil War - and facing it was the picture from the ring.

I didn't know which to read first. My eyes hovered between the two, but were drawn to the picture, which was identified as the rebus depicting an eye and a slip of a fig tree, which was created in stained glass in Westminster to commemorate the origins of a 16th century Abbot of Westminster - John Islip. The ring was still in my bag. I placed the open book on the kitchen table and tipped the ring out next to it. To avoid touching it I rested my head sideways on the table. Even at such an awkward angle it was easy to identify the design - it was less intricate, but unmistakeably the same.

I sat up and shifted my eyes to the right hand page, where the headline read: 'Battle of Islip Bridge'. Of course. I had known that, but I'd forgotten. I read with new interest of how the Parliamentarians had despatched Oliver Cromwell to command the first engagement for the New Model Army to Islip. The aim was to help stop King Charles I from meeting up with Prince Rupert who was believed to be in Worcester. A Royalist garrison was stationed at Islip, where the bridge had strategic importance and made the road the main route if you wanted to avoid fortified Oxford and the wetlands of Otmoor. Cromwell's army attacked and defeated the Royalist troops. It was strange to think of sleepy little Islip being a place of such significance all those centuries ago.

I pushed the book away. My eyes were drawn back to the ring. It was beautiful. But to whom had it belonged and how did it come to be buried in my garden? My hand reached for my phone as if it had a life of its own, like the Thing in the Addams Family. I picked it up and stared, puzzled, at the keypad. Who did I think I was going to call at this time of night? Hardly anyone knew about the ring anyway. I put my phone down, switched off the lights and went to bed.

FOUR

Catherine
Saturday, April 19th, 1645

THE FIRST BEAMS OF LIGHT cast by the weak morning sun bounced through the thick glass of the naked windows and stroked Catherine's face. Her eyes flickered open and she smiled. She had always liked mornings. They brought with them the freshness and promise of a new day. She watched the dust motes swirling under the thatch and reached out a hand as if she would catch them. Through the window, which was at her eye level but separated from her sleeping platform by the void that hung over her kitchen, she could see a pale, pinkish sky. She stretched her limbs, which were stiff with inertia, and cold.

Tilly slept still, cocooned in the thin blanket that they shared so only the top of her head and part of her face were visible. Catherine pressed her lips to her daughter's cheek, feeling her warmth, and then slid from the mattress, tugged on her gown, and wrapped a thick woollen shawl around her shoulders for extra warmth. She trusted her feet to guide her without slipping down the familiar rungs of the ladder into the darkness below, which was yet to welcome in the light of the new day. She unbolted the front door and resurrected the fire.

Her movements were a well-established, daily routine. She didn't need to think about them, which was good, since her thoughts this morning were occupied with her father's words of the previous evening. Whatever he was getting involved with, she had to distance herself and Tilly from it. She stirred the thin porridge, flavoured with dried berries and honey, and remembered she had another problem to resolve. The chain was still around her neck, the ring exerting gentle pressure against her skin. Its presence this morning, though, was comforting. It had the familiarity of a loyal companion. She would talk to her father over breakfast and this time he would listen.

The smell of warming oats soon filled the room. Tilly shuffled down the ladder, yawning and rubbing her eyes. She pulled three bowls and spoons from the shelves, placed them on the table and slid onto a chair. Catherine poured some porridge into a bowl and pushed it towards her. 'Eat, my love.'

A thump on the door made them both jump, even though it was not unexpected. William Bramble grunted a greeting to his daughter and granddaughter. He stamped his feet on the step, and without bothering to remove his boots, claimed the empty chair at the head of the table.

'Good morning Father,' said Catherine, infusing her smile with optimism and energy.

He ignored her and helped himself to a generous portion of porridge.

Was his sullen silence any better than his garrulous, alcohol-fuelled bravado of the previous evening? She watched him scooping porridge into his mouth, hunched over the bowl so the spoon had less distance to travel. His eyes were red-rimmed, whether with lack of sleep or an excess of drink in a tavern last night she couldn't tell. There was a tenseness about the set of his shoulders and he appeared on edge, as if he was waiting for something. Her optimism faded, but even if he would not listen to her, she had to try.

She noticed Tilly had finished eating. 'Will you go and dress my love.'

Tilly nodded and left the table.

Now was her moment.

'Father.' Catherine kept her voice low, hoping her words wouldn't reach Tilly's ears. She had no wish to alarm her daughter, whom she had noticed had begun to show awareness beyond her years to the nuances of adult moods and behaviour.

William Bramble paused, loaded spoon raised halfway to his mouth, cooling porridge dripping from it, like a ball of thread unrolling.

'What you were saying last night. I'm worried ...'

He dropped the spoon and it hit the table with a clatter. Moving with the swiftness of a red kite swooping on its prey, but none of the grace, he half raised himself from his chair and leaned towards her, resting his weight on his right elbow. His coarse grey beard brushed her cheek and she recoiled from his rancid breath. He tapped the fingers of his left hand on her collarbone, beating time with his words, which he enunciated in a slow, loud whisper, lips brushing her ear. 'I know what I'm doing girl.'

Catherine froze, silenced by the latent violence that had risen to the surface. How foolish her optimism of just a few minutes ago now appeared. She couldn't reason with him in this sort of mood. Eyes wide with shock, she watched him retreat across the table. Ignoring his spoon, he picked up his bowl, tipped his head back and poured the remains of the porridge into his mouth before slamming the bowl down on the table. He stood up, shoving his chair so it tipped over and its high back hit the solid floor with a crack. He marched to the door and left without a backward glance or another word.

The house was enveloped in a dense silence. Catherine realised she was holding her breath and exhaled. She massaged her neck, to ease away the impression of her father's fingers, and the cool metal chain rubbed against her skin. Shock subsided, and frustration tinged with anger grew in the vacuum left behind. She had a right to know if he was putting her - and Tilly - in danger. At the thought of her daughter, Catherine's head jerked up. The house was too quiet. She should be able to hear Tilly moving around on the platform above.

She hauled her father's chair back onto its feet and forced a smile into her voice.

'Tilly. Hurry up. Come down here with your hairbrush.'

Almost immediately there was a rustle, and her daughter's thin ankles emerged on the ladder below a skirt that was soon going to be too short. She would have to see if there was anything left on it to let down.

'Why was Grandpa in such a bad mood?' Tilly asked, holding out the hairbrush. Wary eyes probed the shadows before coming to rest on her mother's face.

Catherine took the hairbrush. Tilly coiled her thin arms around her mother's waist and Catherine absorbed the anxiety that oozed from her like butter melting on a hot day. There was something else as well; something close to fear. Catherine trembled with shame. She was failing to do the one thing she had sworn to do, since John had died, and that was to keep her daughter safe. She gripped the hairbrush until the pain of the bristles digging into her skin became too much and she almost dropped it. The anger she harboured towards her father intensified, but she pushed it away. She needed to reassure Tilly, but she didn't know how. Sending a silent plea to John to forgive her attempt to console their daughter with statements that she knew to be untrue, she tried to sound unconcerned with her eventual answer. 'I don't know my love. He must have something on his mind. We can't always be cheerful.' She brushed Tilly's hair until it gleamed and pinned her own in a coil about her head. The normality of the ritual was soothing, and Catherine was relieved that Tilly was soon chattering about seeing her cousins.

'I've got some linens to return to the manor. If you help me load up the cart we'll get to Aunt Helen's even quicker.'

The cart was two-wheeled with a lightweight wooden frame and a harness attached to it - a smaller version of the sort normally pulled by a horse. Catherine brought it in from the back garden and they wiped it dry and piled it high. She would collect it later. They pulled on pattens to protect their shoes, in case the lane to Helen's house was still muddy from recent rain. As she reached for their cloaks her arm brushed against her satchel. She lifted it from its hook and placed it on top of the pile on the cart - she might get some time later, and she still had space to fill on her one sheet of paper.

The High Street was busy, noisy with squawking geese and the clatter of cartwheels. Catherine took Tilly's hand and they turned left, down the hill towards the bridge. A soft grey mist rose from the surface of the river and hovered, as if suspended by invisible wires. To her left, Catherine could see a man on horseback had stopped to talk to the soldiers who were guarding the crossing. She turned right, but Tilly tugged at her hand.

'Mama, can't we go and see the ducks?' she pleaded.

'No, my love, not this morning. We don't have time. You can look for them from Aunt Helen's garden, as long as you don't go too close to the water.'

Tilly dragged her heels in protest but followed her mother onto the rutted, narrow lane, sheltering beneath a canopy of tall trees that followed the Ray, and then the Cherwell, away from the village before petering out in a boggy courtyard at the mill.

It was a few days ago, walking this route with Thomas, that Catherine had become certain that he was seeking her out, and that all the times she'd seemed to bump into him by accident were not chance encounters at all, but by design. His design. She had been walking from the manor to her aunt's house, along the river, when he had fallen into step beside her, leading his horse.

'May I walk with you Mistress Meakin? Monty's gone lame. I'm taking him to the blacksmith.' He'd stroked the horse's long muzzle as if it were a favourite child and the beast had snorted with pleasure.

'I don't know much about horses, sir,' she'd admitted, wishing she could offer a more informed comment.

'Nor I,' he'd agreed cheerfully. 'Stubborn creatures they are.'

They'd walked in silence for a few moments, and then he had asked her the strangest question.

'Are you happy?'

She'd twisted her hands together, trying to prevent a wry laugh escaping her lips. Happiness. It wasn't something she'd considered often since John had died. She wasn't sure what he'd meant by asking her such a thing. She could sense his eyes on her, but she hadn't wanted to show him the confusion that she was sure must be carved into her features by turning towards him whilst she tried to think of an answer.

'I mean, it can't be what you expected from life, to be on your own at such a young age and with a small child.'

'My daughter is my world, sir.' A hard, defensive edge had crept into her voice. She'd raised her eyes to his, and met his gaze without flinching, challenging him to dare question her ability to look after Tilly. That's when she'd noticed his eyes for the first time. They were such a pale shade of brown that they were almost golden. His sharp intake of breath had shattered the moment, and she had turned away and lowered her voice. 'Is life ever what any of us expect?'

'I apologise if I caused you offence. That was not my intention.'

It had been his turn to pause to think. She had been aware of the intensity of his scrutiny as he'd matched his long stride to her shorter steps. It was perhaps fanciful, but it was as though he was trying to reach inside her head, work out what the problem was and weigh up possible solutions to see which would fit. The sensation had been so powerful and intimate, that she'd stumbled in a rut in the lane. He'd caught her arm to stop her falling and she'd muttered her thanks.

'Mistress Meakin, you are correct. Until recently I had thought that life was very predictable, but now I'm not so sure. I must leave you here. Good day to you.' His tone was thoughtful. He'd turned and led Monty up a path towards the church. She'd leaned against the wall, trying to slow her racing heart. What was she thinking, talking to Thomas Marlow like that? Even more astonishing than what she had said was that he had listened to her, and instead of becoming angry when she had expressed her opinion, he had seemed to be thinking about her words.

When she was calm enough to look at his retreating back, he'd turned and waved his hat, as if he had sensed her eyes on him.

Embarrassed, she'd hurried away. And that's when she'd realised it had to be more than coincidence that their paths were crossing with such frequency; the blacksmith's forge was at the other end of the village, in the opposite direction.

Whilst Catherine had been lost in her thoughts, Tilly had skipped ahead. She waited in front of a long, low, stone-built cottage that stood alone and proud, giving the impression of solidity, and the assurance that it had been occupying that spot for centuries and would remain for many more. Catherine caught up with her, tapped on the front door and then pushed it open. She stepped inside and was nearly knocked to the floor as a miniature tornado with a mop of red curls barrelled into her knees and wrapped its arms around her.

'Hello, Aunt Cat,' it said with a giggle.

'Harry! How many times do I have to tell you not to do that? You'll hurt your aunt.' Helen stood in the doorway at the end of the entrance hall, wiping her hands on a cloth. Her eyes were stern but the twitch at the corner of her mouth told Catherine she was fighting to suppress a smile.

The tornado unwrapped its arms and charged down the hall like a dragoon on the battle field, pushing past Helen. Tilly hooted with laughter and followed.

Catherine watched until they were out of sight. 'Always an enthusiastic welcome to be had in this house,' she joked, taking a few steps forwards to embrace Helen. The youngest sister of Catherine's mother, Helen was only a few years older than Catherine herself and their relationship was more that of close friends, sisters even, than aunt and niece. There was little in their appearance to announce to the world that they were related. Catherine had inherited her mother's dark looks, and the one feature she shared with her aunt was the eyes - black and deep, like the pool of water lying at the bottom of the village well. Otherwise, everything about Helen was as different as it was possible to be - she was tall whilst Catherine was short, with auburn hair that fell in wild ripples whilst Catherine's was black and straight. Helen had a smattering of freckles across her small nose, whilst Catherine disliked her own nose - it was too big - and her skin went from pale white to bright red in the sun with nothing in-between.

Catherine tried to step back from the embrace, but her aunt didn't release her. She squirmed under Helen's firm grip and penetrating stare.

'What's wrong?'

Catherine shrugged her shoulders in a pretence that she didn't understand the question. Helen's grip tightened.

'Don't give me that nonsense. You look as if you've been using those charcoal sticks you're so fond of on your face. You're grey.'

'I couldn't sleep.' She brushed an imaginary fleck of dust from the sleeve of her cloak, reluctant to meet Helen's eyes; she should have known there was no point trying to hide anything from her. For a moment Catherine considered confiding in her aunt about the ring, but dismissed it. She knew what Helen would say, and then she'd be facing her scrutiny every time they met.

'Why?' Helen's questioning was insistent, but not uncaring.

'Just something my father said last night.'

Helen took Catherine's hand and pulled her through the doorway into the kitchen that ran along the back of the cottage. It was long, low and cosy, dominated by a fireplace at one end that was as wide as the room and almost as high as the ceiling. Two low-level windows set either side of the back door invited the warmth of the sun in. Helen pushed her into a chair at the table, swept the used breakfast bowls away and sat down by her side. Catherine relaxed into the soothing atmosphere and comforting familiarity of the scene.

'Tell me,' Helen demanded.

Catherine looked around.

'There's no-one here. Ed has already left for the mill, the boys are in the garden with Tilly and the girls have gone to the farm for milk and butter - they'll be in no hurry to get back here.

Making eyes at the soldiers no doubt and thinking I won't get to hear about it. So tell me.'

At the mention of the soldiers, Catherine tensed. She loosened her cloak and let it fall from her shoulders.

'He was talking about the mood of the country, saying people are tired of the demands made on them, from both sides, and are going to start to fight for every man to be equal. When I tried to ask him what he meant, he got angry.'

It was an under-statement, but not an outright lie. She may be deceiving her aunt, just as she had Tilly earlier, but she could not worry them by revealing the extent of her own fear in response to her father's violent behaviour. She crossed her fingers behind her back and watched the procession of expressions marching across Helen's face. Her aunt's ability to pull together strands of information and analyse her thoughts before speaking was a skill Catherine envied, or perhaps it was just patience she lacked. She watched, and waited, drumming her fingers on the side of the table, knowing Helen would say nothing until she was ready.

'This might be something Ed has mentioned as well. Just last night, or the night before. There's a group - I can't remember what Ed called them - who want to change the way the country is ruled, level out the power, make things fairer. There's been some talk of them campaigning in the countryside, trying to recruit rebels.'

'Rebels!' Catherine gasped.

'He doesn't think it will come to anything though,' Helen reached for Catherine's hands and squeezed them between her own.

'And if it doesn't, what will happen to the men who supported it - the rebels - if they are discovered?' Catherine demanded, her eyes searching Helen's for reassurance. They both knew the answer to that. Retribution from those on both sides of this conflict was swift and merciless.

'I know what you're thinking, but you know, whatever happens, you - and Tilly - will always have a home here, with us.' Helen's words were calm, but her eyes betrayed her concern.

'Must we always be beset by men and their stupid wars?' Catherine murmured.

They both stared out of the windows to the neat garden, from where the excited shouting of children was just audible. Catherine longed to linger and draw strength from the comforting presence of her aunt, but she knew she could not. 'I must go. I can't be late,' she said.

She stood, smoothed her gown with her fingertips and pulled her cloak back on.

'Oh, Tilly's hoping to see the ducks.' Her voice softened with the mention of her daughter.

'Well, we'll have to see if we can find them for her then,' Helen followed her to the front door.

Catherine waved to Helen before turning up the path towards the church to cut across the graveyard and avoid passing the King's soldiers at the bridge. She ought to find their presence reassuring, she always had before, and the village was safer with them here. Not two years ago the Royalists had defeated Parliament's troops and sent them scuttling back towards Abingdon. But this morning nothing was the same. This morning their presence worried her. She was sure they would notice something different in her expression, point at her and call her out as ... as what? A traitor? A revolutionary? Someone tainted by her father's idealism?

An idealist.

She almost laughed aloud at the absurdity of the thought.

That's not a label she would ever have given her father.

But what then?

She grasped at memories that were vague, hazy like the horizon on a hot, sunny day and realised how little she knew him. This man, who had been partly responsible for bringing her into the world, but had then shown very little interest in her; until the fever had struck, that is, and widowed both of them within days.

Her memories of the joint funeral and the weeks that followed were clear and sharp, an indelible print inside her head, like an etching on a metal plate. She would never be able to let them go. Mary, her younger sister, had attended the service in church with her husband, George. Catherine had little chance to talk to her, though, because George made no attempt to hide his dislike of their father and had been insistent that they could not linger. She had watched Mary struggling to keep up with her husband's long stride, clinging to his arm with one hand and rubbing at her eyes with the cuff of the other, as he'd rushed her from the churchyard after the service. Catherine knew they had a long walk home to Beckley, several miles across the fields skirting the edge of Otmoor, but even so, she would have welcomed the opportunity to spend some time with her sister. She saw so little of her.

Nor had she given up hope that her older brother, James, would somehow have heard of their mother's death and turn up at the church unannounced, even though she had no idea where he was, or even if he was still alive. She had cricked her neck with her repeated glances over her shoulder during the service, expecting to see him silhouetted in the church porch, but he didn't come. Weighed down by grief at the loss of her husband and mother, she had never been so alone.

Some days later her father had emerged from the river of ale in which he had immersed himself. Her surprise at his expectation had been so complete that she thought she must have misheard him.

'The sooner you move back home the better, girl.'

She'd been sitting by John's grave, which was just a mound of raised earth, no marker stone and even the grass had not begun to grow. She had scattered some poppy seeds over the bare soil to give him some colour. He had loved colour. Her father's tread had been so silent she hadn't even realised he was there.

She'd turned around and tilted her head to look at him. His skin was tinged with grey and he was neither close-shaven nor bearded. Why had she not considered that he would provide for her and Tilly? She'd turned back to the grave. All she knew was that the thought had never crossed her mind. Providing for Tilly was her responsibility now, and although the ground seemed to be crumbling beneath her feet, threatening to sweep her away with it, she was not going to fail her daughter. The only solid and reliable thing left to her was her home; the home she and John had created, with love. She was not going to let it go.

'What do you mean Father? I have my own home. Mine and Tilly's. I'm not leaving it.'

'Don't be silly, girl. You can't live there alone. It don't make any sense, especially now.'

'I'm not being silly. I've already spoken to the estate. The tenancy is mine now. I can earn enough money at the manor to pay the rent and put food on the table.'

She had spoken with more confidence than she felt. 'I hope,' she'd whispered. She had also been offered a live-in position at the manor but had refused it because she couldn't have taken Tilly with her. The best solution for both of them was to stay in their own home for as long as they could.

She wasn't sure how long he had stood there. She didn't turn around again and at some point she had sensed she was alone by the graveside.

That he was angry she had no doubt, but it wasn't long before he had started presenting himself at her door at mealtimes. They had fallen into a sort of routine that, whilst it was not perfect, they had both accepted and a relationship of sorts had been established.

But now his behaviour was worrying, and he was getting involved with something that threatened to destroy the security she was fighting to build for Tilly. She clenched her fists under her cloak, forgetting for the moment that she too was guarding a secret, such was her frustration with the knowledge that they could both be judged by her father's actions, but she was powerless to do anything about it.

His words, though, did have a ring of truth to them. Her conversation with Helen had brought back fragments of information that she had heard and not given any thought to before, such as stories of supplies being foraged, often from people who had little enough to start with, to support the troops. How could that be a fair system? There had been talk of a man from a village on the other side of Otmoor having been thrown in prison in Oxford for refusing to provide food for a party of Royalists, because it would have meant taking it from the mouths of his own family. An unusual atmosphere was hanging over the village. Was it a sense that ordinary people were beginning to pay too high a price for this King's struggle for power with his Parliament?

'Mistress Meakin. I have something for you.'

Catherine looked up in surprise. She had been so deep in thought that she hadn't noticed she had reached the market. The activity and noise shattered her thoughts and gave her the strangest sensation of being dropped into the middle of a blank canvas that had, without warning, burst into motion around her. She stretched out a hand and clutched a low branch from a nearby tree to steady herself.

'Are you quite well?' The cloth merchant's kind, plump face was full of concern. 'Take my arm. Let me help you to a seat.'

'No, I'm fine,' she shook her head. 'Thank you, sir. My mind was elsewhere, and you startled me.'

'If you're sure.' He sounded relieved and doubtful at the same time. 'Maybe this will help to cheer you up.'

He handed her a bundle of wrapping paper. She seized the package and only just stopped herself from grasping the merchant's hands as well in her eagerness.

'Thank you, thank you. I have only one sheet left.' Excitement tinged her voice. Her fingers ached to close around a charcoal stick and allow her thoughts to escape across the paper.

'You must let me pay you, but I have no coins with me.'

'There is no need. I told you, I have no purpose for it,' a hesitant smile lit his eyes. 'But I would be honoured if you would be kind enough to use one sheet to sketch something for me.'

Catherine had given him a sketch once before to express her thanks, although it was presumptuous to think that anyone would want to look at something she had drawn. Hiding her surprise that he should request another, she nodded and beamed at him. 'Good day to you then, kind sir.'

She hurried home, where she unfurled the bundle of wrapping paper and weighted it down on the table, using bowls and mugs to stop it curling. Then she dragged the heavy cart through her front door, attached the harness and set off down the hill. It took all her strength, pushing back on the cart, to stop its weight propelling her into a trot before the gradient levelled off on the long driveway to the manor.

The drawbridge was down, and the guard nodded to her from his position in the gatehouse. She waved to him, crossed the moat and entered the large, rectangular courtyard. The imposing manor house with its own chapel attached occupied one entire width directly opposite. Outbuildings sprawled along the two lengths. To the left, a groom was saddling a horse, chickens scratched in the dirt and a goat was bleating. Catherine turned right, towards the kitchen buildings where a low archway led into another, sheltered, irregular-shaped enclosure. It was bordered by the kitchen on the left, a dairy and outhouses used for preserving meat in front, and a high wall which plummeted into the moat on the right before curving around to meet the archway. Although smaller than the manor's imposing courtyard, the space was still substantial. This was the kitchen garden, where herbs and other vegetables were abundant in tidy rows occupying flat, deep beds. Catherine inhaled the fragrant air in which the scents of rosemary, thyme and lavender failed to overpower each other and instead united to produce an intoxicating perfume that lifted her spirits.

Leaving her cart to the right of the archway, she entered the building through the scullery where she pulled on an apron and tugged a cap down over her hair, taking care to push any loose tendrils beneath it. She could hear the familiar clatter of pans and a cook's raised voice in the adjacent kitchen. Mary, the scullery maid, looked up from the bowl of swede she was peeling. 'Mr Dawson said to go see 'im as soon as you get 'ere,' she said.

Unease pricked at the edges of Catherine's mind and she rubbed her temples. Mr Dawson would not approve of whatever her father was getting involved with. What had Helen called them? Radicals. But he couldn't have found out so soon. Could he?

She tried to sound casual. 'Oh, did he say why?'

Mary shrugged and turned her attention back to the swede.

Catherine hurried along the dark passageway to the butler's office. She hesitated before tapping on the open door, reminding herself that whatever he may have heard, she had done nothing wrong. Mr Dawson looked up from the ledger he was studying, put his quill down and flexed his fingers.

'Ah Mistress Meakin, I need you to work on Monday evening - her ladyship is organising a dance for Lady Frances - it's her birthday and we're short of staff.'

Catherine stared at him. She'd been preparing to defend herself and it took a moment for her to realise that she wasn't about to lose her position.

'Is that a problem?' Mr Dawson was watching her, expecting a response.

'No sir.'

'Good. Well, what are you waiting for? I expect you've lots of linens to sort out and put away.'

She backed out of the office. The extra money would be useful. She might be able to buy some cloth to stitch a new gown for Tilly.

Mr Dawson picked up his quill and returned his scrutiny to the ledger. 'Be here by two on Monday.'

Some hours later she had finished her work and was trying to reload her cart with more sewing, including a set of heavy drapes that needed their hems re-stitching. She heaved them onto her cart, but before she could strap them on they started to slip off the other side. After three attempts, she paused for breath. She needed someone to help her but was reluctant to go and ask Mr Dawson, Mary would be of no use and to ask any of the cooks would be frowned upon. She heard voices and footsteps approaching from the courtyard beyond. Perhaps she could ask them for help.

She was moving towards the archway when a gruff voice that she didn't recognise said, 'I hear Thomas Marlow spoke for Ellis.'

Catherine froze, and pressed herself into the wall, fingers flat against the cool stone, and held her breath.

'Aye, word is he'd still be in that rathole now otherwise, and then how would she be coping with all those kids and her laid up in bed and all?'

The footsteps were moving away, the voices growing fainter. Catherine peeled herself from the wall and dashed through the archway. Two men in the livery of servants carrying a loaded trunk between them were crossing the courtyard. She opened her mouth to call after them but closed it again. If Mr Dawson heard she had gone chasing after footmen she would lose her position for sure.

She returned to her cart, filled her lungs with the perfumed air and redoubled her efforts with the drapes. This time she managed to loop a strap around before they slipped off and soon she was ready to leave. She hung her apron and cap on their hook, collected her satchel and retraced her steps past the gatehouse and over the moat.

Her thoughts now were full of what she had heard about Thomas Marlow. They must have been talking of the local man who had been thrown in jail for refusing the King's men food. But Thomas Marlow was a Royalist, why would he speak for someone who had not acted for the King?

The cart was even heavier than it had been before, and her shoulders were soon aching. She paused to stretch her back and looked up. Two girls were ahead of her on the drive, walking towards her, followed by one of Lady Gilder's companions. She recognised Lady Frances, but the other she didn't know. They were giggling and talking behind their hands, which were held up close to their faces, as if sharing a secret. A white handkerchief drooped from Frances's fingers. Catherine stepped aside to let them pass. As they drew level, Frances dropped the handkerchief and stopped. She turned to Catherine with a haughty expression and blue eyes that were cold and soulless, like a piece of stained glass pretending to be a precious stone.

Catherine shivered under that frosty stare. She wasn't sure what she was expected to do, but she knelt, picked up the handkerchief and held it out to the girl. Frances kept her eyes fixed on Catherine's face, took the handkerchief, taking care to hold just one corner of it between the tip of her forefinger and thumb, as if it were contaminated. Then she turned her head, took her friend's arm, and strolled away. Catherine watched them go, trembling with anger and humiliation. Her face and neck prickled with heat, and she imagined Lady Frances tripping on the path and falling to the ground, crying with pain, and holding her ankle. She gripped the harness and stamped away, kicking out at the stones and clods of earth in her path and not slowing down until the grounds of the manor were behind her, replaced by the tranquillity of the meadows bordering the river.

The sun was beginning its gentle slide down the sky towards the horizon, casting shadows over the bridge and onto the surface of the water. Catherine unhooked the cart, sat down on the trunk of a felled tree, and loosened her cloak, letting her hood fall back. The air was still, the environment calming, and she pushed her anger away. She didn't have much time before she would need to collect Tilly and return home to cook supper and face possibly another confrontation with her father. A few precious minutes was all she needed. She reached inside her satchel for her paper and charcoal sticks, and, using the satchel as a hard surface to support the paper she began to sketch.

Although the colours of the afternoon were beautiful, it was the contrast between different shades of light and dark that fascinated her. She sought to capture them by varying the strength of her strokes on the paper. Working with precision and care, she bit her lip in concentration, and flicked an occasional glance towards the bridge to make sure she didn't miss any of the detail.

She was so absorbed in her sketching, losing herself and her worries in the simple action of applying charcoal to paper, that there was no room in her head to ponder what she had just heard about Thomas Marlow, or what she should do about the ring, or even her father. Nor did she hear Thomas approach, so when he sat down next to her on the tree trunk he startled her and the charcoal skittered across the surface of the paper leaving behind a harsh line.

'May I join you?' He removed his hat.

She brushed at the line with her fingers.

'I'm sorry. Is it ruined?'

She shook her head. Her heart was pounding, but she remained focused on her sketch. 'No, it will come off. That's one of the problems with charcoal - it smudges too easily. It doesn't stay where you put it either.'

He peered over her shoulder. She attempted to move her sketch so he couldn't see it, but he was too quick for her. He reached out and seized the corner of the satchel. Her skin tingled where he allowed his hand to rest for the briefest moment on hers. He moved his head in closer until it was almost touching her elbow, then sat back. 'It's really very good. But it isn't what's actually there. You've changed the view. You haven't drawn the soldiers.'

'I know.'

'But why leave the soldiers out?'

She shrugged. 'I didn't want to put them in.'

'But why?' He persisted.

Catherine turned the charcoal around in her hand, wondering how to answer him. She couldn't explain how the presence of the soldiers in the village no longer seemed reassuring to her, because it would mean confiding in him about her father's words, which she dare not do.

'I ... I just don't feel comfortable with them,' she said.

'With soldiers in general, or with this particular variety?'

'In general,' she replied, keeping her eyes lowered. The charcoal stick danced between her fingers, as if it had taken on life of its own.

'You can say what you think. I don't bite.'

Catherine turned the sketch back towards her. Holding it so he couldn't see what she was doing, she drew a cluster of bluebells beneath a tree. She handed it back to him and regarded his expression as he looked across to the tree and drew his eyebrows together in a question.

'The bluebells aren't really there. It's the privilege of the artist, to take what we see and use it as we will. What we draw does not have to be a faithful reproduction,' she said.

'I've never encountered anyone quite like you, Catherine.' His tone was gentle and she looked up. His face was close to hers. His beard was unfashionably close-cropped, but his hair was thick and wavy, sandy brown in colour. His eyes were fixed on her with an intensity that made her gasp.

The breeze had tugged at her coil of hair, loosening a strand from its grips. He reached out and tucked it behind her ear. She knew she should reprove him for his actions and use of her first name. She should move away, but she was locked in position, as if she were in a trance and unable to move. It wasn't fitting to be seen like this with a man who wasn't her husband or a relative. She had learnt that as a young widow she had to be even more guarded with her behaviour to protect her reputation. People were so quick to judge and slow to forgive.

He appeared to sense her discomfort and leaned back, turning away, directing his eyes now to the bridge.

'Do you still have the ring?'

'Yes,' she nodded, one finger reaching inside her collar. This was the perfect opportunity to give it back to him. She started to pull the chain free of her gown and then stopped, struck by a reluctance to part with it.

'Good.'

He picked a long blade of grass, held it between his fingers and blew on it, making a sound like a trumpet in the hands of an incompetent trumpeter. He laughed and let the grass fall to the ground. She allowed the chain to slip through her fingers and the ring brushed her skin as it settled back between her breasts. Maybe she would look back at this moment and regret her decision to keep the ring, for now at least.

'What did you mean about there being darkness around me?'

'I'm not sure. I can't explain. It's just a feeling I get sometimes.'

Catherine waited for him to say more, but he remained silent. She stole a glance at him. He appeared to be deep in thought, his attention focused on the river and bridge, as if he'd forgotten she was there. She wasn't satisfied with his answer, and wanted to ask him about the conversation she had overheard at the manor, but she couldn't find the words to form the questions. She replaced her charcoal and paper in her satchel, taking care not to crease or fold the paper and slid down from the tree trunk.

'I have to collect my daughter. Please excuse me sir.' She tightened her cloak around her, slipped the harness back on and started to walk away.

He stood and bowed. 'I'll see you at church tomorrow. And please call me Thomas.'

Catherine smiled but resisted the temptation to turn around. She had forgotten what it was like to receive the attentions of an attractive man. The excitement beginning to churn in her stomach, the anticipation of what might happen next, because she could fool herself no longer. Thomas Marlow was showing he was interested in her, she was sure of it. She tried to stamp on these emotions and bring them back under control as she returned the cart home and then hurried back to Helen's house.

'The fresh air has done you good,' remarked Helen. 'You've got some colour back.'

Tilly tugged on Catherine's skirts and she turned to her daughter, grateful to escape Helen's scrutiny. Her aunt found it far too easy to read her, and if Helen thought her colour was due to walking in the fresh air she would not ask any awkward questions.

'The girls bought a goose from the market and it's far more than we can eat. Why don't you all join us after church for dinner on Sunday?'

Catherine's mouth watered at the thought of roast goose.

'Thank you. That would be lovely.'

Catherine embraced her aunt and then turned down the lane, trying to focus on Tilly who was skipping along by her side, chattering about the ducks. She was certain that Helen was watching them still, could feel her eyes and sense her sharp mind working hard, wondering what could have happened to her niece in the few hours that she had spent at the manor.

The village was quiet, and they passed no-one on their way home. Tilly took a piece of chalk and a slate and began to draw at the table whilst Catherine peeled and diced turnips. She was stirring them into the broth when she heard the grating of the front door as it was pushed across the stone floor. She span around in alarm, not expecting her father this early.

'Supper isn't ready yet,' she said, pouring him a mug of ale.

He grunted, sat down at the table, kicked off his boots and stretched out his legs. He drank the ale in one long gulp and held the mug out for her to re-fill.

Tilly slipped down from the table and moved to a corner by the fire. She sat on the floor with her arms wrapped around her knees and her chin resting on them, staring into the flames. Catherine watched her, unease tugging at the fringes of her mind. A heavy black cloud seemed to have descended over the cottage, bringing its darkness inside and extinguishing the light. Her father lit his pipe and the room filled with the thick, bitter smell of cheap tobacco. It stung her eyes and burnt her throat. She opened the back door a fraction.

'Can't a man enjoy a smoke at the end of a day's work?'

His eyes were fixed on her, their expression challenging, inviting a response. A wave of exhaustion pressed down on her, blackening her vision. She leaned against the door frame, lingering to avoid answering him. She didn't have the energy for an argument, but she didn't know what to say to avoid one.

He made a point of turning his back on her and re-filling his mug. She returned to the fire and stirred the pot.

'Helen has invited us for dinner after church tomorrow,' she said, forcing lightness into her tone. 'She's got a goose.'

He grunted.

'And I have to work late at the manor on Monday, so Tilly will stay at Helen's.'

His fingers paused in the action of re-filling his pipe, but otherwise he didn't acknowledge that she'd spoken.

When the broth was ready she ladled it into three bowls and placed them on the table with some bread.

'Come and have supper Tilly.'

Tilly slowly unwound her arms from her legs and shuffled back to the table. She moved her chair as far away from her grandfather as possible and stared at her bowl. Catherine crumbled her bread between her fingers and watched Tilly pick up her spoon and stir smooth circles in her broth, head bowed. She made no effort to lift the spoon to her mouth. Without moving her head, Catherine's eyes flicked to her father. He ate quickly with his mouth open and once he'd mopped his bowl clean with a thick wedge of bread, he pulled his boots back on and got to his feet.

'You're going out?' Catherine asked. Her voice was calm but her insides were churning. Did she want to know where he was going, or was she better off in ignorance? That way if his actions did bring trouble to his door, she could say with all honesty that she knew nothing of them.

He paused and turned to face her. 'Don't try to get involved with things you can't understand girl,' he snarled. He stamped his feet as he crossed the room, shaking bits of dried mud over the floor and leaving the front door wide open behind him.

Catherine took a deep breath. The air that filled her lungs was fresh and invigorating. She smiled at Tilly who sat stock-still.

'Eat, my love.' She fetched a broom and swiped at the mud, forcing it out of her house and scattering it over the path. Then she closed and bolted the door.

Tilly picked up some bread and dipped it in the broth. Soon her bowl was empty.

Catherine was relieved to see Tilly eat, but she had not been mistaken in what she had seen earlier. She could only hope that her interpretation was wrong, because it was very clear to Catherine that Tilly had not wanted to be so close to her grandfather. She had probably picked up on the tension that had been simmering beneath the surface as a result of last night's argument. Catherine wanted to talk to her, to reassure her, but she was reluctant to draw attention to something and make it into a problem where one might not actually exist. Instead, she sought to distract Tilly by plaiting the girl's hair - and her own - into several tight braids, promising it would transform her straight tresses into curls overnight. When she settled Tilly into bed she clasped her daughter in a tight embrace, unwilling to let go.

Feeling her way with care back down the steps, every part of her body seemed to ache with exhaustion. She was beyond tired and it would be sensible to go to bed, but she was certain she wouldn't sleep. Her mind was too crowded. She could hear Tilly singing, her sweet, soft voice trilling like a little bird. Catherine dragged one of the chairs closer to the fire, sat down, leaned back, and shut her eyes, allowing her thoughts to return to Thomas Marlow. She was fidgety with excitement. It was an excitement she had to tamp, before it led to its more assertive siblings, hope and expectation. The more she learned of him, the more she liked him. What did he mean by his attentions to her, and why had he helped that man? Thomas Marlow was not the person he appeared to be on the surface. He was a puzzle, the answer to which eluded her.

She loosened the collar of her gown, pulled out the ring and looped the chain over her head without bothering to unfasten it. She placed it in her lap and studied it again. The stone twinkled in the soft candlelight. Its effect was hypnotic. Her eyelids began to droop and a comfortable lethargy spread over her limbs as she drifted into a restful sleep.

FIVE

Hannah

AFTER I'D HAD BREAKFAST THE next morning I sent Matt an email. He'd said he was going to do some research, so I thought it was only fair to tell him what I'd discovered. I took two pictures, one of each page of the village book and added them as attachments.

I was on my way to the studio I rented in nearby Kidlington when my mobile rang. I answered it on the hands-free. It was Matt.

'That's the design all right,' he agreed. 'But those dates - it says John Islip was born in Islip in 1464 and was Abbot of Westminster from 1500-1532. That's more than 100 years before the Civil War and when those coins were minted, so if they were lost together it wasn't him that lost them.'

In my excitement last night I hadn't noticed the relevance of the dates. Of course, he was right.

'So, the ring must have been passed down to someone in his family after he died,' I suggested.

'Or sold. I'm not a theologian and nor am I particularly religious, but I'm pretty sure that abbots weren't allowed to marry - this would have been before the Reformation, so he wouldn't have had any kids.'

I could hear the smile in his voice when he added, 'At least ones he could admit to anyway.'

I laughed. 'He might have had other family though - siblings, nieces, nephews.'

'True.'

I sighed.

'At least it sounds as though he was quite famous in his day. It shouldn't be too difficult to find out more about him.'

'I'll google him.'

'I've got to go Hannah. I've got a client due any minute and I need to have a bit of a tidy up. Hope you get on okay with Joel. Let me know if you find anything more.'

And he hung up.

I had a quiet start to the morning before clients were arriving - a young mother who wanted some moody black and whites of her two-year old twins. I started editing the photos I'd taken yesterday in my garden. The red kites were the show-stoppers. There was one shot in particular that stood out. The kites had turned to one side, their wings carving through the sky without so much as a flap, exposing that pinky-red underbelly that is so striking. Just stunning. It almost made me want to leave the image in colour. I saved it and then told the programme to ditch the colour, so I could work with the contrasts in black and white. Stunning became spectacular - in my eyes anyway.

There's nothing as simple as black and white in a photo - there are different shades of black and different shades of white, which, the more you look at them, appear to take on hints of blue or green, or even pink, unless that's the eye leading you astray. In this shot the brightness of the sun made the sky light - ultra light. I had zoomed in on the kites so they appeared like enormous sky monsters, with every detail of their intricate markings printed in those glorious shades.

I was still absorbed in my editing when the clients arrived. In seconds, the calming, creative atmosphere of my studio was turned into a chaotic squall of voices as Louise tried to control her cute, but unruly offspring, with limited success, whilst I tried to coax them to sit still and smile.

By lunchtime I'd had my fill of clients - the very young ones in particular. I felt as drained as my car battery in the depths of winter. Anyone who copes with children all day has my full respect. I didn't have the energy to drive into the city centre so I left my car at the Park & Ride, hopped onto a bus and sank, exhausted, into an uncomfortable vinyl-covered seat on the almost empty top deck. I was content to watch the gardens and leafy streets of North Oxford slip past, whilst my imagination popped and fizzed like fireworks on New Year's Eve. By the time I got off the bus I was convinced that in the next half an hour I would have answers about the ring and how it came to be in my garden. Perhaps it was a well-known artefact that had gone missing, lost for centuries, like something Indiana Jones might go on the hunt for, pursued by loads of bad guys all wanting to get their hands on the booty.

Dr Joel Fielding's office was in the history faculty building on George Street. He was a strange man. I'd expected someone similar to Matt for some reason - just because he'd said they were friends I suppose. But he wasn't. He was much older for starters, so they can't have been school friends. And he was shorter - but then most people were - he didn't have much hair and he wore glasses, a combination that gave him that air of the intellectual. But he had a welcoming smile, which punched dimples into his cheeks. I accepted his offer of coffee and we sat in his cramped office with a view over the Odeon cinema and Gloucester Green bus station.

'You want to know something about the Civil War and Oxford, I believe?'

'Yes, although more specifically Islip.' I pulled the village book out of my bag, opened it at the page and placed it on the table. 'I found three coins that Matt - Mr Denton - has identified as Civil War and a gold signet ring with this design engraved on it.' I pointed to the page. 'And this is all I know about Islip in the Civil War.' I pointed to the other page. His eyes scanned the text and he smiled.

'Firstly, you are assuming the two are connected, correct.'

'It seemed ...'

'Yes, I agree, it seems logical, but it presents a problem, does it not, because the dates don't match.'

He had a strange way of constructing his sentences that gave his voice a sing-song quality.

'I know, Matt pointed ...'

'The other problem is that I think it is highly unlikely that this version of the battle in Islip is correct.'

He also had a habit of interrupting every time I started to speak, but now he paused, bespectacled eyes fixed on me as if watching to see my brain connect the dots. I took my chance.

'So, what can you tell me?'

'Firstly, the Royalists were in control of the crossing with an experienced commander. Is it not so that they wouldn't have chosen to fight from such a disadvantaged position, trapped by the river and the village.'

'Maybe they took him by surprise?'

'Secondly,' he continued as if I hadn't spoken. 'Cromwell's own account of the event is that the Royalists had pre-warning of his army's approach and had withdrawn from the village before he arrived on the evening of April 23rd, 1645.'

I couldn't work out what he was saying.

'So there wasn't a battle of Islip Bridge at all?'

He tapped away on his keyboard. I waited, leaning forward in my chair until my nose was almost touching the back of his computer screen, waiting for him to explain. Talk about letting the suspense build for maximum impact. He should have been a film director, not a historian. I coughed to remind him I was still there in case he'd forgotten all about me and gone back to work. He turned the screen towards me and I jerked my head back just in time to avoid a painful bash on the nose. I stared at it. He was showing me a blown-up scan of a letter, written by Cromwell on April 25th, 1645, from Bletchingdon, a village just a couple of miles away from Islip.

I squinted at the screen. The language was old-fashioned, and I had to read it twice to make sense of it. Cromwell wrote candidly that he had learned how the Earl of Northampton's Regiment was stationed in Islip and that he marched his men there, hoping to take them by surprise. When he arrived the Regiment, having been warned that a Parliamentary army was approaching, had already moved out of the village. After staying overnight in Islip, Cromwell was taken by surprise the next morning by three of the King's Regiments. He quickly assembled his troops, and they confronted the Royalists in the fields where there was a battle and a pursuit with Cromwell's army claiming victory along with the capture of around 200 prisoners and 400 horses.

It was a very different account to the one I had read just the night before, which was interesting, but I wasn't sure that the exact details of a battle that took place nearly 400 years ago made much difference to what I wanted to know. I raised my eyes from the screen and Joel took that as a cue to carry on.

'Thirdly, Cromwell was just a lowly General at that point. The New Model Army was just that - new. And is it not so that if he had successfully stormed the village and routed the Royalists, he would have been the first to boast of it to his superiors.'

Fourthly, I thought, how does this help me?

'Finally, as you can see, the Battle of Islip - which was really little more than a skirmish - took place on the morning of April 24th, but I think not on the bridge itself but in the fields between Islip and Oxford, and indeed Cromwell was the victor.'

Jeez, he was worse than my old history teacher at school.

I was wasting my time. None of this was any help. I didn't want to appear ungrateful though. I searched my mind for an intelligent question to ask him.

'So what can you tell me about life in Islip at the time? Who did they support?'

He stroked his chin.

'Most of Oxford was Royalist, after all, the King had made the city the centre of his Parliament had he not. But outside of the city walls it would have been more mixed. Islip was for sure used to having soldiers lodging there, guarding the crossing. And of course, the village has long associations with the English seat of power, does it not, having been gifted to Westminster by Edward the Confessor, but even so, it is likely there would have been support for Parliament.'

'There was a manor house in the village wasn't there?' I wasn't being clever - this was in the book as well and an archaeological dig with TV's *Time Team* programme a few years ago had found what remained of its walls, underneath a field on the edge of the village.

He nodded. 'At one time, your John Islip would have lived there. It would have been quite some place by all accounts.'

'So who would have lived there during the Civil War years? Would they have been descendants of him somehow?'

My mind was racing ahead of itself now. Maybe this hadn't been a total waste of time after all. I leaned forwards, expectation building again, which was quickly squashed by the reproving expression on his face. He held up a finger and wagged it from side to side, like the pendulum on a grandfather clock.

'Young lady, I'm a historian, not a walking encyclopaedia!'

'Sorry,' I muttered.

He waved away my apology. 'I can look it up though, can't I. Just you'll have to leave it with me, I'll need to pull out the peerage records - it's likely they would have been titled, is it not.'

'I suppose so.'

'What has the coroner's office said?'

I didn't know what he was talking about. The coroner has responsibility for dead people. What does that have to do with anything? 'The coroner's office? What do you mean?'

'You have to report finds like this.'

'What are you saying? I am entitled to keep these, right? I found them on my ...'

'It's Treasure law. If a museum wants them, they have the right to buy them ... following a valuation of course. And you have to report the find within 14 days, don't you, or you may get a fine.'

He had to be kidding, didn't he? He removed his glasses and shook his head, eyes reproving.

'Or even a prison sentence.'

He didn't look as though he was kidding. He looked dead serious.

He stood up. 'Very nice to meet you Miss Hannah. I will let you know what I find.'

With a feeling of déjà-vu, I scribbled my mobile number down on the notepad he pushed over to me.

'Thank you.' I shook his hand and left.

For the rest of the day I kept my phone by my side and checked it every few minutes for missed calls and messages, but he didn't ring. I spent what was left of the day at home, helping Dave to finish off my new deck. I'd left him this morning fitting the planks that would form the floor and it was almost complete.

My boat was also waiting for a final coat of paint before I could take it out. I'd rubbed it down and it would be sporting a coat of a deep, shiny blue when I finished. Dave was clearing away his tools when he took me by surprise, asking if I'd found anything out about the ring and the coins. I wouldn't have put him down as a man who was interested in history. I told him what I had learned so far.

'Wow,' he said, when I mentioned the Civil War.

'Course, they could've been lost any time since then,' he added.

He had a point, but if I was going to find out anything about the ring and why I felt such a connection with it, I had to start somewhere. Those coins were the only clue I had at the moment, and besides, I was becoming fascinated with the whole Civil War business.

Dave was hovering around, expectant, and I realised he wanted paying. I went into the house to get the cash I had withdrawn from the ATM for him, whilst he went to fetch his van from where he had left it on the grass verge around the corner. By the time I'd counted out the notes he had loaded up the van, which was now blocking the lane, and he was leaning against it, facing the centre of the village. I followed his gaze and saw protestors gathering at the entrance to the Confessor's Walk.

'What you gonna do if this new road gets the go-ahead?'

It was a very good question. When I'd bought this house I hadn't given the rumours of a new road much thought. It was such a ludicrous suggestion. Why, after years of protecting development in the green belt, fighting to preserve the style of villages like this through conservation areas, would an organisation that doesn't even have a base here be allowed to dig up our countryside and build all over it for their own financial gain?

I shrugged. 'I dunno. Move I guess.' The thought filled me with dread. I'd only just begun to feel settled here.

I handed the envelope of notes to Dave. He flicked through it and squeezed his impressive paunch behind the wheel of his van.

'I'll be off then,' he said, and drove away at a pace that would have shamed a snail, tooting to warn the protestors who had spilled over the road to move.

I poured a glass of wine and strolled down the garden, armed with a beanbag and cushions to spread out on the deck. The beanbag was comfortable and I settled into it, legs stretched out in front of me, head nestling against a cushion, and sipped my wine, relishing the silence of the late afternoon. I watched the sun slide down to the horizon, spreading its glow like molten wax between the clouds, until the lights on the Beckley satellite mast started to wink and I shivered as the sun retired for the night.

After my dinner-for-one-sad-person-with-nowhere-to-go-on-a-Friday-night, takeaway fish and chips from the Red Lion, which I couldn't eat-in because I don't know anyone there - I changed into pyjamas and slippers, curled up in a corner of the sofa and logged onto the laptop.

John Islip was easy to find. Westminster Abbey's own website had a huge section devoted to him. I started a new word document so I could cut and paste anything that might be of interest and soon I had filled several pages. I noted that he did have a sister - called Agnes - and that the family name was most likely to have been Giles. Not very helpful though because chances are Agnes would have married and taken her husband's name. I also noted that the stained glass panel of his rebus at Westminster wasn't presented to the Abbey until 1924.

I topped up my wine glass and switched my search to Agnes-possibly-Giles and the Battle of Islip, but very soon I was going around in circles. One record I found even had the battle dated as February 1645. I was beginning to understand what my unattractive history teacher had always tried to instil into me about reliable source material. Still, it had given me some ideas about where to continue my search if necessary. I rubbed my eyes, which were itching from staring at the screen for so long.

I clicked the computer into sleep mode, turned the TV on and stretched out my now cramped legs. Some chat show or other was on with an actress who looked familiar but I had no idea who she was. By the time I woke up several hours later the chat show had morphed into a quiz show that I couldn't identify, the birds were chirping and daylight was trying to squeeze through a chink in the curtains. I groaned and rolled over. It was too late to bother going to bed now.

When I woke for the second time that morning, with the imprint of the sofa's textured cushions down my cheek and a stiff neck, I regretted that rash decision. I made strong coffee and carried it outside with a folding camping chair to enjoy on my new deck. The sun was already warm on my neck and the river was beginning to look very inviting. Even my boat appeared to be gravitating towards the water, as if in anticipation of an outing. I drained my coffee and went back indoors. The morning had given me a new sense of purpose. Maybe a little trip down the river would help me solve the riddle of the ring.

I threw on shorts, a T-shirt and deck shoes, made a flask of coffee and found a ready-made pasta salad - complete with a plastic fork - and a bottle of water in the fridge. After gathering a fleece, my camera and mobile in its waterproof case and thrusting them into a hiker's day pack, I left the house by the back door, locking it behind me. A large black and white cat was sunning itself on my deck. I hadn't seen it around before. It opened one eye and regarded me with a haughty expression, as if I was invading its space. 'It's okay puss. You can stay on my deck if you want to.' I'd never really been much of a cat person, but I was in a generous mood today.

I took a moment to admire my boat's pristine new paintwork before dragging it into the water, climbing in and pushing away from the bank. We drifted into the middle of the river and I took the oars and started to row upstream, away from the village. The current was strong, and fighting against it was a good workout. The Old Mill retreated into the distance behind me and the river began to meander between open fields. I hadn't seen another human being all morning - fine by me - and the only sounds were the calling of birds and the distant hum of traffic on the A34. I kept my eyes open for a suitable place to stop - by suitable I mean where the bank is low enough for me to get out of the boat and there's a tree to secure it to. It wasn't long before I found a spot. I clambered onto the bank and tied up. With my camera on its strap around my neck and the day pack on my shoulders I ambled away from the river, letting my arms swing by my side to ease the ache from rowing, and stopping to take pictures whenever anything of interest caught my eye.

I turned onto a path between two high hedges almost entirely overhung by trees, dappled with light where it had found a way through the canopy of leaves. As I emerged into another field, in front of me was the most perfectly framed view of Islip church. The top of the tower was all that was visible, surrounded by trees and the odd glimpse of a thatched or tiled roof. It was the archetypal English village, picture-postcard stuff. I clicked away. A huge oak tree, standing proud and alone, dominated the field. How could something as impressive, as majestic, grow from a tiny acorn and how many centuries had it taken? I decided it was a good place to stop and have my lunch. The ground under the tree was springy with moss and leaves. I spread my fleece out to sit on, unscrewed my water bottle and took a long swig. My hand fumbled for my mobile phone and I activated it using my thumbprint but there were still no messages or missed calls from Joel.

I lingered under the tree for some time, eating my lunch, sipping lukewarm coffee, and admiring the view. From this angle I could also see the back of the Old Mill and I wondered how different it would have looked in 1645, with its wheel rotating and dipping into the river, water cascading from its blades and workers bustling around. It was difficult to imagine a scene so different to the tranquil picture of sleepy rural England that was in front of me. And then, in a flash, the scene transformed almost into that vision. It wasn't quite light, but even so I could make out the outline of a huge wheel, and it was turning. The building itself was smaller though and there were no workers. There was a tang of something like bonfire smoke in the air. I squeezed my eyes shut and opened them again. The scene had gone and the Mill was back to normal. I always did have an overactive imagination.

I returned to the boat by a long and circuitous route, feeling virtuous that I had done my 10,000 steps today and more. My phone rang as I was guiding us back home, letting it drift in the current and using the oars as little as possible. I couldn't take my eyes from the river so I answered it without looking at caller ID, expecting it to be Joel. It wasn't.

'Hannah? It's Matt Denton.'

My stomach did a flip. I looked down at it in surprise. Pressed a hand into it to make it stop.

'Is now a good time?'

'Er yes. I was expecting it to be Joel.'

'You sound a bit ... distracted.'

'Sorry. I'm concentrating on steering my boat.'

'Your boat?' Now it was Matt's turn to sound surprised.

'Just a little rowing boat, but I enjoy it.'

There was an awkward silence. I dipped one oar in the water to turn the boat into a meander of the river.

'How did you get on with Joel?'

'Fine. He's an interesting character.'

'He's a really great guy. I'm seeing him later for a few beers.'

This was a strange conversation. Surely he hadn't just rung me to tell me he was seeing Joel later? Maybe he had found something relating to the ring and I waited for him to say more.

'I wondered if you'd like to go for a drink?'

My hand pressed down on the oar and it jerked up, splattering me and the phone with water.

'Hannah? Are you there?'

'Er yes. Just a little accident with the oar.'

'Tomorrow lunchtime?'

'Well ... I ...'

There were so many reasons why I should say no. Pouty Lauren for one. But he was only inviting me for a drink, in the middle of the day. There was nothing wrong with that. If I thought he was asking me on a proper date, well, that would be something different.

'That would be nice.' The words slipped out before I could stop them.

'What are the pubs like in Islip? I don't often get out into the countryside.'

We agreed to meet at 1.30 in the Swan, which occupied one of the best spots in the village, overlooking the picturesque bridge. It crossed my mind that he'd suggested somewhere he hadn't been to before so he could be sure no-one he knew would see him with me, but I pushed it away.

When I tied my boat up for the first time at my deck, the cat was still there, stretched out, basking in a shaft of sunlight. It opened one eye, flicked its tail at me, and closed the eye again.

After cleaning my house and downloading all the photos I had taken recently to my computer, I had a long soak in the bath and applied a deep treatment to my hair, which is long, straight and straggly, like my mother's and my grandmother's. Well, the long and straight bit anyway - mine's also straggly because I'm lazy about going to the hairdresser. With my hair wrapped in a towel whilst the treatment worked its magic for 20 minutes, I chopped up vegetables and chicken for that evening's dinner-for-one, chicken stir-fry. Somehow eating alone didn't feel as depressing as usual.

What was I doing?

I wasn't ready to start dating again - even if it was a date, which it wasn't. But just thinking about seeing Matt was setting my toes tingling as if they were the percussion section of an orchestra. As I rinsed the treatment off my hair, I tried to remember the last time an attractive man had asked me out - even for coffee - and I couldn't.

Now that's a depressing thought.

It would have been nice to be asked, even though I wouldn't have accepted. That's because I don't need a man in my life, since Sean. I am happy on my own. Delirious, in fact. I mean, who wouldn't be? No need to fill my trolley at the supermarket with all sorts of stuff that I would never touch in a million years just because they are someone else's favourite treats. No picking up someone else's dirty underwear from the bedroom floor, or being forced to watch football or rugby all weekend on the TV. Of course I'm happy.

Back in the kitchen, I threw my diced chicken and vegetables into a wok and they sizzled in the hot oil. I stirred, bashing the spoon against the sides, annoyed with myself because I'd let my guard down and memories of Sean had flooded in without my permission.

I'd tried to convince myself I should be grateful that he'd saved me by dumping me just a week before our wedding, muttering something about not being ready for commitment. Last I heard of him he'd gone off travelling with someone called Trixie. Really. How could anyone be called Trixie. I mean, it sounds like a poodle.

What did that make me, then? Dumped for someone who sounds like a poodle.

I tipped my stir-fry into a bowl, sat down, cross-legged on a dining chair and leaned forward, resting my chin in my hands, and pushing the chicken around. It didn't look very appetising. The peppers were tinged with black where they'd caught and the sauce was already congealing.

I took a few mouthfuls and then put my fork down. The walls of my kitchen seemed to be pressing in on me. I swung my legs to the floor, pushed my chair back and reached for the back door. I flung it open and breathed in the crisp evening air. I leaned against the door frame and admired the night sky, which was clear with stars and a half moon, the lights of the John Radcliffe Hospital shining like an enormous beacon in the distance and the glow of Oxford's city centre to their right. It was familiar and soothing. **My** view, from the back door of **my** house. The house that **I** had paid for from the money **I** earned from **my** business.

Sean is in the past and that's where he belongs.

It was time I left him there and concentrated, instead, on my future.

SIX

Hannah

MY USUAL SUNDAY MORNING WAS spent relaxing. No
need to leap out of bed. Read a book for a while. Eventually get
up for coffee and a late breakfast. But today I was twitchy, nervous,
checking my watch and counting the hours to lunchtime. They
stretched for miles, like the traffic queuing on the A34 on a Friday
afternoon. I thought about calling Matt to cancel and several times
my hand reached for my phone, but a voice in my head reminded
me of my resolution of last night and I withdrew it. In the end, I
stuffed the phone in a kitchen drawer to remove temptation.

I still hadn't heard from Joel, so was no closer to learning
anything else about the ring or who might have lived in the manor
during the Civil War years. The thought of trawling the internet
again for any fresh nugget of information that I hadn't already
found wasn't appealing, so I decided to go for a walk. I didn't
go past the entrance to Confessor's Walk. Instead, I turned down
Mill Lane and went up the new pedestrian and cycle bridge over
the railway line. The bridge is long and narrow with high pre-
fabricated concrete sides that I'm not tall enough to see over, but
a path slopes down from each end to the lane, lined with new
saplings and wooden fencing. I crossed the bridge and leaned
against the fence, looking out over the empty, flat fields towards
Kidlington. If Joel was right, the Battle of Islip had taken place
here, on these fields, maybe even on the railway line underneath
where I was standing. I wondered how many men had died here.
Cromwell's letter that Joel had shown me had been vague about
that, mentioning men drowning in the river but not dying on
the battlefield. For a moment I heard the sounds of that battle

echoing through the centuries towards me. The shrill neighing of frightened horses, the hooves beating the ground, the clash and jangle of metal, the screams of dying men. The brutality of it made me shudder. Yet this had been a small battle.

I don't know how long I stood there for. Several dog-walkers passed me and said hello, but I returned the greeting without noticing them. When I did glance at my watch it was already 12.30. Not only was I not ready, but I hadn't even decided what to wear. What do you wear for a date that isn't a date anyway? I hurried back home, ran up my short flight of stairs and jumped into the shower. Although I was quick, the bathroom filled with steam - I must get that extractor fixed. I opened the window and tried to waft the steam out.

After flinging clothes around my bedroom for a good ten minutes I settled on some cropped jeans with flowers embroidered down the side, and a pink shirt with no sleeves that tied at the waist. I'm sure I looked a bit like a throwback to the sixties, but I didn't care. I'd stopped following fashion years ago and I like pink - it looks good against my black hair. Anyway, we were only going for a drink in a village pub. Better make a bit of an effort though. I don't wear much make-up, but I applied some mascara, left my hair to dry naturally - no alternative since I don't own a hairdryer - and found some low-heeled sandals that matched the shirt. Ready.

Although the heels were low, I wasn't used to wearing any, so I kept my eyes down as I hurried along Mill Street so I wouldn't trip in any of the potholes. The aroma of roasting meat wafting from kitchen windows mingled with the smoke from barbecues and chased me. The smell was delicious but I had no appetite. My stomach was knotted up with apprehension and something else. Was it excitement? I rejected that thought as soon as it popped into my head.

Matt was already there when I crossed the road by the bridge outside the Swan. He was sitting at one of the cramped tables facing the road. His long legs were stretched out in front of him so they were almost dangling over the low wall. His hair was bandanna-free today and he was wearing long black shorts that skimmed his knees, canvas shoes leaving just a glimpse of a sock and a long expanse of hirsute calves, and a loose-fitting collarless white shirt. He saw me, waved and slid over the wall to the ground so he could greet me, continental-style, with a kiss on each cheek. He stepped back, removed his sunglasses, and smiled.

'Sit outside?' he invited.

I'd rather be in the shade and the front of the Swan is a suntrap at this time of day, but I nodded. Matt went inside to fetch drinks and I tried to manoeuvre one of the plastic chairs so I could sit with my back to the sun, without much success. I adjusted my sunglasses, wishing I'd brought a hat.

'It's busy inside,' he remarked, handing me a glass of chilled rose wine, and squeezing into the seat opposite me. He had a pint of something dark coloured, which he raised to me, smiling. 'Cheers.'

I took a sip of my wine, which was very good, crisp and dry, and tried to relax, but I could feel his eyes boring into me from behind his sunglasses. Not being able to read his expression made it an unsettling sensation. I wished he would say something, but he seemed intent on enjoying his drink. I turned away from him and watched the traffic jostling for space on the narrow bridge.

'I've a message for you from Joel,' he said, putting his glass - now half empty - down on the table.

'Oh. Why didn't he call me himself?'

'He was going to, but I thought I could tell you in person. Save him the bother.'

'So, did he find anything?' Now he had my attention. I leaned in towards him.

'Some names.'

Matt took a piece of paper from his pocket and handed it to me. I unfolded it and read out loud.

Miss Hannah

The manor in Islip - it was owned by the Dean and Chapter of Westminster. It was on a long-term lease and throughout the Civil War years appears to have been occupied by the family of Sir Henry Gilder and his father and grandfather before him. I haven't had time to explore his ancestry, but I will try to find more next week. After the Gilders, the next most significant family was that of Richard Marlow - he had an estate between Islip and Oddington, but records are a bit vague about where exactly. Sir Henry was married and had four children - Henry, Frances, George and Elizabeth. Richard Marlow, a widower, had one living child - Thomas - who was himself in his 30s but unmarried.

Yours respectfully
Joel Fielding

'He's good, your mate.'

'Why do I get the feeling you don't like him?'

'I don't know him well enough to either like or dislike him. He just wasn't what I expected.'

'We met at a conference. I knew no-one, he knew no-one. We were sitting next to each other at the opening night dinner and discovered we both lived in Oxford. Job done. We have some professional interests in common and outside of that we meet for a pint or two every few weeks. We get on.'

I couldn't see his eyes, but I thought he was frowning. Was he offended that I hadn't raved about his friend? Strange, he didn't seem the ultra-sensitive type.

I leaned back in my seat and sipped my wine.

'Can I read that again?' He held out his hand and I passed the letter back to him.

'What is it?'

'The name. Thomas Marlow. Just think I've heard it before.'

He removed his sunglasses and chewed the end of one arm. He had a very expressive face. Right now his eyes were narrowed, squinting into the sun, and his eyebrows flared upwards at the outer corners so they resembled Hercule Poirot's crazy moustache. I swallowed the urge to laugh.

'No, it's no good. I can't get it.'

His eyebrows relaxed and he passed the letter back to me.

'Let's talk about something else. Tell me about you. What do you do for a living?'

I told him all about my photography. He fetched more drinks.

'And why did you end up in Islip? Why not the city?'

'I'm a country girl. Don't get me wrong. I love the city - well, Oxford city anyway, maybe not every city. But I wanted to be on the river and I had no chance of affording river frontage inside the ring road. I was drawn to Islip when I first moved to Oxfordshire. It's difficult to explain. It felt like home.'

I was starting to feel a bit tipsy, but in a mellow, dreamlike way, and I was sure my nose was starting to turn red. My shirt was sticking to the plastic back of the chair and I tried to shuffle into the thin strip of shade appearing as the sun dipped behind the trees lining the river. I switched the conversation to Matt and learned that he had a younger sister, his favourite colour was black, and although he looked like a rock star he was actually tone deaf.

I had nearly finished my third drink and the combination of the heat and the alcohol was making me drowsy, when all my senses were jolted back into wakefulness by a screech of tyres and the honking of a car horn. Looking up, I saw a cyclist on the bridge, one foot on a pedal, the other on the ground, shaking a fist at a white van that was accelerating up the hill on the other side of the bridge, out of the village.

'That was a near miss,' Matt said.

I nodded. 'Not the first one either.'

The cyclist pushed his bike over the bridge and I watched him, noticing the shadows were lengthening. 'I should go.' If I had too much more to drink here I wouldn't be able to move.

'I'll walk you home.'

I tried not to show my surprise.

'No need.' My protest was not very convincing, and soon we were walking - or should I say swaying - down Mill Street.

I was ravenous. I'd had no lunch and the best part of the bottle of wine that was sloshing around in my stomach was demanding something of substance to soak into.

'Early dinner?' I suggested as we reached my front door. My words surprised me because I hadn't intended to take him home, let alone offer to feed him, but I suddenly wanted to spend more time with him. 'Not sure what I've got in the fridge, but I can rustle something up.' Don't be deceived. My style is more school dinners than Nigella, but I'm always prepared to have a go.

'I'll help,' he offered.

I was about to push the door open, but I paused and turned to look at him, trying to gauge if he was joking or if he really did just offer to help. Sean would have helped if asked, but he would never have offered. Matt's face gave nothing away, so I just smiled and led the way to the fridge. He followed and stood behind me. I wondered when I'd last cleaned the shelves and hoped he wouldn't notice. He reached over my shoulder, picking up items. He was stooping a little because of his height, and his arm brushed my hair. I imagined his breath on my neck, could almost feel it.

'You've got chicken, chorizo, mushrooms. I'm thinking pasta. Do you have pasta? Pesto?'

Back down to earth with a crash. Hannah, get a grip. You are not getting involved with this man.

'Mmmm, yes.' I turned and my nose pressed into his chest. 'Erm ...' He stepped aside, a smile playing on his lips. I fetched the pasta and a jar of pesto.

'Coffee?'

'Please. Milk and two sugars.'

I had mine black in an effort to sober up.

For the next half hour we stumbled around my kitchen, which was designed for one and was only capable of accommodating two if they were hobbits. We kept bumping into each other and laughing. Matt made himself at home, opening and closing drawers looking for ingredients and utensils. If he couldn't find what he was looking for he would ask and I would point. We were like a well-rehearsed double act. Cooking had never been so much fun.

I set the table. He carried the bowls and a bottle of red - he'd had no trouble finding my wine rack. I tried to read the label without him noticing, hoping it wasn't one of my bottom-of-the-supermarket-shelf specials - vinegar masquerading as wine. But no, he had good taste. He'd picked the one bottle I had that was worth drinking.

The pasta was delicious.

'Where did you learn to cook?' I tried to keep the amazement I felt out of my voice.

'I like to eat. It helps if you can cook.' His eyes twinkled and I realised he was teasing me. I picked up the empty bowls, grateful to turn my back on him so he couldn't see me blush, and dumped them in the sink.

We carried cushions and the rest of the wine to the deck and stretched out. The wood had been absorbing the sun's heat all day and was warm underfoot. The cat was still there.

'What's his name?'

'No idea. He isn't mine, but he seems to have adopted me.'

Matt leaned over and stroked the cat's ears. It started to purr and rolled onto its back inviting Matt to stroke its soft tummy. It had curious markings - like a Dalmation in reverse.

'He likes you.'

'Mmm. I have a way with cats. And he's a she by the way.'

I leaned back and sipped my wine. I'd chosen this spot well. It was peaceful and private. We could be the only people in the world right now - unless a boat went past of course.

'So tell me, how did you end up dealing in old coins and all that other stuff? I mean, it's not something they teach you at school.'

'Family business. My grandad started it back in the '50s. My dad used to go away on buying trips and I was always fascinated with what he brought back. I used to help him clean the old coins. I learned everything I needed to know from him and took over when he retired.'

'You're so not what I expected.'

He raised an eyebrow and his lips twitched. 'Let me guess, you expected someone about twice my age wearing corduroy trousers and a baggy cardigan?'

Obviously, he'd heard that before. But now he'd planted a vision of Leonard Rossiter as Rigsby in Rising Damp in my head and I couldn't get rid of it. I started to giggle.

'What is it?'

'It's ...' I couldn't speak I was laughing so much.

'What's funny?'

'Rigsby,' I managed to splutter. For a moment I thought he was going to be angry, although I was too busy crying with laughter to worry too much. But then he started to laugh as well. And I swear I don't know how it happened, but the next minute his arm was around me and he was pulling me towards him and his lips were on mine, gentle at first and then more searching, increasing in urgency. He rolled over so I was pressed beneath him, my toes tingling in a way I couldn't remember ever happening before. I made a decision, and I'm ashamed to say that not a single thought of Lauren wandered through my mind. I pushed him away and wriggled out from under him. He sat up and looked at me and I thought I could read his eyes wondering if he'd got it wrong. I held out my hand and pulled him, with difficulty, to his feet, led him back inside and up the stairs to my bedroom.

SEVEN

Catherine
Sunday, April 20th, 1645

APART FROM HER PLAIN GREY working gown, Catherine had only one other. It had been her mother's and was still a simple design, but it was cut from cloth of a deep, rich shade of blue and had sleeves that flared below the elbow trimmed with a paler cuff, the shade of bluebells. The vibrant colours lifted her spirits. Today, she would not be drab Catherine Meakin. Today, she would be someone more exciting and interesting. As she dressed, Catherine wished she had the blue eyes to match. The thought brought back the memory of Lady Frances yesterday and her icy, spite-filled stare. She pushed it away. She wasn't going to let that girl intimidate her - lady or not.

In the kitchen, she brushed her cloak, then Tilly's, cleaned the mud and dust from their boots and massaged dubbin into the worn leather. Satisfied, she crouched down in front of the oak chest and removed a slim, paper parcel from the bottom. The paper crackled as she unfolded it. Inside was a single lace collar, a few ribbons in different colours and a sash. She attached the lace collar to her gown, then she opened the jewellery box, picked up her mother's brooch and held it against her throat. It wouldn't do. Such frivolity would be frowned on in church. Reluctant fingers released it and snapped the box lid closed before trailing over the ribbons, and she remembered the occasions when she had worn them. The carefree happiness of those days, the hope and anticipation. She recognised these emotions within herself again now, welcomed them as long absent companions.

Small hands pressed on her shoulders and Tilly's hair tickled the side of her face. 'They're so pretty Mama. Can I wear one today, in my hair? Please?'

Catherine turned her head and kissed her daughter's nose. 'No, my love. Not for church.'

Tilly's face fell, and her eyes lingered on the ribbons as Catherine stood. 'Come, let's look at your hair.'

Catherine unwound the plaits, and one-by-one dropped the sheets of curls over Tilly's shoulder. She squealed with delight, disappointment over the ribbons forgotten, fidgeting and bobbing her head up and down, watching the curls bounce.

'Be still, my love,' Catherine laughed. 'You're making this much harder, and we'll be late.'

When she'd finished, Tilly stood in front of the small, cracked mirror, twisting her head from side to side to try to see the back.

'It looks lovely,' said Catherine, smiling with pleasure at the excited expression on Tilly's pretty little face.

Tilly insisted on wearing her curls loose and Catherine indulged her, knowing from experience that they wouldn't last for long and wanting her to enjoy them. Catherine dressed her own hair following the fashion of the day, allowing several tendrils to escape and frame her face. She secured the rest in a neat bun at the nape of her neck, topped with a close-fitting cloth cap.

Whilst Tilly admired her curls, Catherine took the sash and tied it around her waist. The pale blue wasn't quite a match for the cuffs of the gown, but it was close. Although they were not yet ready to leave for church, she took her cloak from its hook and pulled it around her shoulders, securing it at the front so it wouldn't flap open.

Catherine always made an effort to dress for church. She had no intention of giving those who would criticise her any grounds for doing so. This morning, though, she knew she was taking more care than usual. She could try to fool herself and invent a reason for this fastidiousness, but she wouldn't. Thomas Marlow had said he would see her at church, and she wanted to impress him. Catherine's skin tingled under the caress of the ring, and its cool chain that never seemed to warm up. She was afraid to admit that she no longer had any thoughts of trying to return it to him.

She busied herself in the kitchen, tidying and rearranging dishes and mugs that were already in perfect order. Her cloak hampered her movements and she hoped Tilly wouldn't question why she was wearing it indoors when it wasn't yet time to leave, but Tilly was too busy admiring her curls to notice anything else. Catherine tried, and failed, to suppress the excitement that was building within her, churning in her stomach, and drying her mouth until her tongue felt as tough and cracked as a strip of old leather. The passing of time had never been so slow. When she could think of nothing else to do, she leaned on the frame of the open back door and stared out at Otmoor, not noticing the view, but allowing her imagination to take her to a different world. In this world there would be no social barriers and no discord between men for their beliefs, status or wealth. She was so preoccupied, allowing her mind to explore this alternative reality that she didn't hear her father's heavy tread on the path. The grating of the front door, followed by a blast of wind announced his arrival.

'C'mon girl. You ready?' He stamped his feet, and his fingers rattled the door handle. Catherine could feel his impatience radiating into the room. She let go of her imaginary world and hurried to help Tilly into her cloak.

He didn't wait for them but marched ahead at a fast pace. Catherine secured the front door, took Tilly's hand and they hastened after him but could not keep up. Inside the graveyard he was greeted by a tall man wearing a long coat and a hat decorated with a sprig of something that looked like rosemary. It was pulled down low at the front making it difficult to see his face, but Catherine didn't recognise him.

'You go in girl,' her father waved them past with a self-important flick of his wrist.

Catherine watched him turn his back and follow the stranger to the edge of the graveyard where they paused. Their heads were close together and they were talking, arguing even. The stranger had an expressive manner; his arms and hands seemed to have life of their own, fluttering by his side like a bird as he spoke. She wished she could hear what they were saying. This stranger must be connected with her father's comments a few nights ago and whatever he had become involved with. They took the steps that led down onto the path and moved out of sight. Tilly tugged at her hand and she turned away.

The church was almost full. Catherine and Tilly slipped into a pew towards the back. Helen, Edward and their four children were already seated in the row in front. Helen turned and smiled at them. Her expression became puzzled as she noticed they were alone. She mouthed 'all well?' at Catherine who nodded, raised her shoulders and her hands, trying to convey that she did not know where her father had gone.

Catherine found it difficult to concentrate on the sermon. It was reduced to a stream of words with no meaning, as her ears strained to hear the click of the heavy latch and the stirring of air that would indicate the church door opening to admit a late arrival. She wanted to turn around and watch the entrance, but she daren't. Her father did not join them. She tried not to dwell on what he was getting involved with and allowed her eyes to seek out Thomas Marlow instead, but his family pew was too far away, and she wasn't tall enough to see beyond the row in front of her.

At the end of the service the vicar led the procession out of the church and the congregation fell into step behind him, pew by pew, like the animals queuing to board Noah's Ark. She wanted to stare at them, looking for Thomas, but instead she focused on the pew in front. Her skin prickled and she raised her eyes without moving her head. Thomas was passing her pew. He raised his hand and his fingers brushed his brow. The gesture was so natural that he could have been scratching an itch, but she knew he was greeting her. She tapped her foot, impatient to follow, but forced to wait in turn.

At last, they were in the church porch exchanging pleasantries with the vicar. Catherine almost choked on her own hypocrisy as she offered the expected compliments on the sermon, whilst her eyes combed the graveyard. There was no sign of her father, the stranger, or Thomas. Pockets of men gathered under the boughs of the yew and lime trees that guarded the graves like sentinels. She and Tilly joined Helen, Edward and the other children who stood in a small group quite close to the stone that marked John's grave. As was his custom, Edward excused himself. Catherine watched as he moved from one group to another. It was clear that he was respected and liked. She pushed away a pang of envy that he and Helen had the life that she and John would have aspired to had he not been taken, and turned to Helen, who was discussing the price of goose with a neighbour. Catherine smiled and nodded to the older lady, who tilted her chin and sniffed the air as though there was a bad smell, but didn't acknowledge her. Gradually people started to drift away. The children were becoming impatient. Tilly had already moved to the edge of the graveyard and was hovering by the gate.

'Shall we go Cat? Your father will join us when he can. He knows where we'll be.'

Catherine nodded, the disappointment that Thomas hadn't tried to speak to her outweighing her worry over where her father might have gone. They caught up with Tilly and she took her daughter's hand. Where the hill flattened out and the river beckoned, the lane was crowded with children crouching in the dust, playing a game with sticks. The cadence of voices from the various taverns beat a rhythm that spoke of men relaxing on their day of rest. Catherine knew the volume and pace would only increase as the day stretched into evening, and men in various stages of inebriation were tipped out onto the streets to pick a fight with a rival, or stumble home. Her father would probably be among them.

She didn't notice Edward had joined them and his voice startled her.

'Helen, I've asked my old friend, Thomas Marlow to join us for dinner. I'm sure there will be enough goose.'

'You'll be very welcome Mr Marlow,' Helen said with a smile, linking arms with her husband

Thomas fell into step beside Catherine, and she kept her eyes fixed on the rutted surface of the track, trying to ignore a peculiar fluttering sensation in her chest. She tightened her grip on Tilly's hand, causing the little girl to gasp.

'Sorry my love,' she said, loosening it. 'I didn't want you to trip.'

'Mistress Meakin,' Thomas nodded to her. 'How did you enjoy the sermon?'

Catherine searched her memory but couldn't recall a single word the vicar had spoken. 'I ... I ... don't think it was one of his best,' she mumbled, wishing she had paid more attention.

'No?' He appeared thoughtful, and she was aware of the scrutiny of his gaze. 'Maybe not.'

Was she imagining the hint of a smile hiding behind his beard? He must find her inability to make conversation amusing. This was her chance, to say something intelligent, or make him laugh, but she was so taken by surprise that he was to join them for dinner that her mind was a blank. Perhaps she could ask him about the man who had been thrown into jail for refusing to provide food for the King's men. She was still trying to frame her question when Edward pushed open the front door, and the aroma of goose that had been roasting on a spit over the fire all morning wafted out.

'Mmm, that smells promising,' Thomas said, sniffing the air. He stood to one side to allow Helen and Catherine to enter the house, and then followed Edward into the front parlour where they sat, drinking and smoking whilst the children played in the garden. In the kitchen, Catherine took the knife that Helen handed to her and started chopping some fresh spring greens and beets. She'd had no idea that Edward was on such good terms with Thomas. The prospect of sitting through a meal together at a table where she was considered an equal was intoxicating, if worrying. Her aunt would be sure to notice that she and Thomas were not strangers to each other. Catherine wouldn't put it past Helen's piercing gaze to be able to see through the fabric of her gown and detect the ring and chain. Her lack of concentration made her clumsy. She nicked her finger with the knife and drew blood.

'Ouch,' she cried.

Helen placed the slice of goose she had just carved onto a platter.

'Let me see,' she demanded.

'It's nothing.' Catherine sucked it to stop the bleeding.

Helen gave her a strip of muslin, took the knife and finished chopping the greens. 'Are you still worried about your father?'

Catherine wrapped the muslin around her finger and nodded. She couldn't admit to Helen that her thoughts had been far removed from worries about her father, and Helen's words were a reminder that he had failed to show up in church. 'He hasn't said anything more, but where is he? He stopped to talk to someone outside the church. I didn't recognise the man. They must have gone somewhere together,' Catherine paused. 'But what could be so important that he had to miss the service?'

'Maybe he didn't want to disturb the sermon by coming in late.' It was a half-hearted suggestion.

'We both know better than that Helen.'

'Ed might have heard something. He might know who that man is.'

'No,' Catherine pressed her fingers into Helen's arm. 'You are not going to ask him. Not now anyway.'

Helen put the knife down, confusion glowing in her eyes. 'Wouldn't you rather know?'

Catherine shook her head.

'My father works for Thomas Marlow's father. It's too risky.'

She bit her lip, thinking.

'We don't have to mention your father.'

'Helen, please. Promise me you won't.'

'If that's what you want, I promise.'

'Thank you.' Catherine pointed at the platter of goose. 'Shall I take this through to the dining room?' She didn't wait for a reply, but picked up the platter and left the room, Helen's shrewd eyes burning into her retreating back. She didn't have to see her aunt's face to feel her unasked questions hovering in the air like a cloud of annoying flies.

The dining room was opposite the front parlour. The door was ajar and Edward's voice carried into the silence of the hallway.

'How's Ellis?'

Catherine froze in the shadows, holding her breath to hear better. She recognised the name. Ellis was the man Thomas had spoken for.

'As well as can be expected.'

The reply from Thomas was curt and there was something else in his tone. Frustration, she thought.

'Dammit. I can't sit back and let a good man rot in jail for trying to protect his family. That doesn't mean I share his beliefs, though.'

'He was being made an example of and you know it. By intervening you may well have drawn attention to yourself.'

'I've got nothing to hide.'

Edward snorted. 'Since when did that matter?'

Catherine heard a chair leg scraping across the flagstone floor and Helen's voice calling the children in from the garden. She needed to move or she would be caught eavesdropping. She ducked into the dining room, placed the platter on the table and made a pretence of attending to the fire, trying to organise her thoughts about what she had heard. Without doubt, Thomas Marlow was more than he seemed.

'Where's your father?' Edward asked, taking his place at the head of the table.

'He ... he,' Catherine faltered. Could she claim he was unwell?

'He met a strange man outside the church,' Tilly finished the sentence for her.

'Tilly,' Catherine's voice was sharp, and the little girl turned towards her, eyes wide with surprise.

'I'm sorry my love, but you shouldn't interrupt adults,' she softened her tone and took Tilly's hand to reassure her.

'Where do you want the children to sit?' Catherine addressed Helen, hoping that Edward and Thomas might not have heard Tilly's words.

'At this end of the table.' Helen took the hint and started pulling chairs out and directing the children.

Edward had been piling goose onto his plate. He paused, and the slice he had speared on the end of his knife wobbled.

'What strange man?' He addressed the question to Tilly. She glanced at her mother and then bent her head. Catherine noticed her hands gripping the edges of her seat.

'Tilly, please answer me.'

'I ... I don't know,' she muttered.

'Tell me what you saw,' Edward persisted.

'He had a twig in his hat.'

Catherine willed her daughter to say no more, but she knew Tilly would not dare to ignore Edward.

'Did you recognise him?'

Tilly appeared to be trying to make herself invisible. Her head was now so bowed that her curls were pooling on the table. She shook it, in a movement so slight it was almost imperceptible. She didn't look up.

Catherine saw Edward and Thomas exchange a glance. 'There are always strangers in Islip, passing through or visiting the market,' she interrupted. Helen passed her a plate and she took a small helping of goose. Tilly raised her head a fraction and Catherine smiled at her.

'Eat, my love,' she said, placing some greens onto a piece of goose and raising it to her mouth.

'They don't usually turn up in the churchyard on a Sunday though,' Edward remarked, lowering his knife to his plate.

Thomas leaned forward and his eyes roved from Catherine to Tilly before settling on Catherine, one eyebrow raised into an elegant arch.

'Mistress Meakin, had you seen this man before?'

She sighed and shook her head. 'No.'

'What did he look like?'

'His hat was pulled down so low that I couldn't see his face.'

'Tall, short, fat, thin?'

'Tall and thin.'

'What business did your father have with him?'

Thomas had taken control of the conversation with quiet and unchallenged authority. Catherine dare not avoid answering him, but now she hesitated, not sure how much to say. Could she trust him? Would he report back to his father that he was employing some kind of radical? After what she had just heard, she thought not, but she couldn't be sure. And what would he think of her if he knew more about her father? She glanced around the table. No-one moved. Three pairs of adult eyes were focused on her, waiting for an answer. She fancied that even the room itself was holding its breath.

'Cat, you must tell Thomas what you know,' Edward prompted.

She swallowed. Helen caught her eye and frowned. Catherine sensed she was trapped. If she didn't tell them what she knew - even though that amounted to nothing - Helen's duty to Edward would compel her to speak, promise or no promise.

'My father has been saying some strange things of late,' her voice was gentle, but she raised her head and met Thomas's eyes with a confidence that she hoped wasn't bordering on familiarity.

'About what?'

'I'm worried,' she admitted. 'Maybe I just haven't noticed before, but he's angry. He seems to think that change is coming and he's determined to be involved.'

'Involved with what?'

'There's this preacher who's been saying things. Father's all stirred up about it. He's talking about the mood of the country and saying men like him are not going to put up with what he sees as this unfairness any more.'

Thomas drew his brows together in a thoughtful expression.

'And you think the stranger in the churchyard might be involved?'

Catherine shrugged. 'I don't know sir. Truly I don't.'

'It's true that no-one knows how long the King can hold out for in Oxford, but even if Parliament defeats him I'm not convinced much will change for most people,' Edward said.

Thomas shook his head. 'Most of Parliament's men are landowners. They want power as much as the King does.' Catherine was surprised at the bitterness she heard in his voice. He spoke like a man disillusioned.

'I think for my father the choice is no longer King or Parliament,' she said.

A heavy silence hung over her words. She wished she could take them back, wrap them up and bury them in a safe place where no-one could find them. Where no-one would be able to use them against her or Tilly. She sought Helen's eyes for reassurance, but Helen was watching Edward.

'Go on,' Thomas prompted.

'I ... I don't know anything more. I swear.'

He turned to Edward.

'Levellers? Are they active here?'

Edward inclined his head.

'Fools,' Thomas slammed his fist on the table. 'Even if Parliament defeats the King, they'll never go as far as the Levellers want them to.'

Catherine pushed her plate away and wiped her brow, which was moist with sweat. Levellers. That must be what this group called themselves. The walls around her had taken on life of their own and were swaying. Her lace collar was pressing against her throat as if it would choke her. Her breath was trapped inside her chest, unable to beat a way out. She had to get out of the room.

'Please excuse me,' she said, stumbling to her feet and avoiding eye contact with anyone. She rushed through the kitchen and into the garden, gulping air like a frog. Her boots crunched the loose stone on the path and then she was into the orchard, weaving her way between the trees. She didn't stop until she reached the river and could go no further. She loosened her collar and leaned forwards with her forehead and hands pressed against the mighty trunk of a horse chestnut. Its reassuring warmth and solidity seeped through her skin, into her bones. Her breathing returned to normal, as if she were pulling on the tree's invisible essence to restore her strength. She heard soft footsteps approach and swivelled around, expecting to see Helen, but it was Thomas. He was just a few feet behind her. She turned back to face the river and hugged her arms across her chest to stop them shaking. He moved to her side and stood, feet apart, hands resting on his hips.

Why didn't he speak? She wanted to ask him about the Levellers. Who they were. What they stood for. But she was afraid of what he might say.

'Sometimes the ducks paddle down here. Tilly loves to see them,' she murmured when she could bear the silence no longer.

'Shhh,' he said, turning towards her and putting a finger to her lips. His eyes, warm and serious, scanned her face and it seemed that time stood still, and life was reduced to the two of them, cocooned in that moment. They weren't even touching, but the intensity of the emotion flowing between them was more powerful than anything Catherine could remember experiencing, except her love for Tilly. 'You're worried about what might happen to you and Matilda aren't you? If your father is involved with something that may be dangerous?'

At the sound of his voice the connection between them dissolved, and Catherine stepped away, moving closer to the river.

'Is that so bad? I have to keep Tilly safe. I cannot be held responsible for my father's actions.'

'Your father is well known in Islip as a bit of a hothead.'

His comment was so unexpected that she was unable to suppress the bitter laugh that burst from her. It released her tension like flood water that increases its pressure on anything that stands in its way, until the resistance yields and it bursts through in a triumphant gush.

She'd never considered before that her father might have a reputation. That someone like Thomas would have taken notice though was a surprise.

'I think he can take care of himself, but if he is embroiled in something that may have repercussions for you and Matilda, nothing bad will happen to you. The ring is my promise.'

He stared at her, unblinking. His golden-brown eyes glowed and she could almost feel them burning into her skin, burrowing down below the surface and setting fire to her veins.

'Trust me,' he said.

Could she? She wanted to. She searched his face as if she could find the answer printed there. Failing, she twisted away from him, and allowed her gaze to rove over the garden to the house. She could see Helen at the back door. It was a reminder that the afternoon was drawing in and the shadows were lengthening. 'I need to go. Time to get Tilly home.'

'Wait one moment.' She turned back. He stepped to one side so he was positioned between her and the house and pulled a small parcel wrapped in cloth from his coat pocket. He held it out to her. 'For you.'

Catherine stared, but kept her hands by her side, remembering the last time he had insisted she take something from him.

He grasped her hand and pressed the parcel into her palm, then closed her fingers over it with a warm smile.

'What is it?'

'Open it and see.'

Although she knew they were alone in the garden, Catherine's instinct was to look around to make sure no-one was watching. She thought she saw a flash of movement - something dark against the green of the field across the river. Whatever it was disappeared behind the hedge. Probably a hare. A kite hovered overhead. Thomas followed her gaze. He screwed his eyes up and shielded them with his hand. Had he seen it too? She looked down at the bundle. Handling it with care, as if it were a tiny baby, she unrolled the cloth. Inside was a selection of chalks, fresh charcoal sticks, inks and a quill.

She stared at them. The ring was no doubt valuable, but these were of far greater value to Catherine. So many times she had wished she had better materials to work with, and Thomas had just gifted them to her. She picked them up one-by-one, enjoying the feel of them between her fingers, and was overwhelmed with longing to be in front of a blank sheet of paper, to see what she could create.

'I ... I don't know what to say.'

He put his finger to his lips, smiled and turned away from her. 'Draw me something beautiful.' he said. He walked with purpose back to the house. Catherine quickly re-wrapped the parcel, pushed it inside her sleeve and followed.

Helen was still in the doorway, watching them. She said nothing, but Catherine didn't miss the unasked question in her aunt's eyes and twitched with guilt for not being honest with her. She called Tilly to get her cloak and they said goodbye.

The village was quiet, the lanes and the High Street deserted as they walked the short distance home. Catherine wondered again what had been so important that her father had missed church, and who the man he had met in the graveyard could be, but she was unable to find any answers.

It wasn't quite dark when her father returned. Tilly was sitting on the back door step wiggling her fingers in an effort to attract a skinny black and white cat that was lying just out of her reach, swishing its tail in the dust.

'Don't you let that filthy animal in here,' he growled at her.

Tilly jumped to her feet and ran away. Catherine watched her skid to a halt at the wall at the bottom of the garden. The cat held its ground.

'It's doing no harm,' Catherine defended the cat. 'And Tilly likes it.'

She met the cat's eyes and decided she liked it too. There was something soothing about its calm presence. It might be small, but it wasn't intimidated.

She wanted to follow Tilly, to make sure she was all right, but her father blocked her path.

'Is there any supper, girl?' Phrased like a question, Catherine knew it was a demand.

He slumped into a chair at the head of the table.

'Why didn't you join us at Helen's for dinner?'

She unwrapped the cloth in which Helen had placed several slices of goose, removed two and re-wrapped the remainder. She put them in a bowl with a hunk of bread and pushed it across the table towards him, taking nothing for herself. Although she had eaten very little, she was not hungry.

'Business to attend to.'

'On a Sunday?'

She could feel his eyes following her as she poured him a mug of ale, but he said nothing.

'Who was that man?'

'What business is it of yours girl?'

Her back was half turned towards him, so she could only see him in profile, but that didn't stop her being able to sense his mood. The air teemed with tension. It seemed to bounce off him, hit the wall and do a turn around the kitchen, gathering strength, before settling back on him, like a cloud. The way he'd snapped at Tilly and was now sitting, watchful, alert and biding his time, made her think of a wild animal about to strike. It was a warning not to push any further. She took a deep breath and pushed anyway.

'It's my business if your actions endanger Tilly.'

'A man has got to stand up for what he believes in. Even that sop you married knew that,' he snapped.

She gasped and swivelled around, her eyes searching his face. Why would he say such a thing?

'What do you mean? John was loyal. A Royalist.'

He threw back his head and laughed. It was not the joyful laugh of someone relishing life, but the bitter, strangled sound of one person trying to inflict hurt on another.

'You see, that's why you shouldn't try to get involved with things you just don't understand girl.' His laughter died away and his mouth settled into a smirk. He held out his mug for more ale. She couldn't look at him. Abruptly, she turned away and a bunch of herbs from the beam brushed her face. She swiped at them and they twisted, like a body hanging from a gibbet.

The wild animal had just dealt her a dangerous blow. She hadn't been wrong about John. Had she? Was no man what he seemed to be? Her father, Thomas, and now John as well.

Out of the corner of her eye she saw Tilly creep back onto the step. She was being careful to remain out of sight of her grandpa and Catherine pretended not to have noticed.

'I hear Edward invited that Marlow fellow back for dinner.'

'He did.'

Her head was still whirling with thoughts of John and she was unprepared for the sudden change in direction of the conversation.

'I'd have thought Edward would have more sense. I don't trust him. You stay away from him, girl.'

He waved his finger in front of her face and she recoiled, her instinct screaming at her to get away, but the room was too small. There was nowhere to go. He angled his head to one side and studied her, a strange expression shrouding his features. His mouth was moving, as if he was trying to work something out, but he was not speaking. Her eyes flicked to the doorway. She could see that Tilly had drawn her knees up to her chest and buried her head in them with her hands clamped over her ears.

His accusatory voice dragged her attention away from Tilly. 'Why did you wear that gown? It was always your best. You always did look good in that gown.'

Puzzled, Catherine held out her arms, looking at the sleeves.

'You wouldn't have me go to church in my working gown would you? This is the only other I have.'

He lunged forwards and reached for the sash, seized the end of it and examined it, turning it over in his calloused hand.

'And what's this? There's no place for vanity on the Sabbath girl.'

In a sudden, quick movement, he tugged the sash, and Catherine stumbled towards him. She planted her hands, palms down, on the table and leaned backwards. The sash tore and she staggered, keeping her balance by gripping the back of a chair.

He unfurled his fingers and let the sash fall. 'You're throwing yourself at him.'

Catherine glanced at Tilly. Even with her hands over her ears she must be able to hear his voice, and his anger. Catherine longed to go to her daughter, scoop her up and run, putting as much distance between them and her father as possible. Something inside her snapped with the unfairness and irrationality of his behaviour. 'I was only being polite,' she hissed. 'It isn't my place to be rude to someone else's guest.'

He slammed his hand on the table. 'You heard me. Stay away.'

He stood, and his chair legs screeched over the stone floor. He lurched across the room to the front door, rammed his hat so low on his head that it hid his eyes and stamped out.

Catherine hurried to the back door, crouched down on the step and pulled her daughter towards her. Tilly lifted her head. Her eyes brimmed with unshed tears.

'Why was Grandpa so cross?'

'I don't know.' Catherine wrapped her arms around her. She was beginning to question whether the darkness Thomas could sense was somehow connected with her father and his moods that seemed to be getting blacker by the day. Sometimes, when he looked at her, it was as if he wasn't seeing her at all, but someone else. They sat on the step until the cold from the stone began to chill her and the sky over Otmoor darkened into an inky jet pierced with stars. A half-moon appeared, wearing wisps of cloud like a veil. She stood and pulled Tilly indoors.

'Let's do some drawing. Would you like that?'

Tilly nodded. Her eyes widened when Catherine showed her the bundle of charcoal sticks and chalks and invited her to choose what she would like to draw with. 'Mr Marlow gave them to me. He said he wasn't going to use them so maybe we could.' It was the second time in as many days that she had misled her daughter, which shamed her, but the deceit worked. Tilly smiled.

'I like him,' she said. 'He showed me how to blow a piece of grass like a whistle. You hold it like this.' She held her hands up to demonstrate. 'And then blow as hard as you can. Like this.' Tilly put her mouth close to her bunched fingers and blew, producing a rasping sound that made her giggle.

Smiling now and relaxed, Tilly chose a fine black charcoal stick and some chalk and Catherine gave her one of her new sheets of paper. She took a fresh charcoal stick for herself but she sat with a blank sheet in front of her, chewing her nails and unable to draw a single line. She couldn't concentrate. Her mind was full of her father's behaviour and her memories of John, now tarnished by his words. He was wrong. He had to be. And what did he mean by warning her to stay away from Thomas? She twisted the charcoal stick in her fingers, puzzling over that question and why he disliked Thomas so much. Was it as simple as him being Richard Marlow's son, and therefore the enemy? She thought of the ring that Thomas had insisted she wear, his kindness in giving her the drawing materials, and the forgotten feelings that he was awakening within her, how she wanted to live again. She had a sense of duty to her father, but she would not allow him to dictate to her about who she could talk to.

After a while she looked down at the sheet of paper and was surprised to see she had sketched something after all. There was Thomas on the left, recognisable from his close-cropped beard, holding a blade of grass between his fingers, and John on the right, faded and somehow lacking in substance. Between the two stood her father, face grey-tinged and eyes wild. In his hand he was holding the torn sash from her gown.

Catherine studied what she had drawn for a few moments, her fingers tracing the charcoal lines. It expressed her confusion but did nothing to alleviate it. She glanced at Tilly, who was shading in the outline of the cat she had drawn, creating black patches on the off-white paper, a smile on her face, earlier anxieties seemingly forgotten already. Watching her draw, Catherine wondered when Thomas had spent time with her daughter and how she hadn't noticed.

EIGHT

Hannah

I KNEW AT ONCE THAT something was off-kilter. It wasn't just that I ached in a pleasant sort of way, there was more to it than that. It took me a few seconds to work it out ... I wasn't alone in my bed.

I stretched out my arm, seeking with my fingers, which met with a firm, well-muscled stomach. I snatched my hand back, half opened one eye and snapped it closed again.

What had I done?

I started to inch very slowly to the edge of the bed, but a hand on my hip stopped me.

'Where do you think you're going?'

The hand moved down my thigh and up again. But I was awake now and I was having none of it. This wasn't supposed to have happened. When I'd agreed to have a drink with Matt, that's all it was. Just a drink. In the middle of the day. Safe. Sleeping with him had not been part of the plan - even though he made my toes tingle.

And I don't steal other girl's boyfriends. Even if the other girl is pouty.

I squeezed my eyes into a tight ball that made my nose wrinkle, hoping I was dreaming, and if I could wake up again, Matt would have disappeared and I would be on my own.

'We shouldn't have done this.' I opened my eyes and he was still there, looking at me, puzzled. He rubbed the stubble that had sprung up across his face overnight like a new lawn.

'What about Lauren?' I asked, surprised that I had to spell it out. He laughed.

Now it was my turn to pout. 'I don't see what's funny.'

I moved with the speed of an athlete, swinging my legs out of bed and sitting up, but he was even faster. An arm circled my waist and pulled me back down. I scowled at him.

'Lauren's my cousin,' he said, tucking my hair behind my ears and holding my face in his hands.

Really, that old chestnut. Was that the best he could do?

My disbelief must have registered in my face.

'I swear to you Hannah, she is my cousin.'

I didn't know what to say.

'I don't cheat on my girlfriends.'

His eyes were locked on mine, unblinking, shining like my mum's polished silver teapot. For a few seconds we stayed like that, frozen in a moment of time. I wavered. I believed him. Then I felt stupid. Embarrassed even, for making assumptions. My mouth was dry and tasted of last night's stale alcohol. I needed coffee.

I sat up and this time he didn't try to stop me. He watched me pull on an old T-shirt that doubled as a nightshirt - I never could be bothered with pyjamas.

'Coffee?'

'Please.'

I went first to the bathroom. One glance in the mirror told me that my worries about my sunburned nose were all justified. Wreckers could have used it to lure ships onto the rocks. I rubbed some moisturiser into it, brushed my teeth and went downstairs. When I returned with coffee and a plate of biscuits on a tray, Matt was sitting up in bed, phone in hand, presumably checking for messages or emails. I wondered what time he was supposed to open up the shop.

'Thanks,' he said, taking one of the mugs and putting the phone down.

I climbed back into bed, being careful not to spill the coffee. 'I'm sorry,' I said, feeling awkward.

'Why? Is the coffee as bad as that?'

I was about to reply when I realised he was teasing me. His

mouth was twitching as he tried to appear serious and suppress a smile. He failed.

'I shouldn't have jumped to conclusions.'

'Forget it. It's not important.' He drank some coffee.

'Hannah, you said you got a shock from touching the ring when you found it. Have you had a shock from it since?'

I shook my head. 'I haven't touched it again.'

He was looking at me in a curious way.

'You want me to try, and see what happens?'

'Only if you want to.'

Of course I want to touch something that's going to pump god knows how many volts into my body! It was a stupid suggestion. But then it might be different if I tried again. Whatever had caused the reaction might have passed. I might even be able to wear the ring, but then I remembered what Joel had said about not being able to keep it and I bit my lip. I still hadn't reported it because I wasn't ready to give it up yet. I wanted to hold onto it for myself for a bit longer and see what I could find out.

Matt was watching me, sipping his coffee. I put mine down, opened my bedside cabinet and pulled out the two jewellery pouches. I tipped the ring and chain onto the duvet. It landed with the engraved surface facing us, sparkling, the 'eye' fixed on us, radiant and glowing, as if it were alive. My finger hovered over it for a few seconds, then I shook my head and let my hand drop to its side. I didn't want to do this in front of Matt. It may sound silly, given what we had done last night, but it felt too intimate, as if I would be exposing something of my inner self, something that I should not share – not yet anyway.

I knew Matt's eyes were still on me. I could feel them, burning into my skin like a branding iron. When I turned to face him, his eyebrows flared.

'Sorry. I don't think I want to.'

Matt reached for my hand and enclosed it in both of his. 'No, I'm sorry. I shouldn't have asked you to.'

We sat in silence, both of us looking at the ring.

'Joel said he didn't think you'd reported this yet.'

'I didn't know I had to until he mentioned it.'

'Yeah, I should have made it clear. I doubt they'll be that interested in the coins, but this, well, this is different.'

Matt drained the rest of his coffee. 'I have to go,' he said, reaching for his clothes and pulling his shirt over his head. 'Buy you a proper dinner tonight?'

He pulled me towards him and kissed me, twisting my hair around his fingers. He didn't wait for an answer, clearly didn't expect me to say no.

Would I have said no?

I sat on the bed for a while after he'd gone, legs crossed in front of me, focusing on the ring. It was no good. I had to know. In one quick movement, not giving myself time to change my mind, I stretched my left hand out and touched it with my little finger.

'Ow!' I snatched my hand back. The shock was as bad as the first time. I clenched my fist into a ball. I had my answer then. Whatever it was hadn't gone away.

When the pain in my finger had subsided, I fumbled the ring and chain back into the pouch without touching them. I showered, dressed, wrote a shopping list and went to the supermarket. Matt's words about the ring were spinning circles inside my head. I hadn't thought about it before, when he'd dismissed the coins, but now it struck me that the ring was not only of historical significance, but possibly also valuable. I wasn't that bothered about how much it might be worth. My main interest was in its connection to me - because I was now convinced that there had to be one. I felt quite protective towards it, as though it had been buried for centuries and had waited for me to discover it, trusting me to uncover its secrets, and now I had a responsibility to keep it safe. I made a mental note to find a better hiding place for it than my bedside cabinet. Although Islip was a very low crime area, you could never be too careful.

As I filled my basket with fruit, yoghurt, cold meat and smoked salmon to go with salads, my thoughts turned to Matt. Telling myself that Sean was in the past and it was time I moved on was one thing. Throwing myself into another relationship was something else entirely. Was that what I was doing? I wiped my clammy hands on my jeans and tossed a packet of prawns into my basket.

I liked Matt, there was no doubt about that. Did I want to risk my heart again?

'Take a chance Hannah.' A woman in the aisle next to me looked startled and I realised I'd spoken out loud. I smiled at her and hurried past.

Matt arrived at 7. I'd had the usual wardrobe crisis, and had spent so long pulling out one outfit after another and discarding it that I'd run out of time. In a panic I settled on a floaty summer dress that I'd bought on an impulse that insisted I must have something feminine to restore my self-pride after Sean dumped me - but I'd never worn it - and high-heeled sandals. I was just applying a little lip gloss when I heard Matt's car pull up outside. I ran down the stairs, carrying the sandals, grabbed a light summer shawl from a hook in the hallway and rushed out of the house. He reached over and pushed open the passenger door. The bandanna was back and tonight it was red. I relaxed into the comfortable leather seat and we swapped stories about our day.

For the second night running I didn't miss my dinner-for-one. Matt had chosen a tapas restaurant in Jericho that I hadn't been to before. The walls were covered with pictures of flamenco dancers and matadors. It was so loaded with atmosphere that I could almost hear the castanets and smell the Brylcreem from the slicked-back hair and well-oiled moustaches. We followed the waiter's recommendations and soon the table was full of small plates of the most delicious tapas.

I speared a prawn that was swimming in a lemon, chilli and garlic broth, and as I popped it into my mouth I caught the triumphant expression that Matt was wearing.

'What?' I asked. 'Why are you looking like that?'

He picked up a chunk of bread and took his time mopping up the garlicky juices.

I put my fork down.

'You know I said yesterday that there was something about Joel's information that sounded familiar to me? Well, I've remembered. Before I joined the business, I did a degree in American history. A Thomas Marlow was one of the men that helped establish England's colonial claims along the east coast of America in the seventeenth century.'

'And do you think he's our Thomas Marlow, from Islip?'

'Could be. I did a bit of digging and the dates work - he apparently arrived there in July 1646.'

I spooned some chicken and rice onto my plate, trying to work out how this could help me find out why the ring had ended up buried in my garden.

'Even if he is, it doesn't help. We don't know that he was related to John Islip, or that the ring was his. And if it was, why isn't it buried in a garden in America instead of here?'

'Hannah, don't be so black and white. Think of it as one piece of the puzzle. Did you never do jigsaws as a kid?'

'Yes, of course.'

'Then you know you might pick up a piece and you don't know where it fits - in fact it doesn't fit at all - until you've slotted some other pieces into place and then it suddenly becomes obvious.'

'Or, it's a piece from another puzzle.'

He laughed and reached for my hand across the table. 'Mixed up jigsaw puzzles! That's the sign of a muddled and untidy childhood.'

'Mmm, maybe,' I agreed.

'So you won't want to look further into any possible connection?'

There was a trace of a smile in his eyes.

'I didn't say that.'

'Good, because there's an exhibition of early American history on at the American Museum & Gardens, near Bath. I thought we could go - maybe tomorrow?'

A voice in my head was telling me to slow down, but I ignored it. Wild geese and Otmoor were at home together after all, and I was prepared to go chasing after any number of them for the prospect of a day out with Matt.

'I'll just have to pop into the studio first thing,' I said. I had an appointment with the twins' mother. I'd edited the photos and she wanted to go through them with me to choose which ones I would mount for her. We agreed he would pick me up from there at 11 and I wrote the address down for him.

We finished our tapas and moved to a wine bar nearby where Matt steered me to a cosy table for two in a dimly lit corner.

'So how come you're on your own?' Matt asked me.

'I could say the same to you.'

'I asked first,' he said. He relaxed into his chair, exuding confidence, his fingers playing with the stem of his wine glass.

I took a sip, followed by a deep breath, and told him about Sean.

I told him how we met. As I spoke I closed my eyes and I knew I would see Sean as I had that first day. On the beach. Sun-bleached hair and blue eyes that twinkled like the sea in a shaft of bright light. Wearing knee-length swimming shorts with a pattern of palm trees and surf boards. Not that he was a boarder. He worked in a bar by night and on his tan by day. I was travelling and I'd planned to spend just a few days in Pattaya before moving on - that part of Thailand being a bit too touristy for me - but I'd ended up staying for weeks and eventually we'd moved on together.

'Go on,' Matt prompted me.

'When we returned to England we rented a flat in Banbury, got proper jobs, got engaged. I thought that was it and I was excited about a life together. Mr and Mrs Average.' I hoped I didn't sound too bitter.

'I thought I knew him. I thought he'd worked that need to doss around the world with no responsibilities out of his system.'

How wrong I had been. How had I not understood that Sean was not the settling down sort? How had I failed to spot the warning signs? They must have been there.

'I was devastated when he left.'

I stopped. I couldn't tell Matt how sometimes even now I ached with longing for him and missed him so much, in spite of how he'd hurt - and humiliated - me. It was strange, talking about it now I was beginning to feel that I was letting go of the hurt. It didn't feel as eviscerating as it usually did when I tortured myself with memories, and the vision of Sean that I still held in my head was fading and slipping out of focus, as if it were an old sepia photograph.

Matt was a good listener - too good. He sat in silence until I stopped pouring out my life story, my words stuttering and faltering like water from a rusty, disused pipe.

'How long had you been together?'

I gulped some more wine.

'Six years and we were engaged for two of them.'

'It must have been tough for you.'

I thought for a moment, trying to find the right words to explain how my life had fallen apart, without making myself appear pathetic.

'It was a surreal time, with Sean. We had a big circle of friends, all in couples. A Noah's Ark of an idealistic society - black couples, white couples, mixed race couples, single sex couples, we had them all - but no singletons, no divorcees. There weren't even any toxic relationships, or not that I knew about, just happy people drifting through life throwing dinner parties and going on holiday. Lots of holidays.'

Matt's eyebrows flared, questioning, waiting for more.

'When he left, everything changed. I no longer fitted. I felt I had become a taboo element for our group - a single person.' I paused to drain my wine, and the memories of that time washed over me, threatening to knock me off my feet, like that extra strong wave on the beach that my mum used to say was every seventh one. I used to count and run away before it could get me.

'After Sean had dumped me, my friends also drifted away. It was as if our lives had diverged. Trains switched onto different tracks, and I was now on the sidings puttering along aimlessly like a Sunday driver, while they were all still on the fast line to somewhere more exciting in the future.'

There I go again, saying too much. I'd just laid out all my angst and vulnerability in front of this incredibly attractive man when I should have held something back, woven an air of mystery about myself, kept him guessing and wanting to know more. But I never was any good at playing those kind of dating games. I'd sent more than one man running a mile faster than Roger Bannister like that. I really hoped Matt wouldn't be one of them.

'Yeah, it was tough. But I'm over it now.'

Not true, of course. There are times when I doubt I will ever be over it.

I wanted to rub at my gritty eyes, but it wasn't a good idea because I was wearing mascara. Instead, I closed them and the room seemed to swirl around me. The effort of talking, of dredging up and confronting all of those emotions was exhausting.

'You look done-in.' Matt finished his drink and stood up, pulling me to my feet. 'I'll take you home.'

He stopped the car outside my house and killed the engine but made no move to get out. He leaned over and brushed his lips against mine. 'Get some rest,' he told me. 'I'll see you tomorrow.'

Exhausted though I was, disappointment that he didn't ask to stay surged through me. It took me by surprise, to realise I would have been quite happy to curl up by his side and sleep. My toes no longer had the energy to tingle, but to have somebody else there, by my side, appealed to me in a way it hadn't for a long time.

Maybe he was already trying to remember where he'd left his running shoes.

I slipped out of the car and lingered in my porch, listening to the purr of his car engine retreating down Mill Street and wondered if he would turn up tomorrow as planned. As I pushed open my front door, something furry brushed past my ankles and ran into the house. I jumped and flicked the light switch. Then I relaxed as I realised it was just the cat that had been making itself at home on my deck. She was now purring louder than Matt's car engine, already stretched out on the deep-pile rug in front of my fireplace.

'Come on, you can't stay here.' I tried to lift her but she dug her claws into the pile, determined not to let go, and looked at me through half-open, lazy green eyes.

'All right, you win. I don't have the energy to argue with you tonight,' I told her. 'But don't think this means you can stay for good.' I wagged my finger at her, and she swished her tail and flicked her volume switch a notch higher. I turned my back and went upstairs, closing my bedroom door in case she had any ideas about joining me overnight.

NINE

Hannah

I WOKE EARLY THE NEXT morning feeling refreshed and alert. An unfamiliar noise from somewhere in the house teased my ears. I stretched and tried to identify it. Of course, the cat. I leapt out of bed and ran downstairs. She was by the back door, mewing and scratching. I pushed it open and she ran for the nearest flowerbed.

I made coffee and sipped it, leaning against the doorframe and watching the birds dance around the fat balls I had strung from the apple tree and the squirrel-proof seed-feeder. The cat was watching them too, crouching low in a patch of long grass. I shook my head at her. 'Don't even think about it,' I said out loud. Her ears pricked and she turned towards me. I threw her what I hoped was a stern look and she gave a haughty flick of her head. A sudden breeze stirred the branches, the birds flew away and the cat stood up, staring at the river. I followed her gaze, wondering what had caught her attention, but could see nothing. I turned my back, drained my coffee, dumping the mug in the sink and went upstairs to shower and dress.

Wardrobe crisis time again. I sighed. Why did choosing an outfit have to be so complicated? I decided on dark grey, tight capri pants and a slim-fitting pink tunic top that finished mid-thigh. I had the perfect earrings and pendant set to match. I flipped open my jewellery box. The set I was looking for was on the top layer - pinks, purples and reds. A pair of blue earrings had found its way into the wrong place. I tutted and moved them to the second layer - blues, greens and ambers. There is a third layer, for neutrals - blacks, silvers, whites. I know, it sounds obsessive, but jewellery is my big weakness. With one or two exceptions they are all cheap trinkets, but I can't resist them. I'm a magpie. I pulled on flat sandals and used a pink scrunchie to tie my hair back in a long ponytail.

Ready. I could feel the pleasant churn of excitement and anticipation about the day ahead somewhere deep down inside me.

When I arrived at my studio, Louise, the twins' mother, was waiting for me, on her own I realised with relief. Cute though the twins were, I hadn't been looking forward to the prospect of trying to keep their sticky fingers away from my cameras and other equipment whilst we went through the photos I had taken.

'Sorry, am I late?' I checked my watch. 9.30. Right on time.

I switched the computer on, made more coffee, and for the next hour we went through photo after photo, dismissing the ones she didn't like for whatever reason, until she had decided which she wanted turning into prints for framing.

She had only just left when Matt arrived. He was dressed casually in black jeans, black T-shirt and today's bandanna was white. At least we wouldn't clash, I thought, suppressing a giggle. He was as gorgeous as ever, but there was a tension hanging around him this morning that hadn't been there over the last few days - or at least I hadn't noticed it before. It was rippling off him in invisible waves, souring the atmosphere like a toxic gas.

'Just give me five minutes. There's a couple of emails I need to reply to and I haven't had a chance.' I pushed a chair towards him. 'Sit down.'

He didn't. He stood by the door, looking uncomfortable and out of place in my small studio, tapping his foot and jingling his keys.

In the car I tried to get him to lighten up, chatting about the cat, but he snapped at me. 'Hannah. This roundabout is tricky. I need to concentrate.'

It didn't look tricky to me. I wondered why he was so irritable, and my excitement about the day ahead drained away - like the air from a punctured tyre - leaving me deflated. Maybe this had been a mistake after all.

I did as he asked, stopped talking and watched the Oxfordshire countryside unfurl itself from the ring road at Botley, impeded at intervals by new housing developments that appeared as livid, ugly scars against the beautiful canvas of nature. We were almost at Swindon before he reached over and squeezed my knee. 'Sorry. Didn't mean to snap. I didn't sleep well.'

I put my hand over his. 'It's okay,' I said.

For the rest of the journey we chatted with the ease of well-worn friends, and by the time we reached the museum his mood seemed to have lifted. I took his arm and we headed to the café first for lunch - my treat this time.

I don't know much about American history. I could have wandered around those displays, reading the boards, examining the exhibits and learning, but doing that with someone who knows a lot about the subject adds a whole new dimension to the experience. Soon I was absorbed in the challenges faced by the early settlers, trying to clear land to farm in an unfamiliar and at times hostile climate, their conflicting hopes and aims and the uneasy relationship with the native Americans, which soon degenerated into war. The exhibits were throwing out information as if they were actors on stage in a pantomime scattering the audience with sweets, but Matt was embellishing it with detail that brought it all to life for me in a way no static display ever could.

We turned a corner into a gallery of paintings. I was ahead of Matt, who had lingered over an exhibit in the previous room. He was just catching me up when I stopped so abruptly that he walked into me. I staggered, and he reached out and grabbed me. 'Sorry,' he said. 'I wasn't expecting you to stop so suddenly.'

I heard his words but they were meaningless because my entire focus was on what I had seen, and I couldn't believe my own eyes. My knees wobbled and I gripped Matt's arm. 'What's wrong?' He whispered into my hair. I couldn't speak. Instead I pointed, with a shaky finger. I sensed him raise his head and look at the portrait on the wall, willing him to see what I had seen. My vision started to blur and I tightened my grip on his arm. I felt his hand on my back steering me towards a bench, then gentle pressure on my shoulders pushing me into a sitting position.

'Wait there,' he said.

Where did he think I was going to go? I was in no state for a quick jog around the grounds.

Matt reappeared with a grey-haired lady, wearing the Museum's uniform, at his side. She handed me a glass of water. I took it gratefully and drank.

'Are you okay my dear?'

I nodded and she held out her hand for the glass. 'No food or drink allowed,' she said, as if an explanation was necessary. People were beginning to stop and look at me, blatant curiosity shining in their eyes. I felt like an exhibit.

'Thank you,' I mumbled and gave her the empty glass.

Matt sat down beside me and squeezed my arm. I looked up at him and I could see my shock reflected in his eyes. Like a pair of synchronised swimmers, we turned towards the wall and stared at a striking portrait ... of me.

TEN

Catherine
Monday April 21st, 1645

THE NIGHT SKY LIGHTENED INTO an enthusiastic dawn, accompanied by the rising crescendo of birdsong. Huddled inside her thick shawl, sitting on the cold step outside her back door, Catherine inhaled the crisp, clear, early morning air with its strong scent of wild garlic. Dew glistened on the long grass, transforming it into a shimmering carpet of light in which buttercups shone like gold. She ought to be starting the breakfast and her chores, but she had turned away from the fire, craving the solace of being outdoors.

The house martins were beginning their return for summer, building their nests under the eaves of the tallest buildings they could find. Their tiny black forms dotted the pale but cloudless sky as they soared and swooped. She watched them for a while, wishing she too could take flight, until a gentle mewing sound attracted her attention. The cat, which had been the innocent cause of such offence the night before, approached her, step by cautious step. It was so thin, she could spare it a little milk. She returned to the kitchen, poured some into a bowl and placed it in front of the creature. It hesitated and its nostrils flared, then its small head disappeared into the bowl. When it re-emerged, the bowl was almost empty, and its whiskers and the tip of its nose were smudged with milk. Still wary, watching Catherine from a safe distance, it licked up every last droplet its small, pink tongue could reach before stretching out in a patch of sunlight. A sound very much like a snore rose from its fragile frame. She smiled.

'Don't get too used to that,' she warned.

'It's happy Mama. That's what cats do when they're happy.'

Catherine moved over, allowing Tilly to snuggle in to her side. 'Is that so?' She smoothed Tilly's hair back from her eyes, which were heavy still with sleep.

'Do you want to go and see the ducks this morning, my love?'

Tilly nodded, sending her hair flying back into her face.

'Come and help me then and we'll have time.'

Catherine was as eager as Tilly to leave the house and go to the river. She wanted to forget all of her worries - whatever her father was involved with, who the Levellers were, his recent aggression, Tilly's nervousness around him, even Thomas Marlow and the ring.

Immersing herself in drawing was the best way she knew to relax, but the house was stifling. It seemed to be trapping all of her problems within its walls, shrouding her in an iron grip from which she was unable to break free. Her fingers played with the chain around her neck, and she felt the weight of the ring shift. Although she'd added it to her list of worries, she no longer thought of the ring as a problem. It was as much a part of her as her fingers and toes.

Tilly helped to bake the bread and make breakfast. Catherine was on edge, listening for the arrival of her father, but he didn't come. She was grateful that Tilly would not be upset further, but she couldn't help but worry. It wasn't like him to miss breakfast. It wasn't like him to miss church either, but he had. What could she do though? She wasn't his keeper. If he had got himself into trouble, he would have to get himself out of it. She could have no part of it. Deep down inside, though, a sense of foreboding was gathering strength. Could this be the darkness that Thomas spoke of?

She made a pie crust, filled it with sauce from the stock pot and the last of the leftover goose chopped into small pieces, and placed it into the cooking chamber built into the side of the hearth. Whatever time he came for his supper it would be ready. Catherine knew if she was not there with the door bolted her father would let himself in to her house. She left the warm bread under a muslin cloth on the table. He may not remember that she was working late this evening, and that Tilly was going to stay at Helen's, but as she was unable to remind him this was the best she could do. She placed some stale bread in a pouch tied around her waist for Tilly to feed the ducks.

One of Catherine's favourite places on the river was a quiet spot a little further down the track from Helen and Edward's house where the Ray met the Cherwell, well away from the bridge and the soldiers. Tilly whooped with delight, running across the bumpy triangle of land that bordered the two rivers. A flock of ducks ventured out from the shelter of the riverbanks. Catherine spread her cloak out on the grass, sat down and watched Tilly distributing the bread, trying to make sure they all received an equal share. From here she could just see the ancient square tower of the church rising above the tallest trees, with its miniature steeples on each corner appearing to survey the land surrounding the village. She began to sketch, using one of the finer charcoal sticks to begin with, which she would then ink over. Thomas had asked her to draw something beautiful for him. She wasn't sure he meant a scene of the village, but there was something peaceful and soothing about the view that suited her mood. Her fingers relaxed their grip on the charcoal stick, and she sketched quick, fluid lines whilst allowing her thoughts to wander. Would she meet Thomas 'by chance' today?

When Tilly tired of the ducks, Catherine took her hand, and they retraced their steps to Helen's. There was no raucous welcome today, as the children were all eating in the kitchen. Helen pulled a chair out for Tilly to join them. Harry raised his arms, inviting Catherine to pick him up. 'You need to finish your breakfast first little man.' She hugged him instead.

When the children ran off to play hide and seek, supervised by the two older girls, Catherine and Helen sat on a bench in the garden enjoying a brief interlude of peace and quiet, interrupted by the occasional excited shouting of a child having discovered the hiding place of another.

Catherine watched a red squirrel run along the branch of a tree. When it reached the end, it leapt to the neighbouring tree and continued its progress, stopping every so often to sniff the air. She envied Helen's garden. Whilst her own patch of land was functional and consigned to growing only what they could eat, Helen's was an oasis of colour. Gently sloping towards the river, primulas clustered under the fruit trees in a shade of pale lilac that was almost white. Closer to the house, beyond the level to which the river sometimes swelled, a square flower bed, bordered with lavender and filled with honesty, poppies, hellebore, roses and various wildflowers was surrounded by a path. In the borders to each side, rambling roses and honeysuckle mingled with box and dogwood. From where she was sitting Catherine could not see the vegetable and herb garden, but she knew it was just as well-tended. Helen was knowledgeable about plants, not averse to working in the garden, and she could afford to pay a boy from the village to help.

Catherine dragged her eyes away and turned to Helen who was leaning back on the bench, face upturned. She wore her red-gold hair loose at the front in the fashionable style that her curls fell into with such ease, but which for Catherine and Tilly required effort and planning. It reflected the sun, creating a sort of halo around her head.

Catherine's fingers plucked at the fabric of her gown. Questions to which she hoped Helen might have some answers tumbled over each other inside her head and she selected one. 'Helen, when John was alive, did you ever suspect that he might have been against the King, secretly I mean?'

Helen's eyes widened and she shook her head. 'No, never.' She turned towards Catherine. 'John was loyal to the King, but not only that, he was too honest. He displayed his thoughts across his face for everyone to see. He would not have been capable of deceiving you - and everyone else.'

Such a confident rejection. Helen's memory of John's character appeared clearer than her own. But then Helen hadn't been there last night, hadn't heard the scorn in her father's voice.

'Why? What makes you ask such a question?'

'I tried to ask my father about the man in the churchyard, but he wouldn't answer. He said he knew what he was doing and that even John would have agreed with him. He ... he laughed at me when I said John was a Royalist.' Catherine shuddered, the memory of her father's tone sending barbed fingers crawling along her spine. 'But it wasn't just that he laughed, it was the way he laughed, as if anyone who had believed John was a genuine supporter of the King had to have been really gullible.'

'That's most of us then. Cat, I'm sure he's wrong.'

They sat in silence for a few moments.

'How did my mother come to be married to my father?'

Helen stroked her curls, casting her mind back to a time when she would have been around Tilly's age. 'As I remember it, he was from Bletchingdon, I think. I can't recall how they actually met, but he started passing through the village quite often - probably on purpose to see Cathy. He used to talk about some benefactor he had, who he was going to go into business with. He was ambitious. And handsome.'

Helen's words conjured an image of her father inside Catherine's mind that she struggled to reconcile with the man that she knew. She closed her eyes and tried to imagine him as her mother would have known him.

'Our father was not a wealthy man - he was only earning a school master's wage - so I think he was quite relieved to get one of us married.' Helen paused, frowning. 'And then something went wrong. The business was all off. His benefactor had lost everything in some deal. I never knew what - Cathy was reluctant to talk about it - but I always thought it was something to do with a boat that was sailing to the New World. It went missing. All the cargo and the men on board were lost and with them your father's hopes. William had no money of his own, but by then he and your mother were already married, and your mother had fallen pregnant with James. Richard Marlow gave him work on the farm, labouring, and the house. Your father kept saying he was worth more, but he wasn't educated, and he had no money of his own - or if he had he'd invested it in the project as well and lost it all. Cathy ... well ... I think she came to realise it was all talk.'

Catherine had heard some of this story before, but not this last bit. She waited, impatient for more, hands gripped together. Helen appeared to have slipped in time, lost in her own memories. She stared, unblinking, at the trees that met the river at the bottom of the garden, but Catherine could see nothing there.

'What could she do though? For better or worse, she had made her choice. She couldn't leave. There was no way out from that tiny house. It wasn't what she had expected, or what he had led us all to believe he could give her. And in spite of all that, I think she still loved him.'

The sun went behind a cloud. Helen shivered and shook her head. It was a gesture full of sadness and wistful memory, and Catherine was reminded of Helen's anguish at losing an older sister whom she adored.

'I'm sorry. I forget how much you loved her too.'

'Why do you ask?' Focused again, Helen turned towards Catherine and their eyes locked, pools of infinite black mirroring each other.

'I was just wondering if he's always been like this or if it's life that's made him so bitter.'

Catherine dropped her gaze and her hand went to her mouth. Helen reached out and pulled it away.

'When did you start with that again?'

Catherine stared at her nails, surprised to see she had bitten them down to the quick. After John had died, she'd chewed them so badly that she'd made them bleed, but she'd broken that habit. Dismayed, she pushed her hands under her skirts so she couldn't see them.

'What's wrong Cat? You're not just worried about what he might be getting involved with are you?'

Helen's concern was palpable and Catherine was tempted to unburden herself of everything that had happened in the last few days. Lay all of her problems at Helen's feet and let her aunt take over, as if she herself were a child again. Where should she start though? The burning sensation of unshed tears pricked behind her eyes. She blinked them back.

'It's Tilly. I think she's scared of him ... No, I'm sure she's scared of him. Yesterday, he was so cross with her for stroking this cat. She wouldn't come back inside until after he'd gone, and she was crying.'

Helen frowned. 'If mine were upset every time Edward snapped at one of them, I'd spend all day mopping up the tears. Come, tell me.'

'He didn't just get cross with Tilly.' Catherine fidgeted, fighting the temptation to chew her nails again, and trying to keep her voice steady. She didn't want Helen to dismiss her worries as the product of an over-emotional state of mind.

'He was so angry with me for talking to Thomas Marlow, and with Edward for inviting him to dinner. He was shouting, thumping the table. He warned me to stay away from Thomas. Tilly heard it all.'

'Even so ...' Helen left the sentence floating. Her sharp eyes now appeared opaque, blurred with her thoughts like river water clouded with mud.

'It isn't just Tilly,' Catherine's voice was almost a whisper. 'I'm scared of him too.'

'Oh Cat, you've always been a bit scared of your father. He's got a temper, especially when he's in his cups.'

'No. This is different.' Catherine paused, trying to find the words to explain what she didn't understand herself.

'I've noticed it over the last few days. His behaviour is ... oh, I don't know Helen. It's strange, almost as though it isn't really him. As soon as he comes into the room, something changes in the air. It becomes as tight as the strings on Edward's fiddle. Tilly senses it too. It's more than just the drink, Helen. I'm sure of it,' Catherine's eyes pleaded with her aunt to believe her.

'It may be that his mind is occupied with this group, the Levellers and whatever they are doing.' Helen suggested. 'Why doesn't he like Thomas?'

'I don't know. He said he doesn't trust him. It's probably just who his father is, what he represents, which is everything my father seems to be opposed to at the moment. Authority. Landowner. Being related to Sir Henry.'

'The Marlows have been good to your family. If Richard hadn't given him employment and somewhere to live all those years ago, who knows what would have happened to Cathy. And Thomas Marlow is a kind, considerate gentleman. Everyone likes him ...' She paused, and Catherine squirmed under the new intensity in her gaze, the opaqueness of a few moments ago wiped away as though it had never been there. Catherine dropped her eyes and Helen's widened.

'Cat! I knew you were hiding something yesterday. You two. Talking in the garden. That wasn't coincidence was it?'

Catherine shook her head, not trusting herself to speak.

'Come on Cat, you have to tell me.'

Helen's tone was gentle but insistent. She leaned towards Catherine so their foreheads were almost touching. Waited.

'I don't know what to say, because I don't understand what's happening,' she admitted. 'He seems to like me. Goes out of his way to find me and talk to me. And I like him. A lot.'

Helen raised an eyebrow, waiting for more.

'Yesterday, he said whatever my father was involved with, he wouldn't let anything bad happen to me or Tilly.' Now was the time to mention the ring and the drawing materials he had given her. She took a deep breath, but Helen interrupted.

'He's an honourable man, that much I do know. He wouldn't say anything he didn't mean. But Cat, what does he mean?' A frown troubled Helen's brow and she tugged at a lock of hair that had fallen across her face.

'He likes me Helen. I'm sure of it,' Catherine insisted. She leaned back and raised one hand towards the collar of her gown. 'And, look ...'

'Oh Cat. You've done so well since John died,' Helen burst in, her voice rising in pitch and frustration creeping in. 'You've proved to everyone that you can cope by yourself, that you and Tilly are just fine together. You can't afford to lose that. Don't risk your good name.'

'I like him. I can't send him away.'

Helen reached out for Catherine's hand, which hovered still by her collar, and enclosed it in a tight grip. Her eyes bored into Catherine's, and she seemed to be choosing her words with great care. 'You're an amazing, generous, beautiful - and stubborn - woman and I love you. You know that. I can understand him being attracted to you. But he's never married and when he does, he will be expected to marry someone ...' she faltered, and there was a slight wobble in her voice.

Helen's words made Catherine pause. She was not so sure of herself any more. She freed her hand and studied her mangled fingernails, all thoughts of telling Helen about the ring forgotten. 'So he's playing me false then?'

'I don't know,' Helen admitted. Then her eyes flashed like polished jet and she added fiercely, 'If he is, it'll be the last time he eats my roast goose!' The mood lifted and became as mellow as the morning light rising over Otmoor.

'If ever I need a champion to fight my battles, I'll look no further than you,' Catherine laughed and flung her arms around her aunt.

Helen's words repeated in a loop in Catherine's head as she walked to the manor, taking the path that followed the river from the bridge, past the soldiers, whom she hardly noticed. Her feet dragged, but her mind raced. How should she respond to Thomas's attentions? Should she stay away from him, as her father had instructed and Helen thought would be sensible? The longer she considered it the more she rejected the idea.

'Men,' she pondered out loud. Why did they have to make everything so complicated?

Why couldn't Thomas be straightforward, like John? Helen had said John was too honest. But had he been? Was the John she remembered just a figment of her imagination? In spite of Helen's reassurance, Catherine was not sure, but she would not let her father's words change how she remembered her husband.

A light breeze ruffled her skirts as she walked, and tugged at the trees, teasing them into waving their multi-coloured, blossom-laden branches in a gentle dance that made Catherine think of swirling skirts. She remembered dancing with John around the Maypole as the village enjoyed the annual celebrations for the arrival of summer. It wasn't possible to hear the choir singing from the roof of Magdalen College here in Islip, but nevertheless the village always marked the occasion with a festival. Workers were given the day off, the taverns and inns were open from early in the morning and a hog was roasted on a spit, courtesy of Sir Henry, for all to enjoy. It had been the last time she'd managed to squeeze into her favourite gown - the one her mother insisted she have for Helen and Edward's wedding. Its deep pink bodice faded into a paler skirt, colours that were a striking contrast with her hair, and the effect had made her feel dramatic and exotic. She'd let the gown out as far as she could and hoped the seams would hold. John had been a good dancer and he'd put her stitches to the test, spinning her round and round on the village green, the pink ribbons she'd twisted into her hair streaming out from her head like writhing serpents, until she was dizzy and they had collapsed on a bale of straw to recover.

She'd worn a garland of bluebells, an act of open defiance that she wouldn't dare repeat today. Had John known that wearing such an ornament compelled one to tell the truth, when he had asked her if she thought she could love him? She could still see the hesitant expression in his eyes, hear the slight tremble in his voice. There had been no hesitation in her reply, and by the next May Day they had been married. Now, just eight years later, she was on her own, and those memories were so old and faded they could have been borrowed from someone else. A different Catherine, the wild and free Cat, who no longer existed. She wouldn't be dancing with anyone this May Day, although if she could she had no doubt who she would choose.

She reached the kitchens and looked around, surprised that she was there already. Mr Dawson asked her to clean some silver before preparing the dining room. 'Make sure you do them properly - I want to see them shine,' he barked.

The manor house was connected to the kitchen buildings by a dark corridor, which split at the end into two short flights of steps. The set to the left led to the grand entrance hall. Catherine turned right and emerged behind a screen at the back of the dining room. She placed the silver on a tray and carried it to the scullery where she had set up a table. After an hour she could see her face in the silver, but she could no longer feel her fingers, which were frozen in their grip around the cleaning cloth. She unclenched and wiggled them, wincing through the pain, until she was confident she could carry the silver back to the dining room without dropping it.

After replacing it all in the cabinet she started preparing place settings for 14 at the vast elm table that was longer than her entire house. The chairs that surrounded it were high-backed and solid. She pulled one out and perched on the edge of the seat, which was hard and uncomfortable, trying to imagine what it would feel like to be a guest eating at this table. The room was by far the grandest she had ever been in, with its high ceilings, dark wood panelling and a magnificent chandelier. Grand it might be, but welcoming it was not. It was like an empty shell abandoned by the animal that had inhabited it.

She'd almost finished laying the table when she heard voices in the corridor outside. She recognised Lady Frances' high and tinny whine. The other was deeper, masculine.

'I'm so excited about this evening. Let's just have a look at the table - come on Henry, please.'

Catherine froze, for no reason, as she had every right to be there.

The door to the dining room swung open and Lady Frances entered on the arm of a tall, blond, handsome young man, probably in his early 20s, whom Catherine recognised as her brother, Henry.

'Oh, what are you doing in here?' Lady Frances demanded, frowning.

Catherine curtseyed. When she stood, she stretched her body, pushing her shoulders up and raising her chin. Even so, she was several inches shorter than Henry, but she was almost at eye-level with Lady Frances. She would not be intimidated by this girl. She clenched her fists behind her back and raised her eyes, unblinking. 'I've just been doing the table setting for supper my lady.'

The girl stared at her, but Henry seemed to look right through her as if she were so insignificant as to be invisible. His eyes rested on something behind her. She turned and realised his attention had been attracted by the door to the silver cabinet, which she had forgotten to close. He looked down his long, aquiline nose at her, wearing a haughty, superior expression.

'I hope we aren't going to find any items missing,' he drawled.

Catherine tightened her fists until what was left of her ragged fingernails dug into her palms. 'No, sir. I've been cleaning them and just replaced them all,' she answered, trying to sound calm although her heart was battering her ribs like a sledgehammer. Henry grunted.

She turned around and closed the cabinet, curtseyed again, and walked away with as much dignity as she could muster, trying to ignore the unpleasant sensation of Henry's eyes burning into the back of her neck, until she slipped out of sight behind the screen. If it had been a door she would have slammed it and suffered the consequences.

Inside she was seething. It was so obvious that he didn't believe her. Did he think she'd stuffed a teapot under her skirts? A few spoons under her maid's cap? The idea that she may be walking around with the contents of Sir Henry's silver cabinet jangling within her under garments was so funny that if it hadn't also been unfair to the extreme, she would have laughed. She may be poor, but that didn't make her a thief. For a brief moment she understood how years of being treated as someone of no consequence, just because of the fortune or misfortune of their birth, could make a person bitter, like her father. She pushed the thought away and swallowed her anger, even though it threatened to choke her. If she didn't have her work at the manor she wouldn't be able to maintain her independence, and then what would she do? She would not - could not - turn to her father. Tilly was reliant on her, and her alone.

By the time the guests began to arrive Catherine was exhausted, insufficient sleep and the emotional energy of the last few days seeming to conspire against her, sapping her strength. She stepped outside for some fresh air. A bucket of water drawn from the well stood by the door. She cupped her hands, plunged them into the water and splashed her face. The tingle of the cool liquid was refreshing against her hot skin, but she had no time to savour the not-unpleasant sensation. Mr Dawson was calling her, his voice tense and impatient, and she hurried back inside.

'There you are Mistress Meakin. The guests are all taking their places. It's time for service.'

Catherine straightened her cap and fastened the ties on a clean apron. She picked up a serving tray laden with dishes and took her place in the short procession of staff retained for the evening. The dining room was transformed in the flickering light shed by the candles in their ornate cups, which filled it with life, creating the illusion that the room itself was moving. The heavy drapes at the windows were closed, muffling any sound from outside, and giving the room the sense of existing, isolated, in its own cocoon. There was a buzz of voices and the tinkle of laughter. Catherine kept her eyes down, as she had been instructed to do, carried her tray to the sideboard and stood to one side. She risked a glance at the guests around the table. It was a scene rich with colour and glittering with precious jewels, but Catherine's attention was drawn to the pair of extraordinary eyes that were fixed on her. Thomas was seated next to Lady Frances. Catherine's stomach plummeted, landing in her boots, and she stifled a gasp. He too appeared shaken. He spluttered mid-sentence but recovered in an instant, disguising it as a cough. It was the first time she had seen him wrong-footed, not in control of the situation. She lowered her head and clasped her hands together to stop them trembling.

Lady Frances was looking very pretty, the low-cut bodice to her crimson gown showing off plenty of creamy white skin, blonde hair in ringlets falling about her face and pinned at the rear in a pearl-studded clasp with strings of pearls looping from it. The sleeves of her gown were full, slashed with the palest grey silk and embroidered with silver thread that sparkled like hundreds of tiny diamonds. They were drawn together below the elbow with matching lace.

She would be beautiful if it wasn't for those mean little cold blue eyes. They were almost the shade of Catherine's best gown, which she had worn with such pride only yesterday, but which she now realised was just dull. How foolish she had been to think she could impress Thomas by wearing it. Why had it not occurred to her that he would be a guest at the dinner? From her post by the sideboard Catherine was able to observe them, her gaze surreptitious, protected in part by her maid's cap. It was obvious that Frances was trying her best to impress Thomas. She was laughing at his jokes and listening with forced concentration, frowning, when the conversation turned serious - to talk of the King in Oxford and his chances of meeting up with Prince Rupert who was rumoured to be heading towards Worcester. When Mr Dawson signalled to her to start clearing the first course Catherine moved around the table, feeling as invisible as she knew she would be, to most of the guests at least, but listening to every word.

'If they can only unite their forces they may be able to secure a victory over Parliament's troops,' Sir Henry said, his booming voice echoing around the room.

'What kind of victory though?' That was Thomas. 'One battle or two? It's not enough. There's no planning or strategy to any of this. Both sides are making it up as they go along. It's no way to win a war.'

'Hmph.' Catherine wasn't sure whether that meant Sir Henry agreed or not.

'I hear there was a bit of trouble in Kidlington last night,' Richard Marlow said.

'Oh, what sort of trouble?' Sir Henry indicated that he wanted his wine glass topping up and Catherine moved to his side.

'Some of Northampton's regiment were set upon by a group of local men.'

'Roundheads?'

'Apparently not. They said they would oppose the armies of either side who believe it is their right to take from honest, hard-working men.'

Catherine backed away from the table, seeking the obscurity of the shadows where she hoped no-one would be able to see the fear that she was sure must be evident on her face. Was that why her father had not come for breakfast this morning? Had he been involved in this trouble?

'Scoundrels, the lot of them,' Sir Henry glared around the table as if daring anyone to challenge his view.

'Most of them are what they claimed to be - honest, hard-working men, who, like many of us, have had enough of this country tearing itself apart.' Thomas sounded frustrated and his raised voice earned him a hard stare from Sir Henry and provoked a rebuke from Lady Gilder.

'That's enough talk of war please. This is a birthday celebration for Frances.' She smiled with fondness at her daughter and the girl simpered and giggled, batting her eyelashes at Thomas.

'You should take care Thomas, or you'll get a reputation,' Henry dared to disobey his mother and raised his glass to Thomas in a challenging gesture. 'What was that fellow's name - Ellis wasn't it? One more renegade safely behind bars until you intervened.'

Thomas turned his head towards Henry, and as he did, the candlelight caught his golden-brown eyes and gave them the appearance of being on fire. There was a tense set to his shoulders and a sudden silence fell on the room, which was broken by Lady Gilder.

'Henry, I said enough.' Her tone was sharp, and her eyes snapped from Henry, to Thomas, and back.

Henry nodded in acquiescence, although the expression on his face was far from compliant. Lady Gilder started to question Richard Marlow, and Henry turned away. Soon the room was buzzing again with convivial conversation.

Catherine wasn't sure how she was going to get through the next hour or so. How long would supper take anyway? She daren't look at Thomas, but she was aware of his attentiveness to Lady Frances, watched with a smile of approval by the girl's mother. It was very clear that there was an understanding from most of the guests that Frances and Thomas would be a good match for each other. She remembered Helen's comment earlier about the marriage expectations of Thomas and clenched her fists. Of course, Helen had been right. Catherine's thoughts were whirling a jig inside her head, but she had no time to think. She was aware of the ring, scorching its impression onto her skin, as if it were trying to tell her something. Fanciful notion, but nevertheless it gave her strength. She was also aware of Thomas trying to catch her eye throughout the evening, and she refused to play his game. Henry was watching his sister and Thomas. Catherine wasn't sure if it was her imagination, but more than once she had the uncomfortable sensation that his eyes roved over her as well, before switching back to them.

She was almost giddy with relief when Lady Gilder stood and led the ladies to the adjacent parlour, leaving the men to smoke and talk. In her haste to clear the table and leave the room, she dropped a spoon. Balancing a large serving dish on her hip, she bent to pick it up, but Thomas was there before her. He held it out and she tried to take it but he didn't release it, forcing her to look at him. His eyes were pleading.

'Thank you sir,' she said, tugging at the spoon and he let go. She turned her back on him, piled the remaining dishes onto her tray and returned to the kitchen, the sound of men's laughter echoing down the corridor behind her.

Mr Dawson was waiting for her. She swapped her tray for the one he handed to her. 'We'll serve the ladies some drinks and once the dancing starts you may go home Mistress Meakin.'

Catherine nodded her thanks. The thought of her small room and her less than comfortable bed had never been more appealing. She climbed the steps from the kitchen, this time emerging into the grand hall. Someone was picking out the tune of a popular country dance on the grand piano in the parlour. She kept her eyes to the floor, careful not to trip on the uneven flagstones, wavering light cast by candles in enormous sconces mounted along the walls lighting her way. In the parlour, she placed the drinks tray on a table as instructed and left the room.

Catherine hung her apron and cap on the hook in the scullery and stepped outside into the now cool night air. She stood still, inhaling slow and deep, clearing her lungs and her head of the oppressive atmosphere of the evening. Had it really only been a few hours since she'd arrived at the manor this afternoon? It could have been weeks.

The sky was inky black, studded with stars. At least the brightness of the half-moon would light her walk home. She strode away from the house and with every step she shed a bit more of her meek, maid's persona and her anger took over. Thomas owed her nothing, but she had allowed the seed of expectation to plant itself in her mind and had nurtured it with her imagination, enabling it to grow. What a fool she had been, and this evening's humiliation was the price she had to pay for that folly.

She had left the security of the courtyard, crossed the moat and was halfway up the long drive when she thought she heard footsteps behind her. Turning around to double check would slow her down. Panic snatched at her breath. She quickened her step until it was almost a trot, wondering if she had anything about her person that she could use to defend herself.

'Catherine, wait,' it was Thomas's voice, low and urgent.

Legs aching, and breathing in short, painful bursts, she slowed to a rapid walking pace. Thomas wouldn't attack her. Of that she was certain. But she didn't want to talk to him. She was exhausted, and didn't know what she could say, or even what she wanted to say. In a few seconds he had caught her. His hand brushed her elbow and she stiffened. She kept up her pace, eyes focused on the path ahead. He stayed with her, his hand now planted on her arm. She tried to shake it off, but he tightened his grip until the pressure of his fingers seemed to meld into her bones.

'The dancing will have started. You'll be missed.'

'I won't. I pleaded the onset of a cold.'

Catherine dug her heels into the ground and swivelled to face him.

'What do you want with me, sir?' She demanded. She thought she saw a faint smile beginning to play around his mouth before he made an effort to look serious.

'Come with me,' he said.

She hesitated. She could refuse. Run for home. But if he pursued her she could not hope to outpace him. If anyone was about in the village and saw her being chased by Thomas Marlow, her father would be sure to hear of it, and then what would he do? She didn't want to think about that.

Thomas either didn't notice her hesitation, or chose to ignore it. He turned away from the manor, taking long strides across the meadow bordering the river. His hand still gripped her arm, and she stumbled after him.

'Where are we going?'

'Somewhere we can talk.'

He stopped at the fallen tree trunk where he had found her sketching two days ago. He made a pretence of brushing the surface clean and waved his arm with a half bow to invite her to sit. It was a theatrical gesture that she found comical, but she was nurturing her humiliation and was in no mood to laugh. She sat and he lowered himself down beside her. The moon cast a shaft of silver across the surface of the water, making it glitter with the ripples of the current. They sat in silence, and she waited for him to speak.

He turned to face her. 'Do you like me Catherine?'

Whatever she'd expected him to say it wasn't that. Two days ago she would probably have lowered her eyes and then admitted, feigning shyness, that yes, she did like him, but the actions that she had been forced to witness this evening, and the realisation that followed had changed that. She was reminded again of John's voice, asking if she could love him, but she was not wearing a garland of bluebells now, and Thomas had none of John's humility.

'Please, don't treat me unfairly ... sir,' Catherine snapped, emphasising the word 'sir'.

Confusion flitted across his face. 'I'm not aware of being unfair and I apologise if that's the impression I have given you.'

He paused, and she was aware of him scrutinising her face, as if searching for answers. 'Do you like me?' he repeated, his tone determined. 'Because I like you, very much.'

'You can't say such things to me.'

Her eyes, dark like ink, refracted the moonlight, transforming it into white-hot shards of sudden anger. Anger that was directed at him. He flinched.

'What about Lady Frances?' She fixed her eyes on the river and shivered. As she pulled her cloak tighter around her shoulders, her fingers brushed the collar of her gown and the coolness of the chain reminded her she was still wearing his talisman. She should rip it from her neck and throw it at him, but much as she was angry with Thomas, she could not bear the thought of parting with it.

'Look at me Catherine. Please.'

The silence grew between them. The skin on her neck itched and she knew he was watching her. She wanted to resist, but she needed to hear his answer. With reluctance, she turned back.

'She's my cousin - second, third or even more removed, I've lost count - but you know that anyway. Everyone does. And yes, her parents and my father would like nothing better than for us to marry. But she's just a child. There is no understanding between us and I have not led her to believe there ever will be. I'm a grown man, old enough to make my own decisions.'

His eyes continued searching her face. She found it difficult to look at him. Whatever he may say, it was clear to her that Lady Frances and her family did not share his view. He reached out and the light touch of his fingertips stroked her cheek, resting on her jaw before raising her chin with the gentlest of movements and forcing her to look at him. With his other hand he reached for hers, prised the fingers to uncurl them and brought her hand to his lips. She waited for him to recoil from the roughness of her skin and her mangled nails, but he seemed not to notice either. His beard tickled as he kissed her palm, not taking his eyes from hers for one second.

Catherine couldn't move. Daren't move, in case she broke whatever spell she was under. It was as if she were poised on the edge of a precipice - one step in the wrong direction and she would go hurtling into oblivion - but which was the wrong direction?

'You have to believe me, Catherine.' Thomas begged, his voice infused with frustration. His habitual self-confidence had deserted him, replaced with the uncertainty of a child unsure how to proceed in an unfamiliar situation.

'I ... I don't know what to believe,' she muttered. 'I'm so confused. I don't know what you're saying. I just don't know anything.' She snatched her hand back from him and leaned forwards, making a nest of her palms in which she rested her head.

'All right,' he sighed, his shoulders slumping. 'I understand. You're angry. I'll escort you home. But promise me one thing. Meet me in the churchyard tomorrow morning, early. Leave your house when the clock strikes 6am.'

Catherine raised her head, looked at him, puzzled.

'Promise me.'

Too exhausted to argue further, she agreed.

He stood and strolled back across the meadow. She followed. At the end of the track that led to her house he bowed to her. 'Remember. The churchyard. Tomorrow,' he whispered.

She nodded and walked the remaining few steps to her front door alone. The only light inside the kitchen was that cast by the moon, revealing the dirty bowl and plate from her father's supper still on the table. She ignored them. Weariness overpowered her, like the heavy black clouds that would descend from the sky sometimes and refuse to move, squeezing out the light from its rightful place and trapping the village in a day of night. She climbed the narrow steps to her bed. Certain she would lie awake for hours, she stretched out under the blanket and blissful sleep overcame her.

ELEVEN

Hannah

MATT HELD MY HAND. 'THIS is the time to confess that you are the secret travelling companion of a Time Lord whose Tardis is parked just around the corner.'

I was grateful to him for trying to make me laugh, but the sound that escaped from my mouth was shaky and uncertain. I shook my head, and studied the portrait. It was of a young woman. She had my hair - long, black and I suspected straight, although there was an attempt at a wave in the tresses that fell from a sort of lace cap to frame her face. She had my pale, sunburn-prone complexion. She was smiling and she had my gap between her front teeth. She also had my eyes. I probably haven't mentioned it before, but they're black, and so are my mother's and my grandmother's. It's a family thing. It's in the genes. It's also quite rare.

'Who is she?' I turned to Matt. He knew so much about early American history that it was quite possible he knew, although a part of me did realise that if he had seen this painting before - even a reproduction of it in a book - he would surely have recognised the likeness to me and mentioned it.

He shrugged. 'Dunno.' He got up from the bench and walked over to read the plaque that was screwed to the wall by the side of the painting. He stood there for a few moments, twisting his bandanna and making his hair wriggle like Medusa's snakes. When he turned around his face was whiter than his bandanna.

'What is it?' I asked, wondering what could be so bad he looked as though one of those snakes had taken a nip at him.

He sat back down by my side and drew both my hands into his. I was starting to shake again. His behaviour was very odd.

'It was painted by Thomas Marlow.'

I gasped and one of my hands jerked from his to cover my mouth. He didn't move.

'What? There's more?'

He nodded.

I replaced my hand in his and locked eyes with him. 'Tell me.'

'It's a recent piece acquired by the museum and not much is known about it. They are still researching. No-one knows who the woman is - Thomas Marlow arrived in America, alone, in 1646. There is no record of him ever having married - there or here. On the back of the canvas are the words 'My love'.'

We both stared at the unknown woman in front of us, who smiled back, frozen in time, captured on canvas.

'Tell me if I'm jumping to conclusions here, but this woman has to be an ancestor of mine.'

'I'd say that's a pretty fair bet.'

'So,' I paused, struggling to control my thoughts to follow some sort of logic because none of this made any sense. 'We've got coins dating from 1644 with a ring engraved with the rebus of John Islip buried in my garden, and it's a fair assumption that they were lost together - or deliberately buried?'

'They were only low value coins even in those days. Why bury them?'

'Kids messing around?' My head was beginning to ache. I longed to lean on Matt's shoulder, bury my head in his chest and forget about all of this. 'We've got someone who would have been one of the most important men in the village and could have expected to have a comfortable life, but instead he goes to the other side of the world. He starts again. We have no connection between him and John Islip - except the village itself, but separated by a couple of hundred years.'

'Maybe he liked adventure, and there might not be a connection.'

'True. But now we also have a mystery woman who's the spit of me. And he loved her, yet he never married, or at least there's no record of him marrying. Why not? He has to have been eligible, a catch even.'

'Maybe she was married to someone else.'

'And, there's a connection between me and the ring and between me and her. Surely it's too much of a coincidence?'

I pulled my hands away from Matt and stood up, relieved to find my legs felt much more solid than they had a few minutes before. Even so, I faltered as I approached the painting. I studied her face. Her chalk-white skin was a stark contrast to her hair and brows, beneath which her eyes sparkled with life and energy. I've never understood what people mean when they say something has given them goose bumps on their spine, but at that moment, standing in front of that painting, I got it. I was aware of Matt behind me, so close, as if he thought I might topple over. His hand brushed my waist and I gave in to the temptation to lean against him.

'Who is she?' I whispered. 'And what happened to her?'

We stood there, motionless, for several minutes. I couldn't drag my eyes away from the painting and this unknown woman's eyes, which seemed to bore into me, as though they were trying to tell me something, if only I could read them. Her expression was ambiguous, somehow neither happy nor sad, and there was wariness to her, an aura of something like a diaphanous cloak floating from her shoulders, yet pulling her down with its invisible weight.

The warmth of Matt's body seeped into mine, as if by osmosis, and the connection between us was so strong that I could imagine leaning on him for ever - not just in a physical sense, but emotionally too. I didn't want to move. It had been a long, long time since I'd felt like that about a man. I forgot all about his earlier grumpiness, but the moment had to pass.

He turned me around to face him, kissed my forehead. 'Are you okay?'

I nodded.

'Do you want to see any more or shall I take you home?'

'Home please, Parker.'

My head was too full to concentrate on the rest of the exhibition. I tried to smile at Matt, but it was a poor effort. The he was off, long strides propelling him towards the gift shop, but I lingered and turned back to the painting. I studied her face, and the strangest feeling crept over me, that I was letting her down. That's when I realised I didn't want to leave her. Abandon her. A swift glance over my shoulder revealed the attendant was busy at the other side of the gallery. I whipped my phone out of my bag and, ignoring the signs printed with a camera and a big red cross, took a few quick shots before anyone had noticed. I put the phone back in my bag and hurried after Matt, who was waiting at the exit watching me with an expression of mock horror.

'I hope they don't have CCTV,' he murmured in my ear, taking my arm.

'It's hardly the crime of the century if they do,' I whispered. His mouth twitched as he tried not to laugh.

I felt guilty so I bought a notebook and some postcards in the gift shop.

'What do you know about your family history?' Matt asked once he'd navigated us through the country lanes and we were back on the M4.

'Not much. Not beyond my gran anyway.'

Truth is that I've never been that interested. My gran used to talk about 'the good old days' - growing up after the war when people were grateful to be alive and to have enough money to feed themselves and their families, before technology took over and life got so complicated. I used to tune out, just nod in the right places, but I wasn't really listening. And there was still the small matter of several hundred years between my gran's childhood and the Civil War. My gran died a few years ago, but I was overdue a visit to my mum. Maybe I would go and see her at the weekend.

We drove the rest of the way in silence.

It was early evening when we arrived back in Islip - road works on the A420. Matt pulled up outside my house, which was already in shade. I suddenly didn't want to be alone. 'Stay with me tonight?'

He leaned over and kissed me. 'I didn't think you'd ask. But I'm glad you did.'

We found food in the fridge and cooked. The evening had none of the fun and excitement of two nights ago. When we went to bed we made love and he was gentle with me, as if I was made of glass, and I drifted to sleep, curled into his side with his arms forming a protective bubble around me.

I was woken by the thump of rain slamming into the plastic gutters, and a sloshing, gurgling noise as it overflowed and rushed in torrents down the window. The heat wave had been short-lived.

My alarm clock said it was 7am, but it was so dark it could have been midnight. Matt was still asleep, stretched out on his back, one arm flung over his head. He was so tall his feet were sticking out from under the duvet at the bottom of the bed.

I lingered for a few minutes, my thoughts already full of the discoveries we had made yesterday. I slipped out of bed, showered, and made coffee. Matt came into the kitchen behind me, circled his arms around my waist and nuzzled the back of my neck.

'How you feeling?'

'I'm okay.'

'Honest?'

'Honest.'

My car was still at the studio so Matt gave me a lift.

'You sure you feel up to work?'

'Yes, I'll be fine. I haven't got a very busy day.'

'What next?'

'I don't know. I can't stop thinking about her, whoever she is.'

We had stopped at red traffic lights. 'Have you reported the find to the coroner's office yet?'

I shook my head and watched the windscreen wipers doing their job. If only life were as easy. One minute it was impossible to see through the screen, the glass impenetrable with rivers of water. The next, it was perfectly clear. That's what I needed. Something that could take this muddled canvas that I was failing to make sense of, give it a quick wipe and present it back to me with everything in its place, all crystal clear.

I could feel Matt looking at me. He didn't ask why I hadn't reported it, but I knew he wanted to. The truth was that I felt an even stronger connection with that ring than I did before and I just wasn't ready to give it up.

'I'll call you later,' Matt promised when we reached my studio. He leaned over and gave me a quick kiss.

I tried to concentrate on work and not keep looking at the photo of the portrait I had taken yesterday. I had the prints to organise for the twins, some of which needed enlarging. There were several emails to answer - some of them wanting quotes for work, including a photo shoot at a nearby hotel and restaurant, called The Bear, that had just been refurbished and wanted new photography to re-launch its website and menus. I remembered going there for dinner with Sean years ago when we'd only just returned to England. It had been a stuffy, old-fashioned kind of place. The dining room had had a patterned carpet, matching tables and chairs set out as if by Roman road builders - straight lines and neat intersections. Absolutely no atmosphere. I remembered how we'd laughed through our prawn cocktails and chicken Kievs, and had to pass on dessert altogether when we read the menu, which offered a choice of trifle, Black Forest gateau or Arctic roll. If it had been a 1980s theme night, I'd have said their attention to detail was bang on, but it wasn't. Scanning through the jpgs they'd attached to their email, taken on a smart phone, I could see it was very different now. Perhaps I should suggest to Matt that we go there for dinner sometime, but then it would feel weird going there with another man when I had such potent memories of the evening with Sean.

In spite of myself I was soon wrapped up in the present and I jumped when my mobile rang mid-morning.

'Miss Hannah?'

'Hi Joel. How's things? Have you found something?' I tried - and failed - to keep the excitement out of my voice.

'Well yes. I believe so.'

Knowing he could teach the Thames a thing or two about meandering, I forced myself to be patient.

'Sir Henry Gilder was born in 1593. His father was also Sir Henry - but known as Harry - and his mother was Margaret - they married in 1586, had a son in 1590 who died when our Sir Henry was just a child, and then several daughters. Sir Harry had a sister, who married a Richard Marlow from Oddington.'

'You mean, she was Thomas's mother?'

'No, grandmother. Her oldest son was also Richard Marlow and his son was Thomas.'

'So that makes Richard and Sir Henry ...'

'Cousins, yes. But this is where it gets really interesting. Harry's father - another Sir Henry don't you know - what is with you English people that you give all your children identical names,' he chuckled and I could imagine his cheeks dimpling.

'Anyway, this latest Sir Henry - who would have been our Sir Henry's grandfather - was born in 1520 to parents Letitia and ... yes, you guessed it, Sir Henry. Letitia's maiden name though was Giles.'

I was struggling to follow this. 'Wait,' I said. 'Let me get this straight. We think Giles may have been the family name of John Islip. But I thought his sister was Agnes?'

'You are correct. But Sir Henry's family line goes back to Letitia, not Agnes. Letitia herself appears to be a bit of a mystery, does she not. She was given the Giles name and brought up as part of the family, but the details of her birth are not clear. So unclear, in fact, that I cannot find a record in the register. She may have been a half-sister to John and Agnes, or she may have been a poor cousin who was taken in by the family. I cannot say for sure.'

My brain was trying to catch up. 'It doesn't really matter though, whoever she was, our Sir Henry and Richard and Thomas Marlow, are all descendants from John Islip's family?'

It was another connection and my mind was already in a whirl.

'Miss Hannah? Are you still there?'

'Yes Joel. Sorry. I'm just trying to work out what all of this means. You see, Matt took me to this American museum near Bath, and there was a portrait of this woman - I don't know who she was, but it could have been a photo of me. And it was painted by Thomas Marlow.'

We were both silent for a while, and the mobile line connecting us crackled.

'Miss Hannah. I'm going to think about this some more. Can I ask something for you?'

'Er, I'spose. What do you mean?'

'Be careful.'

The line went dead. I stared at the phone in my hand. What did he mean by that?

I could feel yesterday's headache beginning to pull at my temples again. I scrolled through my contacts list for Matt's number. It was answered almost immediately.

'Matthew Denton's phone. This is Lauren speaking. Can I help you?'

The pouty cousin.

'Is Matt there?'

'He's with a client at the moment. Who is it calling please?'

How many of his clients would call him Matt I wondered. 'It's Hannah.'

'Hannah who?'

Now she was really starting to wind me up.

'Hannah Whittaker.'

'And may I tell him what it's concerning?'

'No, you bloody well may not,' I snapped and hung up.

I was still cursing Lauren and pondering what Joel had told

me when my door buzzer interrupted the silence of my studio, making me jump. I wasn't expecting anyone.

'Delivery for Miss Hannah Whittaker,' the tinny voice on the other end announced. As I pressed the button to release the door I realised I knew that voice. I knew it very well in fact. But it couldn't be. I swivelled my chair around so I was facing the door when it swung open. Standing there, looking almost exactly as he had when I last saw him two years ago, was Sean.

TWELVE

Hannah

'SURPRISE,' HE SAID, HOLDING OUT his hands as if he was about to applaud.

If you only knew how many times I had imagined him turning up on my doorstep like this. How many times I had willed this to happen. And now it had. In my imaginings he would beg me to forgive him, swear that leaving me had been the biggest mistake he'd ever made and vow that he would never do it again. I would then fall into his arms and we'd be back together. No recriminations. No questions asked.

And now here he was, just a few metres away from me, and I was glued to my chair, with no desire to throw myself into his arms and forget how he had treated me. I studied him, not trusting myself to speak. He was still a good-looking guy, that was for sure, but his features no longer hung together the way they used to. There was a hint of grey in his sun-bleached hair, which was neither short nor long but somewhere in-between, that gave him an unkempt appearance. His chin was beginning to descend into his neck, and the buttons on his shirt were straining a little with some additional weight.

Drinking too many cocktails on the beach no doubt.

He had once emanated a vibrant aura that made people want to be with him, but that had faded, like the paint on a red car that's seen too many years of exposure to UV rays. My toes were numb.

I stared at him, fascination and revulsion roiling in my stomach.

He closed the door behind him and leaned against the wall, nonchalant and full of himself, smiling as if the last two years hadn't happened. As if he'd just popped out to the shops. He didn't rush to apologise. Well of course he wouldn't. He never did.

'You need a haircut,' I said.

'Is that all you can say Han? I thought you'd be pleased to see me.'

'Pleased to see you?'

Had I heard him right?

I hoped my voice sounded as incredulous as I felt. He'd dumped me. Humiliated me. Destroyed my life. And he was still sure I'd be pleased to see him. I found it uncomfortable to admit that for a long time I would have been pleased to see him, no matter how badly he had hurt me. In fact, if I hadn't met Matt ... no, I wasn't going to allow him back into my life.

'How's Trixie, Dixie, Pixie, or whatever her name is?' I asked with a sweet smile that didn't reach my eyes.

'Oh, you know, easy come easy go.'

Had he always been this arrogant and I hadn't noticed, or had it grown on him, like barnacles on a rock? I narrowed my eyes and channelled as much contempt as I could manage into them. But Sean's skin had always been thick. 'Oh my god Han. I didn't mean you. You can't have thought I did.'

'I don't know what you mean or what you think any more Sean. I'm not sure I ever did.'

He didn't look so certain of himself now.

'What do you want?' I asked, turning back to my computer and tapping randomly at some keys. I didn't need to see him to know that he was ambling towards me, casual and confident, never any doubt that he would get what he wanted. He stopped in front of me - the computer between us. He was blocking the light. I sighed and raised my eyes.

'We were good together,' he said, leaning over the screen. Close up, I could see that the lines around his eyes were carved deeper into his suntan than I remembered. He smiled that slow, lazy smile that I had loved so much, that cleaved his face into two parts, topped by twinkling eyes. But all I could see were his teeth, ultra-white against his skin, giving him the appearance of a cartoon shark on the hunt for supper. The twinkle was no longer

143

there. I pushed my chair back and leapt to my feet. I needed to put some distance between us.

'We were. But it was you who smashed us up,' I reminded him.

'We could try again. I'm willing if you are.'

I marched to the door and flung it open. 'I'd like you to leave now.'

He raised his eyebrows in shock. I wanted to punch that smug face. How could he think he could just walk back into my life like this and I would let him? I flushed with embarrassment that he had read me so well. No wonder he had walked out on me. I must have seemed pathetic to him - easy to please, happy to wait for him wherever he may have decided to leave me. He strolled towards me and paused. Reached out a hand to touch my face. But I stepped back and kept my eyes fixed on the door, willing him to get the message.

He stepped through. 'See you soon,' he threw over his shoulder as his parting shot.

I slammed the door shut.

What did he mean?

Surely he wasn't intending to turn up on my doorstep on a regular basis.

I returned to my desk, slumped into my chair and stared at the computer screen, telling myself I should go back to work, pretend nothing had happened, but my fingers were trembling. They stumbled over the keyboard like a clumsy drunk. I snatched them away and sat on them to keep them still, looked again at the screen. It was a jumbled mess of letters and symbols. I swivelled around on my chair, eyes seeking reassurance from my familiar surroundings. My safe haven. It felt tainted, polluted by Sean's lingering presence. My powers of concentration deserted me.

Why now? Why had Sean chosen this moment to try to re-insert himself into my life, just as I was starting to move on?

I switched the computer off and locked up for the day. The rain had stopped and the sun was making a feeble attempt to break through the clouds. I decided to drive home and risk taking my boat out.

I changed into waterproofs, collected my camera bag and went out through the back door, almost tripping over the cat who was sitting on the step. It made a move to dart past me inside but I was faster. 'Not right now puss,' I said, kneeling to stroke it. 'Maybe when I get back.'

I pushed off, steering the boat downstream towards the village in the opposite direction to that I'd taken just a few days ago. I didn't go far - I could just have walked along the lane and then the river, but I needed the soothing feeling I always get from being on water. It would help me to evict Sean from my head and quell my own self-disgust that I had once loved him so much that I had thought my life was over when he left.

How could I not have seen through him?

I pulled up onto a shallow hollow under a tree - a favourite spot for kids fishing. My phone pinged and I reached for it, hoping it was Matt. It wasn't.

'missed u xxx' It was Sean. I just managed to stop myself throwing my phone in the river. Matt wouldn't be able to reach me if I did that.

I wondered why he hadn't called me back, but then it struck me that pouty face probably hadn't even told him I'd called.

I pulled my camera out and took some shots of the river, the water in shadows under a weeping willow, with the sun beginning to peep through the branches. Then I scrambled up the bank onto a section of the Confessor's Walk and captured the view towards the village, of the Norman church tower and its four steeples rising above the tree line. Nothing very exciting, but fulfilling nevertheless.

Whilst I was framing shots and changing the settings to manipulate the light I tried to control my thoughts. They were like a boomerang, insisting on returning to Sean as soon as I released them. My anger was building again. It was a suffocating sensation, rising in my throat, choking me.

Breathe out. Let it go. I clutched the sides of my boat and forced my mind to focus on something else. On what Joel had told me, just before Sean turned up. I hadn't had time to think about it yet. What it meant.

There were now too many connections for me to believe in coincidence. If Thomas and Richard Marlow, as well as Sir Henry, were all descended indirectly from the family of John Islip, and were living in the village during the Civil War, the ring must have belonged to one of them. Maybe they had lost it one day whilst out walking and didn't know where, couldn't find it again. That was plausible. Or it could have been stolen and dropped by the thief who was fleeing the village pursued by soldiers. That was also plausible.

What either of these explanations lacked was anything to explain why I felt such a connection to the ring - not just the physical shock, but the sensation that there was a mystery that I needed to find the answer to. And that mystery had to revolve around the woman in the painting - although I couldn't imagine what it might be. It was a man's ring, not a woman's, but even so, I struggled to shake off the conviction that if I could only find out who she was, the rest would fall into place.

I remembered Matt's comments about the jigsaw. Were the pieces starting to fit together, or was I was forcing them into the pattern that I wanted to see?

My mobile rang. I was tempted to ignore it, feeling sure it was Sean, but caller ID revealed it was Matt.

'How you doing?'

'Fine. I tried to call you earlier.'

'Oh, I didn't get a message.'

'I didn't leave one. Don't worry. It's been a hell of a day.'

I told him about the conversation with Joel and how I felt sure the unknown woman held the key.

'Maybe,' he conceded. 'So what's your plan?'

'Who said I have a plan,' I laughed. 'I might go and see my mum though.'

I wanted to ask Matt if he was coming over, but I thought it might appear too pushy. I examined my fingernails, noticing that I'd broken one, while I pondered how I could hint that I would love to see him.

'I'd really like to see you again soon,' Matt beat me to it and I hugged a smile to myself. 'But I have some paperwork that I must do tonight or Lauren will have me strung up from the Carfax Tower.'

'Oh.' What was I supposed to say to that?

'I'm joking. I'd have to fetch my own coffee and muffins though.'

I knew he was smiling by the tone of his voice. I imagined his eyebrows doing that Poirot thing. His mouth twitching as he teased me.

'I might be at my mum's tomorrow night.'

'The day after then? It's Friday. I could take the afternoon off and we could go for a long walk, pack a picnic maybe, hang out like teenagers on Port Meadow?'

'I'd like that,' I said.

After I'd hung up I wondered why I hadn't told him about Sean.

I rowed back home, taking my time, feeling much more relaxed than I had earlier. I left the boat in the water, secured to its mooring post. As I was walking towards the house, I could have sworn I heard someone call my name. My first thought was that it was Sean and he'd followed me home, but it wasn't his voice. I stopped and looked around. I was quite alone and the silence in the garden was thick and heavy, as if its life had been subdued by the rain. I went inside and checked the front door, but there was no-one there. Ears playing tricks on me. I shrugged it off, and changed into comfortable jogging bottoms and a worn old vest top before calling my mum. She greeted me with her usual torrent of words. When she paused for breath I leapt in.

'I thought I'd come and see you tomorrow, and stay overnight if that's okay?'

'Of course it's okay ... but what's wrong love?' She knew me too well.

'Nothing.' I tried to reassure her. 'It's a long story and I'll tell you everything tomorrow, I promise, but I'm fine, it's nothing to worry about.'

Whilst we were talking my mobile pinged again with another text message. *'we could try again'* ♥😊👍😊♥. With a flash of anger, I hit delete.

It was a return to my dinner-for-one that evening. I wasn't very hungry, but I made myself an omelette and a salad and opened a tin of tuna for the cat. She seemed determined to adopt me and had sat mewing outside the door until I took pity and let her in. It was nice to have company, even if it was only a cat. I'd have to give her a name if she was going to insist on living with me, I couldn't carry on calling her Puss.

She curled up by my side on the sofa and I flicked through the channels to find something on TV, eventually settling for a repeat of an old episode of Midsomer Murders. As I was watching, something felt wrong. It took me a while to realise what it was that was bothering me. The photos in their frames on the shelf above the TV were in the wrong order. I frowned. I always put them back in the same places. You might think it's obsessive and maybe it is, but if they are out of position it annoys me. And they were definitely out of position. I got up and readjusted them, and then I started thinking about yesterday morning when my earrings were in the wrong compartment in my jewellery box and a realisation hit me.

Someone had been in my house.

THIRTEEN

Catherine
Tuesday, April 22nd, 1645

CATHERINE WAS TRAPPED IN A maze of high walls built from a cold, grey stone. Disorientated, panic was snatching at her breath, stealing her composure, and compromising her ability to make clear decisions. Every turning she took ended in a new wall of solid grey. After the first few dead ends she began tapping the wall, fingers seeking a hidden door handle, peering up as far as she could and kicking out with her feet. There must be an opening somewhere.

There was nothing.

She wanted to run, but she feared she might miss something vital for her escape. Instead, she crept, hands stretched out to either side, feeling for something, anything, that might indicate an opening. She turned a corner and there, at last, was a wooden door set into the dead end. She lifted her skirts and hurtled towards it.

There was no handle.

She ran her hands over the warm wood, feeling the grain and pushing her fingers into the occasional knots, desperate to find something she could pull or turn. She tipped her head back and screamed for help. Was she destined to remain here for the rest of her days, every turning promising release but failing to deliver?

She slumped to the ground, tears pricking her eyes. Then a voice boomed at her from somewhere above, commanding her to get up and fight. She leapt to her feet and pounded the door with her fists.

Catherine was twisting and turning in bed, tangled up in her blanket, moaning. A loud knocking punctured her subconscious. Someone was hammering on her front door. Tilly. There must be a problem with Tilly. But it was her father's voice, gruff and impatient that brought her to full consciousness. 'Open up girl. A man needs his breakfast.'

It was not yet light, the moon still cast its silvery glow through the tiny window. Rubbing her eyes, Catherine stumbled out of bed, pulled on her gown and a shawl, and climbed down the steps. She unbolted the door and he pushed past her, followed by a blast of chilly morning air. He looked around the room. There was something wild about his expression and the way he swivelled on the spot that unnerved her, and she was grateful Tilly was at Helen's. His nose was swollen and one of his eyes was half closed. Did he get that in Kidlington a few nights ago, or in a tavern brawl here in Islip? He had a canvas bag that she didn't recognise slung over one shoulder. He dropped it beside the ladder, and she looked at it with a mixture of fear and curiosity; she had never known him to carry a bag before. She moved across the room towards the hearth and he followed her. Instinct cautioned her not to turn her back on him, but she needed to tend to the fire. She started to edge away, trying to position herself so the table was between them, but he grabbed her wrist and pulled her towards him.

'You were late last night, girl,' he snarled, holding her wrist in a vice-like grip. His weight pressed her up against the table. She tried to wriggle free, but couldn't move. Her hands were clammy, and ice-cold tentacles infused her veins. She would not let him see she was afraid.

'Father you're hurting me. Please let go.'

He raised his voice. 'I said, you were late getting home last night.'

'I was working - you knew that. Now please let me go.' Catherine forced herself to look at him and almost cried out in fear. His face was grotesque, deformed, but that wasn't what terrified her. His one good eye was fixed on her, staring. Devoid of emotion. Her flesh crawled and she wanted to look away, but she was held in thrall. Then he blinked and the spell was broken. He dropped her arm like a burning coal, settled into a chair and swung his feet up onto the table.

Catherine rubbed her wrist, as if she could erase what had just happened, the way she would remove a charcoal line from a sketch, or blur it to soften its impact. Her hands were shaking. She didn't know him at all, or what he was capable of. She stepped away, out of his reach, and stoked the fire. Its glow was the only light in the room and the shadows remained so dense they could be hiding monsters. She wanted to press herself into them, make herself invisible and hide from the monster that she could see; her father and the stranger he had become.

She cleared away his supper dishes, stretching over the table to avoid standing too close to him in case he should decide to take another sudden lunge at her. She was aware of his eye following her movements as she prepared and served breakfast.

He ate with gusto, his head bowed towards his bowl, so Catherine could not see his face. The silence stretched out between them, as heavy and impenetrable as the fog that would descend on the village on a winter's day. She could sense his mood shifting but was unable to predict whether for better or worse. She tried to eat, but her stomach was churning, anxiety about her father and what he might do next, and apprehension about meeting Thomas competing and conspiring to remove her appetite. If she hadn't made Thomas a promise, she would not go. Her anger had cooled overnight, but her resolve had strengthened. This morning, she would give the ring back and forget him, along with her foolish thoughts of what could have been.

Catherine got up from the table. Keeping as much distance between herself and her father as possible within the confines of the small room, and not taking her eyes from him for one second, she crept past him and back up the steps to finish dressing. That was a hint that it was time for him to leave, but he appeared not to notice she had moved. He had finished eating and now sat, immobile, staring into the fire. The church clock struck six, yet still he lingered. She re-tied her garters, and took her time pinning her linen cap into place. Only when she heard his chair scrape across the stone did she start down the steps. He hoisted the bag onto his shoulders, and she watched him pat it like he might a favourite child before he pulled the door open and walked away with a swagger in his step. She had never been so relieved to see him go.

Even though she was going to be late, Catherine waited a few minutes before pulling on her cloak, so she could be certain not to run into him once she rounded the corner. When she reached the High Street there was no sign of him. She dashed across the road, passed the great elm tree and swept through the gate in to the churchyard. Expecting to see Thomas waiting for her, she slowed to a walk, eyes darting left and right, but there was no-one in sight.

A cluster of bluebells swaying beneath a tall yew tree caught her eye and she paused, tempted to pick them. What was she doing here? Her legs were now as heavy as the lead on the church roof. Promise or no promise, she should not have come. She should have given him the ring back last night, after she had seen with her own eyes that he was capable of playing games with the feelings of others. If he had told her the truth, his behaviour towards Lady Frances was raising that girl's expectations only to knock them down in the cruellest fashion. That he was capable of that sort of duplicity made her realise she didn't know him at all. If that wasn't bad enough, society would dictate she could not become involved with him. She should heed Helen's advice.

She passed the graves of John and her mother without stopping. She didn't want to seek counsel from either of them at the moment. Neither would have approved of her recent actions. Her mother would have shared her own worries about Thomas, although magnified tenfold. And John, would he be willing to let her go, even from beyond the grave?

Catherine reached the wall on the far side of the churchyard and leaned against the damp stone. She decided to wait for five minutes and if he hadn't arrived by then she would leave. If she could salvage nothing more from this situation, she would save her dignity and insist he no longer seek her company. Then she would return his ring and go back to devoting herself to Tilly. She turned around to check the time on the church clock and saw Thomas striding across the graveyard. Her resolution faltered. A broad smile lit up his face and her heart refused to obey her head.

Hell and damnation.

'Catherine.' He stopped in front of her and bowed.

She turned back to face the lane.

'How beautiful the light is this morning,' she murmured, more to herself than to him.

'I didn't ask you to meet me to discuss the sunrise,' he moved to her side. 'Look at me Catherine.'

Slowly, she twisted her head and raised her eyes to his. She wanted to see something in them that would vindicate her decision to walk away from him. Instead, she found herself noticing that the golden-brown irises were flecked with pale green, the shade of an unripe apple, and once again she thought they were pleading with her, but for what?

'You're still angry,' he said.

She shook her head. 'I have nothing to be angry about, sir.'

'Yes you do, and damn it, will you call me Thomas,' he stroked his beard, and she noticed his fingernails were clean and neatly trimmed. 'You think I've misled you, and I admit ... last night ... I cannot blame you. I was playing a part and it was wrong of me, because I feel nothing for Frances.'

'You owe me nothing ... Thomas. I've enjoyed our conversations, but I understand ...'

'You understand nothing, Catherine. Will you listen to me. Please.'

He reached for her hands, enclosed them in his and their warmth soaked into her skin. What was left of her resolve evaporated, like a snowflake hitting the surface of the river. She waited for him to say more, but now he appeared nervous.

She heard footsteps on the path that crossed the churchyard behind them and jerked her hands back to her side. Thomas had heard them too. He stepped away from her and leaned with his back against the wall.

'Good morning, Henry,' he said.

'Thomas,' replied Henry Gilder.

Catherine could feel Henry's eyes resting on her, sense his suspicion, aroused, assessing the meaning of what he had just witnessed. What had he seen? She wanted nothing more than to fade into the shadows, become invisible for the second time that morning, but keeping her eyes lowered, she willed her feet to move, to turn around so she didn't appear guilty.

'It would seem you have had a miraculous recovery from the ailments that caused you to retire so early from my sister's little soirée yesterday evening.' Henry's tone was curt, lips set in a hard line.

Catherine was holding her breath. She forced the air from her lungs and hugged her arms in front of her so he wouldn't be able to see her hands shaking. Thomas kept his composure. He flashed his charming smile at Henry. 'I think I spent too long out in the fields yesterday - inhaled too much dust. I'm so glad to have bumped into you though. I was going to come to see you later, but there's no time like the present. Mistress Meakin, please excuse us. We have some business to discuss.' It was Henry's turn to look confused, so well had Thomas disarmed the situation. He started to draw the younger man away, across the churchyard.

'Of course, sir,' she bobbed a quick curtsey to his retreating back. Forcing herself not to hurry and at least appear calm, in case Henry was watching, she let herself out of the small gate set into the wall and onto the path. Her thoughts were racing though, like fluffy white clouds being chased across the sky by a brisk wind. What had he heard and seen back there in the churchyard? She wasn't comfortable with the idea that someone like him might have knowledge that he could use against her, should he choose. She was still smarting from his insinuation that she might have stolen some of the silver. He would not fail to make trouble for her if he had any idea of what had passed between her and Thomas, or had overheard any of their conversation. What's more, she had failed to return the ring.

She reached Helen's house, and before she could even knock the door swung open and Tilly flung herself at her mother as though they'd been apart for weeks, not just one night. Catherine was desperate to talk to Helen but pushed her worries aside and concentrated on her daughter instead. Tilly was full of the evening she'd had, playing charades and being fussed over by the older girls as if she were a doll. She wanted to tell Catherine all about it. They sat together for a while, Catherine laughing with her daughter, trying not to think about what had happened in the churchyard, and the quizzical expression on Henry's face as he'd looked at her and Thomas between narrowed, suspicious eyes. She was certain he would be drawing his own conclusions of what he'd seen, even if that had been very little. Just the fact he had caught them together, alone, at such an early hour, would be enough to fuel his imagination. She could not stop her hands trembling as the realisation of how serious a position she was in, through her own actions, took root in her consciousness. What a fool she had been. If only she'd listened to Helen. She felt her aunt's eyes watching her and knew she would have to tell her everything and beg for her help.

When the older girls claimed Tilly and Harry again to play a new game of dressing up, Catherine tried not to show her relief. 'Of course you can go and play my love,' she said in answer to Tilly's anxious request that they stay longer. No-one was in any hurry to return home.

'What is it?' Helen asked as soon as the children had left the room. 'You came in here with a face whiter than a priest's surplice, so what's wrong?'

Catherine kept her eyes on Helen's face. With shaking fingers she pulled the ring on its chain from beneath her gown, looped it over her head and placed it on the table.

Helen gasped.

'What ... Where ... Where did you get this?'

'Thomas Marlow gave it to me.'

Together they stared at the ring. Catherine was struck anew by its beauty, and there was something else. It seemed to have an aura, a shimmering energy hanging around it. Helen appeared transfixed. Catherine pushed the ring towards her and watched her pick it up, gingerly, as if it might burn her fingers. She held it at eye level and the green stone glowed as the sunlight bounced from it, reminding Catherine of the flecks in Thomas's eyes. Helen replaced the ring on the table and pushed it away, as though she would distance herself from it.

'You know what this is, don't you?' she demanded.

Catherine's eyes widened with surprise that Helen was able to identify what the ring and its engraving symbolised. By her aunt's expression and sharp tone she was certain what Helen was about to say would only make her own situation worse. She shook her head.

'It's the rebus of John of Islip.'

Catherine frowned. 'What's a rebus? I don't understand Helen.'

'It's like a drawing that describes who you are. John of Islip was high up in the church at Westminster - the old church that would have been - I think he was the Abbot - over a hundred years ago, but he was born here, in Islip. There's an etching of it in the church - you must have seen it.'

'No. I've never noticed.'

'The Marlows are descendants of John of Islip's family. I'm not sure of the exact relationship, but I do remember our father teaching us about local history and who's who. Whether this ring ever actually belonged to John, or someone else had it commissioned I don't know, but that design marks it as belonging to the family. When ... and why, did Thomas give it to you?'

'A few days ago. I'm sorry Helen. I didn't know what to do.'

'You didn't think to refuse it, or talk to me about it?'

'I tried.'

'Really?' Helen arched an eyebrow. 'Not hard enough. Cat, you must know what this will look like, if anyone finds out about it.

You're wearing his ring. Not only his ring, but a very special ring, in secret, and there is no formal agreement or understanding between you. Or is there?'

'No. No, it's not like that.'

'What is it like then? Tell me.' Helen's tone was now so sharp it could have sliced with ease through Sunday's roast goose.

'He said it's a talisman, to keep me safe. He said he senses a darkness around me.' Listening to her own words, Catherine knew she sounded ridiculous. Little wonder that Helen looked disbelieving. 'Some talisman. It's more like an ill omen. Everything has gone wrong since he gave it to me.' Catherine was unable to prevent a bitterness creeping into her voice.

Helen clasped her hands in her lap, looking thoughtful. The ring remained on the table between them.

'And you were right,' Catherine caught a sob in the back of her throat and swallowed it down. She didn't want Helen thinking she was playing for sympathy.

'What was I right about?'

Catherine picked up the ring and turned it around in her palm, hesitating. Helen watched in silence, waiting.

'At the supper last night. It was so obvious they all expect Thomas to marry Lady Frances.' Speaking her thoughts out loud somehow made them more real. Catherine was surprised how much it hurt.

Helen's eyes widened. 'Cat, you'd better tell me everything. From the beginning.'

She didn't need to add 'and don't try to fool me with any nonsense,' because it was stamped all over her tone of voice. Catherine spared Thomas no blushes when she recounted the dinner party, but tried to withhold her own excitement and growing attraction towards him. When she had finished, Helen got to her feet and started pacing across the kitchen. Catherine could tell from the set of her shoulders that she was angry, but she was unprepared for the ferocity in Helen's expression when she stopped pacing and swung around, hands on her hips. She towered over her niece, eyes flashing, hair flaming, and the air around her seemed to quiver in suspense.

'So, let me get this straight,' Helen said, in a voice of pure ice. 'You've accepted a unique and probably very valuable ring from a man with whom you are developing a close, secret friendship. You walked alone, late at night with this man, who you suspect has an understanding with the indulged daughter of Islip's most powerful landowner. You met him by choice this morning - not by accident - alone again, even though you're not sure if you believe him or not, and you were discovered by the young lady's brother.'

Catherine nodded, uncomfortable beneath her aunt's sardonic commentary. She had been chewing her nails and one of them was bleeding. 'You make it sound very underhand, but it wasn't like that.' Her attempt to defend herself sounded unconvincing, even to her own ears.

Helen waved Catherine's protest away with a dismissive flick of her wrist.

'Cat. What did I say about being reckless and throwing away everything you've worked to achieve since John died? How could you be so foolish?'

'Perhaps I was foolish,' Catherine conceded. 'But he's asked me to trust him and you said yourself, he's an honourable man.'

Helen snorted. 'He's also a man of property and expectations.'

'What would you have me do?' Catherine cried. 'I didn't ask for this.'

'Surely you can see you are encouraging him?'

'No,' Catherine shook her head, anger bubbling up with the harshness of Helen's words. 'I have done my best to give him no word of encouragement. Last night, I was angry with him, and this morning I tried to tell him that we had to stop, that I understood if he had an agreement with Lady Frances, but he said he cared nothing for her. I was going to give him the ring back, but then he took my hands and he begged me to listen to him.'

'And what did he say?'

'Well, nothing. That's when Henry interrupted us. But why can't I hope?'

'Hope! Hope for what?' Helen spoke with the rising impatience of someone trying to reason with a recalcitrant child.

'I ... I don't know.' Catherine groped for the right words to describe her feelings, but the depth of her own confusion was too great. 'I may have behaved foolishly, but that is my only crime.' She said eventually, and put the ring down. 'I'll give it back to him, tell him I can't keep it.'

Helen moved closer to her, placed her hands on Catherine's shoulders. 'You do know that I'm only saying this because I care for you, and for Tilly. I don't want to see you get hurt.'

Catherine pulled away before Helen could embrace her. She slipped the ring and chain over her head and let it slide beneath her gown. Satisfied it couldn't be seen, she gathered her belongings and called Tilly. Helen watched but made no effort to detain her.

'Mama?' Tilly tumbled into the kitchen, hair tousled and cheeks rosy from whatever game the children had been playing.

'Time to go home, my love,' Catherine told her.

'I want to stay longer.'

'No, we need to go,' Catherine insisted.

Tilly protested as they walked back through the village, but Catherine wasn't listening. She was already regretting that she had argued with Helen, the person whose friendship - and opinion - she valued more than any other.

Once at home, she followed Tilly out to the garden. The cat jumped down from the wall as soon as it saw them and strolled over, mewing for attention, or maybe more milk. It was a sweet creature. Tilly's good spirits were soon restored, and Catherine sought solace in attacking the weeds. Jabbing at them with the hoe, her hands operated under their own momentum whilst her thoughts went to Thomas and what he might have said had Henry not interrupted them. Helen's words replayed in her head. She didn't know what Thomas was thinking. The hope she had spoken of was based on nothing stronger than her interpretation of his behaviour towards her. And instinct. Like that of a fledgling leaving the nest for the first time and plummeting through the empty air until it flaps its wings and takes flight. Would she fly or crash?

The more she went over and over Helen's words, the more she had to admit they contained many truths. She chewed her lip, planning how she would apologise and beg her aunt's forgiveness tomorrow. She would do as she had said as well and return the ring to Thomas at the earliest opportunity, to show Helen she was serious.

Tilly brought her back to the moment.

'I'm going to call it Splodge, mama.'

'That's a good name my love.' The cat's white fur was interrupted by random black splodges as if it had been splattered with soot. Splodge purred his approval.

Catherine leaned on her hoe and watched her daughter for a few minutes, envying her carefree innocence, her ability to take pleasure from the moment with no concern about what might be coming. Her thoughts turned to her father and she lifted the hoe again and took her fury out on the weeds. What was he involved with? Had he been there in Kidlington, tussling with the Earl of Northampton's men? His face told its own story, but was she jumping to conclusions? And what had been in that satchel he was carrying as though it were a priceless artefact?

She realised she hadn't even told Helen how her father had frightened her that morning. Over the last few days his behaviour had become more threatening. After this morning, the last vestige of doubt that she was being over-sensitive to Tilly's reactions had vanished.

Rubbing her back, which was aching from bending over, she straightened up, letting her muscles relax, and propped the hoe against the wall. She fetched her unfinished sketch of the church, sat on the step and held it at arm's length to study what she had drawn. With careful strokes, she adjusted some of her lines to improve the perspective and applied inks in brown and black over the charcoal outline. A smile spread across her face. The effect was thrilling. On a sudden impulse, she added a clump of bluebells in the foreground.

Her father was late that evening. As soon as he crashed through the door, Catherine knew he was drunk. The swelling around his eye had gone down, but a dark bruise had risen in its wake. His nose was still swollen. She was thankful that Tilly had gone to bed, happy, delighted with her stay at Helen's and demanding to know when she could go back for another. 'Soon, my love,' Catherine had said whilst tucking her in and kissing her goodnight.

She placed a bucket of warm water on the table for her father to wash and watched him, wary, senses alert. His movements were rapid. He lunged across the kitchen and pushed the bucket with some force. Water spilled over the rim and sloshed onto the floor, soaking the hem of her grown. She was cornered. There was no way past him. She could smell the stale sweat on his body. Alcohol on his breath. He leaned in towards her, even closer. She tried to shrink backwards, but she was pinned against the wall, hemmed in by the hearth. There was nowhere for her to go.

'Father, you're frightening me,' she spluttered.

'I thought I told you to stay away from that Thomas Marlow,' he growled at her in a low voice, but it was the expression on his face that chilled her, made her want to run and run, not stop until she was far away. He was angry, but he wasn't in a rage. That would have been better. She knew how that mood fizzled out with as much speed as it rose. It was like a sudden breeze whipping through the village, stirring the tree tops and sending leaves skittering down the lane before deserting Islip and moving on to the openness of Otmoor. No, this was different. He was in control. His eyes were cold and calculating. If she hadn't been standing in front of him she would have sworn they belonged to someone else. A stranger. She searched for a response, something to offer a defence that would not inflame his anger further. She could think of none. He had forbidden her to see Thomas. She had gone against his wishes. Disobeyed him.

He reached behind her, loosened the clasp that held her hair in place and the long tresses tickled her neck as they fell like a sheet of silk beyond her shoulders. He took a handful of it and yanked hard. Her head jerked back and she yelped in pain. She tried to twist away from him but he grabbed her waist with his other hand.

'Cathy, Cathy, you're so beautiful.'

Her eyes widened in horror. She managed to gasp, 'I'm not Cathy.'

He tightened his grip on her hair and she knew her words had not shocked him out of whatever delusion had afflicted him. Even if she was Cathy, is this how he used to behave? Is this how he used to treat her mother?

He pushed himself against her even harder and fumbled at the bodice of her gown. She stretched out her hands, feeling for anything that she could use as a weapon. They flailed around returning fistfuls of air.

'Father, please,' she begged. 'Don't do this.'

'What, not good enough for you aren't I?' he sneered. 'Yet you've been whoring after that Cavalier scum haven't you?'

Desperate to bring him back to his senses, Catherine spat in his face. His eyes bulged with rage. He released his hold on her hair. Trapped, she watched him pull his right arm back and clench his fist. The only part of her body she could move was her head. As his fist came towards her she twisted it as far as she could to her right. His knuckles glanced across her left eye and cheekbone. Her head slammed into the wall. Even deflected, the blow was enough to stun her and pain exploded behind her eye. Dizziness threatened to sweep her away into unconsciousness. Her vision rippled like a scene from her dreams. She was held upright by his weight wedging her against the wall.

But the force in his punch had spun him off balance. He staggered just enough for the pressure of his body on hers to ease.

Her legs wobbled and she gripped his shoulders to stop herself from falling. Her heart was pumping hard. Pure energy infusing her veins. Conscious thought deserted her, and with it, fear. Acting on instinct alone she brought her knee up with as much force as she could into his crotch. It was his turn to howl with pain as he dropped to his knees, then rolled onto his side, curled into a ball, groaning.

Catherine stepped around him. Her whole body was trembling. She grabbed the table edge to steady herself. Her vision began to clear and the dream turned into a nightmare as Tilly's small figure took shape, shaking, on the top rung of the ladder. Her hands were gripping the sides, her eyes were wide open, staring, and her mouth was moving, shaping words that she seemed unable to articulate. Catherine dashed across the room. Bunches of drying herbs brushed their ghostly fronds against her face like the fingers of the long-dead. With a physical strength she didn't know she had, she scooped her daughter up into her arms, and without stopping to collect anything else, not even their cloaks, she ran from the house.

The sky was shrouded in thick cloud. With no stars or moon to show the way, Catherine tripped and almost fell on the rough track from the cottage. Fear returned. She wasn't sure how long it would take her father to get back on his feet and chase her. She stumbled down the hill past the King's Head as quickly as she was able, hampered by Tilly's legs, which were wrapped around her waist, and the child's weight pulling at her arms. Some drunken men outside shouted after her, causing the soldiers guarding the bridge to look up. She kept her head lowered and hurried past, ignoring them all, and didn't stop until she reached Helen's house. Edward opened the door to her furious pounding.

'What the devil ...' he started

She fell into the room. 'Quick, close the door,' she gasped, panting. 'He might be following us.'

'Who?' Edward asked, shaking his head in bewilderment as Helen appeared in the doorway behind him.

'My father,' said Catherine, and burst into tears.

FOURTEEN

Hannah

I STOOD STILL, STARING AT the shelf, mind racing, until my legs seemed to dissolve beneath me and I landed on the sofa with a jolt. The cat opened her eyes, flexed her paws, and settled her head onto them with a contented sigh.

Nothing was missing though - I'd have noticed, wouldn't I?

My mind ran through a list of everything of value I had. It didn't take long. My camera and all my lenses and other kit were where they should be - I knew that for a fact because I'd only just put them all away. I leapt to my feet, bolted upstairs taking them two at a time, and checked my jewellery box. Everything was there.

Maybe I was being paranoid. But maybe not. What if someone had been in the house? They hadn't ransacked the place like your average burglar had a habit of doing. What if they were looking for something in particular and wanted to do that without alerting me to it. What if they were looking for the ring?

I had moved it to what I thought was a better hiding place. I slid back down the stairs and into my kitchen, where I fell to my knees in front of the cupboard under the sink. The plinth here was loose, although you wouldn't realise from looking at it. It was another of those little jobs that I needed to get someone in to fix. I pulled it away from the unit and extended my hand into the void beneath. My fingers closed around the bundle of cleaning rags that I had pushed almost to the back wall. I dragged them towards me and shook them out on the floor. The jewellery pouches containing the ring and coins were still there. I peeped inside to satisfy myself that they hadn't been switched for some random items that felt the same. The green stone glowed, like a lump of Kryptonite.

I leaned against the kitchen unit, clutching the pouches in my hand, and feeling my heart beat slow to a more normal pace. Then I remembered Joel's last words to me yesterday morning. 'Be careful,' he'd said. It had struck me at the time that it was a strange thing for him to say, but Sean's arrival had shocked me so much that I'd given it no more thought. Why did Joel think I needed to be careful?

I remained on the kitchen floor, impervious to the cold seeping through the flagstones and uncertain about what I should do, until cramp in my foot forced me to move. I looked around, feeling vulnerable for the first time in my own house. The darkness outside was deepening, and if there was a moon it wasn't showing itself. Anyone could be lurking out there. In the shadows. Waiting for me to switch out the lights. Had I been here before when whoever it was had broken in? That thought made me shiver with fear, but then I reasoned with myself - if someone had come into my bedroom to go through my jewellery box whilst I'd been asleep I would have woken, so I had to have been out. It might even have been during the day when I was at my studio. I closed the kitchen blinds and checked the back door was locked, sliding the bolt into place with a shaking hand. That was when I realised that I didn't want to be alone. I called Matt.

'Do you want me to come over?'

I was grateful he'd offered and I hadn't had to ask.

'What about your paperwork?'

'I'll be with you in 20 minutes.'

Whilst I waited for Matt to arrive I went around the house, drawing curtains, checking window locks where I had them, and trying not to let my imagination conjure up monsters under the bed or ghouls tapping on the glass to be let in. I was as jittery as a teenager on a first date. Back in the kitchen I saw the jewellery bags where I'd left them on the floor. After a moment's hesitation I re-wrapped them in the rags, pushed them back under the cupboard and replaced the plinth.

When I heard Matt's car I ran to the door. He reached it at the same time I did, knocked, and shouted my name. I fumbled with the bolt and the latch, pushed the door open and stood aside to let him in. I leaned towards him, he held me tight and I clung to him as if I were a child hanging on to my mother's knees.

'Sorry, I'm so spooked,' I muttered.

'Hey, it's okay,' he murmured into my hair.

We stood there for a few minutes until he eased himself out of my grip and walked with more purpose to the kitchen. I followed. He had a small bag with him and he reached into it, pulled out a bottle of wine and held it out to me, his eyes asking a question.

'Good idea,' I said. I unscrewed the top and poured us both a glass. 'Let's go sit in the lounge.'

'Someone's making herself at home,' Matt pointed to the cat, who hadn't moved from her spot on the sofa. Her tail swished as if she knew we were talking about her, and her purr was so strong it sent vibrations through the cushions.

'Yes, she seems to have moved in. I was thinking I need to give her a name.'

Matt thought for a moment, sitting down next to the cat. She tipped her head back and exposed the soft, vulnerable fur on her throat for him to stroke. He obliged. 'How about Trespass?'

I laughed, and it felt like a release of pressure inside, like the 'phhht' when you open a new bottle of some fizzy pop. 'What a great name for her.' I joined Matt on the sofa.

There we were, relaxing in my lounge like an ordinary couple - like I'd imagined Sean and I would become - with a happy cat stretched out next to us, well, next to Matt to be more accurate - and a glass of wine in our hands. The dark didn't seem so threatening any more, and my home was safe and welcoming again. I was suddenly aware that I must look a complete mess and wished I'd thought to get changed before he arrived.

Matt seemed not to notice. He turned his attention away from Trespass, swung his long legs up onto my coffee table and pulled me into his side. 'Tell me what happened.'

'Maybe I over-reacted,' I said, beginning to feel embarrassed.

'Let me hear the story first,' he said. 'Why did you get so spooked?'

I told him why I was convinced that someone had been in my house.

He sounded bemused. 'You mean you really noticed that something was just slightly out of place? I wouldn't have thought you were obsessive - what is it called, OCD?'

'I'm not. I don't think it's that unusual, is it? I just like things arranged in a certain way.'

He shrugged and I nearly spilt my wine. 'I'm pretty sure I wouldn't notice.'

We were silent for a moment.

'And you think they were looking for the ring?'

I nodded. 'Especially after what Joel said earlier.'

His arm pressed closer around me. 'What did Joel say?'

'He told me to be careful. I thought I must have misheard him. I mean, why would he tell me to be careful?'

'Why indeed? I'll ask him tomorrow. But let's think about this logically. Let's assume that someone has broken in. They might have been looking for something else altogether.'

'But what? I haven't got anything worth pinching, except my camera stuff and they left that.' A thought occurred to me. 'I suppose they might have broken in whilst I had it with me, like when I was on the river, or in the studio.' It was so plausible that I almost began to believe it. 'But no, there would have been some of it left here. I never take it all unless I'm on a proper shoot.'

'Maybe they didn't know it's valuable - or don't have a way of selling it on.'

It was my turn to shrug. It was possible.

'But why target me then?' My mind searched for, and found, the obvious objection to that theory.

'Have there been other break-ins in the village recently?'

It was a good point.

'I don't know,' I admitted.

'Maybe that's something to find out.'

Matt shifted his position and I curled my legs up beneath me on the sofa and snuggled into him. His heart reverberated in my ears, its beat strong and reassuring and my panic of earlier started to feel like paranoia.

'How did they get in?'

It was such an obvious question, but I hadn't thought to ask it. I sat up with a start, pulling away from him.

'I don't know.' I was feeling spooked again, my eyes flitted around the room as if someone could even now be hiding in the shadows watching us.

'Someone who notices pictures and stuff being arranged wrongly would notice if a door had been kicked in or a window broken.'

I stiffened at the tone of his voice. 'Don't be sarcastic. I'm really worried.'

'I'm sorry,' he said and pulled me back towards him to plant a kiss on top of my head.

'Does anyone else have a key?'

'No.' And then it hit me. 'But I'm not very security conscious and I often go out and leave the bathroom window open. The fan's broken and it steams up in there. And Islip is such a safe place.'

Matt grunted. 'There's no such thing as a safe place these days.'

He put his wine glass down and stood up, pulled me to my feet. 'I think I can remember the way to the bathroom,' he said, his mouth twitching. 'Let's go and have a look.'

When he'd examined the window, leaning outside and twisting his head from left to right, he slammed it closed and turned to me. 'You might as well have left an invitation,' he snapped.

'What do you mean?'

'Anyone could get through here - it's above your kitchen extension so all they would have to do is climb onto the kitchen roof - probably using that water butt you've put there to help them, and from there it's just a hop, skip and a jump and voila, they're in your house.' He clicked his fingers and turned to me, the silver flecks in his eyes glittering. 'Fuck's sake Hannah. You need to be more careful.'

'I never thought about it.'

'Well you should.'

I leaned against the wall, blinking back emotion-fuelled tears, wishing I could just close my eyes and go to sleep. Matt sat down on the edge of the bath.

'Let's assume then for the moment that someone did break in, through this window, and they were looking for the ring. Who knows about it?'

'Hardly anyone.'

He waited.

'You, Joel and me, that's about it.'

'Well, it wasn't me.'

'I know,' I said, dismissing the voice in the back of my mind that was asking me how I could be so sure. A few days ago I hadn't even known Matt Denton existed. I screwed my eyes tight shut and then opened them again in a flash.

'Oh and Dave.'

'Who's Dave?'

'The builder who was operating the digger when we found them.' Matt raised an eyebrow and looked at me as if to say 'mystery solved'.

'No,' I said. 'Dave's well known in Islip. I asked around before I got him to quote for the job. Loads of people have used him. No-one's had any problems.'

'Even so ... ' he let the thought hang there for a moment. 'And you haven't told loads of girlfriends?'

'No,' I shook my head.

Who would I tell? I no longer have any girlfriends to share secrets with.

He looked at me, a disbelieving expression on his face. Or was it pity?

My phone pinged. Not Sean again please. I closed my eyes,

hoping Matt hadn't heard it, but when I opened them he was staring at me, expectant. 'Aren't you going to check that?'

I pulled it out of my pocket and glanced at the screen. *'y u ignoring me han'*

'Problem?'

'No. I ... ' I slumped down onto the floor, knees pulled up to my chest, phone dangling in my hand. I couldn't take my eyes from his face. He reached over and grasped the phone. His eyebrows rearranged themselves into the Poirot position as he read the screen.

'He's got a way with words this Sean of yours.'

'He's not my Sean.'

'Really? I seem to remember you telling me just the other night how devastated you were when he left. Looks to me as though he's back.'

Now those silver flecks were flashing like the strobe lights in a nightclub. His eyes flicked from the screen to me, and back again.

'He turned up at my studio earlier today.'

'Why didn't you tell me?' he demanded. 'Why am I here?'

'I don't know, and because there's no-one else I would rather have with me right now, who I feel safe with.' The words spilled from my mouth before I could stop them. There I go again, laying my soul bare to be trampled all over.

'Go on,' he prompted, still holding on to my phone.

'There's nothing to tell. I haven't seen him since the day he left me and he just walked in through my door this morning as if nothing had happened, ready to pick up where we'd left off.'

'And?'

'And, I threw him out.'

He leaned towards me and there was a flicker of something in his eyes that made me think that maybe I hadn't completely blown it. Something strange was happening with my breathing. It was being forced out of me in short gasps.

'That's not the first text he's sent me since. I've deleted the others,' I managed to splutter.

'What did they say?'

'That he missed me, that he wanted to try again.'

'What do you want to do?'

I raised my head and met his eyes. 'Honestly. If he'd turned up a week ago I might have said yes. But not any more.'

I watched his expression change. His mouth started to twitch as he typed a message and handed me the phone back.

I read *'fuck off mate, you've had your chance, she's with me now'*

He raised an eyebrow, his eyes inviting me. So I hadn't blown it. I pressed send and forced out a deep breath.

He took my hands, pulled me to my feet and folded me into his arms. I fell into them, grateful that he'd dismissed Sean from my life once again, and hungry for his attention, toes tingling with longing and anticipation. The tensions of the day fell away like something jettisoned from an aeroplane, plummeting beyond my feet and leaving me feeling several pounds lighter.

At some point we must have made it to the bedroom, because when I woke up in the middle of the night we were wrapped together in a tangle of limbs and duvet in bed. I extricated myself carefully so as not to wake Matt. The landing was suffused with the twinkle of lights reaching up from the lounge. I pulled on my old T-shirt and padded downstairs. Trespass hadn't moved from the sofa. She opened her eyes, blinked at me a couple of times and closed them again. I heard a noise behind me and spun around, nerves taught, half expecting to see an intruder. Matt was standing in the doorway, his hair tousled, rubbing his eyes, completely naked. He looked even more gorgeous than he had the first time I'd seen him.

'We left the lights on,' I said, flicking the switch.

I followed him back to bed, curled into his side and fell asleep almost instantly. When I woke again I was alone, the smell of coffee brewing was wafting up the stairs and the room was light with the promise of a bright, sunny day. I stretched, yawning, pulled on a bathrobe, and padded downstairs. Matt had set the small table on my patio for breakfast and was busy doing something with eggs in a bowl. Various of my jars of dried herbs were on the work surface by his side. As I watched, he threw grated cheese into the bowl and gave everything a good battering with my hand whisk.

I stood behind him and looped my arms around his waist, rested my head on his warm shoulder. He was wearing jeans but his chest and back were bare.

'Breakfast is ready m'lady. I couldn't find any bread though.'

He twisted his head around and kissed my forehead.

'Go and take a seat,' he waved an arm towards the patio. 'Coffee is already out there.'

I did as he instructed, sipped my coffee, which was delicious, and admired the beautiful morning. I couldn't imagine a bigger contrast to yesterday's rain and cloud. The sun had carved a shaft of light across the river through the trees and birds were flying in and out of it, creating a continuous moving swirl of shadows. It made me want to reach for my camera, but I didn't. Nothing should break the perfection of that moment. There was a gorgeous man in my kitchen cooking my breakfast, who, last night, had indicated that he felt our relationship was more than just a casual fling. I had a home I loved and was proud of because it was my own hard work and effort that paid for it. I had a boat and river access and could spend as much time messing around on the water as I wanted to. And I had my career - not just a job, but a career. Trespass rubbed against my ankles. Oh, and it appeared I also had a cat. I wondered what she would do whilst I was away at my mum's. Go back to her real home maybe.

'How does the world look this morning?' Matt placed two bowls of cheesy, herby scrambled eggs on the table and sat down opposite me. He had pulled his shirt on but it was buttoned up unevenly.

'It looks amazing,' I admitted. 'I'm sorry I was so spooked last night. I feel a bit daft now.'

'I'm not sorry.' His hand crept across the table and his long fingers locked with mine. 'If you hadn't been spooked, I wouldn't be here this morning.'

We ate our eggs in silence.

'What do you think about Joel's information?' I asked him, pushing my bowl away and pouring more coffee.

'I think there's an obvious theory that you have overlooked so far.' He paused, appearing to think it over. I waited for him to continue.

'The ring must belong to the mystery woman from the painting and that resemblance between you and her means you must be descended from her and that's why you feel such a connection with the ring and get a shock from it.'

'But I have no family connection with John Islip.'

'Do you know that for sure?'

'No. I suppose it's one of the things I need to find out. Starting with my mum.'

I stared into my coffee mug. It was my turn to think.

'Okay, here's another angle on that theory. It might have been given to her as a gift - as a token of affection - perhaps by Thomas Marlow even,' Matt suggested.

'But it's a man's ring. It's not the sort of ring you would give to a woman you loved. A ring they can't wear.'

'Hannah, it was on a chain. Doesn't that tell you something?'

I must have looked bemused because he carried on. 'Whoever it belonged to wasn't wearing it on their finger.'

Now I was with it and kicking myself for being so dumb. 'They were wearing it around their neck,' I muttered.

I puzzled with that thought for a few moments. 'It still doesn't make sense though. If he loved her, why not give her a ring she can wear in public?'

'Maybe it was a temporary thing. Or maybe the relationship was secret.'

Matt checked his watch. 'I have to go Hannah, or Lauren really will have me strung up from Carfax Tower. And I need to get changed.'

'I think you should go as you are,' I said, getting up and walking around the table, letting a mischievous smile play on my lips.

'Particularly with that shirt done up all wrong. That would get her thinking.'

He frowned and glanced at his shirt. I was about to sweep past him but his arm darted out with the speed of a lizard's tongue and he pulled me down into his lap, laughing. I twisted my arms around his neck and he kissed me, long and slow, then pushed me away. 'Begone, temptress. I have to go to work.'

I pulled a face. 'And I have to go to my mum's - she's expecting me before lunch.'

'I'll call you later,' he promised, following me indoors. I watched him leave and then cleared up our breakfast dishes, showered, dressed, packed an overnight bag, and loaded all my camera equipment into another holdall - I wasn't going to leave that here overnight in case some lowlife decided to have another go at me.

There was no sign of Trespass. I locked the back door. She would have to find somewhere else to sleep tonight. Then I retrieved the ring, chain and coins from their hiding place and zipped them into my handbag.

FIFTEEN

Hannah

THE DRIVE TO MY MUM'S took about an hour. I put an audio book on - Delia Owens, Where the Crawdads Sing - and lost myself in the raw, unspoilt and natural beauty of the marshlands of North Carolina, and Kya, the Marsh Girl. It only felt like five minutes before I was turning into the drive of the modern, two-bed semi that Mum called home.

The front door swung open whilst I was pulling my bags from the boot. Mum stood on the threshold, smiling a welcome, and I caught my breath. How could she have aged so much since I saw her at Christmas? I should explain that except for the eyes, my mum looks nothing like me. The black eyes, black hair combo often skips a generation or two - or one sibling might have it but the other doesn't. My grandma had it. I have it. Mum's hair was a deep shade of red, but that was the henna she used; I suspected it had given in to grey long ago. What shocked me though was how her clothes hung from her and the skin on her neck was wrinkled like the 1980s legwarmers I'd seen her wearing in countless old photographs.

She greeted me, effusive as ever, her voice breathless and husky.

'You've lost weight Mum,' I said, when she paused for breath.

She brushed my comment away as if it were an annoying fly. 'Gallstones,' she said, pulling me inside.

'Lunch is nearly ready. Put your bags in your room, there's a love.'

Lunch was delicious. I have to hand it to her; my mum is a great cook. In my mind I could see her with Matt in her kitchen, both wearing festive hats and creating the most amazing Christmas Day lunch. The image almost made me laugh out loud, because

I couldn't imagine Matt wearing anything on his head except his bandanna. Maybe he could have one decorated with holly leaves or figgy pudding or something. I put the brakes on my imagination, tried to focus on Mum's chatter instead.

She pushed her empty plate to one side and leaned forwards with her elbows on the table and her chin cupped in her hands. 'What's up then?'

I told her everything. Well, almost everything. I might have missed out the finer details of the relationship that I hoped was developing with Matt - I wasn't ready to put that into words yet. Nor did I tell her about Sean, although for the first time I would probably have found her expletive-fuelled opinion of him amusing. I might even have agreed with her.

'What does this ring look like then?'

I pulled both jewellery pouches out of my handbag and tipped the contents onto the table. Mum gasped as the green stone blazed, reflecting the sunlight that was streaming through the open French doors.

'It's beautiful.' She ignored the coins and picked the ring up, holding it delicately between thin fingers.

'You don't feel anything then?'

Her eyes wore a puzzled expression. 'Envy, lust, need? What do you expect me to feel?'

'I told you, I get a shock from it. I thought you might too.'

'Why would I?'

'Because you're my mother and if there's a connection between me and the ring somewhere way back in our family's past, it might be the same for you.'

'No, sorry,' Mum said, putting the ring back down. 'So what now?'

'I need to report it as a find and then the powers that be decide if it's treasure or not. I should have done it already, but I didn't want to part with it.'

'Surely you can hang onto it for a while - finders keepers and all that?'

I shook my head. There was something else I had been reluctant to tell her, and I should have known better. I added. 'No, I can't - I could get a fine, but in any case, I think someone has broken into my house looking for it.'

The look she gave me made me feel as though I was five years old again, and trying not to tell her the full story about how I'd broken her treasured record player whilst using it as a roundabout for my dolls.

'I didn't mention it because I didn't want to worry you,' I mumbled.

She got up from the table and fetched her laptop, which she kept plugged in by the oven and hob. That might sound like a strange place to keep your laptop, but Mum only uses it for recipes, cooking tips and so on. She disconnected it and dumped it in front of me on the table.

Now it was my turn to look puzzled.

'Look it up,' she commanded. 'The coroner's office and what you have to do. You're going to get that thing handed in, then if anyone wants to do any breaking in they'll be messing with the authorities.'

In spite of my reluctance I had already googled what to do if you think you've found treasure and I knew I needed to report it to a Finds Liaison Officer. I'd even saved the link - on my own computer, at home. I found the information I needed and punched the phone number into my phone.

It was a very quick process. Five minutes later I hung up with an appointment to deliver the ring and coins to the offices near Witney on my way back tomorrow.

Mum sat quietly, watching.

'Satisfied?' I glared at her. She ignored me.

'You think there's an ancestral link?'

I nodded. 'Let me show you something.'

I scrolled through the menu on my phone to the photo library, found the shot I'd taken at the museum and handed it to her.

Amused, I watched her mouth widen as she looked from the photo to me and back again.

'Oh my love. When you said this portrait looked like you I thought you meant similar. You could be twins.'

She handed the phone back to me.

'What do you know about our family?' I asked.

'Your gran and I did some work on our family tree a few years before she died. When she started to get ill. You know, that emotional journey thing.'

I felt a flicker of excitement stir. Mum read it in my face and shook her head. 'Don't get too excited, love. We barely managed to get back a couple of hundred years - certainly nowhere near the civil war.'

'You've still got it though?'

'Yes. In fact, it's some coincidence. I was only sorting through a load of old stuff in the loft the other day. I came across it. And there's a box full of old photos and god knows what else that I didn't even look through. Pushed it aside for a rainy day. I'll go get them.'

I'd always admired my mum's energy. She was like a human dynamo, rushing effortlessly around the house juggling several jobs at once. Nothing ever seemed to faze her. But now, as I watched her walk across the kitchen her movements seemed slow, awkward, and lacking vitality, as if someone had cut the power cord.

Gallstones wouldn't do that to her, would they?

I cleared the table, loaded the dishwasher, and forced my mind back to when I'd last seen her. Was I imagining a big change in her? However hard I tried I couldn't suppress the niggling worry that all was not well with my mother. It was vying for attention with the excitement that I couldn't help feeling, in spite of her caution, that she might have found something that would help me to identify my mystery woman.

A few minutes later I heard her soft footsteps on the stairs and she came back into the room carrying a roll of something that looked like wallpaper lining under her arm. I helped her spread it over the table and we weighted it down at the corners with cutlery. It was covered with Mum's neat print in black ink.

We sat side-by-side and studied the tree.

'You wouldn't believe how long it took to get this far,' she said and I could see memories clouding her face. Memories of my gran, I guessed. I know my mum still really missed her. When she'd had me as a teenager, on her own, my gran had been there for her, helping her to get through every day.

'We could have gone further, but after your gran died I lost enthusiasm for it.'

I focused on the tree. It was a confusing mass of lines and names - a bit like a crossword puzzle, but with the clues scribbled in the blank squares of the grid instead of neatly to one side or underneath. As I stared I began to notice a pattern. I pushed my chair back and leant over the paper, twisting my hair back in a clip to stop it falling forwards. I traced with my finger, muttering under my breath.

'What is it my love?'

'Just a minute.' I cast my eyes around the kitchen for something I could use and spotted a couple of tea towels hanging from a hook by the sink. I seized one of them and used it to cover one side of the tree.

'That's better.'

'What?'

'See. They're all women,' I said.

I beamed at my mother, wondering if this revelation meant anything at all. It was clear that it didn't. She was staring at the tree, her fingers pulling at the loose skin around her neck. She appeared baffled.

'So, I look like my gran, right?'

She nodded.

'Therefore my mystery woman in the portrait must be somewhere in Gran's ancestry, so we can ignore Grandad's side of the family.' I gestured towards the tea towel. 'Makes it easier to focus.' I said by way of explanation.

'Let me get you a clean tea towel,' Mum suggested.

'It doesn't matter Mum.'

I turned back to the tree and pointed. 'Gran's mother was the oldest daughter, Anne.'

Mum sighed and she turned wistful, sad eyes towards me. 'Lovely, kind and funny lady my gran was. I loved her so much.'

All I could remember of my great gran was a pair of bony but surprisingly soft hands sticking out from a bundle of crocheted blankets in an armchair by a roaring open fire.

'But look Mum, her mother - Sylvia - was also the oldest daughter, and so on, right the way back to 1798,' I pointed to the top of the unfinished tree, 'and Matilda.'

'What does it mean?'

'Damned if I know.' I slumped back into my chair, propped my chin in my hands and tried to think.

'Right. I'm going to leave you to put those little grey cells to work. I have to pop out. I need to get Mrs Mackenzie's prescription for her and pick up a few bits and pieces from the pharmacy. The photos and other stuff if you want them are in shoe boxes on the landing.'

After she'd gone I carried the boxes downstairs and into the lounge. Sitting cross-legged on the floor, I opened the top box and started to flick through. The photos were all in colour. There were lots of me as a child and my mum as a teenager. I pulled one out that I remembered well, of me as a bridesmaid at someone's wedding, missing most of my front teeth, hair swept back in a jewelled band, like a tiara, and falling in straight lines to my waist. I gazed at it for a few moments, trying to see my adult features in the child I once was. I had to be firm with myself. It would be very easy to become immersed in nostalgia, but that wasn't what I was here for. I pushed the box away and opened the next one. These were older, a mixture of black and white and colour. I recognised my grandparents' wedding day and there were various men in army uniforms. I tipped them out on to the coffee table and started sorting through them, checking the reverse for names or dates. There were very few of these, but I put them to one side so that if those names came up again they would be easy to find - and I could compare them to those on the family tree.

Going back through the generations I found many images of women who were recognisably related to me, but in most cases it was impossible to identify whom they were. Very few were labelled and dated.

I found some marriage and birth certificates as well. Mum and Gran had probably referred to these in compiling the tree. There was nothing much of any use to me though. Mum was right.

I put everything back in the boxes apart from the small pile of labelled photos and called Matt.

'Hey,' he said. 'Good to hear from you.'

I could hear the soft click of a door closing and the background noise muted.

'How you getting on?'

'It's frustrating and disappointing,' I admitted. 'I don't feel as though I'm getting anywhere. Mum has done a partial family tree already but it doesn't go back nearly far enough, and she's got loads of old photos but I've no idea who most of the people are. Did you speak to Joel?'

'I tried, but he's been in a conference.'

'This all feels like such a waste of time.'

I chewed my fingernails, waiting for Matt to say something, but he was silent.

'I'm going to have a nice dinner with Mum tonight and come home tomorrow.'

'Are we still on for our picnic at Port Meadow?'

'I'm looking forward to it,' I smiled.

Mum returned whilst Matt and I were making arrangements to meet at The Perch for a drink first at 1pm tomorrow. She lingered by the door and I knew she was trying to work out whether I was talking to a girl friend or someone more significant. She didn't ask though and I didn't offer.

That evening we cooked together. I had suggested going out, but she said she was tired and would rather stay in. I had the job of washing and preparing salad whilst she made a complicated sauce with mustard, dill and capers to go with the baked salmon.

'This Matt fellow then, the one you took the coins and the ring to. Can you trust him love?'

I was slicing a big beef tomato but I paused the knife mid-slice. The question took me by surprise, not least because it wasn't something I had considered.

It's a bit late to start asking that.

My face must have given me away. 'Ha,' she said, screwing the lid back on the jar of capers. 'I knew it. There's something you're not telling me.'

'That's an unfair question,' I protested. 'You deliberately tripped me up.'

'No, you just gave yourself away. I'm pleased for you love. You've been on your own for too long after that waste of space ...'

'I know. I just didn't meet anyone who interested me.'

'Until now.'

'Until now,' I agreed. 'But why ask if I trust him?'

She added a grind of pepper to the sauce and avoided looking at me.

'Because he knew you had the ring, and it might have been him who broke in and tried to steal it.'

'No,' I shook my head.

Mum raised her eyes and I realised I must have appeared too quick to defend him. She probably thought I was heading for another heartbreak.

'For one thing, there's no way he could have got in through that tiny window. He's tall. Very tall. And broad shoulders. He couldn't have. And another thing, his business is respectable. He's got a shop and everything in the city centre. You can't deal in old coins and steal from your clients. His business wouldn't have lasted five minutes.'

'Right. Dinner's ready then. Let's eat.'

Over dinner we talked about neutral subjects. Holiday plans. How work was. I told her about Trespass. The salmon was as delicious as lunch had been, but my mum hardly touched hers. She did a great job of pushing it around her plate and hiding it underneath a lettuce leaf, but I was watching.

'What about you, Mum, what's wrong?'

'I told you, gallstones.'

'I'm not going for that.'

She didn't answer immediately. She nibbled a slice of tomato.

'They're doing some tests. I'll know more in a week or two.'

I frowned. 'Tests. For what?'

'I don't know what they're looking for.'

I glared at her.

'Honest, love. I don't. Who knows with these doctors? They never tell you anything. They've taken some blood and I've got to wait for the results.'

Just like she knew I'd been holding back on her earlier, I was certain now that she wasn't telling me everything. I also knew there was no point pushing her.

I went to bed that night with an uneasy feeling, like a premonition, that this evening could be a turning point in my life in more ways than one.

'Give me a hand with a few bits into the car for the charity shop before you go will you love?'

We'd had breakfast - cereals - my mum had never been big on breakfast - and lingered in the garden. Now it really was time for me to leave or I'd be late meeting Matt.

I followed her into the small utility room where several carrier bags were piled by the freezer and a load of framed pictures were leaning against the wall. I grabbed a couple of bags, carried them to the car and returned for the pictures. I don't know what it was that caught my eye and made me take a closer look at the one in front, but something did and I just stood there, staring at it.

I picked it up. It was drawn with skill in shades of black and brown on biscuit-coloured paper. Whether it was meant to be that colour or had browned with age I couldn't tell. The picture was a countryside view, with a river in the foreground, lots of trees and four miniature church spires rising above a square Norman tower. The frame was plain and simple in wood.

'Where did you get this?'

Mum glanced at it and shrugged, for once misreading my expression. 'Told you I had a sort out in the loft. You wouldn't believe the crap that's up there.'

'No, I mean, where did it come from?'

'No idea.' She took it from me and examined it more closely. 'Why? What's so interesting? It's just a crappy sketch. I've never had much time for black and white stuff, all a bit boring. I need colours. And the frame's knackered. Look at it.' She tapped her finger on a section of the frame where the wood had splintered.

'It's Islip,' I said. I couldn't take my eyes from the picture. Mum might dismiss it as boring, but to me it was beautiful.

I took it back from her, my eyes searching for a signature or some mark that would enable the painter to be identified, but there was nothing.

'How can you be sure?'

'Because I photographed this very scene from the river just a few days ago. I'd bet anything this is Islip.'

My adrenaline was beginning to pump. I felt like a skydiver in that moment before jumping from an aeroplane and plummeting towards the earth. At least, that's how I'd imagine they would feel, not that I'd ever done it.

This was another connection.

'How did a picture of Islip end up in your loft, Mum?'

'I don't know my love. I don't remember seeing it before.'

'Did anyone in our family ever live in Islip before I moved there?'

'Not that I know of.'

'And when you were doing the family tree, did you find any references there to Islip?'

'No. I'd have told you if I had. It would have been quite a coincidence.'

Not a coincidence. There is no way all of this is a coincidence.

'You don't mind if I take this do you?'

'Of course not love.'

I added it to my small bundle of photographs and the rolled-up family tree.

I said goodbye to Mum. My fears from last night, that everything was about to change, hit me again this morning as I hugged her. She stood in the doorway and waved to me and I tried to memorise every tiny detail of her appearance, so that next time I saw her I would know if she had got worse. I wished I could have taken a photo of her so that I had something concrete to refer to rather than my memory, which at times is as fluid as the water in the river at the bottom of my garden, but she would have thought it strange if I asked her to pose for me, so I blew her a kiss and reversed off the drive.

I wasn't in the mood for listening to anything on the drive back to Oxford. I couldn't shake this feeling that something dreadful was about to happen.

I stopped in Witney and delivered the ring safely to the Finds Liaison Officer, who promised to let me know as soon as his report was complete. Parting with it was hard, the connection I felt with it was so strong. I was about halfway between Witney and home, thinking about what to wear for the afternoon's picnic with Matt, when my mobile rang. I almost expected it to be Mum, calling to tell me I'd left something behind. I hoped it would be Matt. I so badly wanted to hear his voice even though I would be with him in a couple of hours. The number that came up on my car screen was unidentified. Probably a client, or potential client wanting a quote. I almost didn't answer it. I didn't feel in the mood for talking to strangers or being polite to customers. Curiosity got the better of me though. It always did. Just as I'm no good at holding back in relationships, I'm also hopeless at not knowing. I'm no good with mysteries. Later, I would think back to this moment and understand that sentiment sums up my life - the ring, the woman in the painting, what's wrong with my mum.

I clicked the switch to answer the call.

It was Judy Daniels, the Neighbourhood Watch co-ordinator on Mill Street. I knew her to say hello to. I wondered how she'd got my number, then remembered I'd stuck my business cards on every notice board around the village.

'You're driving,' she said. Top marks detective I thought, but didn't say it.

'It's fine. I'm hands-free and legal,' I assured her.

'Maybe, but I think you should pull over at least.'

I wasn't in the mood to be told what to do by someone I hardly knew, and I was about to tell her that I was the best judge of whether I could drive and talk. But there was something in her tone that stopped me. And, call me slow, but my brain had suddenly clicked in and was prompting me to question why she was calling me. There was a layby signposted in half a mile.

'Okay. Just give me a moment.'

A few minutes later I was glad I had.

'Dog walkers out this morning noticed that your front door was wide open. There was no sign of your car. They knocked and looked through the front windows.'

A cold fist clenched around my stomach. I knew what she was going to say.

'Do you want me to call the police?'

'No, I'll have a look first - see if anything's missing - and I'll call them. I'll be back in about 20 minutes.'

'I'll wait here, keep an eye on the place until then.'

'Thanks Judy.'

I took a few deep breaths, trying to stay calm. Thank God I'd taken the ring and all my camera equipment with me last night. I was shaky, and now agreed with Judy that I shouldn't be driving, but I couldn't see that I had a choice. I eased back into the traffic on the main carriageway. The next set of lights was on red. I used the hands-free system to call Matt, hating that me ringing him in a panic was becoming a bit of a habit.

He was cool and calm. 'I'll meet you there,' he said.

About 15 minutes later I turned onto Mill Street and I recognised Matt's car ahead of me. Judy was sitting on my doorstep.

'I'm sorry Hannah,' she said, scrambling to her feet and brushing the dust from my unswept porch off her jeans. 'It looks a bit of a mess in there. You sure you don't want me to call the police?'

'We'll deal with it,' Matt said, putting a reassuring hand on my shoulder. I noticed today's bandanna was dark blue, spotted with white flecks - probably birds.

'Thanks Judy,' I said.

'Well, I'll be off then. Here's the number for Kidlington Police Station, but you'll need to call 101 to report it.'

I took the piece of paper that she pressed into my hand.

'If there's anything I can do to help, please call me,' she said.

Just yesterday I would have dismissed Judy as an interfering neighbour, but the kindness in her eyes was genuine and I was surprised how comforting I found the knowledge that I was not alone. I might even have found a new friend.

I watched her walk away, and then turned to face my front door with a new resolve. Whatever I was about to face inside my house, I would deal with it.

'Do you want me to go first?' Matt asked.

I shook my head, took a deep breath and stepped through the open door.

It was like landing in another world - a dream world where everything is familiar but not in the right place. I picked my way across the hall floor, which was strewn with coats and scarves and into the lounge where the devastation was complete. Everything was on the floor - books, magazines, cushions, photo frames, paperwork from my desk, CDs and DVDs. Every shelf had been emptied. The contents of every cupboard had been dragged out and piled up in a heap, on top of which was the remote control for the TV, placed with neatness and precision in the centre, like a flagpole on top of a mountain.

People talk about the violation they feel after a burglary, but until this moment I'd never truly understood what that meant and how bad it could be. This was my safe place, the place I'd retreated to and which had given me the space and time I'd needed to rebuild myself and my life after Sean left. And here it was stripped bare and piled up like a load of old rubbish waiting for its final journey to the tip or the bonfire. If there had been a cushion left on a seat I would have slumped down on it and burst into tears. Instead, I bit my lip in an effort to stop myself crying out, but a strangled sound between a gasp and a sob escaped. Matt reached for my hand, but I ignored him and stumbled into the kitchen.

The pattern was repeated. Tins and packets of food had been swept out of cupboards and left where they'd landed, the cutlery drawer had been emptied into the sink, and plates, glasses and towels were on the floor with cleaning products. The fridge and freezer doors were open and a puddle of water was pooling into a series of mini lakes across the uneven flagstones. And then I saw there was an interesting addition to the chaos that chilled me even more than the careless display of disassembling my life. Spelt out in pebbles on the kitchen table was a single word:

B I T C H.

SIXTEEN

Catherine
Wednesday, April 23rd, 1645

'I DON'T WANT GRANDPA TO come to our house again, Mama. Ever.' Tilly tilted her head and looked at Catherine, a fierce expression shining in her eyes like dark stones on the riverbed, glistening and polished smooth by the flow of the water. Catherine swallowed back darts of nausea, not helped by the smell of warming milk wafting towards her from the pot set over the fire. She had vowed to protect her daughter, but through her own selfishness, she had failed.

She tightened her arms around Tilly who was curled up kitten-like on her lap, and leaned back into the cushions on the wooden settle in the corner of the kitchen on which she had spent an uncomfortable night. She was aware of Helen preparing breakfast, stepping with care around Harry who was squatting on the floor playing a game of soldiers with pieces of wood, and was grateful Helen had refused her offer of help. Her left eye was swollen and half closed. She could only see a fraction of the room. It was as if the drapes on her window to the world had refused to open. She wished they would hide her completely, keep her safe in an imaginary place. Behind her eye her head was throbbing with pain, and she knew there was no safe place. She focused her attention on Tilly.

'Please say you'll stop him. Please.' Her daughter's voice was muffled. Tilly's head was pressing into Catherine ribs, adding to her discomfort.

'Oh my love. I won't let anyone hurt you.' She spoke from the heart, but they were just words, lacking in substance. Her mind was clouded with doubts, former assurance forgotten. How could she be true to that promise?

'Please, Mama. Please.'

The anguish in Tilly's voice was almost too much for Catherine. She wanted to cry out, to beg for forgiveness, anything to keep her daughter happy. But to whom would she beg? The God that she knew did not appear to be compassionate. Her mother? John? Who would help her now? She had brought this onto herself by her own vanity and foolishness. She had opened the doors to the world, dared to live again and this was the result. Was it even her actions that had awakened the bad humours in her father? Perhaps, if she hadn't encouraged Thomas, it would not have upset her father so that his mind slid into such confusion. If she had told Thomas with absolute solemnity that she would rather he left her alone. He was a gentleman. He would have done as she requested. None of this would have happened.

No. She must accept some responsibility for how she had behaved with Thomas, but she rejected the idea that she was also to blame for her father's actions with every ounce of strength she had remaining. Catherine thought back to when she had first noticed the worrying changes in his behaviour. He had always had a tendency towards violent outbursts, which had without doubt escalated in recent times, but were they all linked with Thomas? His political views and recent actions weren't. They were influenced by his frustration with life and what he saw as its unfairness. The details of his past that Helen had supplied were proof that these foundations were laid long ago, years before he had started to look at her and see instead his dead wife.

Whether she was right or not had no bearing on the decisions that Catherine knew she had to make. She closed her eyes, trying to think with clarity. She had to put Tilly's needs ahead of her own. She would do anything to protect her daughter and remove her fear, but how could she keep her father out of her house? It wasn't unusual for a woman to walk out one morning with a black eye, or worse. No-one believed the cover-up story, whatever it was, but it didn't stop them turning the other cheek in a strange parody of the Bible's teaching.

She stroked Tilly's hair, her fingers teasing at the tangles. She had been lucky last night. She had got away. But she knew it could easily have been very different. Perhaps the ring had brought her luck, because she was now certain that the darkness Thomas had spoken of must be her father.

Helen had stopped stirring the porridge and was watching her, their harsh words of yesterday forgiven and forgotten. Catherine knew she was bursting with questions. Questions that Catherine had not been coherent enough to answer last night. Questions that she didn't know if she was ready to answer this morning. She raised her head to meet Helen's enquiring gaze and shrugged her shoulders. It was a gesture of desperation and helplessness.

A loud and persistent hammering on the front door interrupted their silence. Tilly's head snapped up and she whimpered. Catherine tensed, but could not let Tilly see she was also afraid. She cupped the back of her daughter's head and drew it down onto her shoulder. Her other hand gripped the arm of the settle. Then her father's voice brought back the full terror of last night, the moment when she had realised the danger she was in. A low moan gurgled in her throat, and she tried to concentrate on preventing it from escaping and releasing her panic into the room.

'Come on Norris. Open up. I know you've got her in there. Where else could she have gone to?'

He sounded calm, one man appealing to another. Catherine waited, heart pounding, hardly daring to breathe and hoping Edward wouldn't be deceived into thinking he was dealing with someone rational. Tilly's small body pressed closer against her. She could feel her daughter's fear, like a small animal trapped in a snare. The girl pushed her thumb into her mouth and raised her head, seeking reassurance from Catherine with eyes that were wide and too bright. Helen appeared frozen to the spot. They heard the grating scrape of metal against metal as the heavy bolts on the inside of the front door were drawn back. Then Edward's voice, firm and authoritative. 'Bramble. I think it's best if you don't come in.'

'I don't know what she's told you ... but ... Damn it. A man is entitled to respect. Isn't he?' His voice rose, just a notch.

Catherine could sense his anger, bubbling just below the surface. 'Please Edward, don't listen to him.' Her mouth formed the words, but it was a silent plea, inside her head.

'And surely a daughter should be able to feel safe with her own father?' Edward's contempt was loud and clear in his tone of voice.

Tilly whimpered again. 'Shhh,' Catherine whispered and rocked her in a gentle, soothing motion, as if she were still a babe-in-arms.

'She can't hide here for ever. She'll have to go home in the end. Then I'll be waiting for her. Good day to you.'

Catherine closed her eyes and suppressed a shudder. The calmness of his voice made the implied threat even more menacing. She was too exhausted and bruised to think, but she would not give in to him. Her future, and Tilly's, depended on it.

Tilly was shaking now. Catherine held her tight, wondering how she was ever going to find a way out of this situation, but knowing she had to. She wanted to curl up in a quiet corner somewhere, go to sleep, and then wake up to find it had all been a bad dream. But that wasn't going to happen. Wishing for it would just use up valuable time and energy, neither of which she could afford to waste if she was going to find a way of removing both herself and Tilly from the reach of her father.

'You know you can stay here for as long as you need to,' Helen interrupted her thoughts.

Edward appeared in the doorway and nodded his agreement. 'You are my niece, after all. I am expected to extend my protection to the women in my family.'

'Against their own father?' Catherine asked, managing a weak smile. 'But thank you Edward. And for that too,' she waved a hand in the direction of the door.

'I have to go,' Edward addressed Helen. He took her hand and drew her into the hallway. Catherine could hear them talking, their voices a low rumble, but couldn't make out what they were saying. She closed her eyes and winced with pain.

'Mama?'

'It's all right, my love. I'm going to be fine. Just a bit sore, that's all.'

'Come on. Let's eat,' said Helen, bustling back into the kitchen. She carried a pot full of thick porridge to the table. 'Everyone will feel much better after food.' She went to the door and called the older girls. They clattered down the stairs.

'After breakfast you two can take Tilly and go to see Mistress Taylor. We need a poultice for Aunty Cat's eye.'

Tilly was reluctant to leave her mother's side, but Catherine insisted. 'It's quite safe my love. It will do you good to have a little walk and I'll be right here when you get back.'

As soon as the girls had left, Catherine slumped forwards and buried her head in her hands, deflated like one of the plump cushions at the manor with its stuffing ripped out. 'What am I going to do? I can't stay here - it's not fair on you and Edward. But if I go back home, how will I be able to stop him?'

Helen pulled a chair closer and put an arm around her shoulders. Catherine could almost imagine it was her own mother comforting her. She let the fantasy take hold, weave itself through the corners of her mind and flood her veins. She wanted to cling to Helen and the security she offered as if she were a little girl again.

'Why don't you tell me what happened?'

'I was so scared,' she shuddered, remembering his hands groping her and his anger. 'I've never seen him like that before. It was as if he had lost control of his senses. He looked at me and he was seeing her - my mother - and then he called me Cathy. He would have done it - he would have taken me, right there, forced himself on me.'

'You are so alike.' Helen said soothingly, stroking her hair.

Catherine jerked her head back to face her. 'And so is Tilly.'

Helen's eyes widened with shock.

'In a few years' time, will he look at Tilly and see my mother?' The horrifying thought hung between them like a poisonous vapour in the air.

'I keep thinking this is all my fault. He told me to stay away from Thomas. I ignored him. Have I driven him to this?'

'Cat, no. You are not to blame. Nothing gives him the right to behave like that. Nothing.'

'I provoked him. I should have listened to you. I would do anything to protect Tilly. That she witnessed what happened last night is bad enough. I won't allow him to hurt my daughter.' Her tone was fierce and she wondered how far she would have to go to carry out that pledge.

They sat in silence for a few minutes, both absorbed in their own thoughts.

'What's wrong with him Helen? Has he got bad humours? Has something infected his mind? I mean, you heard him, this morning. Does he know I'm Cat? Last night ... it's as if he's lost his reason,' she stopped, unable to voice the words.

The silence that hovered now was thick and heavy with insinuation.

'What can I do Helen? Edward says he will protect us, but how can he?'

Helen was usually so quick with an answer, but she remained silent, and Catherine felt the enormity of her situation tighten around her. Without conscious thought, she had placed some faith and hope in Helen to have a good idea. To unroll a ready-made plan that she could follow. But it was clear that Helen did not have a plan.

'Maybe I could go to Mary and George.'

'Cat ... you don't really think you could do that, even if George would allow it, which he wouldn't.'

Helen's eyes were troubled and her voice was loaded with frustration.

'Would Edward speak for me? Help me to move to another village?'

'But how would you live?'

'I could still work at the manor. If I went to Oddington or Beckley, I could walk back here.'

Even as she said it Catherine knew that wouldn't be a solution - it would bring her and Tilly back into her father's path every day. Helen's expression told her she was thinking the same.

'I could find other work. I could learn to make lace. Sell it at the market. Start again.'

'Oh Cat. Do you know how hard that would be?'

Catherine lowered her head to hide her face and her swollen eye. She knew Helen was right, and she herself was being unrealistic. As close as she was to her aunt, Helen's sympathy and scrutiny exposed her vulnerability.

In a tone that was quite unlike her usual, assertive self, Helen suggested. 'What about Thomas? He said he would take care of you and Tilly, didn't he?'

Catherine jerked her head up, and studied her aunt through puzzled eyes. 'Helen, don't confuse me further. Yesterday you said I was being foolish, and you were right. Thomas has no place in my future.' She shook her head and winced as the violent motion sent shards of pain like arrows shooting into her head. 'No. There is only one way forwards. I have to go back to how things were, just me and Tilly, and find a way to lock my door for ever against my father.'

There was a steely determination in her voice. It mingled with her desperation. As companions they were as mismatched as the fox and hound.

Helen was not to be put off. 'Thomas is a powerful man, though. He has influence,' she said.

Catherine snorted. 'It doesn't make any difference. Him a single man, and me a widow. You know what people would say. It wouldn't be long before the whispers start and the accusations follow. I would be accused of being Thomas's whore, or worse, of trying to bewitch him.'

Before Helen could answer, a firm knocking at the door made them both jump. Panic darted through Catherine's eyes, which were fixed on Helen, before she realised this was a different knock. It had none of the frenzy of her father's earlier. It was the knock of someone of authority. Someone who was used to giving orders and having them followed - like the soldiers of the Earl of Northampton's regiment on the bridge.

There was something in Helen's expression and the way she refused to meet Catherine's eye as she stood up, smoothed her skirts and tucked her hair into her cap. As she watched her aunt leave the room, Catherine was certain Helen was expecting someone. She heard the door opening and then her aunt's quick, light steps accompanied by the more solid, purposeful tread of a man moving along the corridor towards the kitchen. She couldn't tear her eyes from the door. Helen pushed it open, and Catherine thought she had never looked so unsure of herself. The next moment she understood why. Behind Helen stood Thomas Marlow. He had removed his hat and his hair was sticking up on top giving the impression he had dressed in a hurry. His golden eyes glowed in the dim light of the room and the green flecks flashed. Catherine didn't want him to see her like this. She tried to cover her face with her hand, but she was too slow. Shock reflected in his eyes, followed by anger. He took a step towards her and stopped.

For a moment she couldn't understand why Thomas was here. Had he called for Edward? But he must have known Edward would be at the mill by now. Helen's face gave it away. 'I'm sorry, Cat. Edward thought it was for the best. He called on Thomas before he went to work.'

So that's what their whispered conversation had been about. She should have guessed.

'Mistress Meakin. Catherine,' Thomas bowed.

'Why don't you two step outside?' Helen suggested, her hands twisting in a nervous dance in front of her.

Catherine's gaze travelled between Thomas and Helen, noting their unease, as two conspirators caught out in a plot. She stood and shot a look at Helen that she hoped would convey how let down she felt. It was true that she had wanted Helen to give her a solution to her predicament, but not like this. She wanted a choice, not this uncomfortable sensation that decisions were being made for her, and she was being manipulated like a child, swept along in a drama that was about her life but over which she had no control.

Nor was she ready to face Thomas. Her heart and head were full of the anger that was building towards her father, but she pushed them aside, trying to create some space to think. She knew she should carry out her resolution to tell Thomas that she did not wish to see him again, but now he was standing there in front of her she did not have the strength to even try to send him away. Her stomach flipped a few somersaults at the expression in those extraordinary eyes.

He held his arm out to her. She took it and he led her a little way down the garden to the bench on which she had sat with Helen just a few days ago. It was out of sight of the kitchen window. Catherine sat down on the left side, so he couldn't see her battered face, and rested her hands in her lap, eyes focused on the ground. The wood creaked and the air shifted as he joined her and leaned forwards. She sensed him twisting his hat in his hands as if he were searching for something. The seconds stretched into minutes. Several times Catherine opened her mouth to tell him that she must not see him again, but she couldn't frame the words. She waited for him to speak, her apprehension and confusion growing. What had he come here for?

'I blame myself,' he said finally. From the corner of her right eye she watched him straighten his body into an upright position and place his hat down on the bench between them.

'Wait,' he said, as if expecting her to interrupt him, but Catherine was so surprised by his statement that she was far from having anything to say.

'I'm sorry we got interrupted yesterday.'

His fingers brushed the back of her hand and then withdrew. It was the lightest of touches, but it warmed her skin and she looked at her hand, almost expecting to see a scar left behind.

'I shouldn't have let Henry drag me away. Conceited fool that he is. And the errand my father sent me on which meant I had to ride to Oxford. It could have waited. If I'd been able to return to you yesterday, I could have prevented this.'

Catherine was struggling to make sense of his words. 'You are not responsible for my father's actions, sir,' she said.

'If I see your father I won't be responsible for my own actions, may God forgive me. And call me Thomas, please.' His voice, which had been measured until now, rose in pitch.

'Thomas,' she mumbled.

'Have you got the ring?' Remembering that she had resolved to give it back to him, she reached inside the collar of her dress, looped her fingers through the chain and pulled the ring out. She ran her thumb over its flat surface and started to lift the chain over her head, but he stopped her with his hand, interlocking his fingers with hers.

'Look at me Catherine,' he begged.

Heat surged through her fingers. Skin and bone fused as one with his. The connection was stronger than anything she could remember experiencing before, even with John. She had told Helen people would accuse her of bewitching Thomas, but surely it was the other way around. She must break away, but she could not move. She must not allow herself to dream, but still she lifted her head and turned to face him. He raised his other hand and moved it towards her bruised eye. She flinched and shuffled away, until she was pressed against the arm of the bench.

'Don't Catherine. I'm sorry. I'm not going to hurt you.' He withdrew his hands and leaned away from her. They sat for a few minutes, and she began to relax. The silence between them grew more comfortable, broken only by the tweeting of birds as they fluttered around the trees. She focused on a tame robin perched on a nearby branch, head cocked to one side as if listening for something. Now was her chance to speak. She had to tell him that their friendship must end; that he must stop seeking her out. She remained silent, her fingers glowing still with warmth, conscious of his eyes on her.

'Marry me, Catherine?'

His voice was little more than a whisper. She thought she must have misheard him, and sat, motionless. Not daring to move in case he said something else and she missed it. Not daring to answer lest she make a fool of herself. Her head was as empty as one of her sheets of paper before she allowed her thoughts to unravel across its surface.

'Would you do me the honour of becoming my wife?' Now his voice was more forceful, but she couldn't drag her eyes away from the robin. She daren't so much as blink in case she shattered whatever dream she was in. 'Damn it, Catherine! You must know I love you. Haven't I made it perfectly clear these last few weeks?'

She hadn't misheard, but nothing had prepared her for this. The pain in her head was making it difficult to think. Her defences were being dismantled, block-by-block, stone-by-stone. When she had first allowed herself to start to live again, if she hadn't exactly encouraged Thomas's attentions, she hadn't discouraged them either. Had she ever thought he would propose marriage? Never, even in her most vivid dreams. But now he had. She risked a glance at him. The dream didn't shatter. He was still there, but his eyes were restless.

'No ... I mean, you've taken me so by surprise. I ... I don't know what to say. I never thought ... I mean, men like you don't marry women like me,' she stuttered.

'My father has been trying to marry me off for years,' his voice carried a bitter edge of frustration. 'I've resisted every attempt to throw me at some simpering young fool of a girl who will bring more land and status to the family, and probably years of misery to me.'

His tone softened and he inched towards her. His hat fell to the floor, but he seemed not to notice. 'I'm not that kind of man. I want my wife to be someone I can love, respect and desire. I've never met that person until now. Marry me, Catherine.'

This time it wasn't a question.

She ached to believe his words, which were spoken with such sincerity. He was so close she could feel his breath on her cheek. He was staring at her, expression pleading. There was no hint of humour around the set of his mouth, and she knew he was serious. But was it really as simple as that? A few days ago, before she'd understood the expectation that he would marry Lady Frances, and before her father had attacked her, would she have hesitated? Would he have offered?

'I'm 36 years old and I am not dependent on my father - or anyone - for my home or my income. I'll get married to the person I choose, when I choose. And I don't care what anyone else says or thinks.' Impatience and annoyance mingled in his voice, but to Catherine they were overpowered by naivety.

She closed her eyes and allowed herself to imagine the two of them building a future together. It made her want to skip for joy. But deep down she knew his world would never accept her.

'Say something, Catherine, please,' Thomas implored. 'Put me out of my misery.'

Her eyes snapped open. One of his arms was resting along the back of the bench. His fingers plucked at the flowers in the hedge behind her, which was full of blossom. He shredded the petals into tiny pieces that showered the bench and her shoulders, but he seemed not to notice. His eyes were fixed on her, unblinking and so intense, as though they were peeling back her skin to see into her soul and seek out her answer. But she did not know what her answer should be.

Since John had died, she had fought to keep her house, provide for Tilly and survive in this world in which it seemed everything was stacked against a young widow with a child. Last night had shown her just how vulnerable she was. If she was vulnerable, so was Tilly. She had to protect Tilly.

The robin was joined by another and together they hopped onto a higher branch. Catherine turned to watch them. Anything to give her a few precious moments to think. He was offering her a way out. But was it the right thing to do? Wouldn't it be better just to retreat into herself, shut out the rest of the world and devote her life to Tilly? Not to place her trust and her future in the hands of a man.

The robins took flight. She watched until they disappeared over the river, envying them their freedom.

Thomas abandoned the blossom, took her hand and stroked her palm with his thumb. This time the heat was accompanied by a surge of desire.

'You don't know how much I want to say yes,' she said, without moving.

'Say it then. Why deny yourself?'

He sounded baffled, as though he could not understand why anyone would hold back from anything they wanted in life. He wouldn't understand, because he'd never had to deny himself anything he wanted. But then she remembered how he had spoken for that man, Ellis, who had refused to take food from his wife and children to give to the King's men, and she realised that it wasn't selfishness that drove Thomas's actions; it was that he had the strength to stand up for what he believed in, even if it would earn him the derision of his peers.

There was something else in his voice that convinced her that the chance was worth taking. The decision she made in that moment would shape her future, she hoped for the better. She took a deep breath and pushed her doubts away. She had once had a reputation for being reckless. This might prove to be the most reckless step she had taken yet.

'Yes,' she said.

She turned to him and met his eyes. Relief and joy flooded his face, wiping away the tension that had been building in the fine lines around his mouth. He leapt to his feet, gripped both her hands and pulled her up so she was standing, facing him.

'Thank you for making this the happiest day of my life.' He raised each of her hands in turn to his lips and kissed them. 'And I intend to make sure you will remember it as one of the happiest of yours too.'

Catherine had no doubt that he meant every word, but she also had no doubt that this was not going to be an easy path that they had chosen to walk. She had to put her faith and trust in him to somehow smooth that path and prevent them both from tripping continually in its ruts and furrows. A seed of joy and hope planted itself somewhere deep within her, and she vowed to nurture it so it could grow and flourish.

Catherine knew she could love him, maybe she already did, but that wasn't the only emotion that her acceptance of his proposal had unleashed. Mingled with the excitement and promise of a new life was something else altogether. It was an emotion she had no problem identifying. It was fear.

She blocked it out and turned her face, smiling, towards him as he pulled her arm through his, oblivious to her reservations. Together they walked back to the house, watched by Helen who was standing at the kitchen door. Catherine wasn't sure what she should tell her, but Thomas seized the initiative.

'You need have no more fears about your niece Mistress Norris. She has kindly agreed to marry me, so from this day onwards I will ensure the safety of Catherine and Matilda, and any man who wants to harm them will have to answer to me.'

Catherine watched a succession of emotions parade across her aunt's face and had to suppress a strong desire to laugh. It wasn't often she saw Helen speechless. Her face was a portrait of disbelief and amazement. Questioning black eyes flicked from Thomas to Catherine and back to Thomas again. There was an awkward silence, before Helen's caring and nurturing instincts took over.

'Have you had breakfast? Let me get you some bread and ale.'

Thomas accepted and sat down at the table. Helen bustled about the kitchen. Catherine returned to the settle by the fire. Thomas had recovered his composure and started talking to Helen about Edward and the mill, but his gaze was fixed on Catherine and a broad smile appeared painted to his face, as impossible to remove as it would be to pluck the sun from the sky.

After consuming two mugs of ale and half a small loaf of bread, Thomas rose and bowed his head. 'I must leave you now, as I have some pressing business matters that I have put off already for too long.' He spoke as if it was the last thing he wanted to do. 'But I will return this evening, with your permission of course,' he directed the question towards Helen, who nodded her assent.

After Thomas had left, Helen's power of speech returned. She sat down next to Catherine and bombarded her with questions. Catherine recounted the conversation in the garden.

'Why don't you look happy?' Helen demanded.

'I am happy,' Catherine protested. She leaned forward, planted her elbows on her knees, and rested her chin in her cupped hands. Helen's fingers tapped an impatient beat on the settle's smooth arm. Catherine sighed, exhausted through lack of sleep and the effort of trying to express her deepest emotions in words.

'I don't think he's thought this through. He says he doesn't care what people think and maybe that's true. But he's always been Thomas Marlow. Treated with respect. Men look up to him. He's never experienced anything other than that. It's as if he doesn't understand that for people like me there is a different reality. Will the two be able to mix? I doubt it.'

'Don't tell me you thought about turning him down?' Helen's voice was loaded with incredulity.

'You did! Cat, why?'

Catherine's head was beginning to throb again through the effort of trying to explain how she was filled with both the deepest joy and an uncontrollable fear. She stood and moved closer to the hearth, drawn to the warmth and security of the fire. She turned back to face Helen, the fire between them, flickering flames reflecting in her eyes.

'Have you forgotten all those times you've cautioned me not to expect anything from Thomas? That a future for us together would be impossible?'

'Of course not. But this is different. He's asked you to marry him.'

Catherine laughed. It was a bitter sound that was close to hysteria. 'That doesn't make it any less impossible. Do you think Richard Marlow is going to congratulate his son on his choice of wife? The Marlows might have been good to my father, but there is a line and I'm about to cross it.'

'You're right. It won't be easy. Nothing ever is. But you've accepted him. Now it's up to both of you to make it work.'

'In time, will he come to resent me though? Hate me even? I couldn't bear that.' Catherine's voice was little more than a whisper.

'I can't answer that. I think you have to trust him.'

The girls returned with the poultice and Catherine shook her head to stop Helen telling them. She wanted to explain to Tilly properly, in her own time, just the two of them. She allowed Helen to apply the poultice, biting her lip to stop herself crying out in pain.

Catherine put off going back to her house to collect some belongings until the middle of the afternoon when she dare delay no longer.

'Don't go, Cat,' Helen was uneasy. 'Tilly can borrow what she needs from my girls and you are welcome to anything of mine.'

'I must go,' Catherine replied. 'I have lots of linens that will need to go back to the manor, and I want my sketching materials.'

'Then I'll come with you.'

'No. I don't need a chaperone, or a bodyguard. I'm not going to let my father's behaviour force me to remain behind a locked door.'

'Maybe,' Helen nodded. 'But you could wait a day or two. Once it's known that you are to marry Thomas Marlow, he won't dare threaten you again.'

'I'll be all right Helen. Besides, if I go now he'll either be at work still or in the King's Head, so there's no chance of me bumping into him.'

'Be quick then. If you're not back here in half an hour, I will come looking for you.'

The brave face that Catherine had presented to Helen evaporated in the breeze as soon as she left the house. She set out at a brisk pace, but every step she took with her left foot set off a series of reverberations that travelled through her body and convened as a jarring pain behind her eye.

The village was quiet. Unnaturally quiet. She couldn't see any soldiers over by the bridge, or hear the hooves of a horse, or even the wheels of a carriage rattling in the distance. The atmosphere was brooding. It had the lethargy of a sultry July afternoon when the heat had sent everyone - man and beast - into the woods or down to the river, scuttling for shade in which to sleep, or water in which to cool down. But this was a chilly April afternoon. The sky was dull and the air was heavy with the promise of rain. As she crossed the churchyard she could see a single figure leaning against the stocks at the Cross Tree. After her father, it was the person she most did not want to meet - Lady Frances's brother, Henry. She hesitated, and considered turning around to take the longer route through the village, following the river before turning to skirt past the manor, but it was too late. He had seen her. There was no way to avoid him. She pulled the hood of the cloak she had borrowed from Helen so it was snug around her face, hoping to hide her eye from view, and focused on the road beyond.

'You appear to have had some sort of accident Mistress Meakin,' he said as she drew near, his voice mocking.

She lowered her head. 'I tripped,' she mumbled, hating the lie but hoping he would accept it and let her pass.

He laughed. 'Are you sure you haven't upset someone?' He took a step towards her, blocking her way. 'Lots of people find women like you upsetting. I'm sure my sister would be upset if she knew about the clandestine meetings you've been having with her betrothed.'

She shrank back from him, wondering what he meant. Who was he accusing her of meeting? Then she realised. He meant Thomas. Betrothed. To Lady Frances. The shock of hearing those words spoken, confirming what she had herself discerned about the expectations of others, settled like a lead weight in her stomach and pinned her to the spot. Unable to contradict him, she forced herself to look him in the eye and speak with confidence. 'I don't know what you mean, sir. Please let me pass.'

She cast around hoping to see someone else who might claim Henry's attention, but there was no-one in sight. He stepped aside and she hurried past him. 'I would hate to see my sister hurt,' he called after her in a soft voice that was loaded with menace.

Once again, she felt sullied by his insinuations. She wanted to run, but to do so would imply she was guilty of something, and she knew his eyes were following her. If he wanted to watch her, she would show him she had not a care in the world. She slowed her pace to a stroll and held her head high, maintaining her composure until she was safely behind her own front door, and she had bolted it behind her. Then, she sank down onto the floor, knees drawn up in front of her and took a series of deep breaths, waiting for her heart rate to return to normal whilst her thoughts raced on ahead.

Thomas was an honourable man. He wouldn't have asked her to marry him if he was already committed to another. She remembered his declaration that he loved her, and a reassuring glow spread its warmth from her toes to her fingertips, driving away the chill of the day and Henry's words. Thomas was speaking what he believed to be the truth when he'd told her there was no understanding between him and Lady Frances, and that he had never led her to expect anything from him. But others had a different perception.

Catherine realised she was shaking. A path that had been fraught with difficulties and obstructions to begin with had suddenly become even more treacherous. In agreeing to marry Thomas she had made herself an enemy of the most powerful family in the village. She knew with certainty there was no way they would accept her as his wife. Would they also accuse her of using possibly nefarious and immoral means to steal a rich husband for herself? The husband they had anticipated for their own daughter.

Catherine sought reassurance in her own, familiar space, but it was no longer there. Like smoke when you open a window, it had vanished. The fire had died through lack of attendance. The air was cool, and stale with the tang of meat that was past its best hovering as if trapped in the folds of a heavy cloak. Her bunches of herbs hung lifeless from the beams. She could no longer imagine feeling safe here. She pushed herself to her feet. The table was littered with dirty bowls and an overturned mug. She picked them up and her fingers brushed the dull surface of the table. They stuck to whatever had been spilt there and left to dry - ale probably. She withdrew her hand, and rushed to the back door, opened it and gulped in the fresh air, fighting down the nausea that was rising within her. She looked out at the view she loved. Inhaled it. Allowed it to calm her breathing. The cloud was low, and she knew it would be raining over Otmoor.

Her cart was propped against the wall. Splodge was asleep beneath it. She picked it up and the cat opened one eye. Seeing that his shelter had been removed, he stretched and stalked down the slope of the garden, casting an accusatory glance over his shoulder before jumping up onto the wall in a single graceful movement, his back turned towards her.

'Sorry Splodge,' she said.

She carried the cart into the kitchen and loaded it up with the items she thought they might need in the next few days: Tilly's gown; boots, pattens and cloaks for them both, her sewing materials and all the linens she had been working on for the manor. She climbed the steps to their small bedroom and reached under the mattress.

Her fingers probed the straw until they found the loose patch into which she had pushed the pouch that contained the few valued possessions she had, including the coins that John had left her and those she had been able to save by living frugally. She pulled the pouch out and secured it around her waist with a length of string.

She was halfway back down the wooden ladder when a loud rap at the front door almost caused her to lose her footing and fall the remaining three steps to the bottom. She cowered for a moment, before her reason took over. Her father might knock, but he wouldn't wait for her to answer. He would just push the door. But no-one ever called on her except Helen.

Another rap, louder this time, was followed by a male voice. 'Mistress Meakin. A word with you if I may.'

The voice was polite but there was an undertone of suppressed anger that Catherine detected at once. She also recognised the owner. Richard Marlow. She wished the throbbing behind her eye would go away so she could think. Today wasn't going to get any easier.

'Just a moment,' she called, willing her voice to be calm.

She tucked her hair neatly back into her cap, unbolted and opened the door. He recoiled when he saw her face. Perhaps Thomas had not given him the full story, but she had no doubt about why he was standing on her doorstep.

Richard Marlow's tall, dark frame filled the space, blocking out the light. He towered over her, his neck curving to angle his head so he was looking down on her. He glared through hooded, cold, grey eyes, nostrils flaring. He resembled a vulture looming over its prey. She watched the expression in his eyes change from shock to distaste as his gaze moved over her shoulder and roamed over the cramped room beyond. He did not remove his hat.

She pulled her shoulders back and reminded herself that she had done nothing wrong. 'Sir?'

'I'm sure you know why I'm here. This ridiculous notion my son has that you and he are to be married,' he tapped his cane on the stone in front of her. 'I want your assurance that this is nonsense, and that you understand that a marriage between my heir and a woman like you is out of the question.' He emphasised the word 'you', smearing it with contempt.

Catherine fought to contain her anger - not just with the arrogance of the man, but with her own foolishness and Thomas's naivety. How had she ever let him persuade her that this was possible? She should have listened to her own instinct.

She gripped the doorframe to stop her hand from shaking and answered as confidently as she could. 'I wouldn't presume to speak for the intentions of your son, sir. I am an honest woman. If you are displeased, I beg that you discuss this with him.'

He spat on the doorstep, narrowly missing her skirts.

'I would see you dead before you are married to my son, madam.' He turned and she watched him march down the track, stumble in a pothole, and vanish onto the High Street.

Catherine closed the door and leaned against it, overcome with weariness. With crystal clarity, Richard Marlow's words had exposed the extent of their folly - hers and Thomas's. The likes of Lady Frances, her brother, Lady Gilder and Sir Henry would never welcome her - the woman who mends their laundry - to their dining table. She pictured the scene. Under different circumstances she would have found it funny. Lady Frances with the icy blue stare forced to replace that haughty disdain with polite conversation. Lady Gilder having to wear a smile and entertain the woman who had usurped her own daughter for the affections of the most eligible bachelor in the area.

They would be horrified, but it would be no better for her. She couldn't function in their social sphere - even if they were prepared to make it easy for her, which they wouldn't be. She had nothing in common with people like them.

The church clock chimed the hour. It was four in the afternoon. The effort of defending herself had drained Catherine's final reserves of energy. She wanted to retreat into her own space. That was not possible though. She had to leave, or she would risk her father finding her, either at home or their paths crossing in the village. Legs trembling, she forced herself to cross the room where she closed and secured the back door after throwing the little meat that remained in the stockpot to Splodge, who had forgotten his earlier indignation and was now sitting at the bottom of the steps cleaning his paws. He received it with a purr and sank his incisors into it.

She added a few more items to the pile on the cart, including her satchel containing her precious drawing materials, pulled the harness over her head and left her home, locking the door behind her for the last time.

To avoid another encounter with Henry, and keep her distance from the King's Head where there was a possibility she could run into her father, Catherine walked back along the river. It had been less than an hour since she had left Helen's, but in that brief time the village had woken up. As she had predicted though, no-one commented on her face. A few raised their eyebrows, but most just looked embarrassed and hurried away to avoid engaging her in conversation.

The inns were busier than they had been earlier, men who had finished work already enjoying a jug or two of ale before returning to their homes. The air was still. A clatter of horse's hooves broke the silence. A youth wearing the Earl of Northampton's colours riding a large bay mare at speed crossed the bridge. Catherine watched him urge the horse up the hill. She judged he had probably reached the Prince's Arms before the sound of hooves hitting the cobbles stopped. The harness of her cart was rubbing her shoulder. She adjusted it and hastened back to the safety of Helen's house.

The front door opened before Catherine reached it. Tilly ran out and wrapped her arms around her mother's waist, making it impossible for Catherine to walk any further.

'Mama,' she whimpered. 'You've been gone for so long. I was worried you weren't coming back.'

'My love, of course I'll always come back.' She unwrapped Tilly's arms and crouched down so she was on the same level as the little girl. 'I'll never leave you. Promise.'

Catherine hugged her daughter and stood to remove the harness. 'Help me unload,' she said. They placed all of their belongings in a neat pile inside the door, watched by Harry from the bottom of the stairs.

'Aunty Cat, Aunty Cat,' he squealed when they had finished, holding out his arms. She picked him up, took Tilly's hand and the three of them edged down the narrow corridor into the kitchen where Helen was peeling turnips.

'You're getting too heavy for this, little man,' Catherine told Harry, putting him down in a chair at the table. He giggled and proudly rubbed his tummy.

'Harry, be gentle with your aunt, she's sore.'

'He's all right,' Catherine said, ruffling his unruly red curls. It was true that she was sore, although the epicentre of her pain had shifted. The throbbing behind her eye had subsided into a dull ache, but her head was full of the threats she had just received from two of the most powerful men she knew. Anger, fear and doubt were pressing down on her, swinging from one to another and spinning her around until the effort of trying to put them into some sort of order made her dizzy.

Helen bustled around the kitchen, sending conspiratorial smiles in Catherine's direction whenever she thought the children weren't looking. Catherine was unable to respond. She couldn't tell Helen what had been said by Richard Marlow and Henry in front of Tilly and Harry, but the effort of pretending she was fine for the children was as much as she could manage. Playing a part for Helen as well was beyond her. Helen's smiles faded and instead she tried raising her eyebrows as a question or mouthing 'What's wrong?' With a shrug of her shoulders. Catherine just shook her head and turned away. Although she didn't feel like drawing, she took out a fresh piece of paper and fiddled with a charcoal stick. As it always did, the simple motion soothed her and the effort of trying to avoid Helen's questioning eyes was a relief.

It was nearly dark when Edward burst into the house, calling for Helen. The urgency in his voice sent her scurrying out of the kitchen. Curious, Catherine followed. Through the open front door she could see Edward's horse, head down, sniffing the verge for anything tasty to eat. Edward had taken a few steps into the corridor. His hat was askew, and his cheeks were flushed.

'Soldiers - Parliament's not the King's - have crossed the ford down at the mill,' he panted. 'Stay inside. Bolt the door. Don't open it to anyone except me. I'm going to see what's happening.'

Helen had no chance to speak. He left as quickly as he had arrived, leaping back on to his horse and spurring it towards the bridge. Helen did as he had instructed, dragging the heavy bolts into position. Harry tugged at her skirts.

'Sojers! Want to see the sojers Mama.'

'You see soldiers every day, Harry. These are only different by the colours they are wearing.' Helen sounded calm, but Catherine knew from her tone of voice that she was worried.

'So, my father was right about one thing then,' Catherine observed. 'He said Parliament had a new army. But what are they doing here? Are they going to try to take the bridge back?'

There had been times, in recent years, when the Parliamentarians had held the bridge and occupied Islip, but since the King had been in Oxford, his regiments had been firmly in control.

Helen held her finger to her lips. Catherine nodded, understanding that her aunt didn't want to alarm the children.

'Come, it's time for supper.'

The next hour was tense. They could hear horses and foot soldiers passing within feet of the house on the track outside. Helen closed the kitchen door to shut the noise out.

Harry could not contain his excitement and kept demanding to be allowed to see the 'sojers'. The girls, including Tilly, were scared. They stared wide-eyed at the door as if expecting it to be battered down at any moment. Catherine was also jumpy, dreading the loud hammering that would announce her father's arrival.

'Girls, help with the supper please.' Helen gave each of them jobs to do - some that weren't necessary. Catherine realised that she was trying to take their minds away from what might be happening outside. She shook off her own melancholy and piled more wood on the fire, comforted by its rosy glow.

When Edward did return, Thomas was with him.

'There's been a skirmish on the bridge,' Edward explained in answer to Helen's questioning. She poured ale for him and Thomas and gestured to them to move into the front parlour.

'Keep an eye on Harry, girls, we'll only be a few minutes.'

Catherine smiled at Tilly to reassure her. 'It'll be fine my love,' she whispered. She followed the others, aware of Tilly's anxious eyes fixed on her. The parlour was cold and uninviting. Edward raked the coals in the grate and added some dry kindling to coax a flame.

'Tell us,' urged Helen. 'But keep your voices low. The girls are scared.'

'I don't think they need to worry,' Thomas's soft tone was reassuring, but Catherine was getting better at reading his expressions and she thought his eyes told a different story.

'It would have been worse, but Northampton's regiment had already retreated,' Edward chipped in.

'But why?' Helen's curls caught the light from the now glowing fire as she shook her head. 'They have to guard the bridge, why did they run as soon as they were under threat?'

'They didn't run. Northampton had advance warning somehow that Cromwell was leading his new army this way and knew he didn't have sufficient numbers to engage them, so he retreated.'

'And left us to their mercy?' Helen demanded.

'Cromwell's men are already making themselves at home in

the inns. There's plenty of entertainment to occupy them for the evening. They won't be bothered with much more than that.'

'And what about tomorrow?'

'I expect they'll be on their way.' Edward turned his attention from the fire and moved to Helen's side. He put his hands on her shoulders and kissed her forehead. 'Cromwell is after bigger fish than us. He's got the King in his sights. If the King manages to meet up with Prince Rupert, he will be stronger. Cromwell needs to make sure that doesn't happen.'

Thomas nodded his agreement. 'He's an ambitious man. He isn't going to hang around in Islip whilst he has a chance to make a name for himself elsewhere.'

He turned to Catherine and took her hands in his. 'I heard something else today that I think you should know.'

Catherine looked at him. He was worried about something, she was certain of it. She had thought it was the arrival of Cromwell and his men in Islip, but perhaps it wasn't. Perhaps it was something concerning her. Still reeling from her encounters with Henry and Richard earlier, which she was yet to share with anyone, she wondered what more this day could throw at her. A cold fist of fear squeezed her insides.

Thomas stroked her palm.

'What ... what is it?' She had to force the words out, not sure she wanted to hear his news, whatever it was.

'It's your father. I hear he was handing out pamphlets in Kidlington. For the Levellers. I saw one. Portraying the King and his supporters as living in luxury, profiting from the labour of hard-working men, who, in spite of their efforts, still struggle to earn enough to feed their families. Asking men to join their cause for a more even distribution of power.'

Thomas paused.

'Inflammatory material, intended to stir up ill will, and probably succeeding. The King's men saw him. He got away from them, but he's now a wanted man.'

Catherine exhaled, surprised to find she had been holding her breath. 'Where would he go?'

'There's no place for him to hide in Islip,' Edward said. 'Not after what he's done. I won't protect him and I'm sure Thomas won't either.'

Thomas nodded his agreement, watching Catherine with concern etched into his features.

'It's all right,' she said. 'I'm all right.'

The children were reluctant to go to bed. They ate their meal in the kitchen. Harry's head drooped with tiredness. Edward carried him upstairs. The girls and Tilly were too scared to move, so Helen gave them blankets and allowed them to settle in front of the fire. At the back of the house the night was silent, but from the dining room at the front, the sounds of an invading army settling on the village penetrated the thick stone walls with ease; the rattle of bridles, horses neighing, men's voices raised in laughter or argument, feet in heavy boots stamping past the house. On several occasions Edward went to the window and tweaked the curtains, positioning himself so he could look out but at the same time block Helen and Catherine's view.

Thomas stayed for supper. The talk during the meal was all of the Parliamentarians and what the King's next actions would be. Catherine contributed little to the conversation. Her head was busy examining Thomas's news about her father and trying to work out how she felt about him. She was relieved that he would not be able to carry out his threats, but worried about what might become of him. Try as she might, she couldn't banish the idea that the King's men may have been given information about his activities. Could Thomas have informed on him? If so, did it matter? Whatever he had done, he was still her father, and she didn't like to think of him in danger somewhere. But she was not his keeper.

Her bigger dilemma was how to tell Thomas what his own father had said.

After they had dined, Helen insisted Catherine remain seated. 'Edward will help me clear, won't you dear?' He started to retort, but was silenced by the look she flashed him, and followed her with an uncharacteristic meekness to the kitchen.

As soon as Helen and Edward had left the room Thomas moved to Catherine's side. He positioned his chair so he was facing her and took her hands in his. 'What's wrong my darling? Are you sure you're not thinking about your father.'

She tried to pull back from him, but he wouldn't let her. The tenderness in his eyes carried through to his voice and she blinked and swallowed hard.

'No, it's this. Us. Don't you see it's impossible?'

'What's happened Catherine?'

She stared at the floor, not sure where to start or what to say.

'Tell me,' he demanded. 'Is it your father?'

She shook her head and couldn't help a bitter sound escaping her lips.

'Then what?'

'Yours,' she said. His hands tightened on hers and in the dim light his eyes darkened. 'He made it quite clear to me that under no circumstances would he permit you to marry someone like me. Oh, and that was after Henry had warned me that he would look very unfavourably on anyone who came between his sister and her 'betrothed'.'

Thomas dropped her hands and sprang to his feet. 'How dare he.' He did not raise his voice, but the fury in his tone was unmistakable.

Catherine wasn't sure to which of them he was referring. She waited for him to say more.

'It's my life, not his.'

He paced across the room and leaned against the fireplace, looking into the flames that lapped the crackling logs.

'And Henry. What the devil is he about?' He turned back to Catherine. 'I told you before, there is no understanding between me and Frances. Anyone who says otherwise is lying.'

'But don't you see?' She cried out with frustration. He seemed determined not to accept the difficulties of their situation. 'Whether they are lying or not, if that's what people believe, it puts me in an impossible position. Your family will never accept me, and others will accuse me of who knows what.'

Thomas returned to her side and clasped her hands again. 'I don't care what other people believe. And if my family put their views above my happiness, well, I can live without them as well. We'll go away, start again somewhere else. I've been thinking of late that it would be good to get away from Islip for a while. There are other ways to serve the King, and God.'

He put his arm around her and drew her towards him.

She buried her head in his shoulder so he would not see her eyes filling with tears, and allowed his optimism to wash over her. It was a good feeling, leaning on someone else, and after the tension and seesawing of emotions of the day she longed to give in, to place herself and her trust entirely in the hands of another. But deep down inside, so deep she found it difficult to expose, there was a niggling doubt that try as she might, she could not suppress. Thomas was a harbinger of her future, but whether that was for good or bad she could not tell.

SEVENTEEN

Hannah

I BLINKED AND RUBBED MY eyes as if that would block it out, or when I opened them the letters would have rearranged themselves into a nicer word. But they hadn't. Someone must really hate me.

The room was starting to spin and my vision was fuzzy with black spots around the edges. I backed away from the table, stretching out my hands, searching with my fingers for something to hold onto. I heard Matt's voice, very faint and muted as if from a distance, and then my legs seemed to dissolve beneath me and I started to fall.

The next thing I remember was hearing the gentle lap of water. Even through the fuddle in my brain I knew I was on my deck, although I had no memory of how I'd got there. Strong arms were wrapped around me and I felt warm and safe. I wanted to stay there and not have to think about who had done this, and why. I didn't want to step foot back inside my house.

Matt must have felt me stir.

'Hannah.' His voice was so gentle and there was something else there too that I struggled to identify. Was it worry, or shock maybe?

'You gave me a fright there for a moment. If I hadn't caught you and you'd banged your head on the floor, we'd be going to hospital.'

I twisted around to face him.

'Are you okay?'

'I think so,' I said. 'Who hates me so much that they would do that?'

Matt didn't answer, but tightened his arms around me. For several minutes we stayed like that. I couldn't help thinking back to the last time we had been out here on my deck together and how different the atmosphere had been then. It wasn't even two weeks ago, but so much had happened in that short space of time.

'We need to call the police.'

I shuddered. I knew he was right, but the thought filled me with dread, as if doing so would take away any shred of hope that this might all be a mistake, a figment of my imagination, or a bad dream.

'I'll do it,' he said. 'You stay here.'

I propped myself up on the cushions and watched him walk to the kitchen, pulling his phone out of his pocket as he went. Trespass jumped onto the deck and rubbed her face around my feet, purring. Cats are very perceptive creatures. She appeared to sense my mood. She sat back and looked at me, lazy eyes blinking. Then she stretched out by my side, rested her head on her front paws and went to sleep. It felt good to have her there. It was as if she was offering me her support and affection without conditions or expectations - except perhaps the odd tin of tuna.

I don't know how long we sat like that. Matt brought coffee, which was strong and sweet. I don't take sugar, but he'd obviously read the manual for how to treat someone in shock. At least he hadn't taken it so far as to serve me tea - that I would have found difficult to forgive. I forced the coffee down because I didn't want to appear ungrateful, and I was soon rewarded with the restorative rush of sugar into my system. It wasn't enough to make me want to return indoors, though, so when the police arrived Matt met them at the front door and brought them to the deck.

'Nice spot you've got here,' the female officer remarked, pulling up a cushion and squatting down next to me.

'Not a pretty sight in there though. You okay?' She was tall and very slim with short bobbed mousy hair and brown-rimmed glasses.

She held out a hand. 'I'm PC Fletcher. This is my colleague, PC Jackson,' she nodded at the male officer, who shuffled his feet and seemed awkward, as if he wasn't sure whether to join us on the deck or remain standing. He opted for something between the two and perched on the edge with his feet planted flatly on the ground. His hair was so close-cropped he almost appeared bald but his skin had the smooth texture of a young man. He was probably fresh out of training school.

'We've got another officer inside, dusting for prints.' PC Fletcher flipped to a clean page of her notebook. 'Do you want to tell me what happened?'

I knew she was trying to do that police thing, putting you at ease - victim or suspect - but it was still a strangely worded question. Whether I wanted to tell her had nothing to do with it, and surely it was pretty obvious what had happened.

She scribbled on her pad while I talked.

'What time did you leave yesterday?'

'Mid morning. About 11.'

'Who knew you were going to be away overnight?'

'No-one. Well, my mum of course, and Matt.'

'And what time was the break-in discovered?'

'I don't know. You'd have to ask Judy Daniels. She lives just down the road.'

'We know Judy,' PC Jackson said. He did have a voice then. I was beginning to wonder.

'Have you been able to work out if anything has been taken Miss Whittaker?' PC Fletcher took over again as if he hadn't spoken. Physically she may appear as pliable and insignificant as a young tree, but I suspected she was formidable.

'No,' I said. 'I mean, I haven't gone through everything in there, obviously, but there was nothing here worth taking. I had anything of value with me.'

'Oh, why's that?' I sensed a spark of something in that question, as though she was no longer just going through the motions of an enquiry that we all knew would go nowhere except onto the local crime statistics.

'Because I thought someone had been in my house.' I explained about the pictures in the wrong order and the colours in the jewellery box. Even to my own ears I sounded like some kind of nutcase. She was never going to take me seriously, but she did.

'That's quite some attention to detail.'

She tapped her pen against her top lip, deep in thought.

'What do you think they were looking for?'

I told her about the ring and showed her a photo on my phone. She took it from me and I thought her eyes widened before she bent her head over it - whether to stop me from seeing her expression or to take a closer look I couldn't say. I didn't tell her about the shocks.

'Where is it now?'

'I handed it in to the Finds Liaison Officer in Witney this morning.'

'She also took all of her photography equipment with her.' Matt had watched and listened in silence so far. I wondered why he'd added that. It was as if he was trying to deflect their attention away from the ring. He was one of the few people who knew about it, and knew the house would be empty last night. I didn't want to suspect him, but right now I was seeing villains lurking under every shrub. I wasn't sure I'd be able to stay here tonight.

'It's the only other stuff I have that's worth anything. And it's well known that I'm a photographer - I have my cards up all over the place.'

PC Fletcher grunted. 'Who knew about the ring?'

'Matt, my mum, Joel and the builder who was driving the digger when I found them. That's all. Oh, and Lauren.'

'Joel and Lauren?'

'Professor Joel Fielding - works at the university and is an expert in the Civil War - and Lauren Martin, my assistant at work,' Matt explained.

'What work would that be?' She flicked back through her notebook, searching for something. 'Mr Denton?'

'Denton's Collectibles. I specialise in old coins.'

'I know nothing about old coins,' I said. 'I took them to him to find out what they were.'

'And that's how you two met?'

I nodded.

'I see,' said PC Fletcher. Her tone insinuated that was significant somehow. She was beginning to get up my nose now.

'And where were you last night Mr Denton?'

'At home. I'm a bit behind with some paperwork. I needed to catch up,' behind her back, he winked at me and smiled. I hoped PC Jackson hadn't noticed. He appeared to just be there for decoration, but I bet he was missing nothing and they'd be having a good old chat about us after they left.

'Can anyone vouch for that?' PC Fletcher looked up from her notebook and fixed her inscrutable gaze on Matt.

'No, sorry. I was alone all evening.'

She let her eyes linger on Matt for a moment before turning back to me. 'We can rule your mum out since you were with her last night, but we'll need to talk to Professor Fielding, Miss Martin and the builder.'

'I can give you Lauren's number and Joel's,' Matt said.

'Dave's card is on the corkboard in the kitchen,' I offered.

'Do you think this break-in is connected with the other?' I know it sounded like a dumb question, but it just didn't feel right. And Islip has virtually zero crime. The occasional break-in to an outbuilding or a shed, teenagers messing around by the railway line, or the odd bit of road-rage on the bridge when a cyclist meets a tractor maybe, but not proper crime.

'At this stage we keep our options open, but I would say it's likely.'

'But this is different. I mean it feels different.'

PC Fletcher tapped her pen on her lip again and the sunlight glinted off her glasses. 'Go on,' she said. 'You're right, and I'd like to hear your thoughts.'

'Because whoever broke in before did it carefully so I wouldn't know anyone had even been in the house.'

'How did they gain access?' PC Jackson was rewarded with another scathing glance for interrupting.

'Through the bathroom window.' I pointed. 'That one there. My extractor fan is broken and the window's very small, so I never thought of it as a security risk.'

PC Fletcher grunted as though she couldn't believe the stupidity of some people. 'Carry on,' she invited.

'So, before, they searched as if they were looking for something, putting everything back into place - or almost into place - so I wouldn't know anyone had been in my house. This time, well, I don't know how they got in ...'

'Front door lock forced,' PC Jackson risked it again.

' ... but this time, it's like they've gone out of their way to tell me they've been into every millimetre of my personal space. But it's not frenzied. It's not as if they've thrown things around at random when ransacking the place. The way they've done it feels very precise. And that word on the table,' I shuddered. 'This is more like they're doing it to spook me - and I can tell you it's working.'

'Mmm,' PC Fletcher nodded. 'Can you think of anyone who might want to do that, anyone who might have a grudge against you?'

I stared at her, connections in my brain starting to fall into place. She was watching me as I struggled to find the words, and so was Matt.

'What is it Miss Whittaker?'

I swallowed hard. 'A few days ago, my ex-fiancé turned up, out of the blue, at my studio. He started sending me text messages as well. And then, later that day, I thought I heard someone calling to me when I was in the garden. There was no-one here though. That evening was when I realised someone had been in my house.'

And Matt had sent that text message to Sean as well.

'But, it can't have been Sean - the first break-in happened days before he turned up again and he doesn't know where I live. He's never been here - I bought this house after he'd left. And this ... that ... in there,' I directed my gaze towards the house. 'I can't believe he hates me that much.'

'What's his name?' PC Fletcher was poised with her pen.

'Sean Fitzpatrick.'

'Do you know where he lives?'

I shook my head.

'No matter, we'll find him.' She unravelled her long legs and scrambled to her feet. 'Can we have a look upstairs?'

'You don't want me to come with you, do you? Because I'm not sure I can face it.'

'No,' she shook her head. 'We can handle it.'

PC Jackson followed her into the house. Matt leaned against the deck, arms folded in front of him. A moment later the bathroom window opened and PC Fletcher stuck her head out.

'What's it like up there?' I called, hoping that they might have left it alone.

'Much the same as downstairs,' she said. I was glad she didn't elaborate, although I supposed I would have to face it at some point.

The thought of the police poking and prodding at my personal space was almost as unsettling as the break-in itself. As I watched the house, I could see PC Jackson standing in my bedroom with his back to the window. I imagined him looking at my possessions. What if they'd tipped my underwear drawer out and left all my knickers on display for him to see. I felt a flush creeping into my cheeks and I closed my eyes, hoping to obliterate the image.

We waited in silence for them to finish their inspection. It didn't take long and soon they approached us again, strolling across my patchy lawn as if it was just another day's work. I suppose it was for them.

'I think we're finished here. We'll be in touch Miss Whittaker.'

'I'll see you out,' Matt offered.

I didn't object. Tall as PC Fletcher was, Matt towered over her as they walked back up the garden. Trespass diverted my attention, nudging my hand and purring in what felt like a gesture of solidarity, a girl power reassurance that we are strong and we will survive. I'd forgotten she was there, and I rolled onto my side to stroke her.

Trespass made me feel a bit better, but even so I wasn't ready to go back into the house just yet. At the mere thought of it my palms started to feel clammy and I knew a mild panic was waiting to pounce and knock me out.

'We should sort it out,' Matt suggested. His voice made me jump. 'The police said it's okay.'

'No,' I shook my head.

'Your call,' he said. He sat down next to me on the deck and Trespass rolled over for him.

Traitress.

'So what are we going to do with this gourmet picnic that I slaved over this morning?' I twisted around to look at him. His lips were twitching and he raised his eyebrows. I wondered if he made them do the Hercule Poirot at will or if they just did it anyway.

'You mean Mr M&S slaved over the picnic,' I teased him back. It took an effort but it felt good as well. To act normally. As if nothing had happened. 'We should eat it of course.' I'd had nothing since that small bowl of cereal at my mum's and I was surprised to find I was hungry.

The pristine paint of my boat caught my eye and I knew what I needed to do. The call of the soothing water was irresistible. I pulled myself onto my knees so I could reach up and rest my head on Matt's shoulder with my arms wrapped around his neck. We stayed like that for a few seconds, and the tension that had seized me since the moment I walked into my house earlier and saw the mess started to release me from its iron grip.

Matt was not convinced when I told him I wanted to take the boat out.

'What, that boat?' He asked, with a flick of his head towards the river.

'Yes,' I laughed at the expression of horror on his face. I had to admit that when you looked at Matt next to the boat it did look a bit preposterous.

'I'll go and get the picnic hamper - it's still in the car.' I could hear the reluctance in his voice but I wasn't about to let him off. My brain was chugging back into gear, and I remembered I needed to show him the picture.

'Could you get my overnight bag out of my boot? There's something in there I need to show you.'

I threw him the keys.

We loaded the boat and added some cushions from the deck. Matt offered to row. I admired his chivalry, but his performance had us going around in wobbly circles until I was shaking with laughter. He pushed the oars to me, and the motion of rowing helped to banish my tension even further. I tried to focus on my rhythm and not allow any other thoughts to enter my mind - like the conviction that I would never feel safe or comfortable in my house again. It had been my home, but now it was four walls and a roof through which someone had trampled their hate.

In the field next to my garden two tents had been erected. Not the sort you'd go on holiday in these days. They are all bright colours, lightweight and thin modern fabrics. These were bigger, made of thicker canvas and built to stay standing in proper rough weather - like the sort the scouts or guides would use. My curiosity was piqued. What were the tents there for? The entrance to the field was also the beginning of the Confessor's Walk. The protest banner attached to the gate had come loose and was fluttering in the breeze. If there was going to be some activity for the new road the protestors would be back soon. I would have joined them, but right now I was no longer sure I wanted to stay in Islip. Maybe I should just sell up. Maybe fate was trying to tell me something - that I shouldn't be here. I rowed briskly and with purpose, past the field to the weir and beyond, almost to the spot where I'd taken photos the other day. I steered the boat into the bank and tied it to a tree branch.

'That was hardly worth getting the oars wet,' Matt protested.

'We'll go further. But this is what I wanted you to see.'

I pulled the picture out of my overnight bag and leapt out of the boat.

'Come on,' I urged as Matt remained seated.

He stood, and the boat lurched to one side, but it was in such shallow water that it wasn't possible to tip over.

'Hannah, what are we doing?' He protested, following me up the bank.

'Turn around. Face the village,' I demanded. I removed the picture from the towel I had wrapped it in and held it in front of us.

'Mum had this in her loft. She doesn't know where it came from. Look at this and then look at the view and tell me what you see.'

Matt studied the picture and then tipped his head back. He frowned and his eyebrows poiroted. 'It's the same. Slightly different angle, but still the same view.'

I nodded, satisfied. 'It is, isn't it? I was sure the moment I saw it. But I needed to hear that from someone else too.'

I traced the outline of the church steeples with my fingers. 'When do you think it was drawn?'

Matt shrugged. 'It looks old. The tree line is not so dense as it is now, but even so, there are no houses.' He raised his eyes and shielded them from the sun to study the view. To the right of the church tower there was a cluster of roof-tops. 'Not even those.'

'This has to mean that my family has a connection to the village,' I tried to keep the eagerness I felt out of my voice.

'We know Thomas Marlow was an artist. Could he have painted it?'

I was looking for a connection between me and the mystery woman who was the subject of the portrait, so this was a thought that hadn't occurred to me. I scrolled through the photos on my phone to find the one I'd taken at the museum and held it next to the picture so we could compare them.

'I don't think so,' I said after a few minutes. 'They are very different styles. The portrait is done in oils, but this picture is like a pencil sketch. It's more primitive but in many ways it's also more skilful. There's nowhere for the artist to hide.'

I held it out at arm's length to look at it from a different angle.

'I think it's beautiful.'

A loud growl erupted from Matt's stomach. 'Sorry, I'm starving. Can we eat?' He was looking back towards the boat and the picnic hamper, wearing an expression of longing that I'd be quite happy to have focused on me. We slid back down the bank and I rowed a bit further to a secluded spot under a willow tree where we pulled the boat out of the water and unpacked the hamper. Matt had thought of everything. There was even a blanket for us to stretch out on, to which we added the cushions from my deck. The Prosecco was still chilled, and the single-use glasses had survived the journey intact. The hamper itself folded out to make a sort of table. We spread out all the food and ate. There were tiny sandwiches with the crusts cut off, mini goat's cheese tarts, a pot of cherry tomatoes, a bag of nachos and a dip, with sweet pastries and a bunch of grapes for dessert. It was delicious and I wished that we were on Port Meadow and enjoying this the way we had planned.

I propped the picture up against the tree trunk so I could study it whilst we ate. 'You need to get someone who knows about art to have a look at it,' Matt suggested. 'They should be able to date it - by the paper if nothing else.'

'Would Joel know?'

'Ah, that reminds me. I asked Joel what he meant when he told you to 'be careful'. Turns out it's a language thing. He just meant 'take care'.'

I was relieved. Of course I was. And then I started questioning whether the sense of foreboding that had been growing within me for the last week was all a product of my overactive imagination. I plucked a long blade of grass and twisted it around my middle finger, watched it unwind and tightened it again.

'Do you think I'm imagining things?'

Matt leaned back on the cushions, resting on his elbow. 'What do you mean?'

'You know, all of this: a mystery lost woman, my connection with it all, someone trying to spook me ...'

'No,' he shook his head. 'You haven't imagined that scene at your house. That was very real.'

'But what if it's nothing to do with the ring though? What if it's about something else entirely?' The thought had been nagging at me all afternoon. It just didn't feel the same.

'Got any suspects?' He tried to do a New York drawl but it didn't work. I laughed. He pulled me down next to him and I curled into his side. The late afternoon sun was warm on my face and I felt drowsy, helped by the aftermath of shock, a full stomach and half a bottle of Prosecco. I don't know how long I dozed for but when I woke the sun had dipped in the sky and my face felt tight. I knew I'd have an unattractive and glowing red nose again. I was wrapped in Matt's arms, and although I was uncomfortable from lying in one position for too long I was reluctant to move.

'I didn't want to wake you,' he murmured in my ear, sensing I was awake.

I wriggled around to face him.

'Mmm, nice nose.' He kissed me. 'I think we should be getting back.'

I really didn't want to face my house, but I knew he was right. Daylight was fading, and the way back would be a harder row against the current. It was dark when we arrived at my deck. I had rowed in silence, my head busy with competing theories as to who might hate me all vying for attention. Matt had concentrated on spotting the low branches in the half-light and raising them so they wouldn't knock us overboard as we passed beneath. We unloaded the boat, piling the cushions back onto the deck and Matt carried the hamper and my bag with its precious cargo to the house. I started to follow but my steps grew slower and more sluggish the closer I got until I stopped and stared. My eyes darted from window to window looking for shadows that shouldn't be there. My ears strained for unfamiliar sounds in the gathering darkness. By the time Matt came back out I was shaking.

'I can't do it.'

He had removed his bandanna and his hair was falling over his face so I couldn't see his eyes. He stopped a few steps from me.

'Come on Hannah. You'll feel better once it's all cleared up. It's like when you fall off your bike as a kid and your dad makes you get back on right away. Conquer your fears.' There was an edge in his voice that I hadn't heard before. Was it impatience? Or maybe he was just tired.

'I always thought that was just sadistic.' I was trying to joke but I knew it sounded false.

He took my hand and tried to pull me gently towards the house, but I pushed him away and wrapped my arms around myself trying to stop the shaking that was increasing its intensity, gathering strength like a wind increasing from gale force, to storm force, to hurricane.

'What do you want to do?'

I had an idea, but I was sure he'd think I was bonkers.

'I'm going to sleep out here. By the river.'

It's a good thing I couldn't see his eyes. I could feel them. 'You've got to be kidding.'

'No. I've got a hammock. Would you mind fetching it for me? It should be in a canvas bag in the cupboard under the stairs, so it's probably on the floor in the hall. There's a sleeping bag there too.'

He didn't say anything, turned around and went back into the house, returned with the bag and handed it to me.

'Hannah, this is madness. You'll be much safer in the house.'

'It's no different to camping. It's a double. You can stay if you want to, but I'll also be okay on my own.'

The thought terrified me, but I wasn't going to admit it. I shook the hammock out of the bag. I'd bought it when Sean and I were travelling. We'd slept in it on many an occasion, strung between palm trees on the edge of an idyllic beach, or on a boat travelling to our next destination. I hadn't used it here yet, but I'd had the deck built with two tall corner posts across the diagonal, each fitted with a large metal hook and perfectly spaced so the hammock would hang across the deck. I secured the loops over the hooks and it fell into shape. Around two sides of the deck I'd strung some pretty solar lights. I switched them on, and the transformation from dark and threatening into warm and welcoming was complete. Then I turned to face Matt. His expression was one of resignation, but his lips curved into a hint of a smile.

'You are full of surprises.'

He grabbed my hand and tugged me towards him. I didn't resist, and we collapsed onto the cushions.

EIGHTEEN

Hannah

I'D FORGOTTEN HOW COMFORTABLE IT was, sleeping in the hammock. I awoke in a shaft of weak, early morning sunlight, which was already making my burnt nose prickle. The hammock was swaying in a soothing motion. Matt was still fast asleep, one arm stretched over me, head resting on my shoulder and one long leg dangling over the side, toes brushing the surface of the deck. I had no immediate urge to move. Instead, I allowed my senses to adjust to the new day, enjoying the smell of honeysuckle drifting towards me on the gentle morning breeze, the river lapping at its bank to my side, the tweeting of the house martins and the more persistent call of the woodpeckers.

It's a cliché, I know, but it's also true that everything looks better in the light of a new morning. The thought of going back into my house didn't fill me with me panic like it had last night. Better face it sooner rather than later, especially since I needed the bathroom.

There is no easy way of getting out of a hammock, and without waking up the other person who's in there with you I'd say it's impossible. I rolled over. The hammock swung and deposited me onto the deck. I landed on a cushion, just missing Trespass who was stretched out underneath. She opened her eyes, looked at me briefly and closed them again, no doubt indignant that she hadn't been able to jump up and join us during the night.

There was no sound from Matt, so I slipped on my shoes and made my way across the garden to the back door. There, I almost lost my nerve, but I knew I had to do this. I took a deep breath and pushed the door open. I didn't want to look but I couldn't avoid it. My eyes scanned the chaos that was my kitchen. It didn't look any better than it had yesterday, but I was relieved and touched that someone - had to have been Matt - had removed the pebbles from the table. I forced myself to cross the room, stepping around the mess, and went upstairs. Ten minutes later, when I emerged from the shower feeling refreshed, I was further invigorated by the smell of coffee wafting up from the kitchen. Matt must have followed me in. I threw some clothes on and joined him.

'We could go out for breakfast,' I suggested, taking the mug that he held out to me.

'No, we're going to tidy up this mess, and then, I need clean clothes.' He shook his head. 'No argument,' he added as I opened my mouth to protest that it could wait.

He was right, I knew. With a sigh of resignation I sipped my coffee and watched him picking up tins of tuna and chopped tomatoes and piling them into a cupboard, knowing that I would have to take them all back out again and put them into a proper order or I would never be able to find anything.

'Are you going to help, or just stand there and watch?'

There it was again, that edge to his voice that I'd noticed last night. I stared at his back as he busied himself in my cupboards, irritated and a little annoyed that he didn't get it. Didn't get me. It was my home that had been wrecked. My private space that had been violated. I had a right to feel like this, and if I wanted to wallow in self-pity I would. Some sympathy would have been nice, but it obviously wasn't going to be forthcoming, so I carried my coffee into the lounge, put it down on the table and started tidying. Within a couple of hours my house was cleaner, and tidier, than it had been since the day I'd moved in, and I was grateful to Matt for his help. But he had shown me a side to him that I hadn't seen before and I wasn't sure I liked very much.

Matt stayed for the weekend. He didn't even bother going home to fetch clean clothes. We went shopping at Bicester Village instead, taking the train from Islip to the shopping centre's own dedicated station to avoid the traffic and full car parks.

Talk about role reversal. I was the one waiting outside the changing rooms, fidgeting and impatient whilst he tried on countless shirts and shorts and then insisted we return to the first shop we'd been in. What a waste of time! Give me a good bookshop any day. My toes did tingle though when he finally emerged, wearing the new dark blue slim-fit shorts that ended just above his knees and a crisp white T-shirt, his old clothes bundled into the store's designer carrier bag.

He draped an arm over my shoulders, adjusted his sunglasses, and together we dodged the hordes of tourists from China and Korea wheeling their suitcases full of designer bargains, bumping into them when they stopped without warning to take random selfies with a naked Christmas tree in the background. It reminded me of why I try to avoid this place.

We stopped for lunch at the Farmshop which was already heaving with weary shoppers eating their superfood salads and knocking back nutritious smoothies. Mine was going to be a glass of wine ... large. Healthy be damned. Whilst we were waiting for the waitress to find us a table, I realised we were being scrutinised by a couple walking towards the exit. I didn't recognise them but I glanced at Matt and it was clear he did. His expression was wary. As I watched his face I thought he probably looked like that as a child, when he'd been caught doing something that he knew was forbidden and was waiting for the telling off to start. His eyes were dancing from side to side, but there was no escape.

'How are you mate?'

'Fine, Steve. You?' The handshake was interrupted by the girl, who flung herself on her high platform heels at Matt and kissed him on each cheek. To his credit, he appeared to be trying to keep her at arm's length.

'Matt,' she shrilled. 'How lovely. We haven't seen you for such a long time.'

I was pretty sure Matt didn't share her enthusiasm for the chance encounter. He tried to take a step backwards, but he was already pinned against the wall. He mumbled something that I didn't catch - maybe her name.

'And how is Lauren?' She flicked her eyes towards me at this point, which I thought was Matt's cue to introduce me, but he didn't.

He shrugged. 'She's fine too.'

'Your table is ready,' the waitress appeared at my side and waved a couple of menus at us. 'Follow me.'

'We have to go mate,' Matt addressed Steve rather than the girl. I could feel her eyes tracking us as we followed the waitress across the busy restaurant to a table in a far corner.

She took our drinks order, parroted the specials of the day, and left us. I waited for Matt to say something, but he was absorbed in the menu. I was twitching with annoyance by now.

'Who were they?'

Matt looked up from the menu, feigning surprise - that I should be interested or that I thought the topic was worth discussing, I couldn't say. 'Steve and Debbie,' he said. Just that. No qualification of who Steve and Debbie might be. He returned his attention to the menu.

'Didn't you think it might have been polite to introduce me?'

He put the menu down and reached across the table for my hands.

'I would have done, but the waitress came to take us to our table.'

That was true, but I couldn't help thinking he had seized on that as an excuse to get away. I dropped that line of enquiry because there was another question that I had to ask. I pulled my hands away from his.

'Why did she ask about Lauren?'

'They're old friends. Why shouldn't she ask me about my cousin?'

His smile was forced and there was a tension to the set of his shoulders that told me he wasn't comfortable. I studied his face, wanting to push it further, searching for the right words. He took my hands again and stroked his thumb along my palm.

'You're being over-sensitive Hannah.'

Was I? Maybe. I wanted to trust him and I tried to push my doubts out of my mind. Matt soon bounced back, nonchalant, a pretence that nothing significant had happened, but I felt the atmosphere between us had soured somehow.

'Come on, let's order. I'm starving,' he said.

We didn't refer to this incident again. Matt threw himself into the role of Prince Charming with renewed gusto and I lapped up the attention. My thoughts did return to it though, after he'd gone home on Sunday evening. I liked Matt, a lot, and I could be blissfully happy at the moment, but for that niggling doubt that left me questioning this relationship that I was nurturing - no, not just nurturing, it was more than that. I was reaching out to it as if it were my last chance.

But was he the person I thought he was?

I checked my emails on Sunday evening and was thrilled to see one from The Bear hotel. I had sent them a quote and they wanted me to do a site visit 'the sooner the better - can you do tomorrow?' I replied to say I could squeeze them in late morning, so on Monday, instead of going to my studio, I had a lazy start to the day, breakfast outdoors with Trespass at my feet. She was twitchy and kept pricking her ears and swishing her tail into my legs. Her mood rubbed off on me and I found it hard to shake the sensation that I was being watched. My eyes scanned the garden, even though I knew there was no-one there. Just the spooks of the break-in returning.

I went back inside and called Joel. His phone went to voicemail. I left a message, and whilst I was waiting for him to call back I remembered the family tree that Mum had started to compile. I realised I hadn't even mentioned this to Matt. I fetched the rolled-up paper and box of photographs and spread them out on the table, weighting the corners down with tins. It would be a massive task to complete the research that my mum had started and I wasn't in the mood to tackle it now, but I would later. My thoughts went back to my mum and what might be wrong with her and an icy hand seemed to clutch at my heart and give it a quick squeeze. I'd been so wrapped up in my own problems that I hadn't given her a single thought all weekend. I reached for my mobile and dialled her number. She must have been sitting on her phone, it had only just started to ring and she answered.

'Hello love.'

Was I imagining it or was her voice strained?

'How are you Mum?'

'I'm fine. Just didn't sleep very well. How are you? Have you seen your young man again? Matt, wasn't it? I do hope you'll be careful.'

She was off into one of her torrents of words, but it seemed to me that, although the words were there, the energy was missing.

'Call me when you get the test results, Mum.'

She promised she would and I hung up. My phone rang again almost immediately.

'Miss Hannah. It is a good morning, is it not. What can I do for you?'

I smiled at his idiosyncratic way of talking. I was getting used to it now, the way his words formed a question but his tone made it into a statement.

'I need an art historian to look at a picture I found. Do you know anyone?'

'You are good at finding things, are you not.' I could hear a chuckle in his voice and could see those dimples. I realised I was becoming fond of Joel.

'It just so happens that I do. You can drop the picture in to me - maybe this afternoon - and we'll go along the corridor to my young friend, Marco.'

I agreed that I could get into Oxford in the afternoon. It was a relief to know I would not have time to go to my studio today now. I wouldn't put it past Sean to be camped out in the doorway, or staking the place out from across the road, waiting for me to show up. I was just as reluctant to spend the day in my house. It no longer felt like my home, and I wondered if it ever would again. I remembered Matt's impatience with me over the weekend - he had made it clear that he felt I was being pathetic, and part of me was still annoyed. Surely I was entitled to be a bit spooked?

I had plenty of time, but I was restless. I never was any good at having nothing to do, and especially not when I'm rattled about something. I decided to leave early for my meeting and stop at the bridge on my way. I drove past the gate to the Confessor's Walk and slowed down. The field was a hive of activity, although I couldn't see what was happening. Protestors had gathered and were waving their banners and placards. I saw Judy and raised my hand.

It was a very different scene here when I returned later.

I pulled into the car park at the Swan. It wasn't open and there was no-one else around.

I crossed the road and leaned back against the comforting old stone of the pub walls, facing the bridge. I screwed my eyes shut, clearing my mind and opened them again, trying to see the river and the crossing as it would have been in the 17th century. When I'd googled John of Islip I had come across some history of the bridge, and I knew it had been rebuilt several times with the present structure dating to some point in the 19th century. I imagined the bridge that might have been here before, with more arches, lower and longer. But it wasn't the bridge itself I was trying to conjure in my imagination. It was the scene. I wanted to know what my mystery woman saw when she walked here, because the more I thought about it, the more I was convinced that she had lived in Islip.

The road was there, still winding up the hill on the other side, but between open fields, with no houses, maybe a barn. The surface wasn't modern tarmac but a compact earth and stone, furrowed with ruts where rainwater had carved its own path into the river. It was studded with potholes that may have had stones thrown into them in an attempt to stop the carriage wheels getting stuck or even coming off. The road sign warning of pedestrians wouldn't be there and nor would the telegraph poles, electricity pylons and cables.

There would be a horse and maybe a carriage crossing the bridge. And soldiers. I pictured three or four. All Royalists, with long hair and pointy sculptured beards like an upside-down mountain peak, and feathered hats which would have made them look like dandies on the way to church if it wasn't for the weapons strapped to their waists and across their chests.

And then I pictured a woman with black hair, skirts swirling in the breeze, dress hidden beneath a heavy cloak, maybe carrying a basket. Where was she going? What was she doing? Who was she?

The vision was so real that I could almost hear her voice, an echo through time, reaching out to me. A delivery van tooted its horn and the spell was broken. The scene returned to normal, and I was disappointed that my vivid re-imagining wasn't sufficient to conjure up the answers that I sought.

I sighed and returned to my car.

My visit to the Bear hotel was pleasant but uneventful. I got the job, which I was thrilled about. It would be a great one for my portfolio. My visit to Joel was more eventful. He dimpled at me and greeted me as if we were long-lost friends, continental style with a kiss on each cheek and then back in for a third.

His young friend, Marco, turned out to be 70 if he was a day. A semi-retired Italian who had trained and worked at the Uffizi Gallery in Florence. As credentials go they don't get much better than that.

'Marco. Miss Hannah is in the middle of a mystery and she needs your help.'

Marco took my hand in a vigorous grip, bony fingers compressing mine. 'I do like a mystery. What can I do to help?' His English was impeccable with just the slightest hint of an accent. He peered at me through a pince-nez and I stared. I'd never seen anyone wearing those funny old-fashioned glasses in real life before. Only ever in films or on TV. They gave him a distinguished, elegant air, which was at odds with his mop of grey hair. That was more the eccentric, or mad, scientist.

I removed the picture from the blanket I had wrapped it in and passed it to him.

'I found this in a pile of junk my mum was taking to the charity shop and I'd like to know more about it, if possible.' He pulled on cotton gloves and took the picture from me. I outlined the events of the last couple of weeks and why I was keen to know about it.

'What do you want to know, exactly?'

'Anything you can tell me.'

He turned the picture over and examined it from all angles, front and back.

'The frame is modern. May I remove it?'

I nodded and watched him work. With great care he eased the frame away. The picture was sandwiched between two sheets of card, one with a window cut into it. He lifted it out and the paper crackled with stiffness in his fingers. He scrutinised it through an instrument on his desk that shone light onto it. He didn't speak, other than the occasional, 'um' or 'ahh'. He also was clearly not in a hurry. When he paused to make more coffee from a small pod machine behind his desk, I was almost jumping up and down with impatience. I shook my head when he offered me a cup.

What is it with these history boffins? Why can't they just get on with it?

Eventually, he put the picture down on his desk and beamed at me. 'Fascinating,' he said.

'What? What's fascinating? Is there something special about the picture?'

'One question at a time,' he swirled the dainty espresso cup in his hand and drained the contents. 'The past reaching out to us in the present is what is fascinating. Thank you for bringing this to me. I can never tire of examining old paintings.'

He beamed at me and his eyes twinkled over the pince-nez.

'So this is definitely old?'

'Oh yes. See here,' he started pointing at the picture, 'and here … and here.'

Joel and I leaned over the desk so we could see what he was showing us.

'They're like tea stains,' I said.

'It's called ink burn,' Marco explained. 'It's caused by oxidisation of the ink over a period of many years. It's often found with iron gall ink, which was common in the 17th century. Ink burn can also be used to mislead people - buyers - into believing a picture is older than it really is. In this case, though, it is genuinely old.'

'How can you tell?' I asked. To me it looked like brown splodges on a picture.

'Because I can see it, through the light.'

He stroked the instrument on his desk as if it were a beloved pet. 'Transmitted light,' he added.

I did understand a bit about this principle. My photography course had included modules that covered light.

'That's when you pass light through something to enhance your view of whatever you're looking at?'

'A paper expert could tell you more,' Marco nodded. 'I studied with one in London last year. Fascinating.'

He paused, rubbing his chin and peered at me again through his pince-nez.

'What can you tell me?'

'I can tell you that this is a drawing done in charcoal and ink. That's unusual.'

'Unusual? Why?' I couldn't help jumping in. One day I must learn how to be patient.

'Because most artists would use one or the other, not both.'

I opened my mouth again, but he frowned at me.

'Let me tell you what I can, please. The ink was applied using a quill. The composition of the drawing is skilful, but the application of the ink is not. There is no signature that I can see and the style of the work does not lead me to conclude it was done by any artist who is recognised or well-known today.'

He removed the pince-nez and waved them at me in the air of someone delivering a lecture.

'That does not mean, however, that it is not good, because it is, although I think the artist was unused to working in ink. This may have been an early attempt with an unfamiliar format.'

'The paper is very yellowed. Is that also an indication of age?'

Marco shook his head. 'Not necessarily. The paper would have been off-white anyway. It is not good quality - it is a mix of linen and hemp - old tarred rope or sail cloth - so it would have been buff-coloured to begin with. Also, there is no watermark - if it was a good quality paper I would expect it to have a watermark, from which a real paper expert could tell you more - where and by whom it was made, for instance. When you look at it through the light, you can see the laid and chain lines - that's the wire profile of the papermaking mould on which the paper was made. Again, a paper expert could tell you more, could date it more precisely than I am able by closer examination of the wire profile - that's the frequency of the closely spaced wires and the widths between the wider spaced lines. However, my guess would be that this paper was originally used for wrapping goods sometime in the 17th century.'

I suddenly understood why he found this fascinating.

He beamed at me again and placed his pince-nez on his desk. Without them his face appeared oddly naked and younger. 'That's probably all I can tell you young lady.'

'All! That's flipping amazing. I had no idea that something as simple as paper could give you so much information.'

'There's nothing very simple about paper,' he huffed, placing the picture back in its card mount and frame and handing it back to me.

'Thank you so much,' I said, taking it and gripping his hand in an enthusiastic shake.

'Any time,' he said, settling back down at his desk with his back turned towards us.

I drove home, my head crowded with what I had learned.

The protestors at the gate to the Confessor's Walk stood in a subdued huddle, their placards and banners abandoned. The gate itself and the fence either side were covered with yellow tape, sealing off the area. I slowed down but a woman wearing a high-vis jacket waved me on. I checked my rear-view mirror and there was a car behind me that I didn't recognise as belonging to any of my neighbours.

I parked on my drive, but I didn't go into the house. My curiosity had to be satisfied and I had a funny feeling that whatever was happening in the field was significant. Within a few minutes I was joining the group of protestors. I could see now that a white tent had been added to the others along the hedge, about halfway down the field. It was the kind you see on TV when forensics have been called to a crime scene, with a flap down the middle that serves as an opening, although this one was positioned so that any opening was facing away from the road. I was sure I'd get a better view from my boat.

'What's happening?' I asked the man standing closest to me. I recognised him as someone who lived along Mill Street, but I didn't know his name.

He turned to me. 'They've found bones,' he said.

NINETEEN

Catherine
Thursday, April 24th, 1645

IT WAS DARK, AND THE birds had yet to start their daily rejoicing at the arrival of a new day when Catherine awoke, stiff and uncomfortable from a second night in Helen's kitchen. The girls and Tilly had all been asleep in front of the fire when Thomas had left last night. Edward had carried them one-by-one upstairs. The night had been quiet.

Catherine tested her eyes and was relieved to find the left one opened almost as usual. She brushed it with her fingertips and winced. It was still sore and no doubt she was sporting colours that made her face resemble one of the stained glass windows in the church, but her vision was a definite improvement on yesterday.

Yesterday. So much had happened. Henry, Richard, and their threats. Her father, now a wanted man. Thomas, his quiet determination, and his anger at what he saw as others trying to interfere with his life. She needed to void her mind of it all so she could think with clarity and without interruption.

She swung her legs to the floor and sat there for a moment, stretching her cramped muscles, listening to the intense quiet of the house and inhaling the warm, stale air of the kitchen. It was stifling. She pushed herself to her feet and padded across the cold flagstones out of the kitchen and into the front parlour. The curtains were pulled tight, so not even a chink of the outside could penetrate. She tugged at one edge and peeped out of the window at the lane beyond, looking for any sign of soldiers. The fading moonlight was wispy and swirling, as if stirred by some invisible force. It was the only movement she could detect. Otherwise, she could see nothing out of the ordinary, except a glow in the distance from somewhere near the church.

She returned to the kitchen, pulled on her gown, and tipped a few coins from her pouch into her satchel. She took out a charcoal stick, tore a corner from a sheet of paper and did a crude drawing of her sitting in a field sketching, with a + sign next to it and an arrow pointing to a second drawing of the market. Helen would no doubt be cross with her for going out alone, but Catherine would not be treated like a child, and she would be careful. She could be fairly sure she wouldn't meet her father if he was in hiding, and if Cromwell's soldiers had been drinking until late in the taverns they would be sleeping off those excesses and would not be about on the streets yet either. It was safer to venture out now than later, she reasoned.

She pulled on her cloak, pattens and a cap, unbolted the front door and stepped out into the lane, listening again for any sound that would imply the presence of anyone else nearby. Thick silence hung in the air, which was itself heavy with an acrid smoky smell that made her choke. She screwed up her nose and put her hand to her mouth.

She walked away from the village towards the mill. The further she walked, the cooler and fresher the air became. She couldn't see the river, but was aware of its presence on her left by the shifting texture to the darkness that rippled and lapped against the grassy banks.

Beyond the mill, the track became a path. Catherine followed it for a little way until she found a good, sheltered spot beneath a tree where the ground was cushioned with moss and dead leaves. She sat down, leaning against the solid trunk, and took out some paper, chalk and charcoal sticks. On top of the stack of blank sheets of paper was the sketch she had done a few nights ago, of her father with two faces disappearing into the dust thrown up by the hooves of Richard Marlow's horse. She still didn't understand what her drawing meant, but she feared that her father had some terrible disunity at the very core of his being, which had the power to change him into a person she no longer recognised. Mayhap it even had the power to destroy him and others around him. She put the paper down.

Looking back towards the village she could see the glow she had noticed earlier was coming from the church, and smoke was clinging to the tower, shrouding it in its foul breath. There must have been a fire. Careless soldiers after too much ale, or maybe even a deliberate act.

Her attention was diverted by the changing shades of the sky, which was lightening, allowing a subdued grey to infuse the blackness. The birds awakened and started their morning song. With a little imagination, she could make out the curve of the top of the giant wheel at the mill. Without taking her eyes from the scene, she reached for a charcoal stick and started to sketch, applying broad, confident strokes across the paper. She frowned and rubbed at one of her lines, smudging it so it became softer, less defined. It still wasn't right. The angle was skewed, so the wheel appeared too flat on one side. It wasn't her best work.

She flung it down onto her satchel and felt around her neck for the chain which held the ring next to her skin. She looped it over her head without undoing the clasp, twisted the chain around her wrist and laid the ring in the palm of her hand. The metal was warm, like a stone that had been baking in the sun. Its presence was comforting. It had become part of her. She traced the outline of the design with her finger and hoped that the man about to fall from the tree wouldn't prove to be prophetic. Then she shook her head.

'No,' Catherine spoke aloud. 'This feels right. It's going to work.'

She could still see obstacles and problems in their way, trying to grind them down until they were no longer able to resist, but she had to trust Thomas.

Would he truly be prepared to carry out his suggestion of yesterday evening that they would move, if necessary, away from the influence of his family? She drew her knees up to her chest, clasped her arms around them and used them as a table on which to rest her chin. She closed her eyes and imagined herself in a strange new town, starting out again. In her mind she could see a pretty market square, bigger than Islip's, with more substantial houses, all in a honey-coloured stone like Helen's, not the dirty white daub and timber frame of her own. The smells coming from the stalls and the taverns would be welcoming, of warm bread and meat-filled pies. The skies would be clear, presenting a view that would stretch for miles, dotted with green forests and small hills. Maybe even the ocean, which she had never seen, would be visible in the distance. She pictured it as an impossible shade of deep blue, flecked with tips of white, and boats, so many boats.

In the clear morning air, with Thomas's words of last night echoing in her ears, Catherine knew she was going to fight for this chance for a new life. If he was prepared to go to such lengths so that she was comfortable and they could be happy, she owed it to both of them to commit herself fully. She had always had fire in her soul. For two years she had believed she needed to calm that spirit for Tilly's sake, and she'd locked it away and hidden the key. But when she'd allowed Thomas into her life, she had also broken the lock and now her spirit was free to fly again.

A smile spread over her face and then faded as Richard Marlow's parting threat came back to her. His voice resounded in her head, as loud and clear as if he were standing in the meadow in front of her right now. 'I would see you dead before you are married to my son, madam.'

Catherine shivered. She knew they were just words, but still they chilled her. Her fist clenched over the ring and it seemed to burn into her palm.

The day was now properly light, the sky striated with pink, dark on the horizon, and fading to the shade of the blossom on the apple trees in the orchard at the manor as it stretched upwards. She picked up her satchel, which was upside down, and the coins fell out. She slipped the charcoal sticks, her unsatisfactory sketch and all her paper back inside and groped amongst the dead leaves on her hands and knees until she found the coins. Fingering the cool metal, she became aware of an unusual background noise. She cocked her head on one side, trying to identify it. The noise was getting closer. She scrambled to her feet, stepped out from the shelter of the tree, and was hit by a wave of panic when she recognised it as the thunder of many horses' hooves pounding the hard ground. Matching it, beat for beat, was the clashing of metal against metal. A cloud of dust rose in the distance, from the direction of Oxford. They would be upon her within minutes. Catherine didn't stop to think. She ran, satchel bouncing along the ground to her side, coins and ring still in her hand. She was hampered by her skirts and her pattens made her feet clumsy on the uneven ground. She passed the mill and ahead of her she could see soldiers wearing new red uniforms approaching down Mill Street and stretching out over the fields to her left. She was going to be trapped between the two armies. She skirted right and dropped down to the river where she judged it would be safer - the soldiers would take a straight line.

She didn't notice a figure peal out from the shadow of the mill and follow her, gaining ground, but the back of her neck prickled with the sensation that she was being watched. She daren't stop to turn around and look. Her breath caught in the back of her throat before spilling out in loud, panting gasps. Fear clouded her vision. She stumbled, and then strong arms encircled her waist, hands enclosed in thick gloves, and she was lifted almost off her feet. She cried out and struggled, kicking, but not connecting with anything. Her hands and arms were free and she tried to beat them at her assailant. The ring and the coins slipped from her fingers and disappeared into the long grass where they settled into the soft mud. She was being half dragged, half carried backwards. The hubbub of battle rose and reverberated in the background. Catherine's blood was pounding in her ears. She was fighting as hard as she could but was unable to break free. She screamed, and then she was propelled to one side, and with a splintering pain that seemed to split her head into two, her world went black.

TWENTY

Hannah

BONES! WHAT SORT OF BONES? Are we talking skeletons? I shuddered, wishing I hadn't asked. But there was no going back now.

I scanned the group, looking for someone who might be a bit more forthcoming with information. Perfect, there was Judy. If anyone knew what was happening here it would be her. She must have sensed me watching her because she turned around and waved. I made my way over to her side.

'How are you? I was so worried - the state of your house. But then, at least you weren't alone.' I looked at her in surprise. Why would she care when she didn't know me at all? But her kind face radiated genuine concern, and I decided she must be one of those nice people who get involved with everything that they can because they want to be helpful and useful.

'I'm fine.'

It was obvious she didn't believe me, but there was sympathy in her eyes and I warmed to her even more.

'No really, I am. I mean, I wasn't, at first. But the house is all tidied up now and you wouldn't know anything had happened.'

It wasn't true of course. I did know what had happened and it would be a long time before I would be able to forget, but I didn't want to talk about that. 'What's going on here?' I asked.

'Archaeologists ... routine work before the new road can be given the go-ahead ...'

Judy didn't sound so calm and composed all of a sudden.

'I hear they've found bones.'

She nodded.

'I'm guessing they wouldn't have sent in the cavalry for animal bones.' I swept my arm out towards the field and the forensic tent.

Judy shook her head. 'No. They aren't saying much, but we believe the bones are human.'

I thought I'd been spooked before, over the weekend, but this was a whole new level. Where that tent was positioned was almost bordering my garden. The thought that a person - or persons - could be buried so close by was unsettling. I had never wanted to live next to a graveyard. Going to sleep at night knowing that a load of skeletons might be the other side of a small wall would give me the creeps.

'Recent ... or old?' I managed to ask.

'They're not saying anything at the moment.'

I watched the activity in the field for a while. A trench had been dug that disappeared behind - or under - the white tent. People, archaeologists I assumed, were working in and around another trench, digging by hand to open up the hole in the ground, with others sifting through soil. None of them came near to the group of villagers huddled by the gate. I wanted to know more, but it didn't appear likely that anyone who knew anything was going to share, so I returned home, walking in a daze down Mill Street, oblivious to the blossom in the hedgerows or the smell of freshly cut grass. My imagination was a riot of blood and gore, envisaging a mass grave of gothic proportions. I already had the heebie-jeebies. I didn't need dead bodies as well.

I had to keep busy. Take my mind off whatever horror was lying beneath the ground just the other side of my hedge. I poured a glass of wine, even though it was early, and went down to my deck. Trespass followed me and settled on a cushion, stretching out on her back and flexing her claws. I stroked her, and her loud purr challenged the hum of the motor that was running in the field just a hop, skip and a jump away. A low mumble of voices drifted towards me, but I couldn't make out what they were saying.

I called Matt but the phone went straight to voicemail. I twisted the stem of my wine glass. There was an idea in my head and I pondered whether I dare do it or not.

'Go on, Hannah,' the trees seemed to whisper to me.

'Sod it.'

Trespass cocked her ear but otherwise chose to ignore me. I drained my wine and put the empty glass down on the deck. My boat was tethered to its post, but the way it was bobbing in the current made it appear eager for an outing. I climbed down into it, released the rope and pushed off, letting the flow of the river carry me downstream for a short distance until I was level with the field. I could see the white tent. I stuck an oar into the water, plunging it vertically towards the river bed, sending my boat into a spin which I stopped by releasing the oar. The boat steadied and I guided us out of the current and into the reeds and long grasses at the edge of the field. The motion disturbed a flock of ducks, which flapped and quacked before plunging into the water. The noise attracted the attention of a thin, young man in a high-vis jacket. He walked towards me.

'You can't come ashore here.' His voice was too deep for his skinny frame.

'I wasn't going to. I was just passing by, saw the tents and was curious.'

He peered at me, evidently not convinced by my 'passing-by' claim.

'Are you a reporter?'

'No. I live next door. I like to take my boat out on a nice evening.'

He still looked suspicious.

'That's why I bought a house on the river.' I smiled at him, hoping to show I was genuine, but he remained silent. I decided to push a bit further.

'I heard that human bones had been found.'

He nodded.

'Just one body, or ... or more?'

'I can't tell you anything.'

He started to walk away.

'Please,' I said quickly. He paused. 'It's just, I feel a bit spooked, you know. I live alone and it's ... unsettling to know there might be bodies buried in my garden.'

He took a few steps back towards me. I think he took pity on me. When he spoke his voice was quiet, almost a whisper. 'We're still digging, but it doesn't appear to be a mass grave. More likely it's just one skeleton. Why don't you come over tomorrow - ask for Ben.' He started to turn and then swivelled around again. 'But don't say I said so.'

I watched him walk back to the tents and then eased my boat out into the current and went a bit further downriver before turning around and rowing home.

I tried Matt again and this time he picked up.

'Hey, how's your day been?'

Where to start? I think you know me by now. I'm not very good at leading into things gently. 'The picture's old and they've found human bones in the field next door,' I blurted out, the words running into each other, like the marbles in the game I used to play with as a child.

'Slow down. You're not making sense.'

I took a deep breath and told him about Marco's certainty that the picture was old, and then what was happening in the field. I couldn't help embellishing the facts as I knew them with a little of my own speculation.

'What if the skeleton is our mystery woman?'

'It's a possibility, but there are lots of other possibilities too.'

'This is a small village. I don't think we have a track record of people going missing never to be heard of again.'

'Just because whoever it was is buried in Islip doesn't mean they were from there. The person might have no connection to the village whatsoever.'

I clicked my tongue with annoyance.

'Or it might be a soldier who died in the battle.'

Why did he have to be so reasonable?

Even so, I hoped he would offer to come over for the evening, or invite me to his place, which I hadn't yet seen. I pictured it as a typical bachelor pad - kitchen sink elbow deep in dirty dishes, everything in the fridge out-of-date, worn socks and boxers littering the bedroom floor. Then I realised that vision of Matt did not match the person I had come to know. His flat in the city would be pristine. So why didn't he invite me there?

'Hannah, are you okay?'

I realised he'd asked me a question and I hadn't answered. 'Oh, what, sorry, the line broke up just then. What did you say?'

'I have to take a client out tonight, so are you sure you'll be okay there on your own?'

He sounded concerned, but remembering how impatient he'd been with me over the break-in, I wasn't going to admit to being squeamish about a mere skeleton in my back yard.

'Sure, I'm fine. I've got Trespass to look after me.' Trespass cocked an ear and I thought she was beginning to recognise her name. She rolled over onto one side, more than half asleep, one paw dangling in the air, tail twitching. Great guard cat she'd make.

Matt then proceeded to tell me exactly what he wanted to do with me next time he saw me, which, he promised, would be tomorrow evening and I forgot all about skeletons, cats and everything else.

Before I went to bed that night though, I locked and double bolted the doors and made sure all the windows were securely closed.

The next morning I wondered what time would be considered reasonable for me to turn up at the Confessor's Walk and ask for Ben. I guessed he probably wouldn't be on site much before 9am so I made myself wait. When I did stroll down Mill Street, trying to appear casual and as if it was just a normal morning, it was clear that word had got out. Among the strangers gathered at the yellow crime scene tape were at least two reporters with photographers. It looked as though I'd missed the action though, as they were packing away their lenses into expensive cases. It was too early for them to have given up, so they must have got their story already.

I hung around, waiting for them to leave and then asked today's high-vis jacketed person - not the same kid I'd spoken to yesterday evening - if Ben was available. He caught the eye of a petite and wiry woman with short, iron-grey hair and a wrinkled, weather-beaten complexion. She strolled over to us, with the air of someone who was in charge, puffing on a roll-up. She was wearing loose-fitting army-style combat trousers, a khaki body warmer and heavy boots that made her feet look too big for her slight frame. She had a pencil tucked behind each ear.

'Can I help you?'

'I was after Ben.'

She narrowed her eyes. 'Who are you? We've given a statement to the press.'

'I'm not a reporter. I live next door. I just wondered if you knew anything ... about ... about whoever it is you've found there?'

She shook her head and ground the rollie into the churned-up mud of the field. 'Nothing I can tell you.' She started to walk back to the tents.

'Wait, please. Can you at least tell me if the skeleton is a woman and if it's been there for, say, maybe a few hundred years, perhaps since the Civil War?'

She paused, spun around on her heels and threw a curious glance in my direction. She gestured to the high-vis jacket to let me through.

'Come with me,' she instructed and I followed her to one of the tents - one of the scouts' tents, not the intimidating white one. I couldn't resist a glance over at it, but was relieved that I couldn't see into it. Beyond the tent a mechanical digger was working on a new trench, and to my left at the other end of the field I could just see the head and shoulders of two people who were partially immersed in yet another.

She offered me coffee from a flask but I refused. Inside the tent various trestle tables held what looked like fragments of pottery, glass and the odd coin. I remembered that I was going to get a metal detector to go over my garden and see if anything else was buried there, and then thought that perhaps I'd better not. Who knows what I might find.

She sat down in a canvas chair at a table that was littered with used mugs and crumbs and stretched her legs out, pointing to another chair on the other side of the table. I sat down.

'I'm Ben,' she said, leaning towards me and holding out a bony hand.

The surprise must have registered on my face and I suspected it was a joke that she liked to play on people. Her eyes were twinkling and the creases at the corners lifted in a smile.

'I was christened Priscilla Bentine-Jones,' she explained. 'I know, ghastly isn't it?'

It was, but I didn't know whether to agree with her or not. I shook her hand. Her grip was firm. She leaned back in the chair.

'When I started out in this work a long, long time ago I soon realised that my name was a big disadvantage, and that if I sounded like a man - at least on paper - I would be taken more seriously. So I ditched the Priscilla and became plain Ben Jones. These days I don't need to pretend, but it kind of stuck and I think I suit Ben better than I do Priscilla. So, tell me. What do you know?'

'I ... I, don't know anything.'

'It's impossible to be precise with the dates of something like this, but I would say it is highly likely that this skeleton has been in the ground since the 17th century. The archaeology around the site suggests that the ground hasn't been disturbed recently, and the bits of pottery that we are finding at that level would fit as well. As to whether it's a woman or not, I can't say for sure until we've lifted all the bones and we can't do that yet. That's what I know, so tell me, what do you know?'

So I told her. She didn't once interrupt me, but listened in attentive silence.

'Do you still have the ring?'

I shook my head. 'I've handed it in to the Finds Liaison Officer, but I've got some pictures of it here on my phone.' I scrolled through my photos and handed the phone to Ben.

She held it close to her face and peered at them. When she dragged her eyes away from the screen there was a gleam in them that told me she was as hooked on this mystery as I was. She pushed my phone over the table towards me, pulled a pencil from behind one ear and started twisting it in her fingers, like a majorette with a baton.

'Where did you say you live?'

'Just the other side of the hedge over there,' I waved my arm and turned to the open flap of the tent. 'That's my roof you can see.'

'And you think this skeleton might be your missing woman?'

'It's a possibility,' I nodded, meeting her frank gaze and hoping she wouldn't dismiss me as a fool, looking for connections where they didn't exist.

'I agree,' she said.

I scrolled through my photos again until I found the one I'd taken of the portrait at the museum and gave her the phone back.

'Take a look,' I invited her.

She glanced at the screen, then at me, then back at the screen again.

'Oh my word.'

I watched her press her fingers to the screen, enlarging the image. She studied it, her expression thoughtful, then passed the phone back to me and tapped the pencil against her teeth.

'I have an idea,' she announced. 'As well as being hands-on with this stuff,' she nodded towards the field, 'I also lecture for a course at the university. My students will be involved with writing up the archaeology from this as part of their research projects. You know, linking the archaeology with what it tells us about the past, what we can learn from it. And if this skeleton does date from the Civil War it is a find that will need to be properly investigated and recorded.'

The pencil was twisting again now, so fast it was almost animated, like a cartoon.

'I have a small budget to help students. How would you feel about being the subject of a project? If the bones are that of a female,' she emphasised the word 'if' and then paused. 'We could do DNA.'

I hadn't been expecting that. How did I feel? Scared. Excited. I was aware of Ben's steady, unblinking scrutiny as she waited for me to answer and I realised her eyes were incongruous with the rest of her appearance. Such a deep blue they were almost violet, asking me a silent question.

'Yes,' I said.

'Great,' she leapt to her feet. 'Do you want to see the skeleton?'

Did I? Didn't I? It was the stuff of nightmares, but at the same time it was fascinating in a macabre sort of way.

I realised Ben's question was rhetorical. She was already striding out across the field. I pocketed my phone and hurried after her.

Later that evening I tried to explain to Matt how I had felt inside that white tent. We'd had dinner at my house and were relaxing on the sofa, finishing a bottle of wine. Matt's long legs were stretched out, resting on the coffee table, and I was lying with my head in his lap. He had removed his bandanna - today's was silvery grey to match his eyes - and his hair fell forward over his face.

'It wasn't as gruesome as I'd thought. The skeleton was sort of on its side, but not curled up, more sprawled.'

I didn't tell him how hard I had found it to drag my eyes to that trench and force myself to look down at what it contained. In a funny way, though, it had helped me to feel less spooked. Knowing what was there made it easier to deal with, but there was something else as well. Something I can't put in to words, but I'll try. It was like a release of pressure, you know, when you've been all wound up about something, and then it's resolved and you do that big sigh and the tension vanishes and you sort of deflate. It was like that, but I wasn't the one doing the sighing. I couldn't tell Matt any of this though. It all felt too personal.

'They haven't started to move the bones yet, probably tomorrow, Ben says, but they'll have to work slowly and carefully to make sure they don't miss or damage anything.'

'Are you sure you want to go through with the DNA?'

About that I had no doubt.

'Yes.'

TWENTY-ONE

Hannah

FOR A FEW DAYS EVERYTHING was quiet.

My fears that I might see Sean skulking behind bushes and in shadowy doorways were unfounded. He seemed to have disappeared as quickly as he had reappeared in my life.

I threw myself back into work, spending most of my time either in my studio or working on my computer at home. When I'd had enough of editing photos I tried to make some more progress on the family tree, matching pictures to names but I didn't get very far, there wasn't much to work with.

Then, in the space of one morning, whilst I was pretending to be busy in my studio, I had three phone calls.

The first was from the Finds Liaison Officer and it stunned me.

'Are you sure?' I managed to gasp, after I'd asked him to repeat the astronomical sum of money that some museum would be prepared to pay for the ring, if its provenance was established.

I reached for a chair and fell into it. Okay, it wasn't such a large sum of money that I would never have to work again, but it would enable me to pay off my mortgage, or move if the developers got their way in Islip.

'It's potentially a very special find, Miss Whittaker.' I tried to focus on his words but they were slipping over the surface of my mind like ice cream melting over a hot sponge pudding. There one minute, gone the next, leaving just a hint of flavour behind.

'They might want to talk to you as well. I'll be back in touch in a few days.'

He hung up and left me reeling. I made some coffee and wandered around my studio, picking things up, putting them down again. I felt as if I'd just won the lottery - even though I'd never even so much as bought a ticket.

My head was in a muddle and I knew I would not be able to concentrate on anything if I stayed here, in my studio. I needed to be outside, feel the wind in my hair and the sun on the new skin where my nose had peeled. As I was locking up my phone rang again.

'Hannah? Ben here.'

She carried on in her brisk manner before I could gather my wits enough to say hello.

'The skeleton is that of a young woman. In her twenties I'd say. And almost certainly an unnatural death.'

'Oh.' I left the keys dangling in the lock and leaned against the wall, my legs sagging. 'What do you mean by an unnatural death?' I felt myself flush, even though there was no-one else there to see. What had made me say something so stupid? And to Ben of all people? She didn't appear to notice.

'Her skull had been smashed. Caved in on one side. Quite brutal.'

Ben's voice sounded very matter of fact, as if this was all part of the job for her. It probably was, but to me it was heart breaking. Whether the skeleton was my mystery woman or not, she had suffered a terrible death and then been buried, anonymously, in a field. Someone must have cared about her though. What did they do when she didn't come home one day? My fingers were clammy with sweat and I almost dropped my phone.

'Hannah? Are you there?'

'Yes, I'm here.' I exhaled and drew breath again sharply, trying to sound normal, but my next words came out in a wheeze. 'Do you mean she was ... murdered?'

'I deal in the facts of what the archaeology tells me, not supposition. All I can say is the trauma to her head would have killed her. Whether she slipped and hit her head on a rock or someone whacked her with a heavy object I can't say.'

Ben paused, as if she understood I needed a moment for my brain to process this news. I closed my eyes, fighting off a wave of nausea.

'Are you still up for the DNA?'

I nodded into the phone and then realised I needed to speak. 'Yes,' I muttered.

'Can you come to the tent this afternoon?'

Of course I could. I was no longer in the mood for working anyway, so I finished what I was doing, thinking I would go home for lunch, although I didn't feel much like eating.

There were no protestors at the entrance to the Confessor's Walk as I drove past. The yellow tape was still there, woven into the hedge like a bright thread through a dark carpet. The atmosphere was muted. Even the air felt subdued, like it had done that time before in my garden when I thought I'd heard someone calling my name. I pulled into my drive, and as I was climbing out of the car, my phone rang again. I fumbled for it in my bag, expecting it to be Matt, but the screen flashed up an unknown local number.

'This is PC Fletcher from the Kidlington Police Station.' Her tone was brisk and efficient.

'Do you have some news?' Even as the words slipped out of my mouth I knew it was another silly question. She wouldn't be wasting time ringing me if she didn't.

'We've arrested Sean Fitzpatrick on suspicion of breaking into your house.'

For the second time that morning my legs threatened to give way beneath me. I sank back into the driver's seat. I could feel my mouth hanging open in what was surely a very unattractive parody of Lauren's perfect 'o' when she'd seen the ring for the first time.

'Miss Whittaker?'

'Yes ... I'm sorry ... I don't understand. Why would he do ... that?'

'Can I just confirm, Miss Whittaker, you're quite sure that Sean Fitzpatrick has never before been to your house?'

'No, he's never been to my house,' I shook my head.

'We found his prints all over the place. Not very clever your Mr Fitzpatrick.'

'He's not my Mr Fitzpatrick,' I started to protest.

He'd never been mine. Even when I'd thought he was.

My voice faded to a whisper. Did he really hate me that much?

It wasn't until after she'd hung up that I thought of all the questions I should have asked her. Like why his prints were on record in the first place, and, if it was him, how had he managed to get through my tiny bathroom window on that first occasion when I'd become aware that someone had been in my house? It didn't make sense.

As I walked to the dig site, I couldn't stop thinking about Sean, the ring, the skeleton in the field and what the DNA might reveal. Information overload clogged my brain, making it sluggish. The high-vis jacket waved me straight through. 'Ben's over in the new trench.' I picked my way across the field. She was peering into the trench, pointing at something. Her khaki body warmer was matched by a bush-style ranger's hat.

'Not found any more skeletons I hope?' I tried to make it sound like a joke, but I meant it. I wasn't sure how many more shocks I could take in one day.

'I'll be with you in a minute Hannah.'

She barked out some more instructions and turned abruptly. 'Right,' she put a hand on my elbow. 'Come with me.' She led me past the trench where the skeleton had been found. The white tent that had been pitched over it was no longer there. It had been moved further along the field, closer to the river. I averted my eyes as we passed the spot where the body had lain, undisturbed, possibly for hundreds of years, and I realised we were heading for the tent in its new pitch. Inside there was a single trestle table and a stack of boxes. I didn't want to look, but I couldn't stop myself. The bones were clean now, but I was grateful that they hadn't been assembled into a recognisable form.

'We're boxing them up to take them back to the office,' Ben explained. 'As well as everything we found nearby. That's why I brought you in here. There were the usual shards of pottery that may or may not have been anything to do with our skeleton, but we also found these.'

She picked up a piece of metal and a strip of something that looked like parchment. 'Leather,' she said. 'I think these were probably part of a bag of some sort. They were underneath the bones. The metal is from a buckle - could equally be a shoe. But this strip of leather - I'm sure it's from a bag and my guess is it's only survived because the river floods and this far down is often waterlogged.'

I nodded. 'Above ground it's often waterlogged as well.'

'I can't tell you much more about the skeleton than I already have. It was definitely a young woman, quite a small frame and only about five foot tall. We can tell that from the size of the bones. Trauma to the head. I already told you that. We've dug several more trenches in the area, as you've seen, and found no more human bones, so I'm pretty confident that this is a single burial. We could try looking in the parish records for recorded deaths, but I can't be precise about the date. And in any case, anyone burying a body out here didn't intend it to be found, so it's highly unlikely that the death is going to be recorded. Far more likely to be someone who just went missing one day.'

It was hot inside the tent, although Ben didn't seem to have noticed. I twisted my hair into a rope so it hung over one shoulder rather than clinging to my neck, and wiped the sweat from my forehead with a clammy palm.

'Like my mystery woman,' I said, in a voice that was little more than a whisper.

Ben turned to me, eyes screwed up, head cocked to one side.

'Hannah. Are you all right? You've gone a bit ... green.'

I looked around for a chair or something to lean on, but there was nothing else in the tent except the trestle table.

'I ... do you mind if we go outside?' I didn't wait for an answer, just turned away from her and pushed the tent flap aside. I allowed my legs to give way and sank to the ground, taking several deep gulps of air. I drew my knees up to my chest and rested my head on them. Ben eased herself down next to me and I heard the rustle of paper as she rolled a cigarette. The breeze wafted the smoke past my nostrils and I inhaled its pungent aroma. It was comforting, in the way an open fire makes a cold, empty room feel cosy and welcoming.

'I threw up the first time I uncovered a human skeleton.'

I knew she was just trying to make me feel better. 'I'm okay, honest.'

'It doesn't matter you know. In fact, there'd be something a bit creepy if you weren't affected by it.'

We sat in silence for a few minutes. The fresh air cleared my head and I began to feel a bit foolish.

'I've got a kit in the tent. Do you want to do it now?'

I nodded. Ben pushed herself to her feet and I took the hand she held out to pull me up.

Matt came round early that evening. I was filling him in with all the events of the day when there was a knock at the door. I wasn't expecting anyone, certainly not PC Fletcher and her sidekick, PC Jackson.

'Can we come in?'

I stood aside. 'We're in the kitchen,' I said, waving her through.

'Ah, Mr Denton. I'm pleased to see you here too.'

There was something in her tone that I didn't like.

'What's going on?' I wasn't sure how many more shocks I could take in one day. I sat down at the table, fingering my wine glass. 'Can I get either of you a drink?'

PC Fletcher shook her head. 'No. Thank you. We were passing so I thought It would be easier to give you an update face-to-face rather than over the phone.'

She let that linger for a moment. She should have been on the stage. Pause for dramatic effect. And it was effective. If I'd been guilty of any wrongdoing I'd be confessing it by now.

'I wanted to let you know that we've charged Mr Fitzpatrick.'

'Oh.' I hadn't realised until that moment how much I'd been hoping that they'd made a mistake and it wasn't Sean. I felt a crushing disappointment. In him and myself as well. So much time wasted. He didn't deserve the despair and anguish I had lavished on him when he'd dumped me, or the two years of mourning I had subjected myself to.

Matt reached for my hand, watching me with unwavering eyes. His bandanna - a deep shade of purplish-black - had slipped and was obscuring his eyebrows, but I knew they were doing the Hercule Poirot thing. Suddenly I wanted to laugh, to let go of all of the tension and stress of the last few weeks, since I'd first found the ring.

PC Fletcher was watching us in silence, her eyes flicking from me to Matt. There was something else. There had to be.

'Did he confess?'

'Oh yes,' she nodded.

Her tone now had shifted to one of distaste and I was certain that she didn't like Sean. She was obviously a better judge of character than I was.

'But only to the second break-in. He insists he had nothing to do with the first. He also insists he didn't know about the ring.'

The events of the day must have dulled my responses because it took a few seconds for me to understand the implications of her words.

'So Sean wasn't looking for anything, he just did it ...' I couldn't finish the sentence.

'To hurt you. Or scare you. Maybe both,' PC Fletcher obliged.

I swallowed hard. He must hate me so much, although all I'd done to him was refuse to give him another chance.

'But then, who ...?' I didn't realise at first that I'd spoken aloud.

I turned to face her. Her eyes were fixed on Matt. A feeling of unease bubbled from the soles of my feet and spread.

'Lauren Martin,' she said.

'What?' Had I heard her correctly? I swivelled around in my chair, jerking my hand out of Matt's grasp. His eyes were now locked with PC Fletcher's.

'What's going on?' I demanded for the second time in the space of a few minutes.

'Do you want to tell her, or shall I?' PC Fletcher's eyes were hard as they bored into Matt's, but he was meeting them with steel of his own, darkening from silver to iron grey.

'I don't know what Lauren has told you, but I had nothing to do with this.' His voice was calm. He adjusted his bandanna and turned towards me. 'Honest.'

'Maybe not directly, Mr Denton, but indirectly.'

Now it was my eyes that were flicking from one to the other as I tried to work out what she meant.

It was clear that Matt was not going to answer whatever question she was silently asking him. I tried to concentrate. If he was guilty he should have been PC Fletcher's leading man.

'You were in a relationship with Miss Martin, and when you met Miss Whittaker - Hannah - you dropped her. Is that how it happened?'

'No,' I objected. 'They're cousins.' But even as I said it, I knew from Matt's expression that he hadn't been honest with me.

'We are cousins,' he said, reaching for my hand again. I pushed him away. 'Quite remote, but still cousins. I haven't lied to you. I swear.'

I pushed my chair back and stumbled to my feet. If his eyes were iron grey mine were pure ebony at that moment.

'Lying by omission still counts.' I moved away from the table, out of his reach. The unease I had felt a few minutes ago was solidifying into a solid block of anger in the pit of my stomach. I folded my arms in front of me and glared at him.

'I believed you. But you've been lying to me all along.'

He was less sure of himself now. He fidgeted, adjusting his bandanna, but still he met my gaze - which I hoped was challenging - without flinching.

PC Fletcher's shrewd eyes were still glued to Matt's face.

'I swear to you Hannah. As soon as I knew that we had something special, I told Lauren we were finished.'

'And when was that?' I remembered that first morning after he'd stayed the night and I'd told him, quite directly I thought, that I wasn't the type of girl who slept with someone else's boyfriend. What were his exact words? He'd certainly said she was his cousin and I'm pretty sure he'd said he didn't cheat on his girlfriends.

'As soon as I got to work after that first night I stayed.'

This was as good as an admission that he had lied to me to begin with. The realisation carved a sharp edge to my anger. Could I believe him that he had broken up with her immediately? Could I believe him that he'd broken up with her at all?

I turned back to PC Fletcher. 'Are you sure?'

She nodded.

I exhaled and then snatched in a fresh blast of air.

'But, I still don't understand.'

'Hannah, I'm so sorry. I should have guessed,' Matt interjected. 'She was always greedy. She'd seen that ring and wouldn't be able to resist it.'

I watched his expression as he spoke, unblinking, like Trespass with her eye on a mouse. He had recovered his composure.

'I swear. I had no idea.'

He sounded so plausible. I was wavering, uncertain.

PC Fletcher cleared her throat. 'We'll be off then.'

'Er yes, of course,' I was grateful for the interruption. Matt's eyes scorched the back of my head as I led the police officers to the front door. 'What happens now?'

'We'll keep you informed. But, to be honest, if they both plead guilty, probably a small fine and some community service.'

I watched them walk to the squad car. PC Jackson climbed into the driver's seat and PC Fletcher said something to him that I couldn't catch. She turned back to face me and beckoned to me to join her. Curious, I flipped the latch on the door so I wouldn't lock myself out and stepped towards her.

'How long have you known Mr Denton?' She spoke in a soft voice, as if imparting a secret.

'Not long,' I shrugged. 'A few weeks. Why?'

'You might like to ask him why he and Lauren live at the same address - a one-bedroomed flat in Summertown.'

She watched my reaction as she detonated this bombshell under my feet. Were police officers supposed to deal out this sort of information? Not sure. But I thought I saw sympathy and maybe pity under the invisibility cloak of those stern eyes, before she slid into the passenger seat and they drove away.

My legs had turned to lead, but with the consistency of rubber. My feet had sprouted roots that were burrowing into the ground, fixing me to the spot. My mouth, I'm sure, was gaping open. Through the fog that had descended inside my head, my mind grasped for the meaning behind her words, even though it was surely very obvious.

It took a great effort to peel the soles of my shoes away from the solid mass of my drive and drag myself reluctantly to my kitchen, to face the person who had alchemised the foundations of my world to jelly.

Matt was standing by the back door. With a shaking hand I poured myself a glass of wine and took a large gulp. I didn't offer him one.

He approached me, eyes smiling, oozing confidence, sure of himself and his reception. I hated myself for still wanting to believe in him, but I wasn't going to let myself be pushed around by a man again. It took all of the will power that I had to follow my instinct rather than my heart.

'When were you going to tell me that you're living with Lauren?'

He stopped in the middle of the room, dominating the space, but now he was wary, like the Gruffalo in front of the little mouse.

'It isn't what you think.'

'Really. Is that the best you can do? I'd have thought you'd have had a better line prepared by now. Were you ever even the slightest bit interested in me, or was it just the ring ... and the money?'

I searched his face, seeking for some hint that I might be wrong, but I'd never felt more right.

'I think you should go,' I said, surprised how calm my voice sounded. I wasn't sure if I meant go for good, or just go for now, to give me some space to think. Matt froze. The expression in his eyes turned cold and angry. As he hovered in my kitchen the impression he gave me was not that of a man who has been caught out in a minor deception. A man who needs to grovel and beg forgiveness. It was that of a man who has gambled and lost. He'd been playing me all along, but the final card in the deck was mine.

His shoulders slumped, he picked up his car keys and left. I heard the front door slam, the roar of his car engine firing up and then fading into the distance.

What had I done?

I drained my wine glass and topped it up. I looked around my kitchen and everything reminded me of Matt. The two of us stepping around each other in the cramped space between the fridge and the hob to cook together that first night. Making coffee. Sharing our meals at the dining table. Clearing up the mess after the break-in. I turned my back on it and went out into the garden. The sun was still warm but it was fading. Plants that I didn't know I had were budding and flowering, shaping and defining the borders. There were weeds too that I hadn't noticed before. I needed to do some gardening. Did I even have any tools?

I grabbed a cushion from my deck and climbed into my boat. I stretched out across the bottom where I wouldn't be seen if anyone else rowed past. I lay there, my head on the cushion, watching the sun set and sipping my wine, with one arm draped over the side letting my fingers drift in the cool, silky water.

My mobile was in my pocket. It pinged with a text message. I reached for it without thinking.

'I'm sorry. Didn't mean to hurt you'

I put the phone down. My anger was cooling. Maybe he was telling the truth. Maybe he hadn't meant to hurt me. He had meant to deceive me though. And he'd succeeded. That I couldn't forgive.

But did I want to forgive him? I picked my feelings apart, scrutinising them as if I'd captured them in a photo. Foolish was there, but that's my fault. I can't blame Matt because I fell for his lies. I'd ignored the voices in my head. I'd seen the warning signs but I'd tossed them away and thrown myself into the relationship with him like a brick plunging into water, sinking. Even Joel had tried to warn me. But after that Sunday at the Swan I had barely stopped to think. I must learn to be more cautious.

I heard a mewing from above and looked up. Trespass was staring down at me, her green eyes large and luminous in the gathering dusk.

'Don't fancy the boat huh?'

She stretched out on the edge of the deck. I supposed I should really go back indoors, and I felt ready to. There was just one more feeling to examine. Other than my pride, was I hurt? I poked and prodded at my heart, waiting for it to explode with emotion like it had when Sean had left me, but it remained intact, beating solidly to its own tune. My tune. I didn't need anyone else.

I climbed out of the boat onto the deck and walked back up the garden, Trespass following at my heels like a dog, and the trees whispering their support behind me. As I pushed my back door open and entered my comfortable, familiar space, I realised I should thank Matt for letting me down, because he had given me back control of my life.

TWENTY-TWO

Hannah
Three months later

I'M GRATEFUL THAT IT HAS stopped raining, but my shoes are still sodden from the long, wet grass. After a gorgeous, hot and sunny spring, our weather has decided to skip summer and move straight onto autumn. I pull my pashmina more tightly around my shoulders and throw the bouquet of roses I hold in my hand into the gaping hole of the grave in front of me.

'Goodbye Catherine,' I say. 'I hope you can rest in peace now.'

The corner of the graveyard where the bones of my ancestor are finally laid to rest is cool under the shade of a large ash tree. She is surrounded by ancient gravestones with illegible lettering, worn smooth over the centuries by the wind and rain. It hadn't seemed right to bury her amongst the more modern graves on the other side of the church.

Her grave appears raw and too new. When the ground has settled and the grass has grown over the mound it will blend in. I'm going to plant some bluebell bulbs on her. I don't know why, but I've just got a feeling she would like that, and I'm going to get a simple gravestone engraved.

Catherine Meakin
Born 1619, laid to rest 2019

So yes, I managed to identify my mystery woman, my great, great, great - I don't know how many greats - grandmother. I don't think anyone was surprised when the DNA results proved beyond any doubt that the bones in the field were those of an ancestor of mine. After that, it took weeks of painstaking work. Ben's students helped me. It all added to the story, she'd said, blowing smoke from her roll-up into my face, if we could find out who she was.

We had the family tree that my mother had already started on, so we picked up the trail from where she had left off, going through parish records, registers of births, marriages and deaths. Following my hunch earlier that it appeared to be the female line that was important in my ancestry, we concentrated on the women. It proved to be the right approach and I'm certain it saved us weeks of work. We had to go back to 1776 before we found the Islip connection, when Anne had married Charles in London, but she had been born in Islip in 1759. The closer we got to the 1640s the more excited I became, but it was excitement that was tempered with fear as well. What if we came this far and still failed?

But we didn't. Matilda Dewe, died in 1698, had been born in 1639 to parents John and Catherine Meakin. Catherine was born in 1619, but there was no record of her death. John had died in 1643 along with Catherine's mother, but Catherine had simply disappeared. The dates fitted. It had to be Catherine that the archaeologists had found in the field.

It was me who found the final link. I should have been elated, but I wasn't. I had just sat there, motionless, staring at the ancient ledgers, at the faded, spidery handwriting littering the thick parchment and I'd wanted to cry. Matilda would only have been six years old when her mother disappeared. That was the thought that stuck in my mind. That poor child, who was also my great, great, great something or other grandmother. She would never have known why her mother went out of the house one day and didn't come back. I wondered who she had lived with after she was orphaned and hoped she'd had a happy life.

Once we had identified the bones the real circus began. The media were all over the story - local press and specialist magazines for archaeology, ancestry, British history and heritage. You name it. The local press got bored pretty quickly. What is it they say? Today's headlines are tomorrow's fish and chip wrappers? Or at least it used to be. These days they use clean white paper.

On this occasion the saying proved to be true. But the specialist magazines couldn't get enough of the story. And in the middle of the media circus a bidding frenzy from museums wanting to buy the ring began to spiral out of control. It seemed the provenance - as in me - and the whole story behind it, or what we were able to piece together of the story, made it an even more desirable and valuable item. What had begun as an astronomical sum soon doubled and then tripled. It really was beginning to look as if I would not have to work again if I didn't want to. But of course I want to work. I'm too young to retire.

I saw the ring again. When it was sold, the museum wanted me to be part of the publicity and organised a photo shoot. It felt strange, being on the other side of the lens. I'd taken gloves with me so I could hold the ring without getting a shock. I don't know what made me do it, but I was waiting with the head of PR for the shoot to start and his attention was diverted by the photographer. The ring was in an open-topped, glass box on the table between us. It was like being reunited with a long-lost friend, and it looked so beautiful, all polished up and glowing. The stone seemed to wink at me, to dare me, so I stuck my index finger out, braced myself for the shock and touched it. And there was nothing. I didn't feel a thing. That connection had gone and it was just a piece of metal. Okay, a very special piece of precious metal, but no longer super-charged with energy. At first I was confused, and sad, but then I realised that the ring had done its job. Catherine had been found.

I feel a hand on my elbow and I turn around.

'Hannah. It's time to go.'

It's raining again, and already I can feel the dampness on my skin beneath the pashmina. I turn around and take in my mother's pale face, her gaunt, skin-and-bone frame and I feel guilty that I've lingered here for too long and tired her. I nod to the undertaker, who is hovering in the shelter of the church porch, keeping a respectful distance and sensibly staying dry. My mother takes my arm and leans on me as we pick our way one slow step after another between the gravestones and back onto the gravel path that dissects the churchyard. I pause and turn, unable to shake a sudden sensation that we are being watched. The patter of rain on gravel and susurration of the leaves seem to whisper to me. 'Thankyou, thankyou, thankyou.'

We leave the graveyard by the small gate onto Church Lane and cross to the car park by the village hall. The playground is noisy; children squealing with delight as they scale the walls of the wooden castle and whizz down the slide, or chase each other around the boat. I see people I know, in a group leaning against the fence watching the children, or on their way to the small village shop and I wave. Then I help my mother into my car. If I was alone, I would have walked, but my mother is on chemotherapy and she's weak, although we're hopeful of a full recovery. She's staying with me so I can look after her. My house is too small, but we're getting by - she's in my bedroom and I'm on the sofa - I've replaced my saggy old one with a new sofa bed so it is at least comfortable. I could afford to move to a bigger house, but I'm reluctant, because in spite of my earlier conviction that I would never feel safe or at home here again, it's strange, but I feel safer and more at home than I ever did.

We pass the entrance to the field and the Confessor's Walk. The protest banners have all gone and the scene is peaceful and rural. If I hadn't been here, I would find it difficult to imagine that it had ever looked any different. As it is, though, I know I will never forget that white tent and the horrors it tried to hide. The plans for the new road and bridge have been abandoned. The publicity around the ring caused so much interest in the village and in preserving its layers of history, that the developers were forced to back down.

I park on my drive, open the front door and wedge it before helping my mother out of the car and into an armchair in the lounge. I look around me, feeling once again that thrill, that this is my home, my space and no-one can take it away from me. No-one is going to make me feel threatened here ever again. The sofa isn't the only item of new furniture I've bought, and I've also redecorated every square centimetre - floor to ceiling - not a scrap of paintwork or a corner of plaster has been missed, and I've moved things around, changed the curtains, replaced the kitchen work surfaces. It looks and feels like a new house. I've obliterated anything that might remind me of that dreadful scene that I came home to just a few months ago.

I've also wiped out anything that might bring back memories of Matt. Just this morning, in an example of very poor timing, a postcard arrived from America. It was a sepia print showing the cargo of a boat being unloaded in a harbour by native Americans, whilst men and women in 17th century dress watched. It wasn't signed, but I knew it was from Matt. I tore it up into tiny pieces and let them drizzle through my fingers into the bin.

'I think I'll just have a little lie down, my love.' Mum pushes herself up from the chair, hands gripping the arms for support. I move to her side and hover there, knowing she will want to manage for herself. She moves slowly to the stairs and climbs them, pausing on each step to take breath. I follow in case she slips. I know it's unlikely, but the urge to look after her, as she once looked after me, is one I can't ignore.

I settle her in bed and she closes her eyes.

'I'll make some nice soup for dinner,' I tell her. 'I'll bring you some up on a tray, and then I thought I would go down to the Red Lion later, if you don't mind?'

She nods and pats my hand. 'That's fine, my love. I'll have a little rest and watch some TV up here.'

I go downstairs and out into the garden, down to my deck. It's already weathering and looks as though it belongs here. I've bought a swinging seat. It's like a huge cushion in a chair-shaped basket attached to a triangular wooden frame by three ropes. It's one of my favourite places to sit, with a book and a glass of wine, or just to think. To watch and listen. I sit now and swing gently, lifting my face to the caress of the cool breeze. Trespass strolls over and lies down in the grass, eyes alert, trained on the hedge. Probably got her eye on a mouse.

I think about the times I've spent out here, in the few short months since it was built, and I remember the day I found the ring and the sequence of events that discovery set in place.

Sean and Lauren pleaded guilty but Matt wasn't charged with being involved. There was no evidence against him, so either he was innocent as he protested, or he was good at covering his tracks. But for me, it's a question of trust. I've forgiven him, but that's not enough. When you've been let down as badly in a relationship as I was - by Sean - to commit yourself again you have to know, without doubt, that you can trust that person. Matt deceived me from the very beginning. I couldn't ever trust him. I would like to think that one day I will meet someone who sets my toes tingling and who I can trust, but if it isn't to be, well, I've developed a fondness for cats and they are far less complicated!

There is one loose ending. How did Catherine die? Was it, as Ben suggested, an accident? She simply fell and banged her head on a rock? It couldn't be, could it? Someone buried her. If someone had found her dead in the field they wouldn't have gone for a spade and buried her. They would have raised the alarm. We know she wasn't a stranger. She was born in Islip and had lived here all her life. She would have been known. If someone had found her, they would have fetched her family and she would have been given a proper burial, in the graveyard.

There is another kind of accident. She could have been having an argument with someone and it turned violent. A lover's tiff perhaps - Thomas Marlow maybe, or someone else. The man didn't mean to kill her, but once he had he panicked. He knew he would hang if he was found guilty of murder, so he buried her and kept it to himself. Left the country even.

I'm saying he, but it could just have easily been a woman.

And of course, there is another possibility, and that is the one that still chills me whenever I allow myself to think about it. Someone meant to kill her, and buried her, in secret, hoping that she would not be found.

I've had to accept that I will never know.

TWENTY-THREE

Thursday, April 24th, 1645

HE DUCKED INTO A DOORWAY to avoid a carriage clattering past the Prince's Arms. It was dark. The village was quiet. There were no soldiers - Cavaliers or Roundheads - loitering under the great elm. The inns were full with workers celebrating the Parliamentarian victory and the success of the new army - and its commander, Cromwell - that they had heard so much about. Now they had seen what it was capable of for themselves, and they had new hope for their own futures.

He couldn't afford to be identified though. He would leave the village for good tonight, vanish into thin air like the mist rising from the surface of the river.

He had no time to waste. Already his sister-in-law had been shouting her big mouth off raising the alarm, and that officious husband of hers was supporting her. Edward was organising a search party to go out at first light. He had to make sure they found nothing. Then the rumour that he would start as his final parting gift, that she had been seen leaving the village with a soldier, would take off and spread, like the leaves falling from the trees in autumn, covering any doubt with an artificial, ever-shifting carpet, obscuring and confusing the true landscape.

The carriage passed. He ran across the road, awkward in his long coat, with the spade he had hugged to his body beneath it hampering his progress. He slipped through the churchyard and crossed the path into the open fields on the other side. The ground was battle-scarred, churned up and muddy. He pressed on, each step taken with care, until he could see the dark silhouette of the mill ahead of him. He turned left, crossed the track that led down to the mill and into the field that bordered the river. There was no moon, which he was grateful for.

The stone outbuilding wasn't even a hut. It was large, open on two sides, with a roof. It was used for storing animal grains and even as a shelter when the weather was bad. He took off his coat and seized the spade, relishing the feel of the smooth, cool metal on his calloused palms.

He chose a spot in a dip, where the ground undulated on its descent to the river and he hoped it would not be so obvious that the earth had been disturbed. He removed the top layer of weeds, grass and wild flowers carefully so it could be replaced and appear as natural. The ground was hard and compact. After a day of hiding, he welcomed the physical work. He threw all his pent-up energy into the effort of digging, breaking out into a sweat, and pausing occasionally to wipe his hands on his trousers so he could maintain a firm grip on the spade.

When he judged the hole was big enough he retraced his steps to the outbuilding and looked around him, his keen eyes fully adjusted to the darkness. Satisfied that there was no-one nearby, he hurried to the far corner where the two walls met. A pile of hessian sacks teetered like a flimsy tower of cards. He pulled them towards him. Behind, just as he'd left her that morning, lay his daughter, curled on her side. He sat down beside her for a moment, stroked her hair, which was matted into clumps and not at all like the soft, silky tresses he was used to. She was cold. So cold. He put his arms beneath her shoulders and pulled her towards him. She was stiff, like a doll. He looked into her eyes, which were dull and staring. 'Still so beautiful,' he murmured. 'Oh Cathy, why did you have to do it?'

A tear slid down his rough, whiskered cheek. He swiped it away. It wouldn't do now to get sentimental. She had rejected him. That was it. He stood up and pulled her unresponsive body after him, dragged it out of the outbuilding and to the grave. He laid her in the hole and covered her with soil, stamping it down in layers as he worked and finally replacing the top layer, treading it in. When he'd finished he stood back and admired his work. He was satisfied no-one would be suspicious.

Still sweating, in spite of the chill in the air, he picked up his spade, collected his overcoat from the outbuilding and followed the river towards the mill. He stooped, splashed water over his face and rinsed his hands. Then he waded across the ford and set off at a brisk pace away from the village. After about a quarter of a mile he threw the spade into the river and picked up his pace until he was almost jogging. The dawn was chasing him as he approached the two men waiting for him on the outskirts of Kidlington. Without a backward glance, they turned and headed south, towards London.

A Note from the Author

The Woman in the Painting is a work of fiction. Although I have tried to keep to historical detail where it is known, the absence of records can be both a hindrance and a blessing for the historical novelist, and as such, I have allowed my imagination to fill in the many gaps.

Edward the Confessor was born in Islip, possibly at the palace belonging to his father, King Ethelred, and the village was given to him by his mother. He subsequently gave it to Westminster Abbey in 1065. John Islip, born in Islip in 1464, was the Abbot of Westminster from 1500-1532 and his rebus is as I describe it in my novel. However, to the best of my knowledge the existence of a ring engraved with the rebus is pure fiction, as is the possible lineage to the Gilder and Marlow families, who also exist only in the pages of this novel.

Very little of the village of Islip as it would have been in 1645 remains to this day. There was a pub called The Prince's Arms (subsequently the Plume of Feathers) on the site where I depict it in the novel, opposite the present-day Red Lion which is believed to have been built on the site of the palace of King Ethelred. In 1086, the Domesday Book details a mill on the river Cherwell in Islip, but the working mill was demolished in 1954 and what remains today is a substantial house dating to the early 18th century. The tree at Cross Tree Green today is an oak, the elm having fallen victim to Dutch Elm disease in the 1980s. The tree was thought to be between 300 and 350 years old when it had to be felled, so may not have been there in 1645. Indeed, there may have just been a simple cross, but I have chosen to have a tree in that position. Time Team did do a programme in Islip, which can be found on YouTube. The team had hoped to find Edward the Confessor's chapel. In this they were unsuccessful, but they did locate the manor house built by William de Curtlington in the 14th century, the remains of which lay beneath a field behind Manor Farm. In my novel, this is the manor house where Catherine works, home to the Gilder family.

Cromwell did lead his army into Islip on April 23, 1645, and on the morning of April 24 he was taken by surprise by three of the King's regiments and engaged in a battle, which he won, probably in the fields that surround the present day village to the north and west. Like Hannah, I have been unable to find any original account of a battle taking place on the bridge. Cromwell's letters, and other first-hand accounts from the time, tell a different story.

The Levellers were active in 1645, mostly in London, and presented their manifesto 'An Agreement of the People' - a democratic constitution for Britain to end the civil war - in a series of pamphlets between 1647 and 1649. They believed in equality for ordinary people and tolerance in religion.

The present-day bridge dates to 1877. There are drawings of the previous bridge, but even that is unlikely to have been the structure that was there in 1645, as there are records of orders to destroy the bridge later in 1645 and again in the 1670s. Hence, when I commissioned William North, (an artist who lives and works in a neighbouring village and specialises in scenes of Otmoor), to generate an original piece of art to use for the cover of my novel, we agreed to start with the canvas of the natural landscape and imagine what the bridge itself could have looked like with no buildings around it. The result is stunning, and the original is now hanging in my hallway. Thank you William.

I must also thank Gregg Archer for sharing his knowledge of civil war battlefields, Edward Caswell for explaining how the system for reporting treasure works, Frances Russell for taking me through the work that archaeologists do before planning permission is granted for development in areas where previous discoveries have been made, and what happens when human bones are found, and Peter Bower for his amazing knowledge of paper and what can be learned from it. The usual disclaimer, that any mistakes are my own. I must also thank all of my early readers, especially my sister Tracey, who has now read *The Woman in the Painting* four times and generously says she has loved it every time, everyone at West Oxfordshire Writers Group (especially Gill, Ailsa, Stuart, Doc, Fran and Lela) for all their feedback along the way, and Gill from my book club in Islip whose comments helped me to shape Hannah's character.

I hope you have enjoyed reading *The Woman in the Painting* and would love to hear what you thought of it. Drop me a line via the website, or reach out to me on social media.

www.amandarobertsauthor.co.uk

@amanda_R_author

/Amanda_Roberts_Author

/amanda-roberts-70077720b/

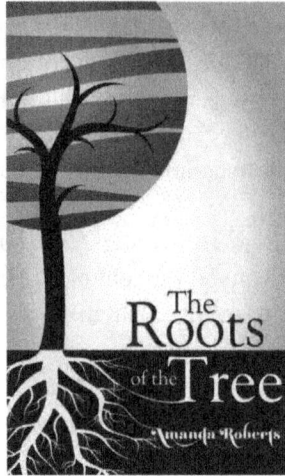

The
Roots
of the Tree

Amanda Roberts

For 63 years Annie has looked up to her father as the one man in
her life who would never let her down. It isn't until after he dies
that she discovers an inconsistency in wedding dates, which leads
her to question every memory she has of her parents and who she
really is.

Shattered by the discovery that the man she spent her whole life
looking up to was not her real father, Annie becomes less and
less able to cope, and it falls to her daughter, Suzie, to pursue the
truth. Delving into the controversial family past, hidden in secret
letters, dusty war records and a neglected headstone, Suzie can
only hope that what she discovers is enough to bring her mother
back from the brink.

Buy on Kindle from Amazon
Paperback from www.amandarobertsauthor.co.uk